EMERALD FIRE
SYN FRASER

To my sister, Jennifer. Without you, I wouldn't have been able to write this story. I'm grateful for your support as a sounding board when things don't read quite right, and for being the voice of reason when I go off the rails and take a detour through the left field. Your friendship has played a crucial role in the growth of Keary and Erin as characters. Thank you for everything.

Also By

Fallen Guardian Series

Redemption
https://www.amazon.com/gp/product/B0C3Y8212Q?ref_=
dbs_m_mng_rwt_calw_tkin_0&storeType=ebooks

Reckoning
https://www.amazon.com/gp/product/B0CBT6L4QN?ref_
=dbs_m_mng_rwt_calw_tkin_1&storeType=ebooks

CHAPTER I

Acaidrin, 1525 A.D.:

By the time Sloan McKenna rides into his courtyard, his shoulders sag. In the past, he'd spread his journey over several days, taking shelter at the small inns along the way. The sense of urgency tarnishing this trip kept him from stopping as often as he'd like, so by the time he spies home on the horizon, his stomach is threatening to eat itself. Just ahead, darkness shrouds his home under a wet blanket, bare of both moon and stars. Fitting, he muses and slows Cahir to a walk.

"Welcome home, Sir."

"Thank you, Ren," Sloan croaks past a dry throat before handing the reins to their new stable boy. Easing himself out of the saddle, his legs buckle the instant his boots touch the ground. The struggle he faces to remain upright and not face-down in the muck catches him by surprise.

"Be sure to give him a good rubdown and extra oats," he instructs, running a comforting hand over the horse's quivering flank. "He's more than earned it this time 'round."

"Jasper said no extra oats."

"Jasper works for me," Sloan snaps, whirling around to confront the young boy. "Which means you work for me." Blue eyes too big for his face widen further. Despite Sloan's size and title, he fights a smile when the child notches his chin upward. The sight is enough to sap the heat from his voice. "My apologies Ren, it's been a long journey. Do not worry over Jasper."

"Yes, Sir."

Thin shoulders turn to lead the horse towards the stable before Sloan heads for the stone keep. Long legs take the wide steps two at a time to beat the ache settling in his body. Stiff fingers fight with his rain-soaked cloak as he reaches the heavy door. As expected, Mrs. Caffey waits just on the other side to trade his wet clothes for a plate of lukewarm supper.

"Bless you, Fan."

"Welcome home Sir. I fear I've sent Miss Darby up to bed some time ago."

"I'll check on her soon." Sloan answers around a mouthful of Brie's biscuits. "For now, will you have one of your lads fetch Duncan for me?"

"Right 'way Sir."

With a nod, he carries his plate to the study until Duncan can join him. He sacrifices sitting at his desk to stand near the fire burning in the giant fireplace and makes quick work of his supper. While he waits, Sloan indulges in sopping up the last of the gravy with his remaining biscuit.

Since his stomach is full and finally quiet, he leaves the empty plate on his desk and pours himself a generous measure of whiskey. Lips tremble silently over a simple toast that ends with him lifting his cup skyward before dumping its contents down his throat. Wincing, he fills the cup once again.

Muscles protest as he returns to the fire. Bracing one hand on the mantle, Sloan waits impatiently for the heat to work its magic on stiff joints now spoiled by age. It's a shame the fire can do nothing for the chill plaguing his soul. Full lips thin as dark thoughts creep in on his homecoming. Duncan's timely arrival grants him a temporary reprieve.

"Good evening, Sir."

Sloan sighs, "Duncan, we've spoken of this a hundred times now. If you refuse to use my name, can you at least use McKenna? You say sir, and I turn expecting to see my father ready to thrash us for the mischief we found."

"Aye" Though the words are dry, Sloan spots a small smile on an otherwise serious face. "I will try, Sir. McKenna."

"Thank you. And thank you for the fire as well."

"The missus feared this foul weather may keep you. If not, you'd be needing warmth. Darby will be pleased to see you."

"Has there been any word in my absence?"

"One of his men came by this morning. I'm to send for him the minute you return."

"Grand. See it done, please Duncan." Raising his eyes from his cup, Sloan notes the strain Duncan carries on his narrow shoulders. "What is it?"

"Beg your pardon, Sir, McKenna. You look tired. Perhaps you'd prefer to sit awhile and gather your wits."

Sloan's lips curl into a small smile. "You think me witless now?"

"Nay, Sir! Never."

"You aren't to be the last old friend." Sloan swishes the amber liquid around the inside of his cup before pouring it down his throat. The cup itself makes a stout clang when he sets it on the mantle with more force than required. "I appreciate the concern, but if I sit now, I'll never get back up again."

"Let me have a bath drawn for you. This business will keep 'til morning."

The mere whisper of a hot bath draws Sloan's ribs tight until his fingers clench. "While my knees would be forever in your debt, we've let them suffer long enough." Even as the words leave his lips, he considers calling them back. "These past weeks have taken a toll on everyone, a few especially." Better to be done with it.

"Yes, sir." Duncan scoops up the empty plate off the desk and turns for the door. "I'll have him brought to the keep at once."

"Oh, Duncan, make sure Jasper is aware the extra oats are for me and see if there's something our new stable boy can do to earn more food."

"Right 'way, Sir."

Sloan smiles at the closed door, wondering if Duncan is aware he never once used McKenna instead of Sir. Old habits.

Now that he's alone, he lets his shoulders droop. With the help of the small space in front of the fire, Sloan paces until most of the ache in his legs subsides. Has he always been this old? Why had he never noticed before tonight? Or that the flames of his fire resemble the long tresses of her hair?

He recalls the look of them brushed smooth to cascade in a burnished copper over an exposed back of ivory skin and his gut knots in response. They carry the smell of lavender when he pulls her close to press soft curves against his hard angles. Thoughts of her since this mess unfolded adds a hitch to every breath.

His wife's behavior in his absence still horrifies him. At first, he'll admit, he'd been unbelieving of the tales. Even as he confronted her with such bold accusations, he was prepared to wipe the tears she'd cry professing her innocence. In a matter of moments, Sloan would see the wild stories against her and their eldest as nothing more than spiteful falsehoods.

The reality made a mockery of his fantasy. His confrontation produced no tears or claims of innocence. At least not from her. In truth, their daughter Geillis shed enough tears for the both of them across the entire journey to the sea. In the time it took him to see to their needs, her splendid face was a mess of red splotches and swollen eyes.

Brigid, however, stood unwavering. Even after he begged for understanding, she never faltered. Her stoic demeanor holds true atop the old nag he allowed for their lengthy trip.

Frigid and calculating, Sloan spent the trip trying to locate the woman he married. The same one he fell crazy in love with. Had it all been a lie? What possessed her to involve poor Geillis in her malicious actions? What of poor Darby? Tightness constricts his heart when he thinks of what their youngest will have to endure without a mother or a sister.

The time he spends there wrestling with his haunting thoughts escapes him. It isn't until Duncan drops a fresh log on the fire before Sloan returns to the present. A shower of sparks spew up from the flames, dancing over the heavy stones long scorched black.

Outside, the gentle rain he'd rode home in gives way to a heavy downpour. Cracks of lightning splits the heavy air before rolls of thunder rattles against the stone manor.

"Sir, he's arrived."

"Thank you, Duncan." Even as he recognizes the itch in his legs to pace, Sloan sets his shoulders. As if a puppeteer pulled his strings, he straightens and locks each vertebra in place.

"McKenna." With a smile and a heavy accent, Bel swoops into the room. A brief pump of hands accompanies the greeting before he spends a moment warming by the fire.

Though Bel's large gathering of followers travel many months of the year, by spring Sloan discovers their camps within his borders. A usually peaceful tribe, they spend the summer only to be gone again before the weather turns cold. It isn't often the nomad leader is so far from his camp. Tonight is a rare exception.

"Thank you for coming."

Though younger of the two, Sloan always felt the opposite was true when visiting with Bel. Not tonight. Tonight, Bel looks every day of his senior years as shadows infest warm brown eyes. Tension pulls the laugh lines around his mouth into tight and fragile cracks. "The least I could do, yes?"

"Have you thought about my proposal?"

"Yes, I've spoken to the elders as well."

"And?"

"Your lady was adamant when she purchased Aoife's particular services." Bel's voice softens, as if to deliver the blow as gentle as possible. "We cannot break the walls that hold them." The hands that withdraw two silver trinket boxes from the folds of his cloak tremble when he places them on Sloan's desk. "That one of my own took part in this, breaks my heart."

"I know what you mean."

"You are a good man, McKenna. No one will think less of you."

"I think less of me," Sloan says beyond the clench in his jaw. "I should've seen the shrewd machinations that hid behind that smile before ever offering my name. Her offenses are mine to carry."

"You're not the first to be blinded by love."

"There must be something we can do. I'd strike a bargain with the Derunid myself if I thought it'd work."

"I fear bartering with them has a steep price, my Friend. The Derunid magic comes with unforeseen consequences. While I cannot break their chains, I can change their prisons."

"How do you mean?" Despite his bleak reality, a promise flutters against his ribs until his heart quickens.

"We thought to just allow them to slumber through their imprisonment. However, the constraints of the spell will not allow such changes. But we may change how their time passes, cut the chance of madness."

"What do you need from me?"

"Just their belongings."

"Done." Poking his head into the hall, Sloan sets Duncan to work on locating their satchels. "What else?"

"Your word that my people will not suffer for Aoife's actions." The hardening of his jaw and the sudden interest Bel takes with the floor tells Sloan it's a hard ask.

"You have it," he answers with no thought of hesitation. "Whatever her reasons, Brigid was the driving force in this. Besides, I believe Aoife's already paid a high enough price for her part."

"Leaving her daughter without a mother."

"Yet another victim of my wife's crime."

"We have a contract, then?"

Sloan nods. "We do. Your people are welcome on my lands for as long and as often as you need."

"Then we'll finish this while the moons still sleep." Bel announces in a quiet voice, setting a small group of papers in Sloan's hands. "Everything you need to know on breaking the spell should the time come."

"Duncan, escort him back to his camp?" A nod of understanding from the somber steward answers the ask, leaving Sloan to climb the stairs to the second floor alone.

Over the last several days, it was easy to lose sight of the victims suffering from Brigid's callous behavior. He knows the women of Bel's camp will surround Aoife's daughter with love, raising her as their own. But the fact remains, Iseult lost a mother.

Then there's Darby. How can he explain everything to one so young? More his child than Brigid's, the fear she won't comprehend settles in his chest.

"Hell, I don't understand it myself," he growls, his hand freezing just outside her door. With any luck, the wee child will be fast asleep, sparing him any explanation until morning.

The scene just inside the room bathes his tired soul in a wave of warmth. Despite the lateness of the hour, his lips transform from thin lines of resignation into a genuine smile. His first in weeks.

Surrounded by a mess of toys, Darby sits in the middle, close to the heat of the fireplace. In her hands, a rag doll rides limp atop a wooden horse as it clops around toy obstacles. Her destination; a knight perched high on impressively stacked blocks.

"Why are you not sleeping?"

"Pa!" Flashing a smile full of charm, she drops her toys to pick a perilous path toward his waiting arms. Once she's close enough, she launches herself at him with a squeal of laughter.

Sloan catches the wild bundle in mid-air and pulls her close, needing the contact as much as her. A moment later, Darby pulls back to frame his face with her tiny hands. "I knew you'd come."

"You did, huh?"

"Yep. I heard Duncan and Fanny arguing over supper."

"What have I told you about being a nosy-rosy?"

"I didn't listen in, I promise. They just talk loud."

"Ah." Sloan snuggles her close once more, burying his face in her cinnamon-colored curls and inhaling their lemon-scent. At once, the weight he'd been carrying on his shoulders, shifts, allowing him to find comfort in her innocent solace. "You couldn't wait for me in bed?"

A pert nose wrinkles in a small face, gray eyes dark. "The bed makes me sleepy."

"That's a good thing." Laughing, Sloan carries her across the stone floor to the enormous bed that dwarfs the room.

"Was the trip grand? What color was the sea this time? Did you find any mermaids? Or bandits?"

"The trip was long, and it rained the whole time. I'm afraid the sea was too dark to spot mermaids. And with a stroke of luck, I didn't come across any bandits either." Sloan lists with patience.

"Darn. Well, Geillis will tell me the good bits tomorrow."

"Nay, not this time, *Cheridish*." Setting her on a pile of blankets, Sloan then turns his attention to the toys strewn over the floor.

"What does cariditch mean?"

Sloan grins as tiny hands plant on what will one day be hips, her childlike face scrunching. He ruffles her curls into an unruly tangle and tweaks the end of her nose. "Cheridish," he pronounces slowly, "it means you are my treasure."

"Oh." A pleased smile flutters across her face, erasing the wrinkles that linger. "And why not?"

"Why not what?"

"Why won't Geillis tell me the good bits you've forgotten?"

"Forgotten?" Setting the last book on a shelf, Sloan moves onto the toys themselves. "You make me sound old, lass."

"Just a wee bit."

"Thanks."

"Why not?" Darby speaks slowly, her girlish voice free of the irritation he's positive she's harboring.

Unable to avoid it, he pauses and takes a breath. Any hope he could stall this conversation until the morning scampers out the window with her steely determination. "Because Ma and Geillis stayed behind to enjoy the summer cottage for a spell."

As she digests his words, a war of emotions skitter across her tiny face. Her smooth brow puckers slightly, her bottom lip quivering a second before she steadies it with the press of her teeth. Standing there, Sloan would rather endure any of the Council's interrogation tactics than the sight of her wee heart shattering.

"They forgot me." Aside from the tremble in her voice, Darby unflinchingly meets his gaze.

"You'll stay with me this time."

"Ma is still cross over the toad," she states with a curt nod and jumps her way to the head of the bed. One last leap plops her near the center in a mess of curls and blankets.

"What toad?" Sloan asks as he sets toys inside the small wooden chest. His grin widens before he levels a knowing look with his daughter and gestures to the imprisoned knight. "Is the princess saving her knight?"

"Mhmm." Darby's worrisome frown eases into an impish smile. "Conall said not every man can rescue themselves. Sometimes they need help."

Her answer lands as a physical blow, forcing Sloan to resist doubling over in front of her. "What brought on that discussion?"

"Brandon refused to let me try his new sword after supper. Said girls shouldn't worry over such things. It's not a real sword," she whispers.

"Yes, tis a training sword. He'll use the wooden one until he gets good enough for a real one."

"Well, maybe you should tell him that." Darby observes, giving her pillow a good whack before settling. "The one William threw into the ma'ure pile."

"*Manure*," Sloan corrects without looking at her. "What did William throw into the manure pile this time?"

"The toad." Her voice takes on a challenging tone, her arms crossing over his inability to keep pace with her.

"Right, sorry. What happened to the toad?"

"I brought it to Fanny so it could have a bath, and she screamed the house down around me. Ma had that wrinkle in her forehead when she sent me to my room with no supper."

The sound of exasperation in her childlike voice puts a twitch in his lip that he's careful to hide. "Mhmm." He knows full well the wrinkle Darby means. The only imperfection in an otherwise flawless face.

"That's why I couldn't go with Ma to the sea."

"No *cheridish*, I wanted to spend time with you."

"You did?"

"Yes." The poor child is going to carry enough shackles in the coming years over her mother's actions. He'll not add another.

"Wait, Pa! He doesn't go into the bin."

The interruption into his train of thought has Sloan staring without seeing at the toy in his hand. Blinking to ease the gloom, he runs a hand along the new wooden horse. "Why not?"

"It makes him sad. So I let him sleep with me."

"Well, he's a handsome fella. Does he have a name?" His thumb brushes over the carved wood, rubbed smooth. Someone took great care in its creation from a rough block of wood, showing patience with the full mane and tail. On the bottom of one foot, he spots a brand in the shape of a star.

"Mhmm. I named him Flynn."

This time, her reply forces his legs to stumble as his body recoils from an attack that makes breathing difficult. "Flynn?" His voice is hoarse as Sloan grasps the wooden figure tightly. Of all the names in the world, she had to pick that one?

"I told Daigh I wanted a horse just like his when I'm big 'nough." Flashing an impish grin, Darby holds out her hands for the cherished toy. "He made it look just like his, so I wouldn't have to wait."

Bile rises in Sloan's throat as he forces his lungs to exchange the now stale air. "That was nice of him." Forcing a smile, he places the toy in her small hands, then rubs a finger against the throb in his temples.

"Will you tell me a story?"

"I'm afraid I don't know many that are fit for little ears."

"Please, Pa?"

"Okay, scooch." Sloan folds his large body in next to hers, giving her a moment to snuggle up close. One small hand rubs over a gray eye as her yawn swallows her face before receding. "Maybe one with an evil queen and the brothers who oppose her?"

It's the least he could do at this point. *I owe them that much.* A tickle sticks in his throat until he can swallow it. With the bob of her head and a wiggle, Darby settles in beside him.

As the story unfolds, his voice softens. Sloan tells his daughter of two brothers, honorable and good, yet betrayed and cursed by magic. Enchanted, they wait for a McKenna to break their bonds.

Night after night Sloan tells the story until it becomes ritual. Since he doesn't live long beyond her childhood years, it's a story Darby holds dear. Soon, she shares it with her own children. Before long, her granddaughter commits it to paper in a small white diary.

Such is how legends and myths form. Still, there's one small camp that knows it to be more than a mere story.

CHAPTER 2

500 years later:

Keary releases a soft sigh as the roar of the waves crashing over jagged rocks below fills the air. Inhaling deeply, she savors the sweet fragrance of her coffee, mixing with the scent of water less than a stone's throw away.

Eight months out of the year, she enjoys the gentle lapping waves off her secluded shoreline. Springtime in Briar means heavy rains and alarmingly high tides. Ferocious waves and higher water level, as a result, soothe the frayed edges of Keary's soul. When she was younger, one instructor after another would blame this wet season on their second moon. Whatever the reason, she finds a strange sense of peace in the turbulent weather.

Overhead, the night sky retreats, dragging the dismal clouds remaining after last night's storm along for the ride. In the hour's earliness, the damp air combines with cool temperatures to burrow a stout chill deep into one's bones. While the effect is enough to keep most people in their homes until the day passes under a warm sun, Keary's always been different.

Different. Out of the many names she's been called over the years, different isn't so bad. Harpy, hag and witch, however, rank high on the list of names she despises. As a child, she wanted nothing more than to shut them up for good. Children and adults alike. As an adult, she makes the conscious choice to take them with a grain of salt.

It wasn't as if Keary or her younger sister chose this small village out of their endless options. With the death of their parents, their father's mother was the last remaining relative. A far better option than an orphanage or group home. Or so Keary thought at the time. Looking back on those hard years, she'd be lying if she said she had no doubts.

Not that her grandmother didn't welcome them with open arms. Though strict, she showered the sisters with constant love and understanding. Since their district holds a higher number of gifted than most other areas, she didn't prepare them for the welcome the sisters would endure.

"Hell, I don't think she was prepared," Keary mutters darkly.

After winning the civil war, natural-born citizens were quick to divide each settlement within Solstier into two ruling groups. The so-called appointed Elders who make their laws and Vanguard soldiers who enforce them. Both groups now restrict their members to those born without "gifts"; natural-born.

The gifted, like Keary and her sister Erin, rank low on the totem pole. Somewhere above slave yet below citizen. Each one carrying the burden of their ancestor's choices five hundred years in the past.

Hell, most gifted aren't able to track their family line that far back. Not that the Elders or other like-minded, natural-born citizens care. If it weren't for our unique abilities, Keary harbors no doubt the Vanguard would've snuffed out every gifted being left alive the instant they won the war.

Giving her head a quick shake, she shakes loose the grip of her sour thoughts. Cradling her mug in both hands, she takes a sip before reclining against the porch-swing back. Gently, it sways forward with a soft creak of chains as the sun climbs out of the horizon.

Tucking one foot beneath her, she leaves the other to hang should the swing need another nudge while she bathes in the sunrise's palette of blush, gold and pumpkin hues. When a stiff breeze comes off the water to trail icy fingers across her skin, she huddles deeper into her sweater.

"Morning Kear."

Soothed by her surroundings, Keary squeaks when Erin's voice fills her head. Judging by the huskiness coloring her usual soft tones, she hasn't been awake for very long. *"Morning Imp. How are you?"*

An impressive yawn slips through the hum of the mind-link before Erin answers. *"I'll let you know once the coffee kicks in."*

"Classes going well?"

"Pretty much. I have midterms just around the corner. How do you always sound so chipper in the morning?"

Keary grins. *"I've been up longer than you have. Not running into any problems then? I can't imagine the Citadel is much like Briar."*

"I'm sticking close to the campus. Still haven't seen those serial killers and rapists you warned me about." There's a slight pause before Erin sends across an image of her tapping a finger against her chin. *"As far as I know, anyway."*

"You're a horrible sister." Keary shoots back, her teeth grinding over Erin's tinkling laughter.

"It's amazing Kear! The hot water that doesn't run out, our markets are full of vendors. The lights don't dim in the evening either. Something about the solar panels they use. Sure you can't come and give the city a try?"

Why am I not surprised? Of course they'd keep the better technology closer to home. Far away from the blight of society. While the heat builds in her chest until she can taste it in her throat, she forces a tight smile. *"Positive."*

"Maybe I'll start attracting a few of those serial killers. Then you'd have no choice but to come out."

"Or I could let them have you."

"Yeah right. Who else is going to put up with you? I've got to go. Love you bunches," Erin rushes to add before severing the connection.

"Love you too," Keary whispers audibly.

After rubbing a finger against a fresh headache, she spends what remains of her morning enjoying the last of her coffee. Just after the mug loses its warmth, she notices the time. The realization she's running late obliterates the calm she's found and purses her lips.

"Time to be an adult." Casting one last look over the railing, her eyes travel over the budding trees to the churning lake just beyond. "Good morning, Nana," she murmurs in a thick voice. The breeze that answers comforts her tired soul.

Figuring she's stalled long enough, Keary steps into her tiny kitchen and rinses out her mug. Leaving it to dry in the rack, she pulls on her favorite boots. Aside from them being a gift from Erin, last yuletide, she adores the swirling knotwork pattern stitched in the sides.

Exchanging her sweater for a light jacket, she stops at the front closet for an umbrella, then begins down the worn path towards her bicycle. When she spots the back tire pressing flat against the damp ground, a groan escapes her lips.

"Really? You couldn't do that tomorrow?"

Jamming the umbrella under the seat, Keary runs to the small shed at the back of her house. Stiff fingers fumble too long over the rusted lock before it finally gives under enough pressure. Once the door swings open, she stands back and eyes the rows of boxes and gardening supplies packed in tight rows.

Huffing loudly, she rifles through the clutter, ignoring the dust clouds forming around her fingertips. When a soft rustling noise reaches her ears, Keary freezes. Peeking over one shoulder, she meets a pair of beady eyes staring back at her from the shadows.

At first, the plump rat continues to nibble on the corner of a box, undisturbed by her arrival. Fingers clench as its large head quirks to the side before he sniffs at the surrounding air. Cutting its losses, the enormous rat jumps down to the packed dirt floor and scurries off in the opposite direction.

Suppressing her shudder, Keary leans over a stack of boxes to glare at the hole in the back wall of her shed.

"Add that to my to-do list," she mutters, then quickly locates the air-pump. Another glance at the time she's wasting has her rushing back to her bike, propping it against the side of the house and getting to work.

The metal pump squeaks painfully with each press of her hand as she fights to maintain a steady rhythm. Sweat gathers on her forehead before her skin pebbles under another gust of a cool breeze. "This is taking too long. Mrs. Tingley is expecting me, and I need the business," she gripes not really expecting her bike to offer a defense. *Never should've dallied this morning*, her head answers instead.

Steeling herself, Keary is ready to walk when the tire suddenly fits snugly against the rim. After a soft whoop and a brief arm pump, she runs back to drop the pump into an open box and reattach the lock to the door. After shoving a hand through her damp hair, Keary climbs on her bike and takes off down the bumpy driveway.

The ride to the heart of Briar's village is peaceful as the road curves around the lake on her left-hand side. While the reflection of the rising sun off the water can take one's breath away, it unfortunately leaves Keary without a direct route into town. However, she figures the mists are in her favor this morning when arrives to find the village still slumbers, except for a few.

The wheels of her bicycle travel smoothly over cobblestone streets that lead into the heart of Briar. Built from rough stone or wooden slats, businesses line either side. To an outsider, their village is both beautiful and fragile. Just like the small rivers that run through the town, an undercurrent of tension builds under the surface.

A gentle breeze stirs the air, disturbing new leaves on a grand oak tree. The nearby bakery, blacksmith and horse paddock creates a mix of aromas. with a combination of baked goods, smoke and fresh hay. As Keary passes Old Man Riley, the scent of his favorite pipe tobacco greets her first. Eyes dance as he spots Keary, and he raises his steaming mug in a silent salute in her direction.

Keary returns the wave with a friendly grin before she veers from the main road. The unevenness of the path from years of use is a stark contrast to the well-maintained main road into town. It doesn't take long for the undercurrent of tension to ruin the tranquil atmosphere. Twice, she notices immense claw marks etching into a wooden or stony surface, prompting her eyes to widen.

The indented marks seem too long to be the work of nature, stretching across the building for several feet before dripping droplets of scarlet onto the ground below. That the businesses tagged are both owned by *natural-born* Keary can't dismiss as coincidence. Like most people, she's heard whispers and rumors about a new group forming in the underbelly of Solstier. Rising from the ashes of an older group, members of Crimson Claw began challenging the harsh treatment of the *gifted*. Oppressed and neglected, their leaders stoke the demands for change.

Keary's grip tightens on her handlebars as she contemplates the possibility of another civil war. Their last one was centuries in the past, but lasted too long and claimed too many lives before it was over. Overnight, it changed the landscape of their society forever, leaving hatred and intolerance for the opposing side in its wake.

"It's not like they don't have a reason to fear us," she mumbles under her breath. Does that excuse their behavior towards us? Not even close. Clenching her teeth tightly, Keary picks up her pace in order to gain as much distance as she can from the Crimson Claw trademark.

Following a series of side roads, she bounces over the uneven ground until she spots the two-story straight ahead. Surrounded by an ivy-covered fence, the stone house stands proud amidst a small grove of trees. The sharp squeal of children draws her attention to the rail line beside Mrs. Tingley's house. As the train pushes hard to reach the primary hub on time, several of the older children race through the fields alongside. The thick plumes of black smoke, the loud clack of the tracks beneath and an occasional blast of its horn shatter the otherwise peaceful morning. Despite the racket, children wave their arms wildly at the engineer.

"Every damn morning!" Bracing her considerable weight against the doorjamb, Mrs. Tingley steps out of her house long enough to send the train a withering glare. "You'd think I'd just sell this place and move on."

Smothering a smile, Keary rests the bike against the side of the porch and loops her satchel over one shoulder. "Why haven't you."

"My late Henry loved this house. When the energy law passed, he spent a week on that roof attaching those solar panels." Mrs. Tingley heaves a sigh. "Walking away from it just feels wrong."

"I understand."

"How was your ride, dear?"

Keary flashes Mrs. Tingley a smirk before she steps into the open living room. "Cold."

The older woman takes a moment to lock the door behind them before settling gently onto her lumpy couch. "I swear this season is colder every year."

Stepping into the house, Keary sighs over the warmth that rushes over her skin. With the fireplace just on the opposite wall, she resists the urge to move closer. Setting her satchel on the floor, she moves closer to Mrs. Tingley. After spending a moment studying her client, her lips pressing tight when a familiar ache settles in her knees. "Arthritis again?"

"It's that or my joints just don't like me. Tea pot should be almost ready."

Before Keary can respond, Erin's voice comes through the mind link. *"Made it to class alive. Though I ran into a guy in the square. Cute, too. Do you think the blood spatter on his shoes is a bad sign?"* Lips twitch as Keary's smile creeps free. "Brat."

The sight of Mrs. Tingley's pointed grin tells Keary she's said that out loud. "Pretty sure I'm too old for such titles."

"I wasn't aware one could outgrow titles. How does that work?"

"You either outlive the ones with the balls for using such names or have so much money that no one else would dare."

One dark eyebrow raises. "You're naughty."

"Mm-hmm. Don't you forget it." Keary catches her wink as she measures out an amount of dried ginger. "How is our Erin doing?"

"Great. She's enjoying school and loving the Citadel."

"Of course she is! Adventure is in her bones, dear. Like your father, that one. What's she studying again?"

"Erin's getting her teaching degree in history. Top of her class, too." Even Keary can hear the boast that colors her words but shrugs it off. *Who wouldn't be proud?*

"Oh boy. I wonder if Mr. Tibbs knows that."

"I think he'd take early retirement if he did," Keary whispers and offers her friend a slow wink.

A sharp whistle signals the tea pot reaching a boil so Keary sidetracks to pour her client a cup. Dumping in the ginger, she adds a small spoonful of honey. "Here you go," she says with a smile, setting the cup on the short table beside the couch. "I added some sweet to cut the bitterness and I've brought some muffins as well. That'll help with the aftertaste."

"I'd better not. At my age, I'd be in the grave five years before I burn off the calories."

"Calories, huh?"

"A nasty word. One that's never cost you a night's rest, I'd wager. Skinny as a rail you are. Your Nana and I had names for your kind."

"I'm sure you did." Tightening the lid on her bottle of ginger, Keary stuffs it into her bag before moving onto one of her ointments. "How have you been?"

"Despite the poking and prodding of our new physician, I'm well. I swear he's disappointed to find me in such good health."

"Maybe he's just editing the paper he intends to write on your behalf?"

"Smartass." Gathering a light crochet shawl tighter around her shoulders, Mrs. Tingley bobs her head once for emphasis. "Now if I could just control my mouth, I'd be golden."

"What's wrong with your mouth?"

"Nothing, dear. But I seem to spend most of my time putting my foot in it, and the rest of my time dislodging it."

"Ahh. Be careful, you don't chew it to nubs while it's in there."

"Hush. You have no room to talk."

"Nope. That's why I avoid most conversations. Harder to offend people that way."

"I'm far too old and set in my ways to walk on eggshells. My late Henry could tell you all about it."

"Don't tiptoe on my account, I prefer your honesty."

"That's because Alex raised you girls right when you came to us."

"Yes, she did." The constant thought of Nana puts a small hitch in her breathing and a twinge in her chest. *I'll pay her a visit today.* "Okay, enough of the dreary! Let's get you up and moving again," Keary declares with a smile.

"The mists bless you, dear."

Lifting one leg, Keary balances Mrs. Tingley's foot in her lap while she lathers her hands with a generous amount of aloe. Not long after she took over as the village apothecary, her visits with Mrs. Tingley grew into a friendship. Out of sorts lately, with Erin away for study, the older lady's sharp wit and warm personality brightens her day.

"Any plans for the weekend?" Mrs. Tingley asks, breaking Keary out of her thoughts.

"Not really. Just going to visit with Nana and maybe catch up on some reading."

"Don't tell me you're making enough money off your medicine to be buying books now?"

Keary chuckles and gives her head a shake. "No ma'am. I'm still working my way through Nana's collection."

"You spend too much time with your nose in a book and your life is going to pass you by."

"So you keep telling me," she replies, using a light touch to rub the ointment into the area surrounding the joint. The more she touches, the more she absorbs the chronic ache plaguing her dear friend.

"When I was your age, I spent most of my weekends dancing." After chasing away a far-off expression, Mrs. Tingley gives Keary a pointed stare.

"I can only imagine."

"Oh, I had moves. Let me tell you."

"You may have to teach me one or two." Keary grins as she sets one leg down before starting in on the other. "Were you the belle of the ball?"

"Oh heavens, no. That was your grandmother. I was more the troublemaker. I had a bit of a wild streak in my youth."

"That, I can believe."

"In my day, I'd give Erin a run for her money." Mrs. Tingley adds with a quick wink. "But those days are long gone."

"They don't have to be. You could organize a dance for the village. Show us kids something new."

"What a wonderful idea! I'll have to talk to the others and see if they're up for it."

"You'll have to let me know how it goes."

"Oh, stuff it, girlie. If I'm dancing. So are you."

Keary's heart drops an inch within her chest. "Oh, I don't think-"

"Your grandmother would roll over in her grave if I didn't pull you out for just one dance. It's settled."

Since arguing with their villages matriarch won't budge the old bird, Keary bites her tongue. No doubt the dance will be a way off. With a bit of luck, she'll figure out a way from the mess she just stepped in.

After a moment of searching with her fingertips, Keary finds the inflamed area and begins massaging the aloe deep into the surrounding tissue. As she works, her mind drifts to thoughts of her grandmother. Some days are harder than others, but most days she just misses her terribly. Since one more conversation with her is out of the question, Keary cherishes her time with Nana's best friend.

"All done, Mrs. T."

A soft gasp jumps from Mrs. Tingley's mouth as she tests one knee and then the other. "You're a miracle worker, Keary."

A flush creeps up Keary's neck as she busies herself with the clean-up. "Call it a fair trade. Your visits are a bright spot for me."

"That's because you're such a good listener, girlie." Mrs. Tingley snags one of Keary's hands between hers long enough to deliver a soft pat. "Being an empath is a rare trait these days. What do I owe you?"

Keary fights to keep her face impassive as she struggles to her feet with suddenly aching joints. Her breath gathers in her lungs until the sensation fades enough for her to plaster a smile on her face. "Well, I'm going to leave you some of this ginger. It will help with the inflammation, so maybe five silvers."

"Let's call it ten since you came to me. You give my best to your sister now."

"I will," Keary promises, slipping the coins in the side pocket of her satchel. After a last wave, she leaves her client resting comfortably on her couch, surrounded by her memories.

Retrieving her bicycle, she scrubs a hand over the back of her neck. She has hours to kill before her next appointment, but the thought of going home to the empty house makes her throat stick.

After a quick battle with indecision, she pedals to the enormous park near the center of their village. Once she props her bicycle against a tree, Keary slides down with her back leaning against the bark and pulls out a book from her bag. Breathing deeply of the fresh-cut grass, she finds the spot where she left off reading the night before.

CHAPTER 3

After swiping her damp palms against her jeans, Erin gives her shoulders a quick roll as the train pulls into the station. Covering her yawn with the back of one hand, she drags the others through her short curls. While passengers filter into the narrow aisle toward the exit, she untangles her legs and rights herself in her seat. Before she can stand, however, the conductor barks out a last bit of instructions.

"In compliance with train policy, passengers in this car will wait until all other passengers are off."

"You mean, wait until all these natural-born are off. Right, mate?"

Erin directs her attention to the young man two seats up on her right. Her ears pick up on the slight accent. He isn't a local. Growing up in Briar, the local speech pattern burned itself into her brain at a young age. Trying not to acknowledge how intrigued she is by something different from what she knows, Erin studies his angular jaw tighten and his dark eyes narrow into slits during his confrontation with the conductor.

With the amount of people already swarming the aisle, there isn't much to do at this point but wait. Retrieving her backpack/pillow from the other seat, she loops it over her shoulders. Through the train's windows, she studies the small depot on the other side. It's been six months since her last visit home. If not for the fact Keary refuses to live anywhere else, she'd be happy never to return.

They drew her back to the situation as the conductor steps into the seat across from her to glare openly at the young man two seats up. "It's our policy to give natural-born citizens the opportunity to get on and off the train, safe from the chaotic nature of you people."

"*My* people," the young man challenges. His eyes narrow so much Erin wonders if he's able to see anything. "Do you mean, *men*? No, that can't be right, 'cause she's sitting here with me," he clips, jabbing a thumb in Erin's direction. "Perhaps *students*? No, again that can't be right because I don't recall seeing this old guy at the University," he openly mocks as he gestures to an older Solstieran. "So what is it you mean then, friend?"

The conductor waits for the last of the passengers to leave, his scowl deepening the sharp features of his face. "As in gifted," he snarls before linking with somebody else on the train. "You may now proceed in an orderly fashion."

Erin remains in her seat as the young man scoffs loudly, then makes a beeline for the exit. She grasps at her short hair, mustering the strength needed to leave the barren carriage. Rising stiffly, she strides down the empty aisle, her bag bouncing off the back of the seats on her right. Near the exit, the tall and slender conductor hovers near the open door with a polished smile. As Erin passes, he includes a slight curl of his upper lip.

Once she steps out into the fresh air, a grin tilts her lips as she stops less than two feet from the train. Tipping her head back, Erin takes a deep breath and smiles as the sun warms her face. For a moment, she allows her mind to drift before the familiar sounds of the village intrude.

A chorus of the boats in the harbor, the distinct smell of fish and squawking birds overhead, serve as her homecoming. The small village she fled nearly two years ago may have been home then, but it never felt like it.

Gradually, the tightness in her chest grows as the bustle of the train station intrudes on her moment of peace. After a glance to check the time, she maneuvers through the throng of people towards a small office near the end of the platform.

Behind her, the conductor's voice booms over the din of noise to begin the trains boarding of all natural-born passengers. A glance over her shoulder shows a group of what she can only assume are gifted passengers, waiting silently for their turn to board. Biting back the sharp retort clinging to her tongue, she weaves through the crowd to reach the office before a line can form. Her hand lands on the polished handle just as another woman attempts to cut her off.

"Excuse me!"

With a bat of her lashes, Erin releases a tiny dose of her lemon and lilac scent into the air. "Oh, I'm so sorry! Are you sure you want me to go ahead of you?"

Pale blue eyes narrow under a set of severely sculpted brows before the woman's hawk-like features tighten. As Erin's scent permeates the surrounding air, the tension leaks from a set of bony shoulders as her thin lips relax. "Of course, child. I'm in no rush."

Erin flashes a practiced smile of innocent charm before murmuring her thanks. She spends the next few seconds reliving one of Keary's lectures with a pinch in her brow. Reigning in her scent, Erin pushes through the wide-set double doors before the woman can change her mind.

Once inside, she scans the room for a sign, pointing towards the ticket booth. Plaques and photos of the area's history decorate the cracked yellow walls under rows of florescent lights humming above her head. The wind from outside gasps and moans within the rafters to smother the room with various smells.

Erin's nose twitches when the unmistakable smell of scorched metal and dirt from the coal train fills her nostrils. Soon, the unmistakable scent of beer and mozzarella coming from the various food stands outside filters in. Her fingers slide along the polished wood surface that creates a barrier between the customers inside the station and the employees on the other side.

Behind the counter, a tall man offers her a friendly smile, causing the toothpick between his lips to falter for a moment. "Good morning." Bushy brows furrow on his weathered face. "Or is it afternoon now?"

Erin covers the distance with a smile. "Since we just passed the noon mark, I'd wager on the afternoon."

"Crazy how hard time is to keep track of when you're stuck indoors."

"I couldn't agree more."

The man slaps his hand on the smooth surface of the counter as he appears to chase away his wandering thoughts. "What can I do for you?"

"I just came in on your twelve-o'clock train and I have a rather large package I need to arrange for delivery." Behind her, the rude woman from earlier heaves a sigh heavy enough to fill the room before making a spectacle of checking the time.

Eyes travel from Erin to the woman behind her before he gives Erin a warm smile. "Well, I can certainly help you with that," he says, the slightest taste of tobacco and coffee on his breath. "Name?"

"Erin McKenna."

"Any relation to Keary?"

Erin's smile becomes more genuine as she gives her head a quick nod. "She's my older sister. You must be new around here."

Eyes twinkle as he runs a hand through his neatly combed salt and pepper hair. "Yes ma'am. Only been here a two or three months."

"Welcome to Briar. It's a nice enough place," Erin grins, "if you like small towns, anyway." Another sigh fills the air behind them, forcing Erin to grit her teeth.

"Big or small, I find it all rests on the people." Plucking the toothpick from his lips, he taps a finger over the sheet in front of him. "Aha! Found your package. Would you like it delivered out to Keary's place?"

"It would be amazing if you could."

"Not a problem. That'll be five silvers."

After dropping the coins in his hand, Erin accepts the hand-written receipt, only to stuff it deep into her backpack. With a quick shake of his rough and callused hand, Erin steps out of line so the rude woman could go next.

"How can I help you, ma'am?"

Her expression troubled, the woman rubs a finger across her brow as if trying to remember something important. Erin decides it's probably better to not tell Keary about this encounter as she slips out of the office and stands in line for bicycle rental. Twenty minutes later, she's walking a bicycle through the busy streets as the sights and sounds of her hometown filter in.

Walking down the winding, cobblestoned street reminds her of how little has changed since her departure. The market offers a familiar scene, with one vendor cheerfully calling out his regulars by name as he hands out his fresh produce. The characteristic smell of fish and cured leather intermingles with that of butchered meat in the air to welcome her home.

The shriek and laughter of children from the nearby school yard barely makes a dent in the hollering of various vendors. However, it's the scent of freshly baked bread and sweetened pastries that draws her close.

Pushing through the designated walkway, Erin searches for an empty rack to stow her bicycle long enough to make a detour. Another minute passes before she locates one just a quick jog from the bakery. "Things would be easier if Keary would just move closer," she observes while digging through her bag for the bike lock near the bottom. "Not that she'll ever leave this place." Once she secures the lock, she rubs a hand over the growing knot in her neck, then sprints back to the smell of sugar and yeast.

In the large bay windows, several displays hold an array of goodies, cakes and other confections. Fine detail decorates some deserts, while others boast a simple elegance that requires no extra effort. When she slips through the door, a tiny bell overhead signals her arrival.

"Well, well. Look at what the mists have brought home."

"Mist indeed." Erin's lips tilt as she greets one of her favorite people. "How are you Mr. Robal?"

"Just grand dear. You're certainly a sight for sore eyes 'round these parts."

"I bet you say that to all the ladies that come in here."

"Only when the wife isn't here and only to those with pretty red curls." Standing mere inches taller than his own display case, his eyes sparkle with laughter.

The air inside is a confectioner's dream, with the scent of baked goods, cinnamon, and sugary sweet delights filling the room. The distinct aroma of coffee draws Erin's attention to a small bar on the far side of the room. "That's new."

"Ah. The missus thought a coffee bar would attract a younger crowd."

Erin grins. "It's a great idea."

"You come to see that sister of yours?"

"I thought I'd surprise her."

"Something tells me she's going to be happy to see you."

Erin nods while inspecting shelves of goodies near the register. "She always is. I keep trying to get her to move out East with me. So far, no luck."

"I don't see your sister fitting in with the bustle of the city."

"Yeah. That and I'm fairly certain that she's turned into one of those old stones from the stories Nana told us."

"Perhaps." His chuckle shakes his ample frame as he pulls out a small white bag from under the display case. "You won't see me complaining about your rotten luck. The more she drags you home, the better, in my humble opinion."

"You'd be *one*."

"The only one that matters, dear," he adds with a soft pat on her hand.

"The market looks good. More vendors this year."

Mr. Robal's smile falters slightly as he casts a quick look over her shoulder at the large window behind her. Before she can count to three, his smile is back, as genuine as ever. "The Citadel granted extra licenses this year."

Erin's brow wrinkles. "Why would they do that? They've only ever allowed ten before."

"Who can really say why those people do anything? I, for one, am happy to see our small market alive with activity. The wife and I don't swallow all that *natural born* rhetoric our Elders push. Gifted or not, everyone needs to eat, dearie." Mr. Robal adds another soft pat of his hand, drawing her back to the reason she stopped in. "Speaking of eating, what treats can I get for you today?"

"Hmm. Are your fritters fresh?"

"See! The mists must've been whispering something fierce in my ear since I just made a fresh batch this morning."

Erin laughs and digs through the coins inside her wallet. "Then I'll take one fritter and one glazed doughnut. Pretty please."

"Put your money away, there's no charge," he declares before folding the bag closed and passing it across the counter.

"Oh, I can't let you do that."

"Let me, huh?" Rounding the case, he encircles her shoulders and walks her to the door. Erin grins, inhaling his scent of spice and sugar. As a child, she could think of nothing better.

"Think of it as doing me a kindness. If the missus finds out I charged you on your first day home, she'd take the hide right off my back."

"Thank you, Mr. Robal," Erin places a chaste kiss to one blushing cheek before tugging open the door. "Give my best to your better half."

Erin makes the quick jaunt to the rented bicycle, with an extra bounce in her step. As exciting as the city is, sometimes the charm of home is its own medicine. She hums a light tune as she rides for home, only to stop short when she reaches the park.

Even if the long black hair piled high on her head, held with pencils, doesn't give it away, the book in her lap certainly does. Setting her bicycle next to Keary's, she's barely out of the seat before her sister is shoving herself to her feet.

"Is everything okay?"

"Of course. Why wouldn't it be?"

"Because you're not due back for months." Keary answers in a tight voice as her face puckers. "Did something happen?"

"Of course not."

"So then, what's wrong?"

"*Oy*, Keary, nothing is wrong. I have a few days off in between classes, so I thought I'd surprise you for your birthday."

"My birthday isn't for months."

"Surprise!"

It takes Keary a full minute to transition out of panic mode. With a smile, Erin counts the seconds it takes for her shoulders to relax and the pinch to soften out of her forehead. She's practically to thirty by the time pear-green eyes flicker and Keary breaks out in a grin.

Laughing, she pulls Erin in for a fierce hug. "You're the best sister ever."

"That's what I keep telling you," Erin quips, her voice muffled by Keary's embrace. "I missed you."

"I missed you too." Pulling back, Keary gives Erin a quick inspection. "You look good."

With a laugh, Erin gives a small twirl. "I have all my fingers and toes and every one of my organs. Promise." Drawing a crisscross over her chest, Erin ends with a wink. "You look amazing! How are you still taller?"

"I told you. I get the height. You get the curves. It's a win-win, really."

Erin's nose crinkles. "I think you're over-estimating the value of curves. Anyway, I come bearing gifts," she announces and dangles the white bag from Mr. Robal's bakery off two fingers. "How 'bout lunch?"

"That isn't lunch. Follow me back to the house. I'll make sandwiches to go with your sweets. Maybe the weather will hold and we can make it a picnic."

"Ooh. See, that's why you're the oldest."

Erin climbs back onto her bike as Keary jogs back to the tree long enough to grab her satchel. Minutes later, Erin's following the ugly blue bicycle with its large wicker basket out of town.

Without a word, the sisters pedal along the familiar, winding road away from the bustle of the village. Around them, trees stand tall, rustling in the soft breeze that carries the promise of blooming flowers over the next few weeks. The closer they draw to home, the more Erin's muscles relax.

As they near the house, their white picket fence comes into view, its paint already peeling from the previously harsh winter. Steering their bikes around the property line for Mr. Soloman's orchard, Keary leads the way up their rocky driveway toward the old farmhouse. A small forest of trees serve as the backdrop before the ground gives way to a rocky drop-off leading to the lake.

The old farmhouse is a porch-wrapped box with three tall windows on each side. The weathered siding is white with blue shutters painted in a simple design, leading all the way to a narrow circle tower in the back corner. Thick rose bushes decorate the front of the house, their branches still bare. Other than the recent addition of solar panels, the house looks the same as it did when they arrived as children.

Resting their bikes against the house, the sisters split up the tasks. Keary makes quick work of a more sensible lunch while Erin fills two large mugs with peppermint tea. Arm and arm, they climb the fat hill next to the house to emerge in a small clearing where a set of worn chairs await them.

While Erin munches on shaved turkey and cheese, she lets her stresses fall away as the wind-chimes that decorate the small grove play in the wind. The heat of the tea in her hands is just enough to ward off the chill in the air as the sky contemplates more rain. When she inhales, she breathes in the lavender they planted two years ago, mixing with wet earth. While they'd both agreed to lay Nana to rest in the town's cemetery; this is where they visit her.

Erin can't count the number of times her grandmother had brought her up here. Often, when life got too hard, she'd patiently teach Erin the dangers of her impulsive nature. Years passed from childhood curiosity to teenage angst. Angry at life, her teenage-self had a rebellious streak that put the Black Death to shame. Unfazed, Nana and Keary stuck with her.

"I miss her something fierce most days." Erin's voice is thick enough to stick inside her throat and she doesn't need to look up to know Keary is watchful. No doubt zeroing in on raw emotions, so Erin fixes her gaze on the cup in her hands.

"Me too, Imp."

Just then, a fresh gust of wind pushes through the grove and sets various chimes to sway among branches. As they dance, they sing songs in their own, unique ways. A few are deep and hollow. Others are light and full. It's a particular one that snags Erin's ear with its tiny, soft notes.

"You hung a new one," she realizes with a smile.

"Mm-hmm. I found it while I was in Harper. You like it?"

Erin meets the green eyes searching her face, looking for a flicker of disapproval before lips quirk in response to her nod. "It's perfect."

"I thought so too."

"Why were you in Harper?"

"Mrs. Tingley asked me to visit a family there. Their little boy was fighting a severe strain of the flu and couldn't get another apothecary to visit."

"One of the gifted families, I take it?" Even as she asks, Erin already knows the answer. Over the last decade or so, the treatment of anyone gifted has grown more negligent. *Not that it was great before*, her mind argues.

"I'm afraid so."

"And how long were you sick after that?"

Keary's eyes flash briefly before she sets her chin defiantly. "Only a couple of days. I'm fine, Erin."

"This time. Without Nana here, you need to be more careful. Taking on their sickness wipes you out."

"You're right." Keary offers a quick nod to smooth Erin's nerves, but even from where she sits, Erin has no delusions about the lengths her sister will go to help someone. Even if that leaves her bedridden for days after.

Her gift of healing came out of nowhere for the sisters. The first of them to show any sign of being one of the wretched gifted. After a little research, Nana found an ancestor or two with minor gifts. Her amiable smile almost smothered the sudden shadows in her eyes because none were as powerful as what Keary displayed.

The two of them had been attending school when Erin *slipped* off the slide and snapped the bones in her ankle. The smirk Sally wore as she stood at the top flashes quickly through Erin's memory. Just like then, her stomach twists and a sour taste explodes against her tongue.

She recalls Keary kneeling beside her, gasping under a wash of angry tears. As children gathered around them, she recalls the laser-sharp focus of her sister's attention. In a matter of moments, Erin went from writhing in pain to stomaching a dull ache. Keary, on the other hand, had spent the next two weeks laid up while her ankle fracture healed. Ever since then, she's been more cautious about her own injuries, hiding them whenever possible.

The darkness of that memory swirls behind her eyes, sucking the energy from her body. Erin takes a minute securing those events behind a soundproof wall before forcing a shaky smile on her lips. "You haven't asked me about your birthday present yet." Wadding up the wrapper from her sandwich, she stuffs it into a pocket of her jacket.

"That's 'cause I know you'll tell me soon enough. Secrets aren't your thing."

"You think so?" Her nose wrinkles despite the air of truth in Keary's words. "You're not even a little curious?"

"Curiosity killed the cat."

"Satisfaction brought it back," she quips. *Funny how two tiny sentences can put a magnifying glass on their distinct personalities,* she muses.

Keary is serious and organized, while Erin is friendly and carefree. As the firstborn in a family with deceased parents, Keary took on the responsibility of the missing role. Because of this, Erin will never understand the heavy load her sister bears. But that weight also makes her reliable. Erin knows she can always count on her sister for a level head, a caring heart and fierce protection.

"I *am* curious," Keary says, breaking Erin out of her thoughts. "But I trust you. Whatever you got me, it'll be perfect. Plus, I consider your visits as presents."

"You're a pain."

"How was the trip home?"

"It rained."

"You did okay, though?" A frown flickers over Keary's mouth before she hides it behind her mug of tea.

"Eh, I made it in one piece, so that's a bonus. The train car was empty for most of the ride, so I slept when I could. And I didn't meet any psycho's or allow the train to stop for hitchhikers." Erin adds to lighten the mood, breathing in the damp air.

"Now who's the pain?"

Suddenly, the skies open up around them. No eerie drizzle this time. This is a hard downpour of water that pummels those foolishly caught in it, drenching Erin and her sister in a matter of seconds. With a squeal, they turn and run for the house. Huddling under the porch roof, Erin laughs while shaking off the excess water.

"What do you want to do now?"

"I have one last appointment."

"You can't reschedule one day?"

"It's Sally Smith's son. If I cancel, she'll drag my name through the mud."

"Sally Smith." Erin hisses the name as if venom coats her tongue. The mention of her childhood bully grips her chest in a vise. The action strangles her breath until Keary speaks in a scolding tone that sends shivers up her spine.

"Be nice. She's going through stuff right now with Tommy Rivers. I hear they're getting divorced."

Good. "Not that it couldn't possibly happen to a better person. I don't understand why anyone wastes the time on marriage? Why can't people just live together?"

"Mom and Dad had a good marriage, Imp."

"Mom and Dad were natural-born." The matter-of-fact tone she musters isn't able to cover the sour scent that leaks out with them.

Rather than calling her on it as Erin expects, Keary ruffles a hand in her springy, wet curls, and forces a smile. "I'm sure you're wiped. Why don't you nap and I'll wake you when I get back?"

"I'm not too proud to say a nap sounds amazing right now."

"Perfect." Pulling her close, Keary swallows her in a hug. "And please, don't leave your boots by the door this time?"

"Got it."

In the time it takes Erin to run through the rain to gather her backpack, Keary holds an umbrella in one hand as she tears along the driveway. *One day, she's going to catch her death parading around in such weather.* As the thought sprints through her head, her chest aches.

After another good shake on the porch, Erin hangs her coat on a hook inside the door and kicks off her boots while ignoring her stiff muscles. "Nice to be home." Though Nana's house isn't the flashiest on the lake, it's by far the coziest.

Inside, the air tastes fresh and warm. Just beyond the thin windows, the wind slips through the trees surrounding the farmhouse with a heavy sigh. Original wood floors creak and groan under her weight as she forces every step forward. When her skin tightens, Erin avoids the rest of the house and cuts through the living room.

A hand drifts over the back of a rocking chair and blows a kiss to a framed painting of her parents still on the mantle before Erin climbs the stairs. A cold wash skitters down her back when she passes the closed door to Nana's room, her skin tingling.

For a second, her hand lifts, only to hang in mid-air. The struggle to breathe without sobbing becomes too real to ignore, forcing Erin to turn and open her own door straight across the hall.

Keary had tidied up since her last visit. Laundered clothes make a neat stack inside a tall hamper. Her small wastebasket under her desk is now empty of crumpled paper, receipts, and the used Kleenex she left behind. She'd even replaced the thick winter curtains with ones made of white lace. Erin suspects she'll find clean sheets on the bed as well.

With a yawn, she plunks her bag near the closet and trades her jeans in for a pair of green cotton shorts. With a thick towel, her small hands squeeze out the last few drops of water from her hair before she scoots under the blankets.

Her feet wriggle across smooth sheets as she snuggles in, pulling her favorite quilt up to her chin. The sun shining through the windows warms the material nicely, chasing the cold from her limbs. It doesn't take long for her eyes to get heavy and droop, as the smell of sun and spring air on her blanket swallows Erin in the warm shelter of being home.

CHAPTER 4

"Okay, Sweetie. I'm almost done," Keary coaxes gently. Judging by the way Simon responds with more scratching and fidgeting, he's missed his afternoon nap. A factor that takes his rabid-dog patience and cuts it in half. Twice now, his restlessness has spilled a good portion of the ointment onto the blanket beneath him. Teeth snap as Keary counts the third.

Peeking over her shoulder, she notes his mother's pacing behind them. Glassy, sharp blue eyes tell Keary she's mind-linking someone. After adding in the rigid set of her shoulders, she assumes it's not a pleasant conversation.

"Won't find any help there," she grumbles and digs around in her bag for a distraction. Pulling the cloth dog from the depths, she grins as Simon's eyes widen in his tiny face. "Want to play with Gruff?" After an excited bob of his head, the boy clutches the toy to his chest. Once he's preoccupied, Keary makes quick work lathering witch hazel over the angry red bumps peppering his skin. The more she touches, the more her own skin itches. By the time she finishes, sweat beads on her brow as she resists the urge to scratch at her own skin.

Lips press into a tight line as she busies herself with packing everything back into her satchel. When she finishes, a soft puff of air escapes her lips to find the maddening aggravation fades into a gentle reminder. "Alright, Bud. You're good to go. But no more playing in the backyard." Deep brown eyes darken a moment before his lower lip juts out from his face. "At least until your dad can clear it. Okay?" Once Simon offers a reluctant nod, Keary pulls a handful of sweet treats from her pocket.

"All done?" Sally's eyes clear as she runs a finger over a wrinkle in her otherwise smooth forehead. Manicured nails drag through her shoulder-length blonde hair as she inspects Simon.

"I got sweets," he declares, opening his small fist to display the treats proudly.

Full, red lips thin before light flashes in the eyes she stabs in Keary's direction. "We don't allow sweets."

"My apologies. I would've asked first, but you looked pretty busy," she answers with smile that's a work of practice and civility. The small voice in her head points out a small kernel of satisfaction when the wrinkle appears on Sally's forehead once more.

"What do I owe you?"

"Eight silvers."

One thin brow arches. "Last time it was five."

"His rash is worse this time, so I'm leaving you some ointment to make him more comfortable." *Not counting all the ointment he spilled.* "I would recommend keeping him out of the backyard until you can clear out the poison ivy."

"He's three. How do you expect him to play?"

"I'd have him rest for a day or two. That'll give Tommy time to clear it."

"Fine." Retrieving a drawstring purse, Sally counts out each silver before dropping them into Keary's palm. Long, boney fingers twitch and curl as if she fights the urge to snatch them back. "Anything else?"

"No scratching. If he breaks any of those blisters, it could cause an infection. If the ointment isn't enough, you could try some cold compresses."

"I can do that." Sally nods, running her fingers through Simon's short hair. "You need to give that," she pauses as if searching for the right word, "toy, back to Keary."

Simon stares up at his mother quietly, his hand tightening on the small dog Keary used for distraction. When he turns them on Keary, unshed tears enhance their dark brown color.

"It's fine," she gushes. "He can keep it."

Suppressing a lip curl, Sally nods. "Very well. Was that Erin I saw riding through town this morning?"

"Mm-hmm. She came home for my birthday."

"Today's your birthday?"

"Oh. No. Not for a couple more months."

"Then she's staying awhile?"

Keary blinks. "I imagine just a day or two."

"Oh good. We get enough foul weather without her influence."

Fingers tuck tight against damp palms. "Pretty sure she left her witch's hat back at University," Keary clips in a cool tone. Another flash of light passes through Sally's eyes, but she remains silent. *Good girl.* Making her way across the living room, Keary leaves a jar of ointment on the tall table next to the front door. "This is for Simon."

"Thank you."

"See you later, Bud," Keary calls, catching his small wave before she steps out onto the long porch. "What a bitch," she breathes lightly once the door latches behind her.

A slight flare of guilt washes over her as she's just lectured Erin about being more polite to Sally. If she rubs her that raw, Keary can only imagine what Sally does to Erin.

Pulling a deep breath, she steps off the porch and toward her waiting bicycle. Walking it in a circle, she points it toward home. *Shouldn't be so quick to judge, especially since I don't know the full story.* Still, there's something about Sally's demeanor that just rubs her the wrong way.

As Keary pedals the bike down the dirt road, she enjoys the warm sun on her back and the cool breeze in her face. Gradually, however, the sun begins to sink lower in the sky. The warm glow that had earlier illuminated the world now takes on a cooler, more comfortable hue. Soon, her light jacket isn't quite enough to ward off the cool breeze coming off the lake as she wraps up her ride home.

A quick stop at the end of her driveway allows her to collect a handful of letters and notices before she rides over her pot-hole riddled driveway. Resting the bike against the porch, she separates letters and bills from the rolled missives they're required to read.

Slipping through the front door, her eyes catch on the familiar scrawl on the top envelope. Fingers curl, the crinkle of paper overly loud in the quiet house. *How many times must I decline? Surely there are other properties that will work?* While trying to figure out how to ignore the growing situation, Keary's foot catches on one of Erin's boots.

Tripping sideways, she over-corrects and stumbles forward, her arms shooting outward for leverage. Envelopes flutter in the air around her so she can catch the corner of Nana's writing desk to avoid smacking into the floor. With a peek through loose strands of hair, Keary pins a glare to the culprit.

"She's going to be the death of me," Keary mutters and places the discarded boots on the rack beside the door. Scooping up the loose mail, she slaps it onto the desk before stomping towards the bottom of the stairs.

"Erin! It's five-thirty," she calls. Seconds tick by with Keary's foot tapping along with each one. "Erin!"

"You know, from up here you sound like a Banshee." Erin observes sleepily, poking her head into the hallway. The wild mess of her hair falling over her face testifies to how well she slept. "I'll be down in a minute."

"Don't go back to bed."

Erin's door stutters. "I won't."

"And don't wear your socks on the stairs again."

"O-mi-goodness! You need a new hobby."

"Nah, keeping you alive is a full-time job."

"That happened one time," Erin clips as she closes the door between them with a sharp click, no doubt declaring herself the victor of their short debate.

"So did the sinking of the Dragon's Call. We all know how that turned out." Keary calls up in a singsong voice, grinning when something thuds against the door.

She doesn't have to hear it to know Erin is grumbling from the safety of her room. Many have accused Keary of being overprotective, but those people aren't even a blip on her radar.

Humming the chorus to a song, Keary makes quick work of the dinner prep. Using a bit of paper to light the kindling in the stove, she waits for the top to warm up. By the time Erin joins her, she has a pot of water on the stove set to boil and the chicken cleaned for cooking.

"I hate it when you use my beloved history to make your paranoid arguments sound logical." Erin grumbles before taking a seat at the island in the kitchen.

"Just stating a fact."

"You realize that ship going down had more to do with the season and the weather than operator error. Despite when some people like to say."

Keary pauses. "Very true." Across from the island, Erin sits with her chin in her hand, her eyes cloudy. Side-stepping the conversational landmines, Keary changes the focus. "Chicken soup, okay?"

"I was planning on cooking dinner for you. I must've been more tired than I thought."

"No worries. I was planning on this, anyway." Keary answers while pulling containers of pre-cut vegetables from the refrigerator. "I prepared everything last night."

"I can see that." Erin gives her a slow grin, her eyes alight with something she finds amusing. "Since when does one *pre*-prepare for dinner? Isn't that redundant?"

"No. Now that I don't have an overgrown Brownie that snacks all day, it saves me time."

"Did you just compare me to an animal?"

"Maybe."

"Gee, thank you?"

The brittle sound in Erin's voice has Keary setting the now empty containers aside. Noting the tightness in her sister's jaw, she arches a brow. "How many times did Gran have to improvise dinner because you came through and ate all the fixings?"

"I don't know. But she bitched about it less than you do."

"That's because she was a saint and had more patience than me." Keary confesses as she makes room on the stove for Erin's teapot.

"I don't think you even know what that word means."

"Patience?" Erin nods. "Depends on the context." Dropping bouillon and salt into the now boiling pot, Keary smoothes the feathers she ruffled with a change of topic. "It's nice to have you home."

"Mm-hmm. It's nice to be home. Even with your grumbling."

"I don't grumble. I bitch."

Erin grins cheekily. "That's the word."

"How're things going with school?"

"Good."

"It'll be nice to have you home for longer than a few days when you finish." The teapot's whistle gives Erin a break, yet Keary catches her sister's sudden fascination with her uneven fingernails. "You're not planning on moving back home, are you?"

"It's an option." Erin busies herself with setting up her cup of tea to pour in the water before meeting Keary's pointed gaze. "If nothing else, I'll be closer than I am now."

"Uh-huh."

"The whole point of the University is to get a job."

"You can't get a job here?" Keary can sense her pitch rising, so she attempts to keep her voice casual. "You love it here."

"I do. But no one is ever going to take me seriously in this town. I'm just Keary's little sister, or Nana's Wild Child. Not an influencer of young minds."

"That's not true." *Where in the world does she get these crazy ideas?* Dropping a spoonful of coffee grounds into the percolator, she leaves it to brew to pull down a couple of bowls.

"Kear, I love you. But not everyone sees me the way you do." One finger bounces the tea strainer within her cup as Erin braces a hip against the counter. "And even if they offer me a job, I don't think I could live here forever."

"No one said anything about forever," Keary muses aloud. Setting the bowls next to the stove, she stirs the bubbling pot. *Why is this topic always so messy to navigate?*

"Keary, if you were a stone, you'd have moss."

"You have a point there." She concedes, laughing when Erin hip bumps her on the way to the table. "I won't lie. It'd be nice having you here. But Nana would tell you to do you."

"Mm, I just wish I knew what that was."

"You'll figure it out. In the meantime, dinner is ready. You grab drinks."

"I brought plenty of tea. It's herbal."

"Ew, no thank you." As if fate decrees, the soft sputter of whistling steam from the percolator rescues her.

"It's six-o'clock. How can you drink coffee this late and not be up all night?" Erin questions while adding cream and sugar to Keary's already brimming coffee mug.

"Practice Grasshopper. First, you must crawl before you can walk."

"You are so old."

"The best of us are."

Erin sets the cup down in front of Keary before taking the seat next to her. "Mm, it smells good," she declares, her face inches from the steam rising off the bowl.

"I hope so. It's the same recipe as always." She waits for Erin to take a cautious sip. The serene smile that reaches her gray eyes is all the answer Keary needs.

"Can't get this at school."

"More reason to come home then." Erin's eyes narrow at the small poke, forcing Keary to wave it off. "I'd make it for you even if you didn't live here."

"I know."

A stretch of silence fills the kitchen as the sisters enjoy their supper, each lost in their own thoughts. Keary isn't sure how much time passes until her stomach warns her it's at capacity and she pushes her bowl away just as a dull buzz shifts in her brain.

"This is a community message. The elder's council is asking all adult citizens to attend a town meeting tomorrow evening."

Once the link is severed, she meets Erin's cloudy eyes from across the table. "Wonder what that's about."

"With the way things are going lately, it could be anything."

"True." Quietly, she mulls over the possible motives behind the message. Their behavior over recent years warrants Erin's quick dismissal. However, Keary can't help but swallow a dark sense of unease. Fingers twitch as nerves stretch just under her skin. Tossing her head left and right, she buries her worries deep into a dark corner for now. "How was your nap?"

"Good. Like I never left. How did the rest of your afternoon go?"

"Could've been worse. I emerged out the other side with my tongue intact after wrestling with Sally and her son."

"That bad?"

"Simon is a charmer, but a little more rambunctious than she's probably used to."

"Oh? Tell me she has her hands full."

Keary blinks at the sudden flare of heat in her sister's eyes. "He sure has a surplus of energy."

"Outstanding!"

"Erin, you two aren't kids anymore. Don't you think it's time to put the nastiness behind you?" Even as Keary asks, she recalls the reaction she had to Sally earlier this afternoon and presses her lips together.

"Nope. It allows me to despise her with all the heat of an adult instead of a child. And don't give me that speech about how Siren's are bitchy. I've met plenty that are rather pleasant. Sally wouldn't know how to be pleasant if it set her panties on fire."

"This is the time Nana would offer a nugget of wisdom." Keary points out, reclining in her chair with a wistful smile. "Something like old grudges spoiling your happy."

Erin's lips thin, her eyes darkening to a cool, gunmetal steel. "I'm not casting a spell over her voodoo doll, Keary."

"Erin-"

"Listen, I appreciate the big sister moment and what you're trying to do. But the day I forgive Sally is the day I become a higher being. And I'm currently rocking the being I am. So, let's drop it, okay?"

"Consider it dropped. Besides, she isn't worth spoiling your appetite over." Keary serves her sister a second bowl of soup and sits to enjoy her coffee. Moments like this are too few for her to ruin it with yet another lecture Erin is just going to ignore, anyway. *Right?*

Erin savors her soup, hungrily gulping mouthfuls with a feverish enthusiasm. Keary's envy intensifies as she admires Erin's total immersion in every moment. Her cheeks pink, she effortlessly savors the warmth and taste of the homemade broth without a care in the world.

Her chest tightens when she considers the freedom in which her sister tackles her world. Fierce and fearless. On the sidelines, Keary calculates every chance of heartbreak or injury her sister can suffer. The hardest part about being the oldest is taking a step back to let her sister learn on her own. Resisting the urge to cover her in bubble wrap or threaten every boy she fancies. *Maybe not every boy,* she amends silently. *Just the worst ones.*

"Why are you looking at me like that?" Erin asks, interrupting Keary's train of thought.

"Nothing, just glad you're home."

Erin nods. The moment passes, and she returns to her supper. A clink of silverware against bowls and the occasional slurp of soup, the only sounds filling the kitchen.

The dinner dishes drip in the rack as Erin excuses herself to barrel upstairs. With a knowing smile, Keary remains at the table with a fresh cup of coffee. Every muscle screams at her to make a run for it, but she battles the urge with a small wriggle in her chair.

It isn't the prospect of being another year older that leaves her itchy, but the attention. Happy to hide in the background, she prefers the passing glances over the limelight. It doesn't help that receiving presents raises the uncomfortable meter attached to her soul. Tucking one foot under her, Keary's mind wanders.

Even from an early age, Erin was always excited about birthdays and holidays. As she's grown older, Keary realizes that her sister's joy in life is infectious. It was foolish to think Erin would let this year slip by unnoticed. "I should've known better," Keary grumbles into her cup.

Erin had just turned five when the two of them came to live with their grandmother. A few weeks later, Keary's world overturned again as her ninth birthday arrived. After declining both a party and presents, she was happy to spend the day quietly, with no form of acknowledgement. Erin didn't agree. Although the present was homemade, Keary couldn't fathom the hours it took Erin to wrangle her untidy nature long enough to produce something she was happy to share. She constructed the number one sister award out of out of red paper, dried flowers and an obscene amount of tree sap. To this day, it stands proudly on Keary's dresser.

The memento brings a soft smile to Keary's face. Her sister's vibrancy is inspiring. Erin had always been the lifeblood of their small family, a burst of sunshine in the darkest of days. She could make anyone smile, even Keary, who's always more reserved. Her sister's enthusiasm is endearing, even if she doesn't fully understand it. A soft creak on the staircase alerts Keary to Erin's return. "Happy Birthday!" Erin calls from the doorway, armed with a beaming smile and brightly wrapped presents. The smile she returns is reflexive while she trips through memory lane for a heartbeat.

Her sister looks much the same as she did all those years ago. Soft bouncy curls like apple cider fall just shy of shoulders, framing her face and accenting flawless ivory skin. Deep gray eyes burn with excitement when she pushes the biggest present across the table in true Erin fashion.

A stab of pain slices through her stomach, knowing how much effort her sister likely put into this. Keary's stomach twists with the idea that her appreciation won't be enough or that Erin will read too much into her reaction. The weight of this emotional landmine is almost enough for her to hit the panic button.

"Stop," Erin murmurs quietly. A smile tugs one corner of her lips as she pushes the larger present closer. "I promise, it doesn't bite."

"You didn't need to get me anything."

"Oh, pish!"

Hands smooth out over colorful paper before Keary pries a fingernail under one flap. The edges are smooth, the folds precise. *No way Erin wrapped these herself with the level of patience the Maker graced her.* First one corner, then the other, and she's able to slide the books from underneath. Their weight considerable, her lips purse as she scans the title of the top book. *Growing Plants Without A Green Thumb.* "Brat," she hisses and sets it aside to read the other. *Mythical Moments In Solstier's History.* In a flash, her fingers tingle to lift the cover so she can thumb through the pages. "I love it!"

"Yeah?"

Leaving the books on the table, she makes quick work of smoothing out the wrapping paper for re-use. "Very much. Though I'm well aware how much silver I sent you to school with, how did you afford these?"

Over the last decade or so, the Citadel clamped down on certain books, making many of them too rare and valuable to afford. Never one to be stifled, their grandmother made it her mission to collect any and every book she could find, regardless of its content. A trait she happily passed on to her granddaughters. This doesn't change the fact that a book of mythology in Solstier had to cost her sister more silver than Keary had provided at the beginning of the year.

"Don't worry. I'm an escort between classes."

"Excuse me?" *What the hell?* Keary searches for a sign that shows her sister is joking. While Erin occupies herself with another cup of tea, Keary studies her face for tiny lines of distress or a twitch of humor only to find nothing.

"I got this," she adds. "My clients are safe and I spend most of my time talking."

"You can't be serious?" Keary's stomach flips as her skin answers with a cold sweat.

"Of course not! I tutor."

"Oh, I'm going to kill you. Eat carefully for the next couple of days." The swell of heat that washes over Keary's face slowly fades to a mild warmth.

With eyes that twinkle, Erin peeks over the rim of her cup. "Should I hire a food taster?"

"You're a brat. I believed you! I wasn't sure if I should lecture you on Nana's behalf or not."

"Ooh, lecture or acceptance, what a dilemma for you."

"Maybe lecture, then acceptance." Laughter dances in Erin's eyes, drawing a chuckle from Keary. "I don't think I forgive you yet, but I love you."

"I know." Her cup sweeps to the books as Erin skips over the terrible joke. "It's time you figured out how to keep our garden alive, and the other one I just knew you would love."

"I *do*."

"Just don't go flashing it around. I'd hate to come home to find they locked you away."

"You make me sound like a criminal."

"Not me," Erin defends sweetly. "You know as well as I do how much the Elders want to keep our history in the past."

"You know it's their way of keeping things running smoothly."

"You mean under their thumb."

Keary releases a dry laugh. "Exactly. We weren't around when things changed. For all we know, this is better than what it used to be."

Even as the words leave her lips, Keary considers how much she believes them. No documentation proving the elders' teaching's survived. Nor did anyone find anything to dispute it, either. It left most people going with their gut on what to believe. Keary needs facts to sway her toward one side or the other. Until then, she'll straddle the lines until that's no longer an option.

"We *would* know if they didn't ban so much of the history prior to the war."

"So, is this a secret rebellion I should worry about? Or just your history nerd rearing its head?"

Flashing a cheeky grin, Erin shrugs. "Maybe a tiny bit of both."

"Uh-huh. Thank you for the books, Imp," she croaks, her throat suddenly tight. "I can't believe you went to all this trouble for me."

"Of course I did," her sister beams. "You're my big sister. Besides, you'd never buy this kind of stuff for yourself."

Keary laughs, feeling her heart swell. Despite all their differences, the two of them have always been there for each other. "Thank you, Imp."

"Hold that thought, there's something else." Erin's grin carries a heavy dose of her charm when she passes the second gift over the table.

The weight of it surprises Keary when she cradles it in her hands. "Did you wrap a rock to go with the books? Just in case I lose my patience with the gardening thing?"

"Yep. One of those dark ones from Mrs. Finch's house."

"That isn't funny." Keary groans and plucks the pretty bow off of the present only to plop it onto Erin's head.

"It's a little funny."

Keary lifts the paper away and her teeth bury into her lower lip as she exposes a plain brown box. "Only until she brings the guards, demanding your arrest."

"She's never liked me."

"*Rescuing* the roses from her prize-winning garden may have something to do with that."

"Whatever, I was eight!"

"Seven. I think. You told Nana the fae made you do it."

"Who says they didn't?" Erin asks with another one of her cheeky grins.

"And her cat chasing you into the river by her house had nothing to do with it?"

"Rufus!" Erin's laugh is a tinkling sound in a quiet house. "That cat was pure evil."

"You mean, is."

"It hasn't croaked yet?"

"Nope."

"See, evil." Hands rub together in a flurry of excitement as Erin bounces from foot to foot. "Come on Kear, open it already."

With a shake of her head, Keary lifts the flap on the box and feels her heart climb up into her throat. On a sharp inhale, it resettles in her chest to clamber out an intense rhythm. Her hands shake when she pulls the silver trinket box from the wrapping.

"Erin," she breathes, "it's stunning."

"I hoped you'd say that."

As the evening sun dips below the horizon, the kitchen lights dim, giving off a soft glow that highlights the silver box on the table. The surface gleams with polish and care as if Erin had spent time buffing it to perfection before wrapping it. Standing proud at three inches tall, and nearly twice as long, it emanates an aura of power that leaves a hint of spice on Keary's tongue. The intricate scrollwork that decorates each surface could only be the work of a patient and skilled hand. At the center of the lid sits a dazzling emerald, catching and reflecting light in a mesmeric display that tightens her chest. Despite its unassuming size, her curiosity is piqued by the box. When she inhales, she pulls in the scent of age, memories, and cedar. As it sits in her hand, the metal isn't cool to the touch. Instead, it hums with a strange warmth that tingles against her skin. "Where did you find this?"

"Friends of mine dragged me to this estate sale a couple of weeks back to find cheap furniture. A woman died up in

Blackstone and left no family behind, so everything went to auction."

"That's sad."

"Yeah, but I got your trinket box and an old trunk for a steal."

"Erin Leigh!"

"Sorry, I'll light a candle for her soul tonight." Erin promises, holding up a hand. "I'm hoping you can restore the trunk."

Her brow puckers. "What do I know about restoring old furniture?"

"You'll figure it out. Pretty, pretty please?"

Figure it out? As her sister sits across from her, Keary notices the sweet fragrance of lilacs in the air. Eyes narrow slightly as she waits for the telltale signs she's familiar with. It doesn't take long before she notes the slightly dilated pupils a second before her smile turns serene.

"Your powers of persuasion don't work on me, Imp."

With a huff, Erin sits back in her seat as the effects of her influence fade. "Fine."

"You need to be more careful, Erin. Anyone aware of your gift could have you sent to the Elders."

"I know."

"They only tolerate the more common abilities. Something like yours will set that council of fools on edge."

"I know, Keary."

"Do you? Because half of them will cry for your execution, the other half will demand using you for their own gain."

Gray eyes darken briefly before Erin blinks away the clouds. Pinning her lip between her teeth, she nods. "You're right."

"Besides, if anything happens to you, I'll end up at the hangman's square after exacting my revenge," Keary explains through her teeth. "If nothing else, being careful will save my neck, as well as your own. Okay?"

A heavy sigh lifts and drops her sister's shoulders before she gives Keary a quick nod. "Okay. I promise I'm being careful. Do you think you can fix the trunk?"

Keary swallows the heavy sigh rising into her throat. "I'll do my best, but don't expect too much, Erin." Satisfied Erin understands the dangers that come with her gift, she turns her attention to her present. Running a finger over the small seam around the top of the box, she frowns. "It doesn't open?"

"Nope."

"Did it come with a key?"

"Not that I found. It came with these old papers, but that's it. Nothing on its history."

"These are letters." Keary observes as she runs a hand over the yellowed pages. Reading through the letters, the fancy loops and curls transport Keary into a different time and place. The handwriting may be old-fashioned, but the emotions seeping through the ink are timeless, connecting her to the person who wrote them. The pages weave intimate stories, filled with secrets that someone has kept hidden for years.

"This is amazing, Erin."

"I was hoping you'd like it."

"Do you have any idea who they belonged to before?"

"No, but I'm sure you'll figure it out. You always do, Keary," Erin says with a smile.

Keary nods, her mind already busy with thoughts as she lays out the letters in front of her. Flipping through the wrinkled sheets, her eyes snag a glimpse of a small riddle scrawled within the back corner of the first page. Tipping the paper toward the meager light, her lips move soundlessly over the bold swoops and neat curls of someone's penmanship.

Three moons to change his fate, a journey of trust awaits.

Fail in this a time by three, and dust he'll forever be.

Who's he? Despite the overflow of random thoughts, Keary succumbs to the pull of the words, the way they beckon her to uncover more secrets hidden within each page. It'll take time and effort, but her body hums just thinking about finding the answers.

"You gave me a puzzle for my birthday," she says, her lips twitching softly as the heat unfurls in her chest.

"Good thing you're good with puzzles, huh?"

Chuckling lightly to herself, she sets the trinket box on the table and sits back in her chair. "Good thing indeed," Keary says.

"Thank you, Erin," she says, finally looking up from the letters. "This is the best birthday present I've ever gotten."

Erin glows, the corners of her eyes crinkling. "I'm glad you like it."

Standing, she pulls her sister in for a tight hug. Resting her cheek on the top of Erin's head, Keary exhales. No matter what the future brings, the one thing she's sure of is that Erin will always be there for her, just like she'll be there for her sister. The two of them have been through a lot together and Keary couldn't imagine it any other way.

CHAPTER 5

When Keary wakes, she discovers the lullaby of rain she'd fallen asleep to, stopped overnight. Propping herself up on an elbow, she silences the incessant ringing of her alarm before it disturbs Erin.

Dragging a knuckle across her eyes, she rubs the sleep clear and stares up at the ceiling. Between catching up with Erin and her new obsession with the trinket box, morning arrives quickly. Covering her yawn, she burrows deeper into the warmth of her blankets and contemplates going back to sleep. Of their own accord, her eyes drift over at the box still sitting on her nightstand. The warm skittering sensation that skips across her skin leaves a wrinkle in her forehead. She can't put her finger on why, but something about the small gift tickles her fascination. The hours she'd spent contemplating it last night, adds a layer of fog to her brain.

With a groan, she pushes the mystery aside and swings her legs over the side of the bed. Breath leaks from her lips as a twinge of pain flares along her lower back. Stretching side-to-side eases enough discomfort to allow her to sit straight. After scrubbing a hand across the back of her neck, Keary weaves her still tangled locks into a messy braid. Her movements are sluggish as she pulls on her lilac-colored lounge pants and tiptoes to the stairs.

When the sisters came here to live with their grandmother, some changes weren't so easy. One bathroom for three girls was a big one. So far from the Citadel, they had to adjust to the limited supply of hot water. In the bigger cities, it's easier to heat and store enough water per household. The smaller villages like Briar struggle with smaller tanks and smaller solar panels. While the person who came up with their plumbing system was a genius as far as Keary is concerned, it's certainly not perfect.

Using the vast natural lake on their left, plumbing fills the individual tanks with water. The waste water then runs through a separate series of pipes for filtering before it returns to the large bodies of water.

Each citizen with a solar panel depends on the energy it creates to heat the frigid water enough for a shower or two. During the cold winter months, cut that number in half. It hadn't taken Nana long to instill the first come, first serve rule. Since the hot water goes to the early riser, the last out of bed suffers a cold one. With that in mind, Keary swallows a short whoop of victory when she reaches the bottom of the stairs.

Just ahead, the bathroom door stands half open. She experiences no remorse as she races ahead to stake her claim before Erin becomes an opponent. When she next emerges, it's on a cloud of steam and to the smell of coffee.

Having replaced her pajamas with jeans and a t-shirt, Keary twists the wet length of her hair into a haphazard pile she secures with a fat clip. Crossing the living room, she nearly knee-caps herself on a rather enormous trunk in the middle of the floor. Pulling in a slow breath smothers the instinctual lecture as she steers toward the kitchen. The sight of Erin curled up at the table, cup in hand, brings a smile to her lips. "I assume that's the trunk you're talking about?"

"Yeah, some men dropped it off early this morning."

"And you thought it best to leave it in the middle of the living room?"

"For now."

Inhaling through her nose, she changes the subject until after she's had coffee. "You're up early."

"Must be," Erin mumbles gently, "especially if I beat you to the shower *and* the coffee."

Rescuing her favorite mug from the dish rack, Keary shuffles to the percolator on the stove. "It was the rain," she confides as she fills her cup. The familiar aroma leaves a purr on her lips as the steam rises from the dark liquid like tendrils of smoke. Leaving just enough room for sugar and cream, Keary joins her sister at the table. "It always makes me sleep like a baby."

"Not me."

Several alarms sound off in her head when she catches the raw rasp in Erin's voice. "Still?" She keeps her question light while her eyes search for the smallest reaction. "It's been years, Erin."

Her sister sighs, the action dropping her shoulders unsteadily. "I know."

"Are you still seeing Dr. Watts?"

"I'm twenty-six years old, Keary. If I'm not over it by now, chances are I never will be."

"It shouldn't keep you from sleeping, Erin."

One shoulder bounces as her face hides behind her cup. Minutes pass in silence before she peeks out, her mouth tight. "The rain is what I remember most about that night. Other than the Vanguard lieutenant that found me telling me our parents didn't make it, anyway."

Keary wants to reach out and hold her sister, let her know she's not alone, but the tension in her sister's posture says it's not the right time for that. Instead, she reaches over and takes Erin's hand, giving it a reassuring squeeze. "I understand." Blowing into her coffee gives her a moment to settle her breathing and collect rampant emotions.

How long since I've thought of that night? A year? Two? Memories flood Keary's mind, each one a jolt of pain as she relives the night her parents died. She can vividly recall the sound of the rain lashing against the windows and the sight of the dozen men surrounding their small porch. Some wear expressions of sympathy or pity, while others can barely suppress their yawns.

Tears prick at her eyes, but she blinks them away, not wanting to add to Erin's pain. A change of topic is vital for her to hedge around the dark memories swirling inside her head. "You head back tomorrow?"

"Yeah. I have an early train so I can make it back to campus before dark."

"Just be safe. You know I worry."

"I'm more concerned about our garden than I am with a long train ride." Erin quips and gestures out the bay window with a swoop of her cup toward the garden.

"What? It seems fine." *It doesn't.* Erin's garden is a disaster, but Keary will swallow her tongue before she admits such a fact to her plant-loving sister.

"By whose standards? Most plants don't produce without sprouting first. What did you do?"

Avoiding her sister's knowing look, Keary swirls her coffee around the inside her cup. "Nothing." The narrowing of Erin's eyes and a slight twitch in her lips squeezes her chest.

"Nothing, nothing. Or didn't even water it, nothing?"

"I watered your damn plants. It could be too early in the year for them to grow."

"One or two should at least have sprouts."

"Well, I didn't do it." Even Keary can hear the shrill tone in her voice that sparks a flicker of amusement on her sister's face. *No better time for a refill.*

"Did you follow the steps for tending them?"

"Kind of." A splash of cream and a spoon or three of sugar distract her from the sudden interrogation.

"So, no?"

"I don't need a list. They're plants. Give 'em dirt, sun and a little water. Easy."

"Uh-huh. So today I'll run into town for more seeds. *And* I'll write up a new list for you."

Keary groans. *Loudly.* "Your plants don't like me."

"How is it you can grow Gran's roses, but a carrot makes you cry uncle?"

"Carrots are stubborn."

"I love you, Kear, but they aren't the only ones being stubborn. Besides, I don't see how you are going to treat people if we run out necessary herbs."

"Fine." Keary lifts a hand in defeat and shakes her head ruefully. Once Erin sets her mind on something, it takes an act of God to alter her course. "Make up your list and I'll *try* not to throw it away this time."

"You're impossible."

"Speaking of impossible," she begins by rejoining Erin at the table with her sweetest smile. "We should look at your trunk today. See what repairs it's going to need."

"I can tell you, it either needs a new lock or a new key made." Erin says over her shoulder as she refills her coffee cup.

"Think we can haul it up to the tower?"

"Why not work on it down here?" Erin's brows furrow, her head tilting gently to one side. "On the *first* floor?"

"Because I don't know what this entire process is going to entail. Or how long it'll take. I can't have it consuming my living room for that long."

"I don't know, Kear, it took three guys from my Lit class to get it on the train. Not to mention the two men that carried it as far as the living room."

"Okay, but how strong are the boys in your literature class?" For all she knows, those three boys compete for the scrawniest college kid award and not the boys sporting any sort of muscle.

"Wow! Condescending much?" Curling back into her chair, Erin tucks one foot beneath her. Her glare never wavers as she blows a breath across her cup.

"I'm only asking."

"Keary."

Though she still wears a smirk, she concedes. "Alright. It's heavy. Can we ask Broc for help?" From where she sits, Keary has a front-row seat to catch warm gray eyes hardening into steel.

"I'll strap it to my back and climb those stairs like one would Mount Mariath before I ask him for anything."

"Whoa, easy killer." Ears pique as Keary straightens to the edge of her seat and searches her sister's face. "I thought things were good between you two."

"They were. Until he cheated on me with some faerie from Dooley."

"Men suck," she clips and brings Erin in for a hug. The sound of sniffling through a runny nose draws her teeth together. Her sister crying is an image that without fail brings out the warrior in Keary, ready to exact a price from the offender.

"I should've listened to you. Long-distance relationships don't work."

"He's a pig. And you deserve better." Her chin rests on top of velvet curls as she breathes in the lemon-scent of Erins soap. "Why didn't you compel him?"

"I shouldn't have to persuade a man to love me."

Keary flinches. "You're right." When Erin draws back to scrub a sleeve down her tear-streaked face, she pulls in a quick breath, her voice tight. "You outgrew him."

"Maybe."

"Well, he's in the vanguard now. So please don't get into trouble."

"Jeepers, I wasn't planning on burning his house down or anything."

"Hmm, I might," Keary answers with a sense of levity she's far from feeling. The heat that flows into her limbs is familiar. Since Erin doesn't appear to find the threat hidden in her words, she flashes a small smile.

"Thank you Keary."

"That's what sisters do. So come hell or high water, we get the trunk up to the tower ourselves."

"Pull!"

"I am pulling! You push," Keary instructs from high ground. Her thighs started to burn a while ago, holding the squat as the two of them fight with the trunk. An image of Erin being steam-rolled by runaway luggage forces her to tighten her grip on its sides.

"I'm pushing, Keary."

"Okay. Stop. I can see the problem." Bracing the hulking weight with her legs, Keary squeezes an arm along one side.

Teeth clench and shoulders strain as she lifts the corner high enough to miss the step. "Okay, push," she hisses.

Like a freshly branded calf; the trunk shoots forward to catch the blanket they laid down to protect the wood floors in the tower. Plush material bunches around the sides as Erin plows into the room. After a loud exhale, she collapses against the doorframe, shooting Keary a disgruntled frown.

"I want that sister award back."

"What?" Keary blinks. "Why?"

"'Cause you just forfeited it entirely."

"C'mon. It wasn't that bad. Besides, it fits up here, don't you think?"

The circular tower is her favorite room in the house, the place where Keary spends most of her downtime. Floor to ceiling windows allow in as much sunlight as Briar's temperamental weather permits.

Original wood floors ooze history and fantasy. Sturdy brown columns reach for the ceiling, the wood dark and polished with years of use. A dozen rows of bookcases made from dark wood fill the gap between tall windows. A collection that is the life's work of generations rest on every shelf. Over the years, the three women scoured barn sales, fairs and bargain bins to fill this room with their favorite stories. Occasionally, they find a book worth replacing a mediocre one, but soon they'll need more shelves. Unable to part from even a mediocre book, Keary began stacking them into random leaning towers on the floor.

For her, the tower tastes like freedom. The familiar fragrance of musty paper, leather and dusty tomes carries a piece of history and centuries-old knowledge.

"How are we going to get it back down?"

Erin's question pierces the blanket of wandering thoughts to redirect Keary to the trunk. "Does it need to leave?"

"Bite your tongue." Erin's voice dips, the threat made clear by the narrowing of her eyes. "Don't even breathe it."

"Oh, c'mon!"

"No."

"But it fits so well here." Keary grins, her arms showcasing where the trunk came to rest. Between the couch and the loveseat, Nana spent a month refinishing, as if destiny had intervened.

"Are you prepared to sleep with one eye open?" Erin challenges, plopping on the couch. With a shimmy, she makes room for Keary to drop next to her, then lays her head back against the cushion, her eyes closing. "Or hire a food taster?"

"Ugh! Fine, you can keep your trunk." Lips twitch and purse as her concession doesn't even warrant Erin opening one eye.

"Gee, thank you."

"You're most welcome."

"The generosity coursing through your veins knows no equal."

She rests her head alongside Erins with a soft chuckle. "I know, but with all my other obligations, it works better if I let Elder Elaine hold the title." That causes one eye to open, her sister offering a begrudging smile.

"You're twisted."

"True." Standing, Keary yanks on one of her sister's arms. "Come on, we can go to town and dig for reclaimed wood."

"What in the world is reclaimed wood?"

"Wood repurposed from barns and stuff." Another tug produces no result. "Why aren't you moving?"

"Can we not find new wood? It's cheaper, right?"

"I suppose, but it won't match."

"And this isn't your OCD talking?"

"Do you want me to work on this thing or not?"

"I just enjoy rattling your cage." Allowing Keary to pull her to her feet, Erin nudges her with an elbow. "After that we can go to the Nursery for more seeds."

The mere mention of the village greenhouse takes the wind out of Keary's sails, leaving them to fall limp. It isn't the prospect of getting dirty, or even manual labor, but that Erin will spend more money on plants that she'll just end up killing later.

Considering her sister's already halfway down the stairs, Keary forces herself to gather up her big girl pants and get it done. "Fine. We can get more seeds *after* we find some suitable pieces of wood."

After an exhausting day lugging Erin's trunk up to the tower, the sisters spent hours in the lumberyard picking over the best pieces of wood Keary could find. Once she arranged the delivery, they made what should've been a quick trip to the Nursery. Keary recalls Fran Sinclair droning on about the fall harvest while Erin took her sweet time selecting their best plants.

The sun was still high in the sky by the time they returned home, so Keary accepts Erin's help to address the poor condition of their garden. Splitting up the tasks, Keary dug up dead plants as Erin pulled various weeds. Once satisfied, Keary took a step back while Erin adds a handful of plants to the garden and the rest to large pots off to the side. Her sister walked her through the daily tending and a strict schedule to stick to for adding new plants. By the time it was all said and done, Keary sends up a quiet moment of gratitude Erin wrote the information down since she'd zoned out more than once during her lecture.

Muscles cramp in her shoulders and back as the sun retires and night steps up to the plate. While Erin attaches the garden instructions to the cupboard just above Keary's percolator, she re-warms last night's supper. Battling with their own exhaustion, the sisters are content to enjoy the simple meal in silence.

Resting her elbow on the table, Keary leans enough to prop her head up with one hand as she pours soup down her throat by the spoonful. *Have I ever been this tired before?* Wincing when her spoon brushes over fresh blisters on her palm, she adjusts her grip with a tight hiss of air. At the moment, she can think of nothing better than the promise of her own bed. Since the town meeting is mandatory, however, she pushes the memory of her soft pillow far from her mind.

At least the clean-up will be relatively easy. Suppressing a yawn with the back of her hand, Erin carries dishes, cutlery, and cups to the sink. In order to speed up the process, Keary arms herself with a threadbare towel ready to dry as Erin washes. Once they return the last one to the cupboard, they exchange a tired smile and head towards the pair of bicycles resting against the house. Just the thought of pedaling into town when even her hair hurts sours Keary's mood for the foreseeable future.

Nearly the entire village gathers inside the town hall by the time Erin and Keary arrive. Handcrafted from both wood and stone, the building itself is a large rectangular room with high ceilings. The floors beneath her feet creak and groan under the pressure of so many bodies filling the open space. With only a few tall, narrow windows, daylight fumbles to light the room during the day. Since the sun set hours ago, the inhabitants rely solely on the dim lights hanging from stout wooden beams.

Keary leads Erin through the mass of people while wrestling with her inner thoughts. On one hand, she wishes the puny solar panels stored enough energy to keep the lights on for the duration of the meeting. On the other; she secretly yearns for a power outage that will send everyone home early. As she finds a section of bench large enough for the two of them, she wonders which scenario would be better.

Scuffed and scarred, long wooden benches stretch from one wall to the other, with the front rows reserved for Briar's natural-born folks. Further back, Keary struggles under the heavy scent of body odor, and musk and the stale tang of sweat and mildew. Long taper sticks jut out from the walls, wafting thin tendrils of smoke to carry a jasmine fragrance to combat the various noxious odors.

Squished between two large men already dozing from an over-indulgence of ale, Keary gives her sister a wane smile. Whispered conversations buzz around the room as Erin fidgets beside her. Too tired to worry over why the elders called this meeting, Keary considers the portraits hanging between the windows. Infused with life, each painting is a narrative of Briar's history. Stories Keary has heard countless time from her grandmother. At the front of the room, above the raised platform, rests an impressive mural depicting their founding members.

Men and women alike pose in front of the thick forest of trees where Briar will soon stand, their smiles bright. In the bold brushstrokes, she senses their determination. A stubborn resolve to keep them going through Briar's many hardships.

Just underneath, someone framed the peace treaty signed at the end of the civil war. What was meant to be a declaration of equality became an order of dominance. A badge of honor and privilege for the natural-born folk to wield against the many injustices at the hand of its gifted citizens.

A soft tinkling bell breaks Keary from her reverie as it signals the start of the meeting. Though the sound barely reaches above a whisper, it's enough to silence the room, drawing all eyes forward. A wave of shuffling shoes and rustling clothes shudders within the room as everyone stands. Wearing a mixture of blank expressions, the elders appear to take their rightful place on the raised platform. Positioning himself in the center, elder Elias gestures for everyone to return to their seats with a flippant wave of his hand. He betrays nothing as his dark eyes scan over the crowd. With a deep huff of air, he tucks his hands deep into the folds of his wool cloak before speaking to the tall, slender lady directly behind him.

"It would seem we're a few people short," he barks. When no one speaks, he continues. "Let's hope this doesn't become a common occurrence." Even from her position near the back, Keary picks up on the subtly veiled threat in his tone. Clearing his throat with a light cough, Elias paces the width of the platform. "For those of you who showed up, thank you. I'm aware it was short notice."

A low hum of conversations fills the room, intensifying as it moves from the front towards the back. Several benches screech as bodies shift in their seats. Searching the faces closest to her, Keary spots similar expressions of fixed concentration.

"Over the last several years, our harvest seasons are falling short. Even with the Lycan hunting parties and the Siren's fishing nets, we're scrambling to last the winter." Speaking clearly, the boom of Elias's voice easily reaches the back wall.

Keary's fingers clench into small fists in her lap as a ripple of awareness shifts around her. One by one, every natural-born head bobs in silent agreement while the gifted citizens bristle, as if mentally preparing themselves for the axe to fall.

"In light of this, we have no choice but to enact a new law. To ensure everyone has adequate rations to survive our harshest months, we require half of the crops from the larger fields."

Amidst mumbles of approval from the front, shock vibrates along the bodies near the back. Seconds tick by before that shock morphs into outrage. Jumping to his feet, Jacob Silver faces the elders. "What do you consider being large?"

Elias's shoulders shift. Tipping his chin, he puffs out his chest as his voice careens over several hushed conversations. "Anything over fifty acres."

One man on Keary's left launches himself off the wall, "That's over half of our community!" The venom in his voice sparks a tidal wave of protests.

"How are we supposed to feed our families?"

"Why can't they grow their own food?"

"I won't share my crop with anyone too lazy to do their own labor!"

One by one, the chaos grows as voices bleed in with the next until all Keary can make out is white noise. From the front, Elias attempts to bring the meeting back to order only for the outrage to swallow his normally booming tone. With a sage nod of his head, dozens of vanguard soldiers take a unified step forward. Squeezing the room with their presence, hands fall to the swords at their hips. Flanking the room, they make an impressive display of intimidation. An effective one, Keary concedes once again: the hall falls quiet. "We understand your concern," Elias declares once he has everyone's undivided attention. "We didn't come by this decision lightly."

Planting a pair of meaty fists on his hips, Jacob's stance remains rigid. "How will the elders distribute this food? Determine who gets what for rations?"

"Natural-born households will receive one share per dependent." Across the front of the room, a wave of heads nod in approval.

"And the rest of us?" With fascination, Keary spies the white knuckles on Jacob's hands and wonders how long before his control is a mess of tattered strings.

"You and your families will receive one half ration per dependent." Even as the words fall from Elias's mouth, his face is a hard mask. Once again, the room erupts into chaos.

"Bullshit!"

"Why are we surprised?"

"Most of us will starve come next spring!"

"So not only do we grow the food, harvest the food and prepare the food, but we get less of it?"

With a sweep of his hand, Jacob calms the rising objections on either side. "If the naturals need more food, then they should put in more effort."

With a tilt of his head, Elias pauses. "What do you suggest?"

"We could always use more hunters. More hands in the fields. Hell, even raising a few chickens would go a long way!"

"If you think I'm going to trust your kind to watch my back in a hunting party, you've lost your mind!"

"That isn't what I'm saying, Mr. Finch," Jacob continues patiently. "There are plenty of ways people can help to make sharing the bounty less of a blow to the rest of us."

"You're saying force the naturals into hard labor?"

Jacob appears to consider this for a moment as he searches the faces beside him. "Only the able-bodied sir, the ones without more pressing commitments and responsibilities."

"You just want us to sink to your station! My family has been here for generations. Please tell me the elders are not actually considering allowing this," Mr. Finch trails off with a lip curl, "this man to dictate terms?"

"Most of our families have been here longer than yours," a voice pipes up from somewhere behind Keary. "You don't see us stealing food from your tables!"

Mr. Finch's face turns red as he sputters before relocating his voice. "It isn't stealing if it's given."

"Not by us, it's not."

Lifting a hand to calm the tempers behind him, Jacob takes a long breath. "With all due respect, it's fair to say we're all in this together. Any suggestions that benefit us as a whole should be worth consideration."

"I think we've heard enough from you," elder Mason snaps. "I suggest you return to your seat."

"Silence!"

Heads jerk as Elias's voice slams against the open room. Once it's quiet, he turns his attention to Jacob. "I appreciate you to provide an alternative, and I thank you for your contribution." When a rush of murmurs ripple through the front rows, Elias hurries to finish his speech. "However, it's not up to me. I must put it to the Council for further deliberation." With a curt nod of his head, Jacob returns to his seat.

"Assigning several hands to the salt and canning processes is easy enough," elder Grayson muses aloud. "We could accept volunteers to help tend to the neighboring farms as well. But I won't support sending naturals out to hunt with Lycans. It's a risk we shouldn't entertain."

The sharp nudge of Erin's elbow draws Keary's eyes to the rippling muscles in Samson's back. While his stiff posture conveys the offense he suffers, his voice remains gentle. "We have plenty of senior wolves better equipped for mixed hunting parties. Any fear of injury would be minimal against their experience and control."

"You'd vouch for their safety?" Elias maintains a smooth mask of indifference over his features, but Keary notes a touch of intrigue in his voice.

"Of course I would."

"Isn't your daughter the Alpha now?" Elder Grayson asks casually. "How do we know she'll honor your word?"

At the mention of his daughter's honor, Samson's voice turns deadly. "If not for her pregnancy, she'd be here tonight instead of me, to give you *her* word. She'll honor any and all promises I make here tonight."

"Thank you, Samson. I don't see why that wouldn't work. This past year has been brutal on our food stores," Elias points out, takes a breath and adds a forcefulness that belies his soft-spoken nature. "We will need cooperation in order to survive our harsh winters."

A low rumble arises from those seated around her. Even Erin's posture carries the weight of her unease.

"For now, we are adjourning this meeting. As the elders, we will watch how things develop over the next few months and reconvene if need be. You're dismissed."

The scraping of shoes and hurried mumbling chases the elders' words. As the room empties, Keary notes that Jacob makes no attempt for the exit. Instead, he hastens to the raised platform where Elias stands. With his back to the room, his ramrod posture is heavy with tension as he converses quietly with his fellow elders.

"I know it may not seem like it right now, but this was a success for us," Jacob explains softly. "The naturals will benefit from our efforts and you've gained some respect from the gifted."

Elias' eyes snap away from the others at the moment he realizes Jacob is addressing him. Eyes blink repeatedly as he regards Jacob with furrowed brows. His mouth opens as if to say something, but then closes again. "Thank you… for your help tonight," he says finally, his voice thick with an emotion Keary can't name.

As she hurries behind Erin for the exit, she considers their interaction. Pausing near the door, Keary peeks over her shoulder to see Elias and Jacob standing side by side. Two men from very different places yet finding common ground regarding what's best for their people. If only it's that easy with all division, she muses.

CHAPTER 6

When she falls into bed that night, just blinking requires more effort than Keary has left in the gas tank. Sprawling atop the covers, she takes the time needed to accept her arms are too tired to fend off the dust bunnies under her bed, let alone braid her hair. So with a pathetic lift of her hips, she peels off her jeans and drops them off the side before doing the same with her bra and the t-shirt covered in dirt and sweat. The mere idea of getting to her dresser on the far wall for a nightshirt has Keary whimpering defeat, so she settles for crawling under her blankets.

Just beyond an open window, more stars wait for their shift to glitter in a clear sky. Pale white light reflects off the tiny slivers of the moons to filter through the lace curtains and land on her trinket box. Even bone-tired with minimal brainpower remaining, the gleaming response of metal wakes a flare of intrigue inside her. Moving as little as possible, Keary plucks it off the bedside table for closer inspection.

"Such a strange thing you are." Turning the box end over end in her hands, she studies it in the waning light. The edges are smooth and straight, near perfect enough she'd bet a ruler could hold its tight angles. "Someone took their time creating you." *So why not make it open?* Keary holds it up to her face and peeks through the tiny keyhole hoping to make out a mechanism or gear. *Nothing.* Was it meant to serve as a visual piece? Something to sit forgotten on a shelf? The many possibilities run rampant inside her head, even as it becomes difficult to keep her eyes open. When Keary lets herself drift off, she's cradling the small treasure in her hands while she dreams of the rolling hills and lush fields. Until her alarm jolts her awake.

"*Holy hell!*"

Forgotten, the trinket box falls to the floor with a clatter while hands scramble in the darkness towards the shrill ringing. Jabbing her finger at the button on the back quiets the incessant noise so her heart has a chance of returning to normal. With a push against the mattress, Keary sits upright to shove the mess of hair away from her face in order to better locate the box. Satisfying herself it remains unharmed, she yanks on a loose t-shirt and a pair of cotton shorts before hurrying downstairs, box in hand.

"Didn't think I'd see you."

Erin's voice prompts Keary to squint into the dark living room and make out her huddled form. Dressed in jeans and an oversized hoodie, she sits on the floor to tie her boots. The duffle next to her tells Keary she was planning to sneak out before the sun even rises.

"Why didn't you wake me?"

"'Cause we had a long day yesterday, and I figured you needed the sleep."

"Why do you always make me sound old?" Though Erin chooses silence as an answer, her pointed look screams an obvious opinion. "Have you had coffee?" Keary asks while she snakes her arms into the sweater she left in the rocker. The fuzzy yarn is just enough to ward off the morning's chill.

"I'm going to stop at Bobby's on my way out of town."

"He doesn't open this early on Sundays anymore. Come on, you have time for one cup."

"Just one. Then I have to go." Taking Keary's offered hand, Erin gets to her feet. She leads the way to the kitchen with a sleepy smile, her curls in a messy bun. "Citadel traffic is bad on weekends."

"I'd imagine traffic in the city is insane no matter the day." Keary points out while she sets the percolator to brew, then retrieves two mugs from the cupboard on the right.

"That's true," Erin concedes, setting the jar of cream on the counter. "Why do you look as if you didn't sleep?"

"I think I laid awake too long mulling over that damn thing." Keary gestures to the tiny box sitting on the counter between them.

"I thought you liked it?"

"I do."

From the corner of her eye, Keary watches Erin pick it up, pitching a knot to lodge within her stomach. For a second, the innocent action sets off a tsunami of ownership raging in her chest. The intensity leaves her gasping for breath until it passes. Instead of yanking the trinket box out of Erin's clutches, she chases the tremble from her hands and uses them to weave her hair into a tight knot.

"It's a curious thing, that's for sure. But not worth losing sleep."

"I know." She waits for Erin to offer before taking the trinket and burying it in a sweater pocket, her gaze darting away from her sister's attention. "It's the questions that nag me. I think."

"Such as?"

"Who made it?" she starts, and settles sideways into a kitchen chair while Erin pours the coffee. "Was it made for someone? Should it open? If not, why?"

"It could just be one of those things people collect." Erin suggests, offering Keary one of the full mugs before taking the chair next to her. "People spend their lifesavings on those types of things. Maybe it's something similar."

"But silver is a commodity. Back then, only the rich could afford to use it so frivolously."

"Only if it's as old as you *think* it is."

Keary's face scrunches over the probability. "Those letters don't look recent to me."

"Yeah." Erin takes a sip of coffee, inspiring her to do the same. "I know very little about antiques, but the spear design on the bottom would be a good place to start."

"What?" Keary lifts the box from her pocket to turn it over. Though faint, and not quite an inch long, the symbol of a spear does, in fact, decorate a bottom corner. *How did I miss that?* "I didn't even see it."

"Well, to be fair, your eyes *are* older than mine."

"Hush it."

"Sounds like this puzzle will keep you busy. Just don't go all *Keary* over it." Erin adds making quick work of her first cup of coffee.

"What does that mean?"

"You obsess."

"I do not."

Erin stands from the table to pour herself another cup with a giggle that follows her to the counter. "Remember when you were fourteen? You begged Nana for weeks to let you paint your room." After four spoons of sugar and a dash of cream, Erin returns to the table. "When she gave in, it took you *six* months to choose a color."

"Color is important."

"Blackstone castle fell in less time." Erin's smile is playful enough to soothe Keary's nicked nerves.

"*Okay*. You have a point." She shakes her head at the memory before they move on to chat over far simpler things. Time whirls by at an alarming pace until the percolator stands empty and there's no choice but to acknowledge the bottom of their cups.

"You'll link me when you get there?"

"I always do."

Standing, Keary drags her sister in for a hug. It's the good-byes that stick in her throat so she doesn't say it. "I'll see you later." She struggles to keep her voice light and focuses on rubbing her chin across the top of Erin's head.

"Of course, I'll try to get home for summer."

"Good."

"See you later."

Another squeeze follows a hard swallow, then she's walking Erin out to the rented bicycle. She huddles deeper in her sweater for warmth as the bright yellow bicycle disappears around the bend in the trees. With a sigh on her lips, she returns to the house, mentally calculating the days until summer.

"Ugh!" Her patience resembles shreds by the time Keary shakes out the cramp in her hand and attacks the lock again. "We both know you want to," she coaxes. As if to say otherwise, the screwdriver slips free and just misses her upper thigh.

Rather than risk catching an artery, Keary sits back on her heels and blows raspberries at the ceiling. The thick layer of sweat that coats her skin sends several drops to follow the slope of ear meeting jaw and jaw meeting neck. "Should've installed that fan," she mumbles, recalling the fight she'd had with Erin. The new electrical they put in was an invisible upgrade that still leaves the tower bare of garish technology. To install a fan, they'd need to remove the iron chandelier, too high a price for Keary. Now, as she squirms under the light racer back tank top, she has second thoughts.

Needing a distraction from the trunk, she takes a minute to open several windows for the spring air. The cool breeze that answers sweeps in to dance across damp skin until she purrs in response. A slow breath restores some of her resolve to bring

Keary back to her new side-project. Brute force seems to work as well as the books she skimmed on picking a lock; not at all. A hand drags over her brow as she weighs the options before waving the white flag.

"Time to call a professional." Ignoring the sharp pain behind her left eye, Keary opens up the community mind-link. Her brain buzzes gently as she presses against the one she's looking for.

"Brandt Lock and Key."

"Afternoon Jeremy." The silence that greets her has Keary tugging on one of the few stray threads that hang off her shirt. Even from her end she can all but hear him tumble through reasons she'd be reaching out to him. *"I'm having trouble with an old lock,"* she offers.

"Oh?" Is that relief she hears, or disappointment?

"Erin found an old trunk and got a hairbrained idea that I'd know how to restore it."

"Sounds 'bout right."

"But I can't get past the lock."

"I see. Scrapping it is your simplest bet."

"I thought of that, but, Erin."

"I understand."

Keary knew he would. Better than most. Few people alive can comprehend the bond she shares with Erin and less than that even try. Since childhood, the sisters bounce between two stages with each other. Best friends and mortal enemies. They can conspire and bolster or tear at each other until they're left with scraps. Should another try to cause harm, however, they will find their end in a bloody crime scene.

"You're going for authenticity?"

Lost in thought, Keary jumps at the smooth baritone of his voice. Her answer is a mute nod until she remembers he can't see her and chokes out a verbal reply. *"That's the idea."*

"Then you'll have to pull the pins and hinges in the back. The lock piece will be easier to remove from the inside."

"Great idea! How long do you need to make a new key?"

"For Erin, a day or two. At most."

"Great. Should I drop it off at the store or can you swing by?"

"I'm having dinner with my parents tonight, but I could come by later. Does that work?" There it is again. A smooth purr of emotion Keary can't quite name.

"Before six is fine." Keary ignores the little voice, telling her to touch on their new friendship boundaries. "Evie is dragging me to May Day."

"That starts today?"

"I guess so. Evie keeps track of that stuff. I'm just her wingman."

"Well, at least you'll have a nice day for it."

"True. Thanks again, Jeremy." Keary severs the link before something innocent gets twisted and releases the air that fills her lungs.

Her thumb nail picks at the outside seam on her jeans as she replays the conversation in her head. She'll admit she'd forgotten how warm his voice can be. But when she searches her insides for a reaction, there isn't so much as a flutter of awareness. "They call it the past for a reason." Keary whispers and distracts herself with the mysterious depths of Nana's toolbox. She empties almost half of it on the floor before finding something small enough to work.

Beads of sweat roll down the narrow corridor of her spine by the time she loosens the first hinge. She spends another ten minutes on the second and fifteen to remove the lock before announcing herself the victor. She'll have to replace the anchor board, but she's able to lift the top free, at least. While weighing a fraction of what it does attached, she struggles to lay it on the couch with any sort of care.

When she turns to address the trunk, her chest tightens. "Oh my stars," she breathes, fighting to comprehend the sheer volume of items stashed in one piece of luggage. Somehow, Keary reigns in the urge she has to dive in long enough to make a trip downstairs.

After a quick shower and a swap of clean clothes, Keary makes her way back to the tower armed with a cup of coffee, paper and a pencil. Using the seat of a chair to lean against, she settles in, inhaling the sweet fragrance of rosemary and cedar, ready to catalog.

CHAPTER 7

"Hello?"

The unexpected greeting draws Keary's attention from the book in her hands and pulls it to the open doorway. Blinking, her head cants at the sight of Evie standing there in full festival attire, leaning on the frame with one hand on her hip. A glance through a window shows a moonless night instead of the sunset she's expecting.

"Damn. What time is it?"

"After ten."

"I'm *so* sorry." Keary drops the paper into the trunk and climbs to her feet as her stomach rolls. "The day got away from me."

"What happened?"

"I got this thing open and then fell through a rabbit hole."

One bare shoulder jumps up in a lazy shrug before Evie drops her lithe frame into a chair. "It's okay. I figured you got lost up here when you didn't answer the mind link or hear me knock."

"You knocked?" Keary balances on the arm of Evie's chair, her smile slowly growing. "How'd you get in?"

"Remember last winter when the heat went out at my place, and you let me crash here?"

"Yes."

"I made a copy of all your keys. I hope to use them when you least expect it to take over your life. Before you know it, I'll be Keary McKenna and you'll be," Evie pauses for dramatic effect, "nowhere."

"Then you'd better brush up on your Erin 101."

A moment passes as her friend seems to contemplate the road ahead. "Um, nevermind," she rushes to say, her slender nose wrinkling. "I'll find someone else."

Keary rests her head against the back of the chair with a laugh. "She isn't that bad."

"No, no, I love Erin." Evie replies, resting her hand on Keary's arm. "She's like my own little sister. But two reckless halves just wouldn't work. There'd be no one to bail either of us out."

"True. I guess I forgot to lock up again?"

"Yep."

"How was the festival?"

"Meh." The tiny frown lines that wink at her with Evie's response draws another laugh from Keary.

"No cute guys this year?"

A lip twitches in Evie's face as she pulls bobby-pins from her bun to drop fiery red hair around a heart-shaped face. "Don't even get me started."

"You did an amazing job on your costume." Keary mentions as she tugs on a ribbon decorating the lace cuff framing a shoulder. "Very demure."

"Thanks. It took hours to nail the whole *virgin* thing."

"I'm sure."

"Some of us are just naturally wanton. Or maybe it's just a phoenix quality," she quips and drops the bobby pins in Keary's hand. "Thanks for these, though."

"Anytime."

Evie exudes confidence like many of the gifted. Rarely is her composure affected by the ignorance of those around her. If the gifted are second-class next to the naturals, the phoenix population is second to the gifted. Most justify this with the phoenix's involvement in jumpstarting the civil war. Keary suspects their harsh treatment is more about jealousy than something that happened a half a century ago.

In school, the envy she felt towards her best friend was almost tangible. Years later, her hair still shines like a beacon of fire, complementing her warm caramel skin tone. Her lips are full and luscious, and her eyes are an arresting shade of gold. Despite being drop-dead gorgeous, Evie is also kind and caring. Qualities which make Keary immensely fond of her friend.

"Jere-my was there."

Keary stiffens at the sing-song tone Evie adapts, and fights to keep her voice normal. "I just talked to him, and he didn't mention he was going."

"Oh?"

"Stop, it's not what you think."

"And what do I think?"

"That I'm going to date him again." Keary states and pushes to her feet while waving off Evie's smug grin. "I only needed his help with the damn trunk." Pulling Evie out of the chair, she leads her toward the stairs.

"And that's it? Nothing more," she winks, "*primal?*"

"Get your mind out of the gutter and have a drink with me."

"Why does it have to be one or the other?"

"Because the last time we did both, it ended with a visit from the Vanguard."

"Oh, yeah. Admit it, the dozen ab muscles between those two gentlemen were stellar."

"They were."

"Do you have rum?"

"Er, I did." Keary retrieves the key to her grandmother's liquor cabinet from on top of the hutch. "But Erin was just here for the weekend, so who knows?"

"*Man*, I swear she was a pirate in a previous life!"

"If I believed in that sort of thing, I'd agree with you."

"Remember that summer we snuck this key and got trashed?"

One eyebrow arches. "Who's we? *You* snuck it," she clarifies while unlocking the wooden cabinet.

"Details," Evie adds, waving off the correction with one hand. "Anyway, I thought for sure she was going to tar and feather us *after* she got us sober."

"That was the longest summer of my life."

"Hey, I'm just glad she didn't tell my parents. Delivering missives was a blessing compared to what they would've done."

"I still can't stomach the smell of tequila." Keary confides, digging through the bottles to locate what's left of the rum.

Evie celebrates Keary's discovery with a dance and a quick hop that allows her to perch on the kitchen counter. "I hate the texture of missive paper now," she mumbles and turns over two short glasses left to dry on the dish rack. "But my parents never found out."

Whiskey in hand, Keary joins her friend on the counter and selects a glass to fill. "Nana was one of a kind that way."

"She could teach our stuffy group of elders a thing or two. I heard they gave Joshua Crait three years in the quarries for selling *banned* books."

Keary's lips twitch as her friend applies air quotes to the word banned. Once the full weight of her words settles, however, it removes any trace of amusement from her face. "Wouldn't the leeching fields be closer for his family to visit?"

"You expect the elders to really care?" After splashing a generous amount of whiskey in the glass closest to Keary, her friend fills her own with Erin's rum. "If he'd been a natural, they'd probably give him a slap on the wrist. Probation at most."

"If he'd been natural, I doubt he'd deal in restricted material," she reasons before dumping the whiskey down her throat with a wince.

"Yeah. Maker forbid we learn the actual truth of our history."

"Evie."

"Fix your face, Keary," Evie coaxes, her hands waving haphazardly between them. "It's not an opinion I'd share with anyone but you, Sugarbutt."

"Maybe we can get some people together and take care of his family while he's gone. It can't be easy leaving a young wife and two small children at home to fend for themselves."

"I'll put some feelers out. With a little luck, we can squeeze a way for them to visit once in a while. The quarries are a two-day trip, one way, in the best conditions. But anything would be better than nothing, I'd think."

As Keary refills her glass, she can't help but stew over the elder's motives. While Evie's opinion about the harsh treatment is best to keep silent, she can't argue with its weight. More than once over the last few years, they'd heard of one natural or another receiving soft punishments for some of their worse crimes, while they make examples out of the gifted. Reasonably, they could've sent him to the leeching fields for the same duration instead of the quarries. Keary liked to think that even one or two would argue that point. Instead, they sent him north. Where the weather is bitter, the snow is deep, and the terrain is impassable in some areas. *Nana would turn over in her grave.*

"Like I said, your grandmother could teach our elders a thing or two. What's it been, two years since she passed?"

"Three this fall." Lips tremble on the words catching in her throat. It's a sound that encourages her to drain the whiskey from her glass with a tight expression.

"I'm sorry, Love."

Keary doesn't have to see her to pick up on the voice change that softens Evie's otherwise animated tone. "Thanks," she forces through teeth. The act of pouring herself a second shot allows her to avoid those watchful eyes.

"You okay?"

"Mm-hmm. Fine," she murmurs and slams down her third shot in a futile attempt to numb the emotions swirling inside her. The liquor burns its way through her body, searing away any solace she might find in the *I'm sorry's* of the people around her. *How many condolences had she heard over the years?* Saying sorry does nothing for anyone except the person saying it. They bask in a hard-won moment of relief, while Keary fights her initial prickly response.

As if sensing the *do not tread* sign nailed to Keary's raw emotions, Evie dances to another topic. "What's so interesting about the trunk?"

"Nothing, yet."

"So much nothing that you forgot May Day and my hunt for a one-night-stand?"

"Right now, it's just a mess of papers and odd trinkets. Though I found an old shawl, you'll love."

"Great! What else are you hoping to find?"

"I don't know." The lie that curdles on her tongue tastes foul, even through the whiskey. *Why not just tell her?* Evie flocks to all things magic. She could prove useful. Yet, for a reason Keary can't name, sharing the trinket box feels a lot like sharing a lover.

"You've always been an odd duck."

"Quack, quack."

Satisfied with her response, Evie prattles on with details from this year's festival and what the new elder is trying to do with their library. If her friend harbors any suspicion over Keary's lack of participation, she never lets on as an hour zips by and they call it a night. Leaving the glasses in the sink, she locks up the liquor cabinet and walks her friend to the door.

"Sorry for flaking tonight."

"Don't be. It's not your kind of scene." Evie turns and takes hold of Keary's hands in a firm grip. "I'm going to say this one time and forever hold my tongue."

"O-kay?"

"Jeremy is a pud. But he's also a good guy and you couldn't do better in this town."

"I know. And I like Jeremy. But I don't feel the same burn that he says he feels for me."

"Love, welcome to being an adult. All the ones that can curl your toes without breaking your heart are extinct."

"That's a very depressing thought." After she places a smooch on her friend's cheek, Keary clicks on the porch light. "You good to get home?"

"You're asking *me* that? Honey, I'll drink you under the table whenever you're feeling sparky." Though her declaration carries a hint of slurred speech, her arms spread wide so Evie can touch a finger to her nose without fail. "See? Nighty-night."

With a comical shake of her head, Keary turns off the porch light and locks up the house. Sometimes Evie can come in like a sledgehammer, mindless of emotional casualties. But it's nights like this that Keary cherishes their friendship. Beyond tired, she stifles a yawn with her hand and climbs the stairs to her room, turning lights out along the way. Sparing time for her nightly routine, she swaps out her jeans and tank top for a t-shirt and pajama shorts and perches on the edge of the bed to brush her hair. Less than a minute later, her brain buzzes gently.

"I made it back, okay?"

"You just now made it back to campus?"

"No, sorry. I made it back a couple of hours ago. I didn't remember to link you until I climbed into bed."

"You're an ass."

"At least you can sleep easy knowing I'm not chained up in a maniac's cellar."

"Good to know. You're barely housebroken. I'd hate to train a new sister."

"Funny! Pretty sure I'm all you get, though. Love you tons."

"Love you more, Imp."

There are moments when Keary could throttle Erin and all her absentmindedness. Still, she can't deny the relief washing over her, knowing that her sister is safe. After a stretch, she switches off the lamp and crawls into bed with a yawn. Feet brush against the cool sheets as a wind chime plays a melody in the gentle breeze. Scrunching her eyes closed, she opens them and groans as the room spins above her.

"One shot too many?" Whether the alcohol or her exhausting day, Keary's eyes are heavy. Sleep won't be far off tonight.

Wait.

Since the rest of the house is dark, the soft glow that comes from the tower room might as well be the lighthouse beacon on Sandy Point. Her grumble stabs the silence as she tosses the covers back and pads barefoot up to the third floor. Seeing the state of the room through fresh eyes pulls a flinch from her.

Papers, tools, books, and trinkets cover the floor from one wall to another. Items she spent the afternoon handling with kid gloves before adding them to a growing list. So caught up in Evie's visit, Keary even left her sweater hanging off one of the bookcase nooks. Her path across the room is tedious to avoid anything fragile underfoot. The indirect path costs both time and efficiency, but it's the sound of crinkling papers under her feet that assaults her like nails on a chalkboard. With just five feet remaining, Keary gives herself an A for effort, until something sharp explodes under her right foot.

As she curses a blue streak that would blister her grand-mother's ears, she hops to the loveseat. Amidst the alcoholic buzz that circles her, she cradles her foot to inspect the dam-age. Though red and tender, she's relieved to see the skin still intact. Fingers absently massage the area while she searches the floor for the assailant.

In any other situation, her breath would catch over the metal hair-comb hiding under loose papers. Large, and with-out a doubt expensive for its time, it's also stunning. When she rescues it from the floor, the hairpiece dwarfs her hand as fingers skim the tiny metalwork that decorates the top. Intricate loops and knots make up an image of a bed of roses with shards of red stones to fill in each miniature petal. Keary's heartbeat slows to its natural rhythm as she removes the sheet of paper stuck in one corner.

Weathered and faint, the bold writing brings to mind a man's cursive instead of the graceful lines one would associate with a woman. After over-indulging on the liquor, Keary resorts to a squinting in order to read the passage aloud.

"*Charmer, charmer, trapped within, tell me true of your sin. Charmer though imprisoned ye be, hear my voice, I call to thee. While I cannot undo your past, my trust will make your respite last. Charmer, charmer, I call to thee. Come forth, so I might see.*" No sooner do the words leave her lips when the room becomes heavy.

A feeling Keary can't put a name to charges the air that surrounds her, pressing in and pushing down. Outside, the gentle breeze kicks up into a furious howl that blasts through open windows to whip loose papers into a tornado. A streak of lightning flashes with a crack sharp enough to raise the hair on her arms and wrestle a squeak of surprise from her mouth. Yet, when she peeks out a window, there's no trace of clouds in the sky. Only brilliant stars that twinkle against the backdrop of night as if all is right with the world.

"It's too early in the year for heat lightning," she muses before checking another window. She's never seen lightning without rain or thunder so early in the year. Despite the blanket of booze and her obvious confusion, Keary notes the start of an itch over her skin as her heartbeat bangs against her chest. Goosebumps accompany her when she spins around on the ball of one foot.

Taller than any man she's ever met, her intruder towers over her. Sturdy legs anchor a hulking frame that dwarfs what little space the room has left.

How dare he break into her house?

Whiskey-laden blood ignites at his sheer audacity. Whether it's panic or outrage that propels her, Keary grabs the nearby bookend and swings it with every bit of strength she can muster.

The sound it makes when it connects with the side of his head before he drops to the floor will haunt Keary forever. Every breath she pulls in is a fight against the pitch of her stomach. Muscles clench with the desire to expel the contents, regardless of where she's standing. Doubling over, she wraps arms around her midsection until the waves of nausea pass. He's unmoving by the time she rights herself.

"Call the guard, you idiot!" It's not until her voice slices through a heady stupor that Keary realizes she's yelling at herself. Careful to not tread too close, she skirts his long frame for the rope she left on the trunk's lid. Frayed and fragile, it's at least long enough to wrap his wrists twice. His manner of dress takes its time to dawn on her, a fact that has Keary wrestling with her own sanity.

A shirt of white linen stretches across the breadth of his shoulders with ease, although the material is near taunt. Hands twice the size of hers are clean, manicured and without gloves. *So not even a competent burglar.* His kilt; a mixture of brilliant colors of greens, blues and yellows, falls just shy of his knees. *A straggler from the festival?*

With the lightning storm growing in its frequency and intensity outside, something stirs in her belly. Wherever he came from, she suspects that the Briar Vanguard won't be much help. Their imprison first, ask questions later policy may not be appropriate. The thought of them torturing him over something so minor leaves her mouth dry.

Instead, Keary takes up a vigil on the loveseat and covers herself with one of Erin's quilts. Armed with her handy book-end, she fights off the shroud of sleep by forcing her eyes wide, ready for any sign of movement. She may not know exactly what's going on, but as she drifts off, she has the distinct idea that this is all Erin's fault.

CHAPTER 8

When Conall comes to, he wishes the ignorance of oblivion would return instead of the agony that claws at his skull. Teeth clamp on the groan that threatens to spill forward long enough for him to creak an eye open. The light that explodes against his temples is sharp enough to turn his stomach and yet, he pries open the other.

Where am I now? Have they moved Daigh as well?

While his view from the floor could use work, Conall can see various improvements. His new cell isn't as confining as the last, nor as damp as Sloan's cellar and he has *furniture!* Most of him can celebrate the upgrades while a nagging thought leaves his mouth dry. *What does she want?*

Since the answer to that question could literally be anything, he shoves it aside for later and moves to sit upright. When his arms don't respond to the action, a flare of adrenaline courses through him until he's visibly shaken. *Did the soldiers finally deliver one blow too many?* A deep ache in his shoulders reassures him otherwise. *Not broken, just tied up and defenseless,* his brain grumbles over the obvious.

His unprotected position carries an uptick in his pulse until his face floods with a heat that spills over to the tips of his ears. Pressure builds inside his chest until Conall can think of nothing else but his hands around her neck. He'd relish in the rush of blood under his hands as the life drains from her face. The image that follows is so vivid it leaves him gasping for air.

Then what? A tiny voice nags, reminding Conall to balance his anger with logic. By now Sloan will have heard of her treachery. After a heated discussion, he'd order their release in time to witness her public execution. That could explain the change in his living arrangements, he reasons and rolls onto his side.

The shift of position immediately restores the blood flow to hands, although his relief is short-lived. With the fresh circulation comes the sharp pinpricks that run the length of his arms, only to throb in the tips of his fingers. Each exhale ends on a hiss through teeth while he waits for the needle-like sensations to subside enough for him to work on the rope that binds his arms behind him.

Fingers pick and pull at the expertly tied knots until sweat beads on his forehead and transform his shirt into a second skin. He isn't sure how long he lay there fumbling with the coarse rope fibers before eventually crying defeat. Closing his eyes, he searches for what remains of his patience while his arms go slack.

Since loosening the knots proves futile, Conall changes tactics and focuses on the ropes' integrity. Wrists rotate and flex to create slack while he gathers the ambition needed to rock upward to his knees. Without hands and his joints stiff from a night on the floor, getting to his feet proves to be a challenge. There's a heartbeat when he readies himself for a crash, only to huff out a breath after the danger crawls along at an agonizing pace.

The jump in his pulse at the sight of countless books lining the walls twists his lips into a sardonic smile. He'd once spent a summer in Elder Murray's library reading as many books as he could, in awe of such a collection. One that now pales compared to the sheer number of books in this room. *Aofie's idea?* As prisons go, he's endured worse. Both comfort and stone, light and dark, warm, and cold. This new one leaves him scratching his head. "Figuratively," he grumbles.

Off to one side stands a pair of chairs decorated with ridiculous pillows and a small table nestled between them. Toward the center of the room, under an iron chandelier, is a narrow bed that holds the top to an open trunk. On his right stands a padded bench meant for dwarves with a mound of blankets testing its delicate frame. None of the pieces appear sturdy enough to support him, let alone to use as a battering ram. The walk to several windows works loose the kinks that riddle his lower half while he forms a new plan.

Outside, soft gray skies chase away the night, allowing Conall to scan the area. In one direction lays a body of water vast enough he can't make out land on the other side. A thick forest of trees makes up the rest of his surroundings, with treetops swaying at eye level. Despite the beauty, Conall's heart drops into his stomach. No way can he risk jumping without serious injury. If by some miracle he didn't break his legs, he can't be sure of a direction to take. The shroud of dawn that mixes with hundreds of trees makes telling north from south or east from west impossible. Oblivious to the cold realization, the budding leaves on the trees closest to the windows that make breathing normally an impossible task.

Spring?

Knuckles tighten and teeth set to shatter in his jaw as that one detail lands like a physical blow. It wasn't yet winter when guards yanked from their beds in the middle of the night to answer wild accusations. They've spent months in her damn prison waiting for justice to be carried out. *No way can Sloan feign ignorance now.*

No doubt he's just as much of a blackguard as the shrew he married. As if he's reliving that night all over again, his breath quickens with the poison of betrayal spilling into his blood.

"Bitch!"

The word is out of his mouth before Conall can call it back. Loud enough to earn him a scathing look from Moira; if she'd been within earshot. Just the thought of her douses his anger and awakens a fresh wave of emotions. *Had she been told? Did they grant her or them that much?* She was already showing her years when the wild lads she took pity on became men. Soon after, her frail form bent at a crooked angle and her once vibrant dark hair silvered. *How many winters can she survive without them to ease her burdens? One? Two?* It won't take long for her body to succumb, and she's left to die broken and alone, buried in a pauper's grave with five or six others.

The sense of helplessness that washes over him puts a pain in his chest as his vision swims. After the kindness the old woman had shown him and his brother, Conall would provide a life of luxury if he'd been able. At the very least, she deserves to know their fate at the hands of Brigid McKenna. Exploding with the pain building inside him, Conall kicks the dwarf-sized bench.

The banshee that shoots out from under the blankets catches him off-guard. Hair dark as night falls around a slender face as she scrambles to her feet with a shriek that could bloody ears. As it is, her unexpected arrival pushes him back a step.

Boots slip and catch on the many items littering the floor until his balance rocks and teeters with an uneasy air. Without the use of arms, Conall is helpless to stop his backward momentum. At the last second, however, he's able to twist at the waist and absorb the fall with the left side of his body.

His collision with the floor sends white-hot pain throughout his shoulder and hip to steal the breath from his lungs. There's a second when he stills, awaiting the sound of breaking bones, his breath a strained groan when it never comes. Teeth set in his jaw, knuckles tighten as Conall pins a glare to the dark-haired witch standing over him.

"Go on then. Finish it."

"Finish what?" Confusion mixes with a slow realization as she looks at the heavy statuette in her hands. The bright blush that follows lends a comely tint to a delicate complexion as her brow smooths. "I'm not going to hit you." His attacker insists in a flurry of words as she sets the weapon on a cluttered surface still well within her reach.

"I believe you already have." Conall notes as the throb in his skull burns with the reminder. *No wonder I have a headache the size of Caridah Keep.*

"That wasn't my fault."

"No?"

"Well, of course not," she insists as hands come to rest on the gentle flare of her hips, drawing his eyes to her state of undress. While the man's shirt engulfs her upper body with mystery, the shockingly short undergarments advertise everything below. The sight of long legs burns their image into his brain before Conall can squeeze his eyes shut.

"*Cor!* Where are your clothes?"

"What?"

"Your clothes, girl. Surely your father doesn't let you parade yourself around grown men in such a state."

"My *father* wouldn't have any say in the matter," her voice snaps. "It's not like I'm stark naked."

Conall opens one eye at a time and pins them to her pear-green eyes, alight with irritation. "Near to it."

"What're you, a prophet?"

"What?"

"A monk," she clarifies. "They're called shorts. People sleep in them. Which is what I was doing until you pitched a fit."

Despite the calm Conall tries to maintain, he can feel himself bristle over her choice of words. "I do *not* pitch fits."

"Since your tantrum jerked me from a relatively peaceful dream, I'll have to disagree." One eyebrow climbs up her forehead to complete a smug expression while arms fold across her chest, inadvertently pulling his attention to the thin material of her shirt and the treasures underneath.

Conall catches the flare of response deep in his gut before it moves on to nudge his impatience. "Maybe it's because I woke up trussed up like a holiday meal."

"Serves you right."

"I see no reason for you to be cross, as I'm the victim here."

"Oh?" Her soft tone cools to match the temperature in the room while she pulls a bright turquoise wrap around her shoulders. He tells himself that it's not disappointment he senses as she perches on the short table not three feet away. Long legs cross at the knees to allow one bare foot to bounce close enough for him to study delicate bones. "Please continue," she clips in a tight voice. "How does breaking into my house and scaring the tar out of me make *you* the victim?"

Huh? Conall chastises himself for falling into the distraction she creates and shoves himself into a sitting position. "Come again?"

"I said you're the one breaking and entering. I should've called the Vanguard on you."

In reality, the volume of her reply wasn't any louder than when Daigh went off on a tirade, but the pounding in his head intensifies it. Conall inhales with the sharp pain that reverberates back and forth between his temples, strangling his words.

"I can hear you just fine, girl, or at least I *could,*" he gripes. "I don't know about now. " More than ever, he wishes he had a thumb free to apply pressure to the throb growing behind his right eye.

"Sorry." When her face flushes pink, it puts a hint of yellow into her green eyes. "I said you scared me when you broke into my home. I merely reacted."

"That's a helluva reaction." *Loathe to see her against a real intruder.* "Wait, this is your home? Not my prison?"

"Why would it be your prison?"

Twisting his shoulders, Conall wriggles his bound hands at her. Her eyes round before a smirk flirts over her lips, only for her to chase it away with the next breath. "Lucky guess?"

"That was necessary."

"Truly?" Despite his current situation, Conall recognizes the warmth expanding inside his chest. "How many bumps do you carry from our meeting?"

"None." Her chin lifts with the one-word reply. "I plan to keep it that way."

"Hmm," he says. "I'm afraid I can't keep up with your reasoning. My head is too muddled."

"*Muddled?* Is that anything like psychotic?"

"I don't know that word." The collapse of his shoulders coincides with her small frown before her furrowed brow drops shadows into her eyes. The effort required to keep up with her gibberish is taxing. "Cor, my head hurts."

"I can help if you like."

"Over my dead body! Fetch Sloan. I wish to know his reasons for keeping me here."

"Um, who?"

"The Lord of your home." She laughs then, and it's a sound that ignites something within his blood to course through his veins. With his skin tight, he sucks in a breath as her smile plays with bow-shaped lips. It's a sight that wets his mouth even after he averts his eyes.

"Unless you're inferring to the elders, there's no Lord here."

She's done away with him as well? Brigid always struck him as calculating and cold, but her feelings for Sloan seemed genuine. *What of Geillis then? Where does she fit in with all this? Or poor Darby?* The thought of the small child suffering is an icy blast that chills him to the bone.

"Where is it you think you are?"

"Last I knew, Meath."

"I don't know Meath, but you're in the village of Briar."

Her softened pitch rolls with the odd accent in a fluid motion that inspires a rash of goosebumps to pucker his skin. "Is that north or south?"

"Er, Northwest."

North is good. We have allies in the north. If he can get word to them, rescuing Daigh will be a mite easier. And should things go sideways, his friends will make sure it all burns. But first, he needs to escape.

"Where is Daigh?"

"Who?"

"My brother. What have you done with him?" Conall asks. While he slips his hands free from the slack rope, he's careful to keep his shoulders from telegraphing the movement.

"I've never seen your brother. Was he at the festival with you?"

"What festival?" Fingers skim over the floor in search of something he can use to escape. The effort to keep the relief from his face when he stumbles on something round and sharp sidetracks Conall briefly.

"May Day."

"What in the bloody hell is *May Day*?"

"It's the celebration of spring." Her words catch as she pushes to her feet and inches toward the only door.

"Where is my brother?" The breath Conall draws in to keep his voice level is pointless as irritation kicks his pitch up an octave or two.

"H–how am I sup–posed t-to know?" Teeth worry over her lower lip as a hand rubs scrubs across the back of her neck. A quick shake of her head catches strands of hair against her eyelashes before she swipes them away with a hand.

Conall spies a tremble along her shoulders as she interprets the change in the air and moves closer to the door, forcing him to act.

Muscles bunch and tendons strain as he throws himself at his target. A squeak of surprise escapes her before he pins her to the nearest wall. One hand encircles her wrists while the other presses the tip of his weapon to her throat.

"Is he dead?" Conall's voice catches on the question, his mind reeling from the thought. The sight of blood that beads against her skin smothers him in guilt before he pushes it down to concentrate on Daigh. "Did you kill him?"

Her jaw drops while all color drains from her face. "Of course not!"

Indignation percolates just beneath her skin, only to tease his senses. While he refuses to dwell on the press of soft curves beneath him, the fragile bones in her wrists remind him to restrain his hold, if only a little. *Have you learned nothing?*

"Why should I believe you?" She's close enough he can smell the rosewater in her hair and enjoy the brush of her hot breath across his skin. He kicks himself for counting the three errant freckles across her smooth brow.

"Because I don't make a habit of killing people." Chin lifts once more while fear and something else flare to life in her eyes. "Although, I admit with *you,* I'm tempted," she finishes through clenched teeth.

Conall tightens his grip at the sign of her temper rising and immediately regrets it when she gasps sharply. Despite the voice warning him otherwise, he loosens his hold. "You're a McKenna, are you not?"

"Why should I tell you anything?"

His smile is reflex. "The answer is in the shape of your mouth and your headstrong air. They speak volumes about your attachment to a devious bloodline."

"Devious? Says the one of us that's armed." Her head tips back to level a glare up at him while her struggle renews. Even with the firm grip Conall keeps on himself, the feel of her curves squirming underneath him demands attention.

"Stop fighting me."

"Oh trust me, I haven't begun to fight you yet."

Something about her words warns Conall to keep his doubts at a minimum, so he resorts to the familiar path of logic. "It's pointless, girl. Not only do I outweigh you, but I have superior strength." While he means to take some teeth from her bite, Conall learns too late. It has the opposite effect.

Fire and shadows darken her face, but now her eyes narrow. Her delicate jaw squares a moment before her struggles resume with a fierceness he's not found in any of the women he's kept company with. When her breasts brush against his chest, it confirms an earlier assumption that they lay unrestrained under the thin material of her shirt. His body shudders with the unexpected contact as liquid heat gathers in his gut until his kilt feels too tight.

"*Cor, girl.* Stop bloody moving!" His words squeeze beyond a tight jaw even as Conall withdraws a step. *That's a mistake,* his mind corrects as one boot catches on yet more of the debris littering the floor to tilt him off kilter. Their impending fall must've shown on his face as her own eyes widen and lips part.

"Whoa, easy there," she coaxes gently.

Too late. Whether from the awkward way he holds her or the various items underfoot, Conall has just enough time to cushion her fall as they tumble backward. His collision with the floor brings a sharp wave of pain to explode in the back of his skull. Hissing, his vision swims until only darkness remains.

CHAPTER 9

"Way to go." The words trickle from her lips, but it's Erin's voice she hears in her head. Luckily, her burglar broke their fall by landing on the bottom. That it also sprawls her across six-feet-something of hard muscle, Keary disregards as unimportant.

Peeking an eye open, she half-expects to find Erin's hobby knife buried in her neck. When she catches sight of it at least three feet away, the shock snaps her other eye open. He must've ditched it when they fell, she reasons. *Why would he do that?*

Scanning his face, she notes the hard planes, high cheekbones, and a prominent jawline. He looks like a man who doesn't waver, so why would he drop his weapon? It's a question she tucks away for now to better address her current circumstances. After cataloging every handsome feature as irrelevant, Keary listens for any sign he's waking up while she works to extricate herself. Drawing in a breath to inflate her lungs, she holds it while sliding her hands free from his lax grip.

Bringing her arms around, she swallows the yelp in her throat when her shoulders protest the movement and plants her hands on his chest to push up on her elbows. Seconds tick by as she exhales through her nose, ready for any reaction. When she doesn't get one, Keary gets to work. Under her breath, she recites the past elders to distract herself from the warm slope of corded muscles resting under her hands.

In order to free her thigh from between his, she resorts to shifting her hips downward before she can inch towards the other side. The flutter of heat that infects her blood only serves to remind her how solitary her life has become lately.

Another breath leaks from her lips as her right knee grazes the wood floor beneath them. Out of nowhere, a sensation of cool air skitters down her body to raise the hair on her arms and kick her fight-or-flight response into overdrive. She catches her lip with her teeth when impossibly thick lashes lift at the same time his hands clamp down on her upper arms. Eyes like her favorite whiskey blink open. Silently, he studies their situation, only to finish with a pinch in his brows from whatever answer he settles on. When he speaks, his words carry a warm lilt that tightens her stomach and curls her fingers.

"You do not listen so well."

"Oh, take orders from a brute holding a weapon at my throat? Yeah, not apologizing for that one."

When his irritation produces a severe scowl, the scruff covering the lower half of his face softens the intensity. "I am not a brute."

"That's right, you're the *victim* here." Keary reminds him in a delicate voice, biting the inside of her cheek when eyes harden and nostrils flare.

"Yes."

"So, why do you react as if I am a leper? If you didn't jump back like you did, we might still be upright."

"Not a leper. I would not insult them in such a way as to lump them in the same category as witches."

The matter-of-fact way he answers, combined with the clench of that sharp jaw, spins her head around. "I'm sorry?"

"I don't believe you."

"Good!" Keary meets his deliberate glare with one of her own. "That wasn't an apology."

"No?"

"Well, of course not!"

One golden brow climbs up his forehead to complete an arrogant glare, his fingers never relaxing in their grip. *Surely his hands have to hurt by now.* "Why not?"

"Because I'm not a damn witch!"

"Says you."

"Why would I lie?" The stress headache merges with the hangover as they both take up residence behind her eyes. Feverfew would be a godsend right now, but she didn't see him letting her go long enough to make a trip downstairs to the pantry.

"You're a McKenna. You lack the fortitude for honesty."

"Fuck you." She seethes until her jaw aches from the pressure. Throwing diplomacy and manners right out one of the open windows, she struggles against his hold. His reaction to her venomous response reveals a set of dimples Keary could've done without witnessing.

"Not too often one hears such language from a lady."

The way his lips curl over the word lady has her balling up her fists until her nearly non-existent nails bite into the tender pads of her palms. "Something tells me you've inspired worse."

His smile is one of pure maleness, reeking of confidence and charm to put tiny dark flakes in amber eyes. "Only in the bedroom. Though I steer clear of the ones that believe themselves to be *ladies*." The deep timbre of his voice softens, oozing over his words like a caress that leaves goosebumps on her skin.

"Let me go and I'll show you the kind of lady I am."

"I think not. The goose egg from earlier is all the proof I need."

Eyes narrow until Keary can feel the heat of her temper warming her face. "Release me and I will make the other side match."

His deep chuckle rumbles beneath her, unleashing an ache inside her that's unfamiliar. The obvious enjoyment he gets from ruffling her feathers soothes some of the harsh angles from his face, making him appear less intimidating. "I must say. I like you, girl. If not for your treacherous bloodline, I'd bed you here and now."

"Stop calling me girl. And you wouldn't live long enough to enjoy the process." The very idea reignites the urge to free herself until it squeezes her heart in an icy grip. Despite the gnawing hunger he's awakened inside of her, Keary will go to her grave, ensuring he regrets that hasty decision.

Her warning results in her intruder laughing to spark another match on her temper. The nature of his laugh isn't helping either. He couldn't settle for a condescending chuckle or a sarcastic giggle. Instead, he rests his head on the floor to ride out a hard laugh that shakes his entire frame.

"Ah," he gasps for breath as he speaks, a trace of amusement still on his lips. "I cannot recall meeting one like you before."

"Then you must've been hiding under a rock for the last hundred years." As quickly as the words leave her mouth, the merry twinkle she secretly enjoys in his eyes vanishes beneath a murky shadow. His jaw hardens under the scruff to thin his lips as his fingers grip tighter.

"As if you don't know," he snarls through even white teeth, the charming lilt replaced with cold animosity.

"Huh?" She's no doubt said something wrong to change his demeanor, but for the life of her, Keary doesn't know what it was. The steady hum that vibrates off of him swarms over her senses to make any coherent thought difficult.

"Do not play games, girl. You'll not like the outcome."

"I have no clue what you're talking about." Teeth chew over her lower lip as she contemplates possibilities until only one remains logical. "I think I hit you too hard."

At her quiet observation, she studies in him in fascination as he calculates that information. Brows furrow in concentration while a pulse throbs in the column of his throat. Eyes dart from her face to the area sporting his goose egg and back.

"Maybe you did."

"I'm a healer. I could help."

"No."

"You could have a concussion." Keary reasons, adding silently that he'd have to release her for sure if she's being of any help. The idea of adding to her own growing headache sits uneasily in her stomach. But at least she'd be free of his iron grip. Leave it to her to have a physical reaction to an escaped mental patient. Maybe Evie is right. *I need to get out more.*

"Not likely."

"How could you possibly know that?"

"I can count all my fingers and toes. Plus, I've been hit harder than that before."

"I can only imagine," she mumbles, resisting the urge to continue her struggles. Not only was breaking his grip clearly impossible without her loyal bookend, but the wriggling is stirring up famished desires to stretch awake after such a long slumber.

"What's that supposed to mean?"

"What?"

"You can only imagine that someone has hit me harder. Why?"

Keary actively searches for her answer to avoid thinking about his thigh inches from the core of her body. Can he sense her reaction to him? The thought of him learning of her reaction would make her list of top ten worse moments. When she lifts her eyes to meet his, she sees no awareness there, only suspicion and quiet speculation. With a shallow breath, she answers honestly. "'Cause you're kind of an asshole." The laughter he erupts into splits the pain in her head to blind her for a few seconds.

"You should meet my brother. I'm the nice one."

"Clearly." Her obvious skepticism only inspires another chuckle from him that Keary tells herself she's not enjoying. She also doesn't notice how the humor takes years off his face, softens his lips or puts a sparkle in his oddly colored eyes. *Nope. Not. At. All.* The tiny voice that lives in her head calls her every version of a liar there is.

"You don't seem convinced."

"Well, you did just hold a knife to my throat."

"Ah, you make a fair point."

"Thank you. Can you let go now?"

"No."

"Why the hell not?" Pleasing to look at or not, Keary is at her wits' end with this man and running out of her reserves of patience. While her question appears to catch him off guard, he's quick to answer.

"Because I don't trust you."

"That's rich coming from the guy who broke into my home, only to hold me hostage."

"*You* tied me up!"

"There are worse things I could've done to the one who broke into my *home*," she counters.

"You hit me with your little knight over there." He shoots back, then casts a dirty look toward her bookend. "I think my skull has a permanent dent in it."

"It would serve you right." Keary inhales and counts to ten. Then counts to ten again. "Maybe we can call a truce for now. You let me go and I promise not to throw anything at you?"

"How do I know you'll honor the truce?"

"I give you my word."

"The word of a McKenna?" Something flashes in his face as fire burns in his eyes, eventually warming his skin. "Is useless."

"Then how about my word as Keary, and not Keary McKenna?" She scans his face, looking for any sign he might relent, and catches the smallest flicker in his mouth before his lips press tighter together. "If I wanted to hurt you, I could've done it while you were unconscious. *Both times*," she adds for good measure as lungs clench on the air of relief when his face softens.

"True. You could have."

Just like that, his hands fall away from her and he lays back to allow her to scramble several feet away. As he sits up, Keary draws her knees to her chest, already missing the warmth he provided. Though he remains silent, she knows he's watching every move she makes. Even now, the hatred he feels for her family still emanates from him to blanket the small room. "Why do you hate my family so much?"

His tawny head cocks to one side to regard her quietly. With a blank expression, his stare burns through the first layer of her skin. Several minutes creep by with no sound until Keary's certain he doesn't plan on dignifying her question with an answer. When he speaks, the raw emotion in his voice pulls her skin tight. "They betrayed us."

"Who did?" Keary can't be completely sure, but there are only a few members of the McKenna line left now. Over time, most scattered so far and wide, she's never met them.

"Sloan McKenna." *Where has she heard that name before?* Soon, the answer itches at the back of her brain as it works its way to the front. Nana talked little about ancestry beyond Keary's father and grandfather, but that name snags an old memory buried under layers of dust.

On an impulse, she shoots to her feet, mindless that it draws him to his full height as well, ready for her attack. Instead of closing the distance, Keary spins about and runs awkwardly across the littered floor, stumbling only once, to the bookshelf directly on her left. With a finger, she guides it along as she scans the old spines until finding the one she's looking for.

The weight of the book itself takes some effort to maneuver as she fumbles through coarse pages to get closer to the middle. The name on the current page sends her back three to read the scrawling names of Sloan and Brigid McKenna at the top. Dread fills her bones as she musters up the courage to bring the book for her intruder to see with his own eyes. Lines tremor across his face before he backs up several steps towards the door.

"I'm not a witch and I'm not cursing you, I promise. I just want to show you something." Keary searches his face until he meets her eyes and she recognizes the agony he's been shouldering. It's the same way she felt when her parents died. The same expression she wears every morning before locking it away long enough to face the day. One that Erin still carries for the world to see.

The struggle he feels to remain still is clear in the trembling of his body. Obviously, his desire to trust her goes against instinct. Eyes narrow when she closes the distance, his hands balling into fists, ready for the first sign of danger. "Is this the Sloan McKenna you mean?" Keary turns the book so he can read the page himself. Eyes scan the page once, twice and a third time before he gives a stuttered nod that drops hair across his brow.

"Yes." An indrawn breath raises his shoulders and stretches his shirt. "But I do not recognize the names after Darby."

"That's because this was almost five hundred years ago." Keary fights to keep her words light so he can absorb the blow mentally. When his eyes shoot to hers, the anguish she sees there twists her gut with sympathy.

His head shakes in denial as he steps back, the color draining from his golden skin until his complexion is gray. When his reaction dawns on her, she drops the book to reach for him a second before he drops like a tree through the door and into the hallway just beyond. In the back of her mind, Keary can hear that little voice calling *timber* as his head collides with the post that secures the banister leading to the second floor.

CHAPTER 10

"You can't be serious!" Judging by the splintered remains of the door adding to the growing items littering her floor, he'll have quite a headache when he wakes up. Incapacitated, there's nothing stopping her from escaping before he can use the iron grip. Lungs prime as her leg muscles twitch. *Why isn't she running?*

Without a doubt, the Vanguard should be her first call. The heaviness in her chest says otherwise. For reasons she can't explain, something about her intruder seems more broken than criminal. The Citadel has a facility for such people, but the thought of involving them rolls her stomach. No, she's on her own until she can figure out what to do with him.

Inhaling to the count of four, she counts to four again before exhaling. Fingers twist as she kneels beside him. While the 4x4 post he struck in his fall sports a dent, he resembles a broken doll.

His head rests at an odd angle, dropping hair across the side of his face. His arms lay splayed as if the thought of catching himself came too late. Long legs that comprise half of his height, rest bent, his kilt hiked against muscled thighs.

Resting back on her heels, Keary absently hums a few lines to a song about a man in his kilt. When she catches herself wondering how accurate those lyrics are, her face heats. The question reveals just how far off the rails she is. Her laughter soft, Keary gives herself a quick shake and pins her attention to the severity of her situation.

In his sleep, he's relaxed. Gone are the lines of tension that creep across his forehead until they pinch the corner of his eyes. His jaw, carved from stone, relaxes in direct contrast to the hard set she's learning to expect. Lips that thin while they bicker ease into a full, kissable shape. Awake, the man exudes an imposing confidence to encourage a disgruntled reaction from her independent nature. Asleep, he portrays a level of vulnerability that lodges a knot under her ribs.

"Okay," she hisses, rubbing the tingling from her hands. "Get a grip." The words sharpen her focus as the half-hearted raspberry she directs at the ceiling settles her nerves. The absence of a blood pool on the floor, Keary accepts as a good sign. Still, her hand trembles when she lifts it to check for his pulse. Being this close to him, envelopes her in a unique mixture of sage, mint, and cedar. A woman would need to be dead to miss the pleasing combination. As her body has been reminding her all morning, she's far from dead.

"You're not dying in my house!" Teeth set, Keary wills herself not to puke as her fingers scramble up and down warm skin. Once she locates the steady throb in his neck, her stomach settles enough for her to release a breath.

"Now what do I do?" If she calls for help, the authorities will either arrest him or commit him. Both scenarios apply a squeeze to her heart, disrupting its natural rhythm. "Figure something out, Keary." *Before your house becomes the crime scene, you've avoided your entire life.* On that note, she fixes her spine.

One hand hooks her curtain of hair across the opposite shoulder so she can lean close enough to assure herself he's breathing. "Hello?" Inches from his face, she pats his chest. "Hey," she pauses, teeth pinching the inside of her cheek, "you never told me your name. Come on, wake up."

When her efforts to be gentle in her prodding produce no results, she sits back on her heels and draws an arm back. The sharp crack of her hand connecting with his face sears across her palm. While he doesn't flutter an eyelash, she resorts to rubbing her hand against her sweater with a hiss.

"Okay, this isn't working."

The rushing sound in Keary's ears grows until a high-pitch ring drowns any hope of a coherent thought. Under her fingers, Conall's skin is clammy and cool. The tawny golden hue she'd reluctantly admired a short time ago, now ashen. Silky hair falls over his forehead, covering the upper half of his face. While his chest still rises and falls, she makes a mental note of the labored action.

After brushing his hair back, Keary rests her palm against his forehead. The instant she explores the pain flooding his head, her stomach twists violently. Snatching her hand back, she cradles her arm against her chest and sits back on her heels.

Whether from knocking him out, the fall they took together or his collision with the banister, the sheer agony inside his skull leaves her speechless. Just the slightest nudge from her powers would've dropped her to her knees if she wasn't already on them.

Breathing deep through her nose, Keary slows the hammering of her heart when a second wave of nausea slams into her. Squeezing her eyes tightly shut, she counts the seconds until it passes. Swallowing against the pain in her throat, her shoulders slump.

"If I don't do something, he's going to die here," she mutters in a flat voice. If that happens, her best hope is that they send her to the leeching fields instead of the quarries or the coal mines.

For over a century now, the elders manage criminals with one of six distinct methods. Of these, the glassworks under Elven rule are by far the most favorable. However, they limit this option for the lesser crimes. The more serious offenders have two options: either they labor in the leeching fields or work in the silver mines. Compared to the coal mine and stone quarry, both compounds are a luxury vacation. Although the work is physically demanding, it's far less dehumanizing than other locations. Even though most sentences range between one and five years, most prisoners don't survive that long. The small fraction that live, return home an empty shell of their former selves. Still, many consider that life a welcome alternative to the hangman's noose.

Keary reflects on her bleak prospects should the vanguard discover a dead body in her house. There's a good chance that Erin's absence will protect her sister from the elder's judgement. Unfortunately, the slight flare of hope sputtering in her chest isn't enough to calm the bundle of nerves just under her skin. Capturing her bottom lip between her teeth, Keary forces herself to get to work. Leaning toward his face, she uses one hand to explore the back of his incredibly thick skull, releasing a puff of air when she finds no traces of blood.

"I'll take that as a good thing. Until you're awake, at least." Reason tells her there's little chance he can hear her, but Keary can't deny that talking as if he can; eases some of the pressure within her chest.

Rubbing her hands together, she waits until the friction replaces the cool chill with a soft flare of heat. Once she's sure there's enough, she places her fingertips against both temples. Squaring her shoulders, Keary closes her eyes and pushes herself to isolate the largest concentration of his pain. While the area under a sizeable goose-egg causes a fissure of throbbing, it isn't enough to steal her breath. After reminding herself to bask in the relief she didn't cause this, she pushes farther until her mind touches the boundaries of his agony.

Ignoring the way her lungs tighten, and her skull threatens to expand and split, Keary siphons away small pieces. When her vision dances in front of her, she merely screws her eyes shut and continues. Muscles in her shoulders and neck tense and twitch with each wave of agony she consumes until she's certain she's leaving Conall with only a dull ache. Opening her eyes carefully, she releases a deep sigh at the sight of his impossibly thick lashes fluttering.

Squinting against the sharpness in her skull, she studies his chest, rising and falling more deeply than before. When he subconsciously leans into her touch, she jerks her hands away. Seconds tick by, mired in proverbial quicksand, while color gradually returns to his face. When his lashes finally lift, he pins those uniquely-colored eyes on her face before searching his surroundings. The instant he registers he's once again on the floor, frown lines appear around his mouth and eyes.

"What did you do?'

"Nothing." A tic pulses in her cheek as she rubs a finger along the pressure against her forehead. "You fainted."

"I do not faint. Women with weak constitutions faint."

"Right." When she considers his massive trust issues, Keary decides to keep her help with his mounting headache to herself. *Chances are, he won't believe me. And if he does, he'll just accuse me of giving him the headache from the start.* "Can you sit up?"

"Of course," Conall grumbles, waving off her helping hand. That he uses strictly his ab muscles to pull himself upright, reminds Keary of the wall of muscle she enjoyed earlier. Coughing calms the quick uptick in her heart rate.

"Did you hit me again?"

"Only to wake you."

His scowl deepens as he rubs a hand across the cheek, sporting a faint handprint. "My head hurts worse than before," he clips harshly.

"Probably because you broke the door and dented the stairs." Gesturing behind him with a furious wave of her hand, Keary assembles what remains of her patience. The full-on banging within her skull makes the task problematic. "I told you, you fainted." Fingers curl tight as she spits her explanation beyond a tight jaw.

As if contemplating her version of events, Conall broods. It doesn't take her long to note the slight green tint in his skin or the rapid bobbing of his Adam's apple. Each one equipped with a separate red flag.

"If you puke on my books, I'm just going to call the vanguard," she mutters. "I don't care if they lock you in a padded cell. It'll save me from being on trial for murder."

"Just give me a moment. I think I broke my head." With an intense scowl, Conall trains his eyes on her face.

"I'm shocked you didn't break my stairs."

Scrubbing one hand across his scruff, the other tightens until knuckles turn white. Silence hangs awkwardly between them before his lips tug into a begrudging smile.

"We need to get you some water. Maybe a few herbs for the headache you're going to have."

"Too late."

Keary offers a gentle shrug, then slips an arm through his. With a grunt, she yanks on his frame, hoping to aid him to his feet. Unfortunately, her efforts fail, falling under the *weighs more than her house* category.

"What in the bloody hell are you doing?"

Heat floods her cheeks as she jumps back. "Helping you to your feet."

"Uh-huh. I can manage." His fluid lilt carries an odd tone. Either he's insulted by the insinuation or amused by her paltry results. When he climbs to his full height, Keary decides the reason doesn't matter, as she's reminded just how big this man is.

"Fine," she snaps, taking another step away. "The kitchen is this way." I*s her voice shaky? Or is she imagining it?* Squaring her shoulders, she pulls her sweater tight across her frame and heads for the stairs.

She's halfway down when she tips her head with an afterthought. "Watch out for the-" The resounding crack of skull meeting floor joist cuts her warning short.

"*Cor*! Bloody fucking hell."

Bracing a hand on either wall, Keary spins around to inspect the damage. First to his head, which he rubs a hand over, then to her house. The lack of dent in either has her blowing out a puff of air. "Are you alright?"

"No." As his hand scrubs over the wounded area, he shoots her a dirty glare. "Your house is trying to do me in."

"I tried to warn you." He grunts a reply as she turns to continue toward the main floor. "Let's get you some water. Maybe an ice-pack." Eyes roll as he continues to grunt dramatically. "Or a helmet," she breathes as a small smile teases her mouth.

Leading the way to the kitchen, she jabs a finger at an empty chair. "Take a seat," she mutters, then fills two glasses with water. "Gently," she adds when he starts to lower his frame into the chair. The thinning of his lips and darkening of his eyes when he accepts the glass from her could peel paint.

After a quick jaunt to the pantry, Keary returns with the small jar of dried herbs. Setting it on the table in front of him, she lights a fire inside the stove and puts the teapot on to boil.

"What is it?" Long fingers pick up the jar making it smaller than when she held it.

"Feverfew. Medicine."

"Medicine for what?"

"Um," Keary eyes the fast-growing lump half hidden by his hairline. "Your headache."

"I'm not taking any of your medicine. Steep some leaves from your peppermint plant and I'll be right as a new babe."

"Yeah. No." She laughs with a quick shake of her head. "Erin will skin you if you mess with her plants. Trust me." When he notches his chin and folds his arms, Keary throws a hand up. "You don't want my medicine, that's fine." Digging out a small container of frozen peas from the freezer, she dumps several into a small cloth bag and set them on the table with a grin. "Put this on it."

"I do not trust you."

"Yeah! You've made that perfectly clear. Several times, in fact." Even if he hadn't made his stance obvious, the venom in which he spits his words at her begins to curl her stomach. "They're peas," she adds while rescuing her whistling teapot from the stove and filling her mug with the hot water. Measuring several spoons of feverfew in, she gently stirs until the powder dissolves completely. "While most people wrinkle their nose up at eating them, I don't see any threat they pose to your head."

Eyes never stray from her as he sits unmoving. "You don't want my help, fine. Suffer." Keary bounces a shoulder and takes a careful sip of her tea. He might feel better wallowing in his misery, but he won't find company in her house. If she thought taking the medicine herself would ease his worry, the frown lines surrounding his mouth say differently. Their standoff continues without a word until a hard rap on her front door spurs him up from his chair.

"Calm down," glancing at the clock on the wall, she waves her hand at his battle stance. Ripples of awareness shoot down the muscles in his arms as he scans her kitchen. *Probably looking for another weapon.* Shaking her head, Keary flaps her hands to settle him. "Just wait here."

Smoothing a hand over wild hair, she rolls her eyes yet again before peeking through the curtain. Jeremy's presence on her porch drops the bottom out of her stomach. "This day has already gone to hell in a handbasket," she grumbles and cracks the door enough for her head to poke out. "Jeremy, I wasn't expecting you."

"Good morning Keary." With a duck of his head, Jeremy studies the wooden planks of her porch. "I stopped by last night, but I must've missed you."

"Right! The lock. For the chest." *You're rambling. Knock it off.* "Um, come on in. I'll run up and grab it." With a hurried glimpse towards the kitchen, she scrambles up the stairs to the tower.

With the trunk's contents, scattered books and a broken door covering the floor, locating the damn lock takes more time than Keary can afford. Getting down on her hands and knees, she's tossing items left and right over her shoulder until she spies it peeking out from under an open book. Clasping it in her hands, she takes the stairs as quickly as she dares only to skid to a halt at the bottom. Her living room shrank considerably in her absence.

From opposite ends of the room, Jeremy and her stranger size each other up. Hands fist at Jeremy's side as Stranger simply folds his arms across his chest. Without looking in her direction, Jeremy speaks tightly through clenched teeth.

"Keary, who's your friend?"

"Friend?" She croaks.

"Conall O'Corr," kilt wearing giant offers in a lovely roll of r's and a brittle smile. One enormous hand hangs in the air a second too long before Jeremy accepts it.

"Jeremy Brandt. I'm a *friend* of Keary's."

Oh, for Pete's sake! Why doesn't he just whip it out and pee on me? She looks from man to man, their expressions full of barely contained hostility. "Jeremy is our local locksmith," she supplies, stepping neatly between the two of them. "He's going to make a new key for Erin's chest upstairs." The murderous glare in Jeremy's eyes doesn't stop her from hooking an arm in his. "I'll walk you out."

Conall O'Corr hangs back as she leads Jeremy out the front door to the narrow walking path towards his wagon. She's almost covered half the distance when he jerks his arm free and rounds on her with a wounded expression.

"One-night stands now, Keary?"

"Excuse me?" Attempting to associate the man she knows with the heat in his voice leaves her head spinning.

"I thought I knew you better than that. Boy, was I wrong."

"It's not what you think." *Why am I even trying to explain the situation? To him?*

"That man is obviously someone you picked up from the festival. Who knows how much he gets around? What diseases he brought into your bed?"

"Jeremy-"

"I'd expect this behavior from Erin. We've all seen how reckless she can be. But I never thought I'd see it from you. You're just like the rest of your kind."

The spit of his barb rocks Keary back on her heels. Acid flows along the tip of her tongue as his emotions slam into her full force. In a flash, fingers clench around the lock in her hand as her chin lifts to drive her eyes to his. "First, he wasn't a one-night stand. Not that it's any of *your* concern. If I choose to ride him like a wild mustang from sunup 'til sun-down and beyond. That's *my* business." Crossing her arms, she takes several steps back. "Second, don't you ever speak about Erin like that again. In fact, avoid her name altogether. Here's the damn lock," she steams, dropping the weight of it into his upturned palm. "Let me know what I owe you for a new key. I'd hate for you to be taken advantage of by *my kind*." Spinning on her heel, she turns toward the house, his quiet voice catching her ears.

"Keary, I'm-"

"Goodbye Jeremy."

Stomping toward the house, she notes the kilt-wearing giant dwarfing her front porch. Feet apart, arms span across his chest to pull the material of his shirt tighter. Even as she closes the distance, he doesn't turn back toward the house until Jeremy's wagon is bouncing over the driveway.

"One of your suitors?"

She closes the door behind them with a growl, spotting the lift of his eyebrow and the quirk in his lips. Ignoring the question, Keary presses a hand to the throb in her head. "I need coffee." Skirting around him, she shuffles to the kitchen.

"Coffee?"

If she'd known a half hour ago the way through his defenses was a dark-roasted bean, she'd have uttered the word the moment she woke up.

CHAPTER II

"You have coffee?"

"Yes."

The near grumble of her reply lifts one corner of his mouth. Turning, he follows Keary to the kitchen, his eyes devouring the long expanse of her bare legs.

A nice pair of legs has always been his weakness, and she flaunts a magnificent pair. Long, and tan with delicate ankles and shapely calves. They're the sort of legs that can easily wrap around a man's body to pull him in and hold him close. The last thought puts an uncomfortable hitch in his step.

Bracing one shoulder in the open doorway, Conall hangs back as she bustles from one end of the kitchen to the other. Lost in her thoughts, probably of her insulted suitor, she's a flurry of activity. He hadn't intended to cause her problems when he poked his head in the living-room earlier; it was mere curiosity he couldn't ignore.

The sight of a strange man in her house put her friend on alert, chasing the smile from his face. The marking territory signal is universal among men, no matter the age, and there was no mistaking it. Conall can admit he found it slightly amusing when the man staked his claim on Keary, and her instant bristling in response.

"Should I expect more suitors to come by?"

There it is. A ripple of frustration creasing her forehead a second before she looks away. "I don't have *suitors*." The way the last word squeaks through a tight jaw inspires another smile from him. "What do you take in your coffee?"

"You don't have sugar, do you?"

A thin, dark brow lifts as she peeks at him over one slender shoulder. "I do."

"Sugar would be grand." Conall can't ignore the little dance his inner self breaks into at the prospect of sweetened coffee. *Do not trust this woman*, his head warns silently.

True, she could've done her worse each time he lay vulnerable, but he's let his guard down before and it didn't go well. That she's smart only heightens his senses as she pours coffee into two fat mugs, adding a spoonful of sugar to both. After a trip to what he assumes is the icebox, she pours creamy liquid in one, gives both cups a stir, then carries them to the round table. When she takes a seat, Conall has little choice but to close the distance, opting for the chair furthest from her. The fact she holds onto the cup with cream settles the raised hairs on the back of his neck. Still, he hones his senses sharply while sinking into the wooden chair.

Across from him, Keary sits sideways in her seat. Propping an elbow on the table, she takes her first drink with a sound that knots his stomach. Hair like a night's shadow falls over one shoulder, a stark contrast to the brightness of her wrap. She bends one leg to recline against the chair's back and

Conall's eyes snag on the smoothness of her knee just above the table's surface. His body is quick to respond, tightening his chest and adding an itch to his fingers.

"I didn't poison it."

"Huh?"

"The coffee."

Conall blinks and stares at the cup in front of him. "I know. I watched your every step." His honesty brings a tightness to the curve of her jaw, but she says nothing. When he takes his first sip, the burst of flavor on his tongue widens his eyes. Holding the cup with both hands, he drinks like a man dying of thirst; mindless of the scalding his tongue suffers. In less than a minute, his cup is empty, his smile genuine. "That's better than Daigh's. Is there more?"

Standing, Keary fetches a tall pot from the stove's top and a small bowl of sugar. Setting them both down in front of him, she passes him a spoon. "I'll let you fix your own. Does your brother make great coffee?"

"More sludge than coffee, but it grows on you." Like a train, thoughts of his brother smack the air from his lungs. His heart quickens as he wonders again where his brother could've ended up.

The notion that five hundred years have passed since that night takes some work to swallow. Conall ticks off all the reasons she has to lie, but he could sense no deceit in her words. That doesn't make her trustworthy, however. Only cunning. If it's *not* a lie, his brother could be anywhere. Including with the Maker.

As if aware of the path his thoughts take, Keary's face softens. Setting her cup on the table, she sits a little straighter, turning to rest her arms on the polished surface. "When did you last see him?" The gentleness in her voice draws him away from somber assumptions.

"*Och*, if I'm to believe you, five hundred years ago." When she responds to his barb with a nod of understanding, Conall feels a squeeze against his heart for snapping at her.

"What were you doing before you wound up in my tower?"

"Soldiers were marching us out to a field. I thought perhaps to hang us."

"Who's soldiers?" Refilling her cup, Keary spoons in some sugar before adding her cream from the icebox.

"McKenna's soldiers." Even as he distracts himself by refilling his cup, goosebumps pepper his skin with the memory. "When they brought us out, Daigh fought. I cannot be sure what they did to him."

"They obviously didn't hang you, so why take you out to this field?"

Teeth clench on his reply as he struggles to fill his lungs with sufficient air. "One doesn't perform dark magic in their homes unless they care not for the consequences." The sound of her obnoxious snort draws his eyes up from his cup.

"I don't believe in dark magic."

"No?"

"Not the kind you're talking about."

"How do you explain me sitting here? If not by dark magic?"

"I'm still not convinced you didn't escape from the looney bin."

The more he talks with her, the easier he finds a path around her strange accent. Her pleasant voice, couples with a sharp intellect to engage him with little effort. But when she uses words that make no sense, the effect is like a dip in an icy lake.

"What is a looney bin?"

"Oh, um, hmm." She draws back, her fingers drumming on the side of her cup. When her teeth chew along her lower lip, his body reacts with a shiver. "It's a house where people mentally incapable of living alone can stay."

"Why?"

"Because most of them can't take care of themselves. We have healers and empath's that look after them."

"You round up all the people who can't care for themselves and give them a place to stay?"

"Well, I don't. The Vanguard does, under the elder's direction. What did your people do with them?"

"Most of society shunned the ones deemed *touched*. Outcast from the civilized, some lived solitary lives. Some they hung for witchcraft."

"Who's they?"

"Only the Lord over the village and the council elders can pass such a sentence."

"That's horrible."

"Most were harmless, yes. But not all of them. And society chews up what it doesn't understand."

"I wish I could say that's changed."

"Are the elders natural-born?"

"Most of them. We have one that's gifted."

Conall's neck is tight as he nods his head. "Then it's changed."

Silence stretches between them, each of them lost in their own thoughts. Conall tries to settle on a plan for locating Daigh, but where to start and how to find him is daunting. To say he's ignorant about surviving in her society is a vast understatement. Fingers form a tight fist as he forces himself to ask the one question weighing heavily on his mind. "Will you help me find my brother?"

Judging by the surprise shooting through her eyes and down to her lax mouth, you'd think he'd just grown an extra head. Seconds crawl by as Keary appears to consider his request. If she refuses, he has no plan B. Her long forefinger taps against the pad of her thumb, increasing the tension in his muscles before she seems to settle on a decision. "I'll help you Conall. But I'll be honest, I'm not even sure where to start." Just then, her eyes alight with a sparkle that has her scrambling from her chair.

As she runs from the room, Conall stands in the doorway, watchful as she searches through a roll-top desk. "What are you looking for?"

"The night Erin arrived; she gave me some pages. They looked pretty old. One of them has a passage written on it."

"A passage?"

"Hah!" Brandishing a sheet of paper that had certainly seen better days, she rushes back to the kitchen. "It must've been talking about you," she explains, smoothing the sheet flat against the table.

"What is?"

"This," clearing her throat, Keary recites the small passage scrawled in the corner. "Three moons to change his fate, a journey of trust awaits. Fail in this a time by three, and dust he'll forever be."

No sooner does she finish before a dark glare replaces Conall's initial confusion. Teeth grinding against the sudden influx of heat, his voice strangles. "Three moons?"

"It must be in terms of the moon's cycles." Returning to her chair, Keary drops with a soft plop.

"Which moon?" The shrug she answers with has him sighing and thinning his lips. *Trust what? Who? The ones who cursed him? Or trust Keary?* The only thing the vague clue inspires is the desire to pull his hair out in clumps. Fisting his hands in his laps to prevent himself from doing that very thing, he takes a slow breath. "A journey of trust?"

"You got me. But according to this your time is severely limited."

"Then we shouldn't waste time squabbling. What other clues do you have?"

"Nothing. And I found nothing magical in the trunk."

"What trunk?"

"Erin found an old chest at an estate sale."

"Erin is your wee sister?"

"Wee?" She laughs. The sound brushes over his skin and awakens slumbering nerve endings. "If you call her that to her face, she'll likely whack you with something, not *wee*."

The mention of her sister melts away her tough exterior. Graceful lines in her face soften and eyes the color of Daigh's favorite apples, glitter. Sitting back in her chair, a smile still on her lips, she nods. The smooth action rustles the silk of her hair until his fingers twitch. *Focus, you dolt.* "D-did she find anything else?" Conall swallows. The crack in his voice tightens his knuckles.

"Just this."

When Keary lifts a silver box from the pocket of her wrap, the air takes on a chill. He forgets to breathe as he takes in the seemingly insignificant item, familiarity smacking him straight in the face. It may have been five hundred years for her, but for him, it was yesterday.

Without the light from their largest moon, the clearing would've been dark if not for the dozens of fat candles someone lit beforehand. Cool air from a recent rain drifts up Conall's bare arms to cause a rash of goosebumps.

They didn't even have the decency to offer a last meal before hauling them up from the cell they've called home for the last several days. Walking in silence, he spots Daigh just over his right shoulder, as rough hands behind nudge him just a stone's throw inside the circle of candles. The lack of witnesses or an elder sends a shiver along his spine.

When the soldiers yank them to a halt, his brother attempts to shake off their hold while Conall scans the area. The large grove of trees on either side could cover an escape. If they can reach it. The strategist in him searches for an opportunity among the dozen soldiers hovering close by. His chest squeezing when he finds none.

Beside him, and despite the odds against them, his brother renews his struggles. Hands bound in front of him, he rocks a shoulder to draw one soldier close enough to headbutt. At once, several men jump forward to subdue their prisoner. Kicking one back, Daigh uses a hard elbow to knock another unconscious.

A spark in Conall's blood surges him into the fray. Ripping an attacker from his brother's back, he drives a knee into the soldier's face. The grunt he exhales echoes through the open field before he crumples in a heap at Conall's feet. Several minutes tick by as the brothers even the odds. Even as the bodies litter the surrounding ground, the soldiers are unfazed in their duty. Eventually, Daigh robs one of his small dagger and uses it to cut Conall's hands free. "Get out of here."

"No! I'm not leaving you."

Silver-blue eyes plead with him to see reason before his brother catches another advance with a hard right hook. "Both of us won't make it. People will believe you 'for they believe me." His groan cuts off whatever else he might say when an attacker plants a shoulder in Daigh's gut.

Three more lunge forward to push him to his knees in the wet grass. Conall's stomach rolls at the thought of leaving him at the mercy of Brigid McKenna. While he fights an internal battle, a tip of a sword balancing at the nape of Daigh's neck snaps his decision in place. Fingers loosen on the dagger, allowing it to drop to the earth as he raises his hands. "Do not hurt him." Conall's surrender of the blade spurs the remaining soldiers to flank him just as pain erupts in his skull. For a moment, his vision dances as he's shoved to his knees in the lush grass.

"Fucker," Daigh hisses, jaw hardening. "You should've run."

After battling the urge to be sick all over the ground, Conall fills his lungs with fresh air. "I've always had your back. Why stop now?"

"Even in death? I always said I was the rational one."

He scoffs as Brigid crosses the enclosure. Daigh the rational one. Who knew? If they're going to die, they'll do it together. As if he speaks the thought aloud, his brother offers a curt nod.

"Are your prisoners under control now, Commander?" *The sharpness of her voice scrapes over his ears to add to the throbbing in his skull.*

Behind him, Commander Riley's familiar tone answers in a brittle voice, her insult obviously striking a chord within the seasoned soldier. "You ordered my men unarmed, M'lady. If you hadn't, they wouldn't have taken out so many."

Eyes as blue and cold as a winter's sky, narrows in her elegant face. Coils of red hair rest atop her head in a tight bun that pulls signs of aging from her skin. With her hands folded in front of her, Brigid raises her chin. "Mind your tone, Commander. My husband can always train another like you."

"I have to ask," *Conall muses aloud.* "Which of your men will serve as my executioner, Riley?"

"No executioner Conall. Lady McKenna gave us her word."

"Yet, you put your hands on my brother and I without qualm," *Daigh counters, casting a withering glance over his shoulder.* "Never should've aided you in training your men."

"Aye. For once, Daigh, your untrusting nature proved accurate. I should've heeded your warnings." *Conall levels a scowl on the haughty face above him, just out of reach.* "If it's not an execution, *what do you plan to do with us, McKenna?" The flinch in her composure rewards his choice to drop her title.*

"I will do nothing." As she steps to his left, she summons someone forward with the sweep of an arm.

Emerging from the night, Conall registers her silver-blonde hair and familiar brown eyes. There was a time he thought himself in love with a girl identical enough to be her twin. Her willingness to take part in this betrayal blankets him under a thick fog. "Why?"

"For my sister," Aoife snaps, withdrawing two silver boxes from under the folds of her cloak. Bare feet whisper through the tall grass as she crosses to set one in front of each brother.

"The girl was batshit crazy long 'for we ever set foot in your village."

"Lies!" Daigh's accusation sends Aoife reeling back several steps, her shoulders trembling. "He wooed her, seduced her, and left her mind broken."

"Nay, Aoife. I would never hurt Etáin or Iseult," Conall urges. "I didn't love her as she loved me, but I would've married her. Even after her condition became known. We could've been a family. It was not me that drove her into the sea."

"He's lying," Brigid spits, stepping close enough to Aoife to whisper something too faint for him to catch. Before him, Conall watches Aoife's shoulders snap taunt, her eyes smoldering with an inner turmoil. Once her accomplice appears to settle, Brigid takes a step back once more. "Naught but a couple of Charmers, these two. My poor Geillis never stood a chance against their advances."

"This again?" Daigh snarls, fighting against his bound wrists. "We never touched the stupid girl!"

"One of you did," Brigid argues. "She was near distraught when she came to me. 'Tis clear, no woman is safe within your company."

"No, Aoife. You know us," Conall reasons quietly, attempting to draw the woman's gaze. Unsure of the lies Brigid would spew to purchase the witch's services, he could only pray logic would be enough to pierce the veil. Unwilling to lay his life in her hands, Daigh's struggles renew. He surges to his feet just as Aoife calls on the Great Mother of Magic.

Overhead, clouds roll in to shroud the twinkling stars in the night's sky. Flames flicker on the candles as a gust of wind whips up outside the circle. Narrow fingers leak through the barrier to snag Aoife's cloak, sending long tendrils of hair against her face. Conall can do nothing but gape as words tumble from her lips, disappearing with the winds' howl before they reach his ears. Beside him, soldiers pummel his brother into a submission he'll never accept. Before he can come to his brother's aid, cold steel lays against his throat, forcing him to watch helplessly when Daigh falls still. Only the slow movement of each inhale and exhale bolsters his hope that his brother still lives once the soldiers retreat.

Around him, candlelight flickers, then grows, its warmth increasing until it sears his skin. His breath catches against the intense discomfort that leaves him a quivering mess on the ground. There's no time to brace himself before the full weight of Aoife's magic crashes down around him. Grunting heavily, blinding pain touches Conall's skin like a thousand burning hands, causing his body to jerk and writhe. Dimly, he's aware that Daigh is incredibly still beside him. Whether from surrender or death, he can't be sure, but the agony radiating from every pore prevents him from checking.

Teeth grind as his vision distorts and narrows to a pinprick of light in a world of black. When the furious waves of heat subside, a whirlpool of energy plucks him from the damp earth. Screwing his eyes tightly shut, Conall's breath leaves in shallow pants as his hands clutch and tear at his hair. Just when he's certain the nightmare will never end, the torture dwindles, allowing him to draw an uneasy breath. Heat ripples through his limbs to ignite an inferno within his core.

Swaying unsteadily, his hands ball into tight fists in the struggle it takes to remain upright. Despite the lingering misery, Conall gasps for air as if he'd just surfaced from icy waters intent on drowning him. Gradually, his awareness returns bringing with it the knowledge that whatever just happened could be a death sentence for both of them.

Three shaky steps bring him close enough to drop to his knees beside Daigh. Shaking his shoulder gently, his brother stirs with a tremulous groan. Conall releases the stiffness in his shoulders when Daigh forces his bleary eyes open. After an incoherent mumble of sounds, he shoves Conall's helping hand away and staggers to his feet. While breathless, his voice carries a deadly intent when it croaks out of his throat.

"What have you done, witch?"

Stepping out from behind Aoife, Brigid claps her hands. In the soft glow of the candlelight, her eyes twinkle. As her icy glare shifts from brother to brother, Conall gapes as her plump lips twist into a haughty smirk. "Since it's a McKenna lady you have harmed, only a McKenna lady can free you." Her soft, bubbly laughter breaks the tension between them. "That day will never come."

Conall's jaw hardens as he digests the severity of the situation. Not death then. His heart twists and shatters as he contemplates their slim chance at freedom before darkness descends. As the sensation covers his brain in a thick blanket, he fights to remain conscious. Sweat prickles at his brow by the time he admits defeat and succumbs to the unknown. The next time they open, the centuries he's lost disrupts the natural rhythm of his heart.

"Conall?"

The lure of her voice guides his eyes from the cup in front of him. Blinking twice to focus, he registers her face instead of the ones burned into memory. With a heavy inhale, he sits back in his chair, physically spent.

"Are you okay? You zoned out there for a minute?"

"Yes," he croaks, jamming a thumb against the ache behind his left eye. "I recall these." Reaching across the table, he brings the silver box closer for a better inspection. "We thought they meant to kill us. I underestimated the true evil in Brigid McKenna's black heart."

"Wait. What do you mean, *these?*"

CHAPTER 12

Keary perches on the edge of her seat as Conall drowns himself in dark memories. As her question hangs in the air, she drums her fingers off the side of her cup. The more seconds that tick by, the whiter his knuckles become. Each breath leaves his mouth in quick puffs of air as he tips his face skyward.

Shifting in her chair, he drew her eyes to the rigid silhouette of his figure. Conall clenches his jaw so tight, a vein appears on his forehead before his lips disappear. Twice, he meets her gaze without a spark of recognition, the chill in his eyes palpable. The danger that rolls off this man intensifies the air between them. *Am I buying this story?* She'll admit it makes more sense than him being a festival-hopping burglar. If he was, her grandmother's house wouldn't be high on his list of targets. Surely one of the more extravagant houses on the lake carries a higher reward of booty. *Booty? Ugh, I'm thinking like Erin.* Her chin notches as she concludes he doesn't strike her as a criminal. However, deranged is still on the table. Conall wouldn't be the first person to have delusions. Probably not even the first to see himself as a warrior of days gone by.

"What have I gotten myself into?" she mutters quietly. *You'll have more than enough time later to weigh the level of shit you've stepped into. First, get some straight answers.* "Conall," she nudges lightly, "what do you mean by *these*? There's more than one? "With a far-away expression on his face, his head jerks a confirmation. "Use your words. Conall!"

The sharp hiss of his name hauls him back to the present. With a deep exhale, the strain in his body seems to vanish as he runs a hand through his hair. "Sorry."

"How many of these are there?"

"When Aoife cast her spell, she set one in front of me and one in front of my brother."

"You're saying she imprisoned you? How?"

"Child's play for someone gifted with sorcery."

Her brain glitches and zeroes in on the words rolling off his tongue. "Why would one of the gifted target you and your brother?"

"At first I thought it was because Daigh and I fought to free the natural-born people from under the boots of the gifted."

"Say that again."

Conall looks up from his cup, blinking rapidly. "My brother and I joined forces with others to create the vanguard. To- gether, we fought in the war against your kind."

"My kind? What makes you think I'm gifted?"

One eyebrow raises, his expression tight. "Are you not?"

"No, I am. Just find it amusing that you would assume such a thing. Basically, you're telling me that it's because of you two, the natural-born have such tyrannical power." Keary's brow furrows as she considers the implications of his statement. Teeth nibble over her lips as she battles with admiration for their success and disgust over the results.

"You use words to addle my brain," he accuses tightly.

"Likewise, buddy."

A smile skirts his lips before he hides it behind the rim of his cup. "The ruling elders kept a tight rein on the natural people. Preventing them from achieving the same level of success as the gifted folk."

"Preventing them?" Crooking her fingers, she applies air quotes to her question before asking another. "How many did the gifted send to slaughter?"

"There's no way to be sure. They said the number was thousands."

"They?"

"Our secret council."

The permanent furrow on Conall's forehead adds a stiffness to her posture. Tapping her thumb and middle finger together, Keary struggles to release the clenching of her jaw. Once she can look at him without imaging a fork protruding from his arrogant face, she responds. "We should change the subject."

"If you wish."

"The gist of all this is that instead of hanging you or leaving you and your brother to rot in some dungeon, my ancestor had you cursed?"

"Yes."

"Doesn't that seem a little extreme to you?"

"Brigid McKenna was an extreme person."

Reaching across the table, Keary reclaims the heavy box. Drawing it close, she registers that the essence luring her over the last two days is gone. "Is that why it doesn't open?" Her eyes narrow as she interprets his lazy shrug as non-committal. "Why would she go to such lengths?" The wide range of emotions fluttering across his face makes it difficult to pinpoint just one. He spends the next several seconds staring into the contents of his cup as if searching for the right words. The sharp knock on the front door offers him a temporary reprieve.

With a glance at her cup, Keary pushes away from the table. Crossing the living room, she peeks out the curtain, half expecting to see Jeremy's wagon in the driveway. A sigh escapes her when she spies the white wagon emblazoned with the council's emblem. Checking to see that Conall remains in the kitchen, she opens the door with a tight smile. "Morning."

"Morning. I'm Stacey, here on council business."

Keary fights to keep her expression blank while a hundred scenarios flash through her head. "What can I do for you?"

"May I come in?"

"Of course." Gripping the flaps of her sweater, Keary steps back far enough for the young woman to enter.

"Thank you." Stacey flashes a practiced smile for good measure while shaking off the morning chill. "The elders have ordered me to hand-deliver a missive to every home."

"You're going to be at this a while then."

"I'm afraid so."

Fingers twist in the soft yarn. "What if someone isn't home?"

"Then I make a note in my report for the council," Stacey answers absently while digging through her satchel. After a moment, her perfectly manicured eyebrows wrinkle. "I may have dropped yours in the wagon."

"Can't you just give me one you *do* have?"

"I'm sorry. No. They addressed each one personally. It makes tracking the ones we couldn't deliver easier."

"I see. Well, take your time. I'm not going anywhere." Shutting the door behind the courier, Keary scurries back to the kitchen. Instead of finding Conall at the table where she left him, he's staring out the far window overlooking the lake.

Just inside the doorway, her eyes devour him without fear of getting caught. A lifetime of manual labor created the strength in his shoulders. The thin fabric of his shirt stretches to its limit around the incredible width. As if carved from tree trunks, his massive legs brace the bulk of his weight with little effort. The material of his kilt encases a narrow waist where strong hands rest. She recalls their rough and calloused texture against the soft yarn of her sweater. As imposing a figure as he is from the back, the effect doubles when he's facing her.

"How cold is your lake? I thought I might wash off the stench of McKenna's cellar."

The realization that he'd been aware of her presence while she ogled him, turns her cheeks red. With a cough, she buys time while her brain replays the question. After a second loop, her brow wrinkles. "Why not just use the shower like a normal person?" His half-turn stretches the shirt tighter against the roping muscles in his back. With a tiny shake of his head, he regards her strangely.

Catching the wrinkle in his brow, she rushes to explain. "It's like," teeth catch her lip as she struggles for a word that'll make sense to him. "Rain! Yeah, rain. In a um," swallowing, she offers a tiny smirk, "box." The eyebrow he lifts elicits a soft chuckle from her. "Let me show you," she says, latching onto his hand. As she pulls him through the house, she tries not to think about his hand in hers, or the incredible warmth it radiates.

Releasing his hand once they reach the bathroom, she scrubs hers against her sweater before flipping the switch for the overhead lights. When a bright wash of yellow light fills the room, Conall flinches before searching the four corners. "I'll explain that later," she promises as she drags the heavy shower curtain aside to expose the miniature bathtub.

"So, um. You turn both handles here to start the water." The sound of water filling the bottom of the tub draws him further into the room, eyes alight. When his shoulder brushes hers, Keary fights the impulse to move away. *Only because another step will put me in the tub.* Dragging in a breath, she clamps down on the moan rising as she inhales the heady scent of him. *Yep, I need to get out more.*

"If you turn the left handle, your water will get hot. If you turn the right handle, it'll get cold. Once you um," she squeaks when he presses closer, her back flush with the wall of his chest. "Once you have the temperature you want, you pull up on this little stopper here."

He jumps when the water crashes against the back shower wall. "Shit," he breathes, placing his hand under the warm spray. "You have rain in a box. Where does the water come from?"

"Most houses have tanks. The solar energy only heats enough for one or two quick ones, however. So I wouldn't waste too much time marveling if I were you," Keary warns as she inches her way from between him and the shower. Once her hand rests on the door handle, she pauses. "Be sure to undress before you get in." His lopsided grin curls her toes and flips her stomach. "There are clean towels in the cupboard here. I'll make breakfast while you, uh, wash up." It's not until she's safely in the hall with the door latched she manages a full inhale. *Cripes!*

A peek through the window of the living room shows the courier rummaging through an impressive pile of bags filling her wagon. Clamping her lips against the offer to help, Keary turns on her heel and moves back to the kitchen to get started on breakfast.

Leaving several pans to heat on the stove, she grabs some eggs from the icebox. Scrambling them in a bowl with butter, her ears stick on the sounds of running water coming from the bathroom. The image of him, naked under the spray of water, puts a jolt in her pulse. Once she realizes she's whipping the eggs with more force than it requires, she sets the bowl on the counter.

Shaking her head, she casts a glance over her shoulder toward the hallway. A few days ago, her biggest worries were a struggling business and whether Erin gets herself killed living in the Citadel. Now she has a stranger in her house spouting ancient ideals of the civil war. *In a kilt!* The worst part is that instead of showing him the door, she shows him to her shower.

"I've lost my damn mind," she grumbles while coating a thick slice of bread with the egg mixture before laying it in the hot skillet. The sharp cracks and pops that follow offers her a short distraction from the traitorous thoughts pinging around inside her head. "I blame you, Erin." After adding a few dashes from her meager selection of seasonings to the toast, she turns her attention to the bacon. *No way she could've known her birthday present would come with a giant-sized leprechaun attached.* Snatching her hands back when the grease begins to pop, Keary gives her head another shake. "True, but it makes me feel better."

Time flies by as she builds a short stack of French toast on a plate, a pile of scrambled eggs and a half a dozen slices of bacon. When Stacey calls out from the front of the house, Keary extinguishes the stove, then dries her hands on a thin white towel as she returns to the front door.

"Sorry that took so long. I don't know how I lost it."

"No harm done, I'm sure."

"I need you to sign for the delivery," Stacey instructs, thrusting a thick ledger into her hands.

Nodding mutely, Keary scrawls her name across the line, then repeats the action on the sheet underneath.

"The bottom is yours to keep for your records."

In an otherwise quiet house, the sound of paper tearing makes Keary wince slightly. She's tucking the folded paper into a pocket of her sweater when a deep lilting voice behind her draws her attention towards the hallway.

"I must confess, I'm gobsmacked."

Keary's jaw drops and her heart falls to her stomach as Conall steps out of the hall, wearing nothing but a towel. His toned body gleams from the morning light streaming through sheer curtains, his dark honey-blond hair clinging to his neck and shoulders. Without asking her permission, her gaze follows the droplets of water as they cascade down his toned body. When her eyes travel and rest on his abs, Keary averts her gaze to something less distracting. Like the floor. Unfortunately, his stride deeper into the room pulls her focus to the flex of muscles. She'll regret it later, but in that moment she can't help but stare as one hand moves through his soaked locks.

Beside her, Stacey's brown eyes grow noticeably bigger, her lips parted on a silent *o*. The rational part of Keary's brain can't fault the woman for savoring the free buffet standing oblivious before them, but the rest of her wants nothing more than to shove her out the front door. With a mental shake to organize her thoughts, she steps in between Conall and Stacey.

"Where are your clothes?" Keary squeaks out from the vise that squeezes her chest.

"They need washing."

When he steps even closer, the combination of soap and musk on his skin assaults her senses. Heat explodes in her cheeks as fingers knot into small fists. "In that case, it makes perfect sense for you to strut around in your birthday suit," she snaps. Her jaw clenches as she grabs the hand not holding the towel in place to drag him toward the back of the house.

"Birthday suit?"

Keary counts to ten as she shoves open a door seldom used. "I'm not having a vocabulary dispute with you right now."

"You mean naked?"

"See, this language barrier isn't so bad when you *want* to understand." His proximity has her sending up a prayer for a normal heart rate. Fingers twitch as she struggles to block out the large presence behind her while tossing boxes from the stack along one wall.

"This bothers you."

"People don't walk around naked. Not unless they want to spend a night behind bars."

"That goes for you as well, then?"

She whips around to face him and her grip tightens on the box in her hands. "Excuse me?" she croaks. The effect of his pointed stare at her bare legs teeters back and forth between fury and desire. A sudden urge to cuff him ignites her blood. A hard tremor cascades through her arms until the feeling eventually passes. *Any more blows to the head might leave him a drooling mess.* "I have clothes on."

"Not so much."

"More than you do!"

The sight of his teasing smile forces her to draw in a calming breath. Laughter twinkles in his eyes as he plants his free hand on the slope of his hip. The second her eyes drop, she chastises herself.

"Not so much." Half-growl, half-mumble, Conall's voice spills over bare skin.

Keary shivers as Conall's gaze heats her from within. The intensity of his eyes hits her forcefully, knocking the air from her lungs. Biting back the moan desperate to free itself and pressing her thighs together from the sudden ache in her core, she counts to ten. Despite the reaction in her body, her brain recovers enough strength to spin her back around, breaking the spell between them. Pulling her bottom lip between teeth, she scrambles to locate the correct box.

"What are you looking for?"

"Clothes," she adds tersely. Endorphins flood her system as she stumbles upon a pair of jeans and several plain tees big enough to fit him. Smacking him in the chest with the stack of clothes, she skirts around him toward the door. "Put these on. Don't even think about coming out until you're covered head to fucking toe."

"You're bossy."

"Buddy, you have no idea," she grumbles, escaping the room before the towel drops. *Coward*! The beast inside her snickers as she all but runs back to the living room. Stacey's lingering presence acts as an immediate cold shower. "Is there something else?"

"I just wanted to make sure you had no questions."

She removed the tie that held her hair back while Keary located clothes for Conall. Now, shoulder-length blond curls frame an oval face as if purposely arranged. She's also undone a few buttons on her shirt to cause attention to well-rounded breasts.

"Not that comes to mind."

"Are you sure?" Stacey stammers, tossing a look around Keary to the empty hallway. "I'd hate to leave you confused about the order."

"I'm sure I can manage." Her teeth grind as she steers Stacey back towards the front door. "Have a great day."

"Oh. Um. Of course, Ms. McKenna. You as well." After a final hopeful glance toward the back of the house, Stacey steps out onto the front porch. "I'm more than happy to-"

With an eye roll, Keary shuts the door on whatever she'd been about to offer. After a second of stewing, she turns the deadbolt for good measure. Stomping to the kitchen, she scowls at a platter of cold French toast and hard bacon. "He can eat it, anyway."

"Better?"

Pulling a breath, Keary peeks over to find him in the doorway, completely clothed. Loose blue jeans ride low on his hips, falling to cover the tops of bare feet in gentle folds of denim. She can almost hear the blue fabric of his t-shirt scream uncle as it stretches over wide shoulders. As the flare of heat pools in her stomach, she has to admit, she liked him better in just a towel. "Yes."

Lips twitch as his eyes sparkle with mischief. "Did your friend leave?"

"I had to scrape her jaw off the floor first," she clips, piling food high on his plate before passing it to him. "But yes, she's gone."

"I don't understand."

"Yes, you do. You may not get the words, but you know full well the effect you had on that poor woman."

Danger springs to life in his expressive eyes as he takes a seat at the table. His intense stare commands her attention from across the room. "Perhaps."

Cripes, I should've called the authorities and had the man locked up.

"What did she want?"

Bracing her hip against the counter, she nibbles on an overcooked piece of bacon. "She's a courier for the elders. Whenever they pass a new law, she delivers them. Apparently, I needed to sign for this one."

"Why?"

"They probably want to make sure they notify everyone about this one because it's going to make some people angry."

Shoveling an impressive forkful of toast into his mouth, Conall chews quietly for a moment. "Why?"

Abandoning the rest of her bacon, Keary scrubs her greasy fingers on the small towel before unrolling the missive she'd dropped on the counter. As she suspected, the elders drafted a long-winded notice confirming their intentions during the town meeting. Pulling a breath in through her nose, she keeps her voice flat. "Because they want our food. At least they're taking volunteers from the natural-born to help with the fields and hunting. That's something."

"Why do they want your food?" With a fresh wrinkle across his brow, Conall studies her with a stormy expression on his face.

Dropping the missive in the trash bin, Keary returns to her lukewarm coffee. Clamping her lips against her initial response, she takes a moment to find calm within the caffeine. When she's certain she can answer without a trace of the acid lining her throat, she meets his eyes from across the room.

"According to the town meeting, our food stores are running shockingly low. To ensure all the natural-born have enough to last the coming winter, they are confiscating a portion the larger farms grow from the gifted families."

"Confiscating?"

"Taking. Without option of dispute."

As Conall mulls over her explanation, Keary refills her coffee cup, relishing in the silence filling the tiny kitchen. Living with Erin day in and day out did nothing to prepare her for Conall's inquisitive personality. *Never thought I'd see the day someone would surpass Erin's needling nature.*

"Perhaps if they are allowed to grow their own crops, they wouldn't need a portion of yours."

Whether it's the highly offensive nature of his reply, or the condescension she picks up from his tone, Keary isn't sure. For one quick moment, her lungs refuse to deflate as tiny lights dance within her vision. Nostrils flare as she bares her teeth. "Let's just agree that you don't know what you're talking about and move on." Releasing her breath on a sigh, she's thankful that she kept her voice from actually spitting the venom coating her tongue. Searching for something to keep her hands busy, she clears away the remnants of breakfast.

"I know firsthand how the gifted lorded over those of us they deemed unworthy of special abilities. Many nights, we went without food. Or even wood for heat that we didn't split ourselves. When our elders asked my brother and I to step up and lead a rebellion, we were proud to do so." Pushing himself up from the table, Conall carries his plate to the sink. "Perhaps it's you that doesn't know what you're talking about. Not me."

"Maybe." Jerking the plate from his hands, Keary soaks it in hot, soapy water. "Maybe you're carrying assumptions from five hundred years ago."

Instead of moving away, Conall takes up a stance beside her to dry the wet dishes she places in the rack. While they work in silence together, Keary remains focused on the task in front of her. When he breaks the silence, she nearly seethes at the gentle coaxing of his voice and the effect it has on her body.

"You're right. I am judging based on how things were when I saw them instead of now."

Rocking back on her heels, Keary blinks. While her mind rebels against the olive branch, it rails at her to refuse the effort while her head simply jerks a nod. "Fair enough," she croaks, containing the urge to filet him with her tongue.

CHAPTER 13

The soothing patter of water echoes off the shower walls as Keary gets lost in thought. It's obvious that Conall carries some strong opinions about "her kind". Are those opinions a result of living under the rule of those who possess "gifts"? Or is it a glimpse into his naturally dark convictions? As she works the shampoo through her hair, she can't bring herself to lump him in with other discriminating people she's met over the years.

Without many details to go on, his reactions give her the impression that life under the power structure he knew wasn't much better than today in reverse. Since history books fall under the tight regulation of the elders, Keary doesn't nurture much hope of finding any actual facts. Whatever the situation, Conall and his brother felt a need to join the revolution that would forever change the seat of power in Solstier. While exchanging the shampoo for the conditioner, she can't help but wonder if he'll ever be able to trust her. Or would her ancestry and "gifts" be an unbridgeable gap? The sudden drop in water temperature snaps her out of her musings.

"Damn. Stupid. Stupid." Fingers ache as she soaps up her body, gritting her teeth together as she musters the nerve to force herself under the cold spray. Since Erin left for the Citadel three years ago, having all the hot water to herself has made her careless.

Turning off the shower, Keary steps out on the mat and bundles up in a thick towel. Teeth chatter as her hands vigorously rub against the numbing pain flooding her limbs in an attempt to get some feeling back. "N-next ti-time Conall h-h-has a t-time limit." Exposed to the cool air, her damp skin tightens and tingles with a voracious layer of goosebumps.

By the time she hangs up the damp towel, small, red splotches stain her skin. Wrapping the second towel around the heavy mass of wet hair, she tucks one end under the other to secure it to the back of her head. Slipping into a bra and a pair of panties, she straightens only to stare at the bluish-purple marks Conall left on her skin. In various degrees of visibility, the patches pepper up and down her arms from his steel–like grip. Under the curve of her jaw lays another area still red and angry after her stand-off with Erin's box cutter. Part of her brain rationalizes the state in which he must've woken up. The other part couldn't care less. After promising herself he'll not leave another mark on her skin, she pulls on her t-shirt and jeans and steps out of the bathroom to find him standing eerily silent in the living room.

As he stares off into the distance, Keary allows herself a moment to examine his profile in the reflection of the nearby window. The sharp angles of his cheekbones and a slightly crooked nose create an attractive silhouette. His hard life hones his body into a sturdy frame and packed muscle suitable for tackling whatever the day requires. Impossibly thick lashes frame sharp amber eyes with the sole purpose of inspiring lustful thoughts. Despite the flaws, his charming ruggedness is hard for her to overlook.

"It still looks the same."

Without turning around, Conall's words fall between them, breaking the tension like the sun peeking through stubborn rain clouds. Keary remains against the doorframe to keep the distance between them. When his eyes capture hers, however, she momentarily forgets how to exhale. After a brief mental shake, she forces herself to offer a gentle shrug of one shoulder. "Here it might. We don't have many people in Briar. I'm sure our cities will surprise you, though. More people and a lot more lights."

"Lights?"

Keary shifts her weight and directs his attention to the small light fixtures on the wall. Once she brushes her fingers over the light switch, he flinches against the sudden wash of light.

Mumbling to himself, Conall takes a step back, his dark expression turning blacker by the second. With a wrinkle in his brow, he looks around as if searching for the source of the mysterious light before settling on the bulb itself. As though captivated, he slowly reaches a hand toward it before freezing in place midway through the action.

Keary grins and steps up beside him. "It doesn't bite." Reaching up, she touches two fingers to the bulb. Conall's jaw hardens, as he scans her face for any trace of pain before copying her actions. "It isn't hot," he murmurs with a slow to grow grin.

"Not yet. The longer they're on, the hotter they become."

"Is it magic?"

Careful to avoid touching him too long, Keary guides Conall to the light switch. Cradling his massive hand in hers, she demonstrates how to turn the light on and off. "Not magic. Science. There are smooth panels that capture energy and store it in a battery for use."

"For your lights?"

"Mm-hmm. Heat as well. We also use it to heat the water for showers. So next time, try not to use all the hot water."

Oblivious to her chastising tone, Conall fires his next question. "Where does the energy come from?"

"From the sun. I'm not a scientist, so I don't know all the steps, but what I know is the panels attract the sun and convert it into energy stored in the battery. Which is why during our winter months, when the days are shorter, most of us still depend on candles for light and wood for heat."

"And everyone has these panels?"

"Most do, yes. Some still depend on candles and wood year 'round."

"Some?" Keary blinks as the twinkle fades from his eyes and a muscle twitches in his left cheek. "Like the natural-born?"

And I'm back to square one. Again. Her hands ball into small fists as Keary tilts her chin. "Actually no. Thanks to the elders, all the natural-born have solar panels, regardless if they could pay for them."

"You had to pay for the panels?"

"The gifted citizens do, yes. Which is why some would prefer to go without. My grandmother had the panels installed here the year before she died."

Conall is quiet for so long, Keary can nearly hear the gears turning in his head. "So these elders charge some people for these panels, but not others?"

"Correct. During the winter months, when the energy level is low, we also give the natural-born individuals half of the candles we make and half of the wood we chop."

"That's very nice of you."

Keary scoffs and grinds her teeth together to stop herself from sparking yet another debate. "Come on, we have work to do."

Meeting her eyes, all traces of tension dissipates from his shoulders. "What do you need me to do?"

"There have to be answers in the trunk Erin found. Our best bet is to start there."

"Before we do that, I owe you an apology."

Raising an eyebrow, Keary crosses her arms and leans off one hip. "For what?"

"For those." His gaze is unflinching. Hard flints of amber in the eyes that he drops to the exposed bruises he'd left on her. When Conall takes a deep breath, she notes the tightening in his jaw. "It won't happen again."

Keary stares intently, her eyes resting on his determined jawline, her ears catching the unyielding pitch in his voice. Taking a step back, she brushes her palms over her bare arms before meeting his gaze again. "It's water under the bridge," she says while softening her expression.

His scowl deepens. "What is?"

"It's a figure of speech. It means I've moved on," she clarifies while biting back the smile flirting against her lips. "I don't hold it against you."

Conall eases some of the severity from his jawline, and he dips his head. "Thank you."

Keary nods in response, and after a moment of silence, she takes a step towards the stairs. "Come on, before we lose the daylight."

Viewing the tower room through fresh eyes lodges a knot just under Keary's ribs. With the amount of clutter she dug out yesterday, she can't fathom how it all fit inside one piece of furniture. Now it lays spread from one side to the other in a mishmash of papers, books, and other random objects.

Taking a deep breath, Keary eyes what remains of the door. Since buying a new one is out of the question, her only option is to get it repaired in town. How she'll get it to town is a problem for another day. "Let's just set this aside for now until I can get it fixed."

Conall nods with purpose before heaving the door onto his shoulder. After several long strides, he crosses to one exterior wall and rests it against the wall without so much as a thud.

Unwilling to blink, Keary watches; her mouth slightly agape over the wavelike movement of muscle across his back and the visible cords along his arms. All too clearly, she recalls the feel of those hard planes hiding under layers of his smooth skin. As if the vivid memory proves too much for her brain to compute logically, her breath hitches as a steady flow of heat creeps over her.

"Where should we start?"

Conall's deep voice brings Keary back to the present moment, and she clears her throat, forcing herself to focus. Gritting her teeth, she redirects her traitorous focus to the mess in front of them. "Might as well work our way in. We'll start two piles. Anything that looks promising will go in one and everything else can go in the other."

Together, they sift through the debris littering the floor. There are old books, yellowed and brittle with age; a rusted dagger; a few ancient-looking coins; and an assortment of other oddities that Keary can't identify.

As they work in silence, the sun sets, casting long, golden shadows across the room. Keary notices Conall rubbing his eyes and stifling a yawn.

"Want to call it a night?" she offers, stretching her arms over her head to ease the cramping muscles.

"Find anything useful?"

"Not yet. There's still a lot to go through though," she mutters, her fingers curling around a tarnished silver band. "What's this?"

"A torc."

The gruffness of his voice pulls her attention from the item in her hand to meet his eyes. "What's a torc?"

"A band worn around the neck. Many wore them are symbols of status."

The torc shaped in an open circle; is cool under her touch. It's heavier than she expected and about the same width as her middle finger. She imagines a time when the metal once reflected the light with a mirror-like surface. Now it lays dark with age in her hands. Even the with the heavy tarnish, she can make out swirling loops and intricate engravings. "It's beautiful," she breathes, brushing her fingertip over the designs.

"The more intricate the design, the higher your status. Finding one like this outside of the gifted community was rare."

Keary's fingers trace the curves of the metal band, her gaze never leaving Conall's face. Tension etches itself into his features, furrowing his brow and the thinning his lips. "Why would someone leave this forgotten in the trunk?"

"It's my brother's," he croaks. "Brigid must've taken it from him before ordering him brought down to the cell."

"Why would she take it?"

"Daigh wore it for protection. He was certain the craftsman warded it against evil. Brigid wouldn't take the chance her scheme would fail." Conall's voice thickens, as if he's reliving it all over again in his head.

"I'm so sorry." *Gee, that helps a lot. I'm an idiot!*

Conall shrugs one shoulder before his eyes flicker up towards hers. "It's not your mistake."

"Why did she want to curse you and your brother so badly?"

"Ah, that's a long story." Stretching his legs out in front of him, he crosses his ankles and reclines back against his hands. "We did some work for her husband, Sloan. Rarely, mind you, but enough we came to know the family."

"What kind of work?"

"Smuggling mostly," the wicked grin lifting one corner of his mouth almost distracts her curiosity. "We spent a few months training his green soldiers too, but mostly we were smugglers."

"What did you smuggle?"

"Food mostly. Fish, or salted beef. Sometimes we'd have enough wool to make a trip for it profitable."

"Oh," Keary mumbles ruefully.

Tilting his head, Conall nudges her with a foot as the corners of his eyes crinkle. "Not what you were expecting me to say?"

Her cheeks warm, Keary shakes her head. "Not really."

"Well, we weren't exactly pirates. We didn't go around looting ships, if that's what you're thinking."

"I don't know what I was thinking." She laughs gently and offers a cheeky grin. "I just thought it would be more exciting."

"Well, we weren't exactly gentlemen either," he confesses with another crooked grin. "Those who had the coin to pay hired us for our specific talents. Whether that meant training their guard or slipping a shipment in under the radar of the gifted elders."

Keary leans in, captivated by Conall's stories. The way he talks about his former profession is almost poetic, and she can't help but feel a pang of envy at the life he led. It's as if he'd stepped out of one of the stories she'd spent her entire life devouring.

But then, all at once, his expression turns serious, and Keary's heart skips a beat. "We were good at our job, but then we made a mistake."

"Brigid?"

"Sloan sent word that he had a shipment ready for the south. All we had to do was pick it up and get it to the ship waiting off the coast for us."

"Sounds easy."

"When we got there, Sloan was away on business. Even though the weather was foul, Daigh insisted we retrieve the goods and get back on the road. I should've listened."

Before she can think better of it, Keary reaches over and rests a hand against his knee. "You couldn't have known."

"No, but Daigh did. He's always been a mistrusting bastard, but he was often right. When Brigid offered us food and shelter to ride out the storm, I thought nothing of it. Figured we'd ride out with the next sunrise."

As Conall recites his story, the stress melts away from her muscles. Either from the richness of his voice, or the smooth melody of his accent. Regardless, she inches closer. "But?"

"By morning, we were prisoners. She'd accused us of seducing her daughter, Geillis. Demanded one of us do the right thing and wed the girl."

"Did you?"

"Never! She had just turned ten and five. Not exactly my type."

"Would Daigh have …"

Although his bark of laughter is rich, the emotion never reaches his eyes. "Daigh couldn't stomach the lass, nor her mother. However, we were both fond of wee Darby."

"Then why would she suspect you?"

"I don't know. Maybe another sullied Geillis. Fearing her mother's wrath, she made up a story? Or Brigid set her sights on landing her daughter a stable husband."

"Okay." Keary ponders over the misshapen puzzle pieces. No matter how she twists and turns them, they don't quite fit. *Something is missing.* Keary's stomach somersaults. "Seems awful drastic on the mother's part."

"Brigid was not accustomed to hearing the word no. We thought to wait out Sloan's return and plead our innocence to him. He never arrived. By the end of the second day, Daigh wrote him off as another of his wife's victims."

"Not according to our records." With a stretch, Keary snags a finger on the book she dropped earlier and drags it towards her. "According to this, Sloan died shortly into the year 1540. There's no mention of Brigid or Geillis for some time before his death. Darby married a Brandon McCall, and they had four children together before she died at the age of sixty."

"Brandon, eh?"

"You know him?"

"If it's the one I'm thinking of. The two of them were mortal enemies, as children." A wrinkle appears between Conall's brows as he appears to consider something. "How do you still carry the McKenna name?"

"That would be my grandmother's doing. When her husband left her on her own with a small child to care for, she refused to keep his name. After a little research and a lot of paperwork, she took the McKenna name and passed it along to her son. My father." With a soft laugh, Keary closes the book with a light thump and sets it aside. "Okay, so Brigid didn't kill Sloan. Do you really think she would've killed you?"

"Yes."

"She would have killed you just for refusing to marry her daughter?"

"Brigid had a vicious streak when crossed. Said we'd brought shame upon her family name and demanded justice."

Keary shudders, unable to imagine the kind of darkness that would drive someone to curse another person. "What happened after she imprisoned you and your brother?"

"At first, the silence and darkness were maddening. I could find no escape." Fingers press tight against the floor as Conall searches for words he needs. "After, it was more of a fog. Counting the days was pointless."

Keary's heart aches for what Conall and his brother must have gone through, trapped in those trinket boxes for centuries. "But didn't anyone come looking for you?"

His eyes turn distant, sorrowful. "I'm sure of it."

"What do you mean?"

"Brigid was smart. She had to know the Northerners would come calling on our whereabouts."

"So, she cursed you before they could arrive?" Conall nods stiffly, his eyes a swirl of heat and shadows. Swallowing beyond the tickle in her throat, Keary gives in to the urge and wraps her arms around him. For a moment, his body stiffens under her touch before relaxing with a sigh. "I didn't think a person could be so evil," she whispers against the warm fabric of his shirt.

"You didn't know her. I should've listened to my brother."

Her eyes water from the heaviness in his voice. "We'll find him."

"It's not as simple as that."

The words linger in the silence between them, heavy with the weight of centuries of despair and regret. Keary wants to say something comforting, something that will make him feel better, but there are some things words can't fix. Pulling away, she meets his intense gaze with a tip of her chin. "I know. But we'll find him," she says firmly, reaching out to place her hand on top of his, giving it a gentle squeeze. Suddenly, there's a soft flutter in her stomach. A sensation she hasn't felt in a very long time. Before those feelings can sidetrack her, Keary clenches her jaw and focuses on the task at hand. "Then we'll figure out how to break the curse."

Conall's eyes brighten at her words. He leans in closer, his warm breath caressing her cheek causing her heart to squeeze inside her chest . "I must warn you," he says, with a hint of caution in his voice. "Breaking the curse won't be easy."

"Challenge accepted." Her gaze skirts to the dark windows and her eyes widen. "It's late. I need sleep if I'm going to get through my morning without committing murder." Pushing to her feet, Keary wraps Conall's fingers around his brother's torc. "I may have to go to town and see if someone can fix my door."

"I can fix your door."

"That's not necessary."

As he stands, Keary resists the sensation in her legs to back up. He's close enough she can clearly make out the individual shades on his stubbled jaw. "I broke it. Only fair, I fix it."

Judging by the thinning of his full lips and the tightening of his shoulders, it's not a topic up for debate.

"Thank you."

His grunt of reply encourages her soft chuckle. As Conall dips his head to stare into her eyes, breathing becomes a chore. Ribs tighten against her heart as heat floods her tummy. The intensity in his eyes clues her in to his intent, giving her more than ample opportunity to step away. While her mind rants at her to move, her body disagrees vehemently.

She inhales sharply just before his head descends, and he covers her lips with his. Warm and soft over hers, Keary's exhale is a small leak of air. The sensation of his lips on hers makes her knees go weak. With a sigh, she leans into him. Strong hands frame either side of her face a second before he takes the kiss deep enough to explore the recesses of her mouth with his tongue.

On a moan, her hands lift to use his shoulders as an anchor. The fierce throb at her core chases away all sense of logic until she's consumed by the inferno he feeds. Heat springs from his lips like electricity and courses through her body. A shock of needing blooms in her chest and spreads through her limbs. Apparently, his grip on control is a little more skilled than hers since he pulls back slightly. A thumb brushes lazily along the curve of her jaw as he stares into her eyes with obvious desire.

Keary's face heats as she snatches her hands from his shoulders and jumps back. With a furious shake of her head, she silences the monster, taking a firm grip on her body's response.

"W-we can't. I c-can't." Arms encircle her waist as she turns and flees from the room.

Once she reaches the safety of her room, deft fingers turn the humble lock before she rests her forehead against the cool wood. The hammering of her heart echoes in her ears until her breath returns to normal. "I've lost my mind," she whispers.

Outside, a faint breeze catches the wind chimes just outside her window. The gentle music that fills the bedroom sounds a lot like a giggle. "Stuff it," she grumbles and strips out of her jeans. After yanking on a pair of sleep shorts, she trades her t-shirt for a loose tank top.

"I can't get wrapped up with this man." Fingers twist and pull her long hair into a simple braid. When the sound of heavy footsteps passes her door and continues to the stairs, her heart skips a rhythm. Sitting on the edge of her bed, she twists a tie around the end of her braid, then trails a finger over her lips.

The man sure can kiss. The instant she felt the touch of his lips, she lost herself. Lost in the heat, drowning in the taste of coffee on his tongue. As her core clenches from the memory, fingers curl. Never has she felt such an attraction to a man so quickly or so fiercely. Evie will tell her its lust. If so, it's the most potent she's ever experienced.

"Stop it," she hisses and dives under the blankets. Squeezing her eyes shut, Keary lays there unmoving until the tension leaves her body. The cycle of shudders and trembles leave her limp and exhausted. *Tomorrow is going to be a long ass day.*

CHAPTER 14

As the days turn into weeks, Keary and Conall begin to settle into a comfortable rhythm. It takes some adjustment and a lot of patience, but they manage to coexist peacefully. The bulk of their days is spent in a flurry of activity, each task carefully designed to keep him occupied. Together, they move with purpose, as if trying to outrun the demons that chase him. Despite being no closer to finding Daigh or breaking the curse, Conall can't deny the growing sense of camaraderie and trust he feels towards his feisty ally. Until today, that is.

Standing off to one side, Conall crosses his arms over his chest as Keary rides her bicycle in large circles. Just overhead, the sun creeps up from the horizon to bathe her in a warm, golden glow.

Mesmerized, he stares openly from the porch as her long, midnight hair captures and reflects the light brilliantly. The chill in the air adds a rosiness to her cheeks and the tip of her nose. Even the wind joins in on his torment to snag several errant strands of her hair. Before he can catch himself, Keary stops and regards him with a slight tilt of her head.

"Is something wrong?"

The fog of his concentration makes her voice sound miles away. When it finally pierces the veil, Conall averts his eyes and scrubs a hand across the back of his neck. "No."

"I know it looks complicated, but I promise it's not." With a gentle smile, Keary beckons him closer.

Making the conscious choice to allow her to think his awkwardness is because of nerves, he stutters a nod and lumbers in long strides to cross the distance between them. "If you say so."

"Give it a try, at least?"

Conall eyes the machine she dug out earlier. The chipped and faded pale blue layer and worn wheels do little for his confidence. "Are you sure about this?"

"Absolutely."

Circling the machine, Conall inspects it with a shrewd eye, as if it's a mythical creature only present in children's stories. As he struggles with the hammering of his heart, his hands clench. "Can't we walk?"

"If we walk, it'll be dark again before we get home."

"Fine," he grumbles and swings his legs over the bicycle, gripping the handlebars tightly. "You owe me."

"You try this, and I'll try something for you." Reading the quick curl of his lips accurately, Keary rushes to add, "within reason."

"Agreed."

"Okay. First things first, this is your brake. Whenever you want to stop or slow down, just give this handle here a squeeze. Okay?"

"Got it."

"Keep your weight even," she instructs, moving to straddle the wheel behind him. "If you lean too far either way, you'll tip."

The cool metal of the handlebars presses against his palms, grounding him in the moment. When the breeze kicks up to carry the scent of rain and the exotic fragrance of Keary's soap to his nose, his stomach flops slightly. Since the night he'd loosened the grip on his control and kissed her, he's made a conscious effort to keep a good bit of distance between them. Having her so close now sends the memory of how her lips felt under his to the forefront of his mind.

"Now you're going to put one foot on the pedal and push off with the other. Once you get going, you're going to bring this foot up to the other pedal. Okay?"

The sensation of Keary tapping her hand against his left thigh instantly dries out his mouth. Since his tongue suffers a lapse in mobility, he settles for a quick nod of his head. When he follows her instructions, the instant wobble of the machine tightens his grip on the handles. Gritting his teeth keeps him from announcing his defeat. Instead, Conall centers his weight and pushes faster with his feet.

"Keep pedaling!" Running along behind him, Keary's breathless cheering covers his frazzled nerves with a soothing balm. "You're doing it."

His heart swells against his chest as he maneuvers into shaky circles around Keary. The sight of her jumping up and down, her eyes dancing happily, replaces the fear in his chest with a slow-burning heat.

For a minute, Conall experiences a passage of time. The years that have come and gone since someone last rode this machine. Unwilling to stop the smile growing on his face, he senses a connection to a long-forgotten memory.

"See?" The instant he comes to a stop, Keary runs up with a breathtaking smile on her face. "I knew you'd get the hang of it."

Standing with his feet on either side, Conall pries his hands off the handles and grins. "You're an excellent teacher."

While Keary secures their bicycles, Conall takes in the sights, sounds and various aromas of Briar. The cobblestone path beneath his feet tempts him deeper into the picturesque scene.

Rows upon rows of buildings line a maze of narrow streets. Most boast the smooth, mirror-like panels Keary described, while others have thin tendrils of smoke drifting lazily from stone chimneys. His head spins with the warm fragrance of bread, and the sweet hint of fresh water nearby mixing with the familiar stench of fish.

Straight ahead, children play within a small field of fresh grass. As they race to see who's the fastest, their sharp squeals barely make a dent in the racket of boisterous merchants set up in the square. Still, his ears strain to listen to the innocent melody of childhood, his mind drifting to his own carefree days. "A lifetime ago," he muses quietly. *Or several*, his mind shoots back.

With every item he finds familiar, he finds two more that are new and strange. To him, the village straddles a thin line between fantasy and reality.

"Are you new here?"

When the sugary voice interrupts his thoughts, Conall turns to find a tall blonde with sharp blue eyes just over his left shoulder. "I guess so," he admits, extending a hand. "Conall O'Corr."

"Sally Smith Rivers," the blonde announces with a full smile. As she steps closer, the scent of her soap burns his nose and sends his stomach into a roll. When she clasps both hands around the one he offered, a chill creeps along his skin. "What brings you to Briar?"

"Oh. Um." Peeking over his opposite shoulder, he sends Keary what he hopes is a pleading glare.

Reading his cue, Keary steps between him and the leech currently clutching at his hand like a lifeline. "He's with me."

Sally's bright smile sours. "Boyfriend?"

"Of course not," Keary laughs while taking a step toward him, giving Conall a reason to back up a step. "He's doing some house repairs for me. Who knows when the last time Nana had any work done?"

Listening to the way she disregards any romantic relationship between them tightens his jaw. While it's true most of their exchanges have been cordial as of late, the memory of their shared kiss flares to life in his head once again. Suddenly, he recalls the smooth velvet texture of her lips and the sweet taste of her tongue. Is it possible his reaction was more visceral than hers had been? *Is it me, or did Keary just stiffen when Sally flashed another smile in his direction?*

"Well, welcome to Briar, Conall. If you need someone to show you around, I'm available."

While her face remains impassive, Keary lifts one dark brow. "Shouldn't you be home with Simon? He's still on bed rest, yes?"

The shift of Sally's curvaceous smile into a scowl that wrinkles her forehead forces Conall to press his lips tightly together. "Tommy has him today."

While she manages to spit her response through clenched teeth, Conall instead studies the serene smile Keary offers in return. The struggle to keep from spinning her around and tasting her lips right then and there steals the air from his lungs.

"I see. Well, enjoy your day off then. I already promised to show Conall around town."

"Of course. It was nice meeting you, Conall. And if you ever need anything, you have my permission to link me. Anytime."

Heat flashes in Keary's eyes so forcefully, it darkens their normal pear green shade into brilliant emeralds. "That won't be necessary, Sally. Have a good day." Enfolding her delicate hand within his, Keary leads him in the opposite direction.

As they walk away, Conall notices the tension in Keary's posture and the way her steps are quicker and more purposeful than before. He wonders what the history is between her and Sally and why it seems to be an unpleasant one.

"Is everything okay?" he asks, keeping his tone light.

Keary shakes her head slightly and gives him a small smile. "Yeah, sorry about that. Sally is just… persistent."

"I gathered," he says, chuckling softly.

"I'm going to have to sit through one of Erin's *I told you so* sessions after today."

"Your sister and Sally don't get along?"

The deep, throaty laughter exploding from her sends a shiver of awareness down his spine. Keary grabs onto his arm to steady herself, and Conall experiences a sudden jolt of electricity surging through his body. It's as if she's touched a live wire. The sensation causes his heart to race.

"I think there's a better chance of the gifted and natural-born living in harmony for eternity than those two having a polite exchange," she explains between gulps of air.

Conall nods, distracted by the buzz of energy from where Keary touched him. *Did she feel it too?*

"Erin is the sweetest person I know. If Sally were to burst into flames, my sister would have marshmallows at the ready."

He raises a brow. There seems to be quite a history between Keary's sister and this Sally character, but he changes the subject. For now. "What does she mean, *link her?*"

Her hand tightens on his arm as her brows pinch together. Tilting her head slightly, his eyes snag on her pursed lips. "She means to send a, um, telepathic thought."

"Telepathic?"

"Like from your head to hers."

"How?"

Keary resumes strolling beside him. The soft creasing of her brow and the fiddling of her fingers tell Conall she's thinking of how to explain it all. Fixing his gaze straight ahead, he steers them around a thin guy unloading bundles of firewood.

"First, you need permission. So, you have my permission to link with me." Keary grins, her fingers drumming on his forearm. "Now give me permission to link with you."

Two weeks ago, her request would've left him skeptical. Opening his mind to someone like her out of the question. Today, Conall stares at the woman without the fog of his past and the paranoia. "You have permission," he mumbles, his voice thick.

When Keary says nothing, Conall returns to absorb the sights and sounds of her small village. Off to his right, a surprising number of people gather into two groups. Lights fill the long, narrow building beside the groups as a tall, slender man comes out to take pieces of paper from one group and then the other. Before he can ask what they're gathering for, Keary's soft, husky voice fills his head.

"This is linking. Sending a thought or an image from me to you."

Eyes wide, Conall digs in his heels. Pulling her to a stop beside him, he whirls her around to face him. "How did you do that?"

"It's a link. The natural born elders in the Citadel had links established hundreds of years ago. Immediate family members can automatically reach each other. New members of a community need to go through a small ritual to reach others in their village. Otherwise, one must grant permission."

"How do I reach you?"

Teeth nibble along the edge of her bottom lip. Just as her nose scrunches, her eyes glitter. "Search for a bond, a tether that stretches from me to you."

Closing his eyes, Conall follows her instructions. At first, the cool breeze and bustling market distracts his focus. When he experiences a slight tug on his mind, like a rope thrown out to him, he grabs hold. Instantly, a connection sparks a flame deep within his chest. Sweat covers his skin as Conall struggles to pull in one full breath.

Next to him, Keary's voice blankets him with her smooth, calming tones. "It's okay, Conall. Breathe and sink into the bond."

Seconds tick by before the anchor lifts from his chest. Seizing the opportunity, he latches onto their connection. Once he's certain they have established a link, he quickly sends out a test. *"Um, hello?"*

No sooner does the thought leave his mind before Keary's husky voice fills his ears. *"Hi."*

Opening his eyes, Conall gazes down into her upturned face, taking in every aspect of her radiant smile. *"This is amazing."*

"Right?"

"So, anyone can link anyone? Gifted or natural?" He asks aloud, as they continue walking through the growing crowd.

"In school, they taught us that the elders wanted open lines of communication for all us citizens. What I'm sure began as an emergency precaution became commonplace." Steering Conall around the young couple waging war with their toddler's jacket, she continues. "Immediate family doesn't require permission and new citizens are introduced by the elders to form a link with the community. When children are born, usually before their third birthday, the elders establish a link with the village."

"But it's not like you can read my mind? Right?"

"No," with a soft chuckle, Keary gives her head a shake. "I can't see inside your head, only what you project through the link we share. Connections outside of immediate family and our community is highly personal."

"So why did Sally give me permission? She doesn't even know me."

His question causes Keary to stumble before she rights herself. Her forefinger taps repeatedly against her thumb as she appears to search for an explanation. "Pretty sure that was to arrange a late-night booty call."

"What's a booty call?"

"It's um, er. It's when two… uh, people get together for um… sex." The blush staining her cheeks adds another level of charm to her natural beauty. Unwilling to meet his eyes, she busies herself with store windows. "I'm hungry. You?"

"Famished."

Even as her face heats further, she pulls him into a charming store chock full of sweet treats. The smell of fresh bread fills the air, mixing with the sweet scent of cakes, cookies and pastries. It's a mixture that has his stomach growling in response. With a warm atmosphere, the bakery shines with vibrant colors. A small section to one side holds small tables and thick wooden chairs.

Responding to the bell above the door, a round man with a cheery smile steps out of a room in the back. "Keary McKenna! By the mists, girl, it's been too long."

Her smile is infectious as Keary allows the man to pull her in for a quick hug. "Good morning, Mr. Robal." When his eyes dance over her shoulder toward Conall, Keary takes a small sidestep. "This is my friend Conall. He's doing some work out at the house. Conall, this is Mr. Robal, the best baker in Briar."

"Good to meet you, Conall," the baker says, extending a hand. "Bout time too. That place needed work when Alex was still with us."

"A pleasure." Conall smiles and gives the offered hand a firm shake.

"This one isn't being too difficult, I hope."

"Mr. Robal!" Keary's sharp gasp turns to into a groan when a smile tugs up one corner of Conall's mouth.

"Just a tad," he replies once he contains his smile.

Mr. Robal heaves a sigh large enough to shake his ample frame. "I expected as much. Hard to budge when she digs her heels in."

"I'm right here, you know," Keary grumbles softly.

In an attempt to smooth her ruffled feathers, Mr. Robal gives her red cheek a soft pat. "Now you know I couldn't love you girls more if you were my own. But if I can't tell you the truth, who can?"

"You make me sound unreasonable." One thin, dark brow lifts as Conall coughs. Arms crossing her chest, Keary shifts her weight to one hip and cocks her head. "What?"

"Not unreasonable," Mr. Robal concedes. "Just difficult. Knew that the instant your grandmother brought you girls to town."

Keary squares her shoulders and tips her chin slightly. "I just know what I want and what I don't."

Leaning closer to Conall, Mr. Robal whispers loud enough for anyone in the store to overhear. "If she gets too bad, give Miss Erin a buzz. No one can get Miss Keary moving quite like that child can."

"I'll keep that in mind, sir. Thanks for the tip."

Mr. Robal chuckles and nods his head. "Just give her time. Keary's always been a bit of a perfectionist. But she's got a good eye for most things. I'm sure she'll be keeping you on your toes."

Conall glances at Keary, who turns her attention to the display case filled with pastries and notices the deep furrow in her brow. *Why does a simple compliment make her so uncomfortable?* The more time he spends with her, the more new questions plague him. "Everything smells amazing," he says, changing the subject. "What do you recommend?"

The baker's eyes twinkle. "The blueberry-filled croissants are a personal favorite of mine. But you can't go wrong with anything in this case," he says while placing two glazed doughnuts in a bag.

Conall nods and spends the next few minutes deciding what to get. As he peruses the pastry case, he can't help but sneak glances at Keary. Her hair falls in loose waves over her shoulders, and a faint blush still lingers on her cheeks. Despite their rocky start, it's been a long time since he's felt this kind of connection to someone.

"I heard what you did for the Crait family," Mr. Robal whispers after giving Keary a gentle nudge. "I'm sure they're grateful."

"It's the right thing. Despite his crime, she has children that need their father."

"Well, I don't see the elders commuting his sentence, but at least now we have a fund that will allow them to visit regularly. Until the winter weather closes the pass anyway."

With a soft wave of her hand, Keary looks over her shoulder toward Conall. "Have you decided?"

"After such a strong recommendation, I think I'll take the suggestion of one of those blueberry things."

When Keary approaches the counter to pay, Mr. Robal waves her off. "Consider it a welcome gift."

Lips thin as she protests, but eventually relents and thanks the baker. As they step out of the store, a comfortable silence settles between them. He takes a bite of the warm, flaky croissant, relishing in the burst of sweet blueberry filling.

Walking down the cobblestone streets, Conall admires the quaint shops and charming architecture. With a hand at his shoulder, Keary gestures for him to follow her towards a small park around the next corner. The sounds of the city fade away as they enter a quiet oasis surrounded by tall trees. Taking a seat on one of the long benches, Conall leans back and enjoys the sunlight dancing off the surface of a small pond.

As the two of them sit in a comfortable silence, his attention shifts to several people pointing in their direction, then rushing off with soft snickers. Studying Keary's profile, her face remains serene as she finishes the last of her treat. Several minutes pass with two more couples exchanging hushed dialogue before running off in the opposite direction.

"Is it me, or are people staring at us?"

"Not us. Me. They're probably wondering what you're doing with one of my kind."

Conall turns to Keary with a frown. "What's that supposed to mean?"

She sighs, running a hand through her hair. "I mean… you're natural born. And I'm… not."

"Why would they care?"

"In some ways, we've made a lot of progress since your time, Conall. In other ways, we've gone backwards. There are some people who believe natural born should stick with their own and not sully themselves with the gifted."

"But Mr. Robal genuinely seems to care for you."

Her smile is small and slightly haunted. "I said *some* people."

Conall's heart sinks wondering just how much discrimination and prejudice she faced in her life. "Is that why you helped that family Mr. Robal was talking about?"

"No. I helped them because they're going to spend the next three years apart. The kids deserve better."

Polishing off the rest of his pastry, Conall's jaw tightens. "What was his crime?"

"He sold a book the elders banned for some reason or another." Shadows darken her eyes before she turns her face upward towards the sun. "Just another way to set an example for my kind."

"I'm so sorry, Keary. I had no idea."

"It's okay," she replies with a shrug. "Most of us have learned to deal with it over the years."

"It's not," he insists, his voice taking on a hard edge. "People shouldn't treat others differently because of something they can't control. This is the very thing the revolution meant to change."

Keary's expression softens at his words. "Come on, we'll finish up our shopping and head home."

Conall nods, but his mind still reels over the treatment Keary faces. As they make their way through the local market, he can't help but notice the looks she gets from other shoppers. It's as if they can sense she's not a natural born, and they're repulsed by her very presence.

He takes a deep breath and releases his balled-up fists, trying to shake the anger rumbling through him. He forces himself to take one plodding step after another, struggling to keep his temper in check. At first, his emotions continues to boil like a forgotten pot on the stove. When he counts to ten slowly, the vise against his ribs lessens and he can breathe a little easier. Pressing his lips tight, he stands close to Keary, creating a wall between her and the hostile glares as the two of them weave in and out of shops.

CHAPTER 15

"I don't need all of this," Conall grumbles as Keary dumps the last bag. What should've been a quick trip, Keary stretched into hours. The sheer amount of items covering her kitchen table forces him to battle his lunch from making another appearance. "None of this is going to help me find my brother."

From the stiff trousers she calls *jeans*, t-shirts, flannels and something she refers to as *hoodies*, Conall's head spins. Any hope he harbors that she'll stop throwing more things on the growing pile, dissipates when she adds a pair of shoes, a jacket, socks and briefs.

"True," she says absently, meticulously folding each article. "Clothes are a necessity. Unless you plan to prance around in your kilt."

"Men don't prance."

The small smile flirting across her lips serves as a momentary distraction. "Let's agree to disagree."

"This is too much."

"You're being dramatic."

"What's wrong with the clothes I'm wearing?"

"They were my dad's. And the few items that do fit you won't last long."

Conall's heart plummets to his stomach. *Way to go, asshole.* Deep in the pit of his gut, a sharp pang grows as his thoughts drift from losing his mother to Moira. He may not have much in common with Keary, but they have this. Shuffling from foot to foot, he forces words beyond a tight throat. "My condolences."

"Thank you," she clips without sparing him a glance. "My point is, you're bigger than my dad was."

"I don't understand."

Her breath escapes in a whoosh of air. "If you sneeze wrong, you're going to pop a button. Or blow a seam. Both of which I'd like to avoid."

"Your eyes say otherwise."

"My eyes can't say anything," she grits through her teeth. "They don't speak."

The corners of Conall's mouth twitch at her reaction. Despite their situation, he's man enough to admit he's enjoying her fiery personality. *Too much*, he reasons. Still, the sight of her flustered with a temper that adds a rosy blush to her cheeks, transforming her eyes to a stormy gemstone green, puts a hitch in his breathing.

As soon as the thought arrives, it takes hold of him in a vise. The image of her consumed by passion fills his head, igniting a fire within him. Her eyes will smolder with lust and desire before sending shivers down his spine. The tanned skin on her neck tinged with pink from the heat of their bodies intermingling while the rest of her glows with sweat. Hair like a dark waterfall would fan out across his pillow as he lays her out before him, every inch of her body bared and open to him.

The vision slams through his brain so completely, Conall could swear he catches her breath quickening before sweet, whispered sighs escape from her lips. The sharp crack of material she's folding snaps him back to the present while the image brands itself into a memory. *What is wrong with me? She's practically an enemy by birth!* He isn't sure if it's the five hundred year long slumber that's causing his hormones to go haywire, or whether the multiple head injuries are affecting his judgement, but something is definitely off.

"You can put these in the back room. That's where you'll be sleeping while you're here."

"Not that I'm not enjoying your amazing couch, but what changed?"

"Nothing, if you'd rather sleep on the couch, I won't stop you."

"That's okay. Thank you." Conall picks up the first of several piles of clothes and makes a hasty exit. As he stomps through the house, his heart pounds and his mind races. "Stay focused," he murmurs to himself and uses thoughts of his brother to eradicate any further images of Keary flooding his mind. Daigh could be in trouble. He could be dead. The last thought douses his raging hormones in icy water. *Can I face living a life that doesn't have him in it?* Conall never considered himself weak, but the small voice in the back of his head leaves him with more than a few doubts.

Stepping in the room, he eyes the narrow bed and a single dresser, chewing up most of the space. Several boxes line the far wall, *Mom and Dad* printed neatly across each one. His heart pinches slightly as he realizes all the memories these walls contain. Despite adjusting his laser focus, he can't help but feel a twinge in his stomach for the loss filling this room. The only thing that breaks the somber atmosphere is a bright painting framed proudly atop the dresser. He sets his clothing down on the foot of the bed before inspecting it further.

By the coloring, he suspects the girl with long black hair and big green eyes to be Keary. Even at such a young age, she sports a slight wrinkle on her forehead as she forces a tight smile for the artist. Behind her stood what must be her mother; tall, slim and elegant. Long, slim fingers rest softly on the narrow set of shoulders, her smile beautiful and serene.

Beside Keary, a tall man sits at an angle, one arm firmly latched onto the small child gracing his lap. No more than two or three; the young child's smile radiates warmth and charm. She boasts eyes similar to a summer storm and curls like apple cider tumble across heavily freckled cheeks. Fingers clench on the fragile frame and his chest tightens as the memory of Darby thunders through his heart.

"They could be twins," he whispers, and before he can comprehend it, moisture blurs his vision.

Suddenly, Keary's voice breaks in. "That's my mom and dad and my little sister, Erin," she supplies, stepping into the room as if sensing his distress. Tears sparkle in her eyes as she stares at the painting, her expression hard yet full of emotion.

Reluctantly, Conall brings his thoughts back to the present. His heart tugs at the pain visibly radiating from her. The need to offer comfort shoots through his arms, but before he can give in to the sensation, she steps back into the hall.

"I'm … sorry." The words feel empty, but he hopes she'll understand his attempt.

Wrapping her arms tight around her stomach, Keary jerks her head toward the kitchen. "There is more stuff on the table."

Tipping a nod, Conall straightens his shoulders and strides out of the room. Can he fault her for being unwilling to open up to him? Not really. But as he follows her to the kitchen, he decides to rectify that.

When he reaches the doorway, Conall stares dumbstruck at Keary's long, graceful fingers moving seamlessly through a growing hoard of goods, seemingly unconcerned with the cost. "I fear those merchants hoodwinked you."

"I've known most of them all my life. They wouldn't do that."

Crossing the floor, Conall braces a hip against the sink. "I see. So, it's because they enjoyed your presence that they sold you all these things?"

She snorts and gives her dark head a toss. "They weren't tripping over themselves for me, Conall."

"Yes, they were very accommodating." After another loud snort, he swallows a grin and attempts to meet her wandering gaze. "Are you jealous?"

Rounding to face him, Keary notches her chin, eyes spitting green fire. "No! You're a grown man. I don't own you."

"True."

She busies herself with wadding up several bags and cramming them inside each other until she's left with an enormous ball. "Who you choose to be friendly with is your business."

"Also, true."

"I certainly won't be losing any sleep over it."

When she retraces her steps for a third time, Conall restrains his grin. "My mistake."

"Damn straight." Her complete lack of eye contact nearly crumbles his effort. "This is your brush, deodorant, toothbrush, and soap."

"You already have soap."

"Yes. I do. Forgive me if I don't want you using all of mine. Besides, mine is girlie. This is better suited for men."

"Is that so?"

"Yep."

On a whim, Conall takes a whiff. Immediately, his nose twitches. "It smells like a barn."

When she finally lifts her eyes to his face, he catches a crook of her lips. "I can make you something else if you prefer. I have to make some for the shelter in town, anyway."

"You make soap as well?"

"Usually just for myself or Erin, but sometimes the shelter runs low on supplies, so I give them what extra I have."

"That's very kind of you."

"For a McKenna, you mean?" Shadows flicker across her face before it softens. Unsure what to do with her hands, her fingers knot together as she searches for something to distract herself with. Before Keary can find it, she gives a quick jump as her eyes glaze over.

"Excuse me."

The weathered boards of her grandmother's porch creak beneath her feet as she latches the door behind her. Inhaling the crisp breeze that blows in from the west, Keary rakes her hands through her hair as she starts up the dirt path to the top of the hill. *"Hello Imp."*

"Hi!" Erin sends across the link, her voice full of curiosity and good humor. *"I was hoping you'd answer."*

She heaves a sigh as she settles herself into one of the wicker chairs. *"Why wouldn't I answer?"*

"Because my head has been buzzing non-stop since you traipsed your new guy around town. Just so you know, they fully prepared me to make an emergency trip home."

"No!" Keary winces at the sharpness of her reply and takes another breath. *"No, I'm fine. And he's not my new guy."*

"Oh?"

"He's just staying with me while he updates some of the stuff we've been putting off in the house."

"I thought you wanted to keep it original?"

Swallowing the soft curse, Keary hedges as she taps her fore-finger repeatedly against her thumb. *"I did. But I'm realizing that original isn't energy efficient."*

"*Can we afford him?*"

"*I think so.*"

"*Okay. Did you check him out? I mean, this guy could be trouble.*"

"*You think I'd let some stranger stay in our house and not do a little research first?*" The lie crawls across her tongue, making her stomach churn. The soft laugh Erin breaks into has her fighting the need to puke.

"*No, that doesn't sound like you at all.*"

"*Exactly.*"

"*So where did you find this handy-man?*"

"*Mr. Robal recommended him.*" Fingers tap quickly on the top of her thighs. *The second lie in less than five minutes,* her brain screams. Smoothing a finger against one temple dulls the noise.

"*Oh. The way some people described him, I expected you to tell me he's a retired prostitute. Or a lumberjack.*"

"*No, nothing like that. How's class?*"

"*Good. I have to write a paper on what sparked the civil war, so I'm preparing to lie my ass off. Just wanted to check in with you before I fall down that rabbit hole.*"

"*I'm fine. People around town need new hobbies.*" Pushing the guilt aside, Keary rushes through the conversation with yet another lie. "*He's asking me something about our solar panels. I'll link you before bed.*"

"*Great. Take care of you.*"

"*You too. Love you.*"

"*Love you back.*"

With a groan, Keary slams her back against the chair and lifts her face toward the sky. The tension eases from her muscles as she soaks up the sun's warmth. With a shudder, she replays every single lie she just told Erin; each one a blade that twists and turns inside her gut. In the trees, the chimes sway with the breeze to mock her with their cheerfulness. Her head spins as she considers the last few weeks. Somehow, she's found herself in an alternate universe, where living with a stranger is the reality, and lying about it is commonplace. The cold revelation doesn't sit well in her overly sensitive stomach.

"I don't know what I'm doing Nana," she says aloud, running her fingers over the denim covering her leg. "I should've given him the boot by now." When the gentle breeze tinkling various chimes is her only reply, Keary closes her eyes.

The headache she's been battling most of the day isn't helping matters. Holding her head in her hands, she attempts to push the thoughts away until she's better equipped to deal with them. When her next inhale carries the distinct smell of smoke, her eyes fly open.

What now? Running down the hill, she makes a beeline for her back door, skipping to a stop when she sees smoke rolling out from the grove of trees on her left. As she changes direction, she links their local fire brigade.

The other end buzzes faintly before a perky voice fills the void with a scripted greeting. *"Is this an emergency?"*

Rounding the yearling trees, Keary follows the thick trail of smoke deeper into the grove. *"I have a fire at the back of my property."* Leaves from the previous fall crunch under her shoes, her eyes rounding when she spies Conall kneeling before an impressive flame. *Trouble indeed.*

"What's your location?"

As she draws closer, Keary stumbles over an uprooted stump. Air hisses against teeth as she stops three feet away from his bonfire. *"Never mind. It's just a troublesome roommate."*

"I have two of those." A soft giggle fills Keary's head. *"Good luck ma'am."*

Severing the link, Keary takes an extra minute to bury her hands into the pockets of her jeans. When her heart is still hammering against her ribs, she gives up all measure of calm and stomps the short distance remaining. "What are you doing?"

Jumping to his feet, Conall's eyes flick between her and the open fire. It switches her concentration from him to the flames scorching her best skillet. "I thought I'd cook supper."

"Planning on hunting a moose? Anything else would be too small for that amount of fire."

"Your woods have a fair amount of rabbit. It won't take much skill to trap one."

The headache behind her eyes intensifies as the full weight of his words takes hold. "A poor, fluffy bunny?" Swallowing the bile rising in her throat, Keary squeezes her eyes tight to keep the angry tears from falling.

"Will it make you feel better if I say that I'll find a gnarly bunny with no fluff?"

"This isn't funny Conall." Marching forward, Keary takes the pan from his hand and kicks black soil over his open flame.

"You say that a lot. Maybe you just don't have a sense of humor."

Jabbing a finger in his chest, Keary's temper finally snaps. "I happen to have a great sense of humor. I just don't think slaughtering woodland creatures fall under that category." When a smile flirts over his full lips, her eyes narrow, silently daring him to let it loose.

As if thinking better of it, Conall removes it with the swipe of his hand. "I didn't mean to upset you."

"This is not upset. It's pissed. Not only are you this close to setting my woods on fire, which will then move onto my house. You're trying to turn my yard into a bunny gravesite. Round up every trap you set before some poor creature finds them." With a final stamp of her foot, Keary assures herself the fire is out before she turns for the house. "I'm going to see if I can salvage this pan and start dinner."

Large hands shove themselves into the pockets of his jeans as he gives a quiet nod of his head. "Yes, ma'am."

CHAPTER 16

The soft glow of the setting sun filters through tall windows to cast a warm light within the tower room where Keary is hiding. The last couple of days have passed in a tense and awkward silence with Keary going out of her way to have as little contact with him as possible. As she replays her harsh words to Conall in her head, her heart shrinks in on itself. *He'd been trying to cook dinner the only way he knew how, and I lashed out like a petulant child.*

"Keary?"

Glancing up from the stack of books in her hand, her breath snags at Conall's presence in the doorway. Shoulders tight, he rocks back and forth on the heels of his boots. Although he buries his hands in the pocket of his jeans, Keary spies the flexed muscles in his forearms. Now that her temper has had time to cool, her earlier reaction leaves her throat dry. Sucking in air, she lets the words tumble free from her lips before he can say anything that will make her feel worse.

"I'm sorry, Conall. I overreacted."

His expressive whiskey eyes snap upward, his lips parting without a sound. With a small crick in his neck, he studies her carefully. "I didn't mean to upset you."

"I know," she whispers. Under the weight of his stare, she suppresses the urge to squirm. "Anyone that knows me will tell you my bitch-button can be overly-sensitive. I shouldn't have snapped at you."

"Apology accepted." Offering an amiable smile, Conall makes cautious progress into the room to sit next to her on the floor. "You've been up here for hours."

"Most of what I've come across, I've added to the proba-bly-not-important pile." Between items Nana collected and the ones she unearthed from the trunk, the room hums with the echoes of laughter and whispered secrets. That none of them hold much promise adds extra weight along her shoulders.

Rooting through the enormous pile of scarves and wraps, her fingers brush against something solid. Pulling it out, her eyes scan a wooden horse. The passage of years and use soften the sharp angles. Gray and worn, Keary can barely make out the intricate details of the mane and tail. "An old toy," she wonders aloud, gasping when Conall rips it from her hand.

With rapt attention, his jagged breaths echo between them. One finger glides from top to bottom of the creature's body, tracing its form reverently. For a brief moment, Keary recalls the way his touch warmed her skin, setting her heart into a furious rhythm. Giving her head a quick shake, she notes the clenching in his jaw as he flips the horse over in his hand and bends low to inspect each hoof, as if searching for something specific. The slight curve of his lower lip is her only clue that he finds what he's looking for.

"Daigh made this."

"Conall, I'm sure there were hundreds of wooden toys left behind in this trunk at one time or another. How can you be sure your brother made this one?" Heat sears her skin as his large paw engulfs one of her hands. Blocking out the sensation of his rough, calloused palm against her soft skin, Keary grits her teeth and resists the impulse to snatch her hand away.

"Feel," Conall breathes, guiding her hand toward the right back hoof.

Extending her fingers, she fixes her gaze on the ceiling to shift her focus away from his touch. When the pad of her forefinger brushes a rough edge, Keary tilts her head slightly before running her finger over it once more. "What is it?"

"Whenever Daigh made anything, he always carved a star deep within the wood. It's been so long the edges are faint, but there." Never taking his eyes from the toy in his hand, Conall releases his grip on her wrist. "This must be the horse he made for Darby."

A lump forms in Keary's throat as she watches Conall gently place the wooden horse on the floor beside him. "He must be extremely patient. Something like that took time."

Conall's chuckle is deep and full of ache. "Daigh could never understand the meaning of patience."

"Tell me about him?"

Eyes flicker to her face before closing, and a small smile tugs at his lips. "Daigh is… complicated. He's stubborn, and has a temper, but there's a kindness to him that not everyone sees. He's always moving. Constantly creating something, or tearing it down to start again." His voice grows quiet, almost reverent in the tower room where memories of the past surround them.

"He's the wild one of the family," he rasps. "He has no patience for anything that doesn't interest him, which is just about everything. But when he finds something he loves, he pours himself into it completely. Like his horse. He spent hours training that horse until every other horseman was green with envy."

"He sounds like quite a character."

"Sitting still and waiting for life to happen isn't his thing. He was too young when we lost our mother. That might be the cause for some of his... less desirable traits."

"How old was he?"

"We lost her the summer before he celebrated his fourth year."

"That must've been difficult for you."

"I'll admit. There were times I thought it best to leave him with one of the families near our village. After we survived the rainy season in the surrounding woods, one of the old spinsters, Moira, took us in."

"That was kind of her."

"When the villagers took our mother away, Moira appointed herself as our Shepard."

For a moment, Keary's hand hovers inches above his arm while she wages a war within herself. In the end, she settles for a genuine smile. "I'm glad you had her."

"Oh, it wasn't all warm love. At least, not at first. She gave us hot food, clean clothes, and a warm bed. In return, we did the trapping and fishing. Later, when we got bigger, we were happy to help with the physical labor."

"You were with her a long time, then?"

"She became a second mother to us."

"Why would villagers take your mother away?"

Shadows war within Conall's intense eyes as he mulls over her question. From where she sits, Keary spots a small tic in his left cheek. "That's a story for another day. You grew up with your grandmother?"

"I was almost nine when Nana brought us here. Erin was five."

"May I ask how you lost your parents?"

A deep wrinkle furrows her forehead as she searches the floor to find something more interesting to focus on than her reaction to him. "We used to live farther south when we were younger. It always seemed to rain there," she states, running her finger along the grain in the wood floor. "They were traveling to a festival in Danburk. I stayed behind for a sleepover with some of my friends. When they didn't come home the next day, my grandmother sounded the alarms and stayed with me."

Swallowing the hard lump growing in her throat, Keary forces herself to continue. "The search party found them several miles from home. A flash flood overturned their wagon, pinning my parents underneath."

"What about Erin?"

"A few Vanguard soldiers found her two days later. Because of the high water levels, she took shelter on a ledge in a small cave nearby. To this day she avoids water deeper than her ankles."

"I'm so sorry."

"Thanks," she mutters tightly through clenched teeth.

"Yeah, I know that doesn't do much."

Keary busies herself with folding some scarves into a small pile, her movements jerky and exaggerated. "People say it to make themselves feel better. Sometimes I get a small taste of their closure or relief, but those feelings aren't truly mine."

"You're an empath."

"You sound like someone who just stepped in a fresh cow patty."

"No," squaring his shoulders, Conall rubs a hand against the back of his neck. "I'm just surprised."

The truth lingers in the air, teasing her senses with its pungent aroma. At first, the scent is sharp and acidic. But as she continues to observe him, it shifts to a coppery tang, causing her heart to race with his fear. Keary simply raises a single eyebrow in response, but the tell-tale flush of pink that stains his cheeks gives away his unease.

"Okay, I lied. Truth is, I've never met an empath before."

"I get it. Most people have the same reaction."

"Most?"

A sly smile tugs at the corners of her lips as she leans in, her voice dropping to a whisper. "Now and then I get a different reaction from the perverts," she says. Conall's nostrils flaring ever so slightly and his eyes narrow to a point that Keary can't help but let out a laugh. "I'm only teasing," she clarifies with a mischievous grin spreading across her face. The air is thick with electricity between them, crackling with an unspoken understanding of their shared humor.

"So, you pick up on every emotion?"

"A better empath might. The emotion needs to be strong to get my attention."

"What am I feeling now?"

Keary's body tenses as Conall's eyes burn with an intensity that threatens to consume her. Once a foreign heat spreads up through her stomach, she fidgets uncontrollably. Shifting in place proves ineffective in ignoring the growing ache within her. When her breath catches in her throat, she drags in the intoxicating scent of sandalwood from his desire. Instantly, it ignites a fire within her, causing her to squirm and struggle against its powerful pull. "D-do you really need me to answer that?"

His unwavering gaze pierces through her like a sharp knife, sending shivers down her spine. The rough rasp in his voice when he answers sets her body ablaze, scorching every nerve ending under her skin. "I suppose not."

"You… you're making it hard to concentrate," she croaks, her voice barely above a whisper.

As he firmly grips her chin in his hand, the heat emanating from his body draws her in like a moth to a flame. The intensity of his desire radiates off of him in bursts of musk and spice. "That's the point," he growls, sending chills down her spine and leaving her breathless.

In this moment, the emotions surging through her body, consumes her entirely. The scent of his attraction fills her senses and clouds her mind. Her heart thuds furiously, every breath she takes, shallow. "This is… isn't a good idea."

Conall's eyes darken as they lower to her mouth. Each second before he speaks drags on painfully. "I'm telling myself the same thing," he admits, his breath tracing across her lips.

"I think it's better if we stick to the task at hand." As soon as the words leave her, her body recoils at the idea.

With a sound somewhere between a groan and a growl that has Keary regretting her hasty decision, Conall pulls back. "You're right. Daigh comes first."

Resisting the itch in her fingers to pull him close and bury her hands in his hair, Keary releases a shuddering breath. Turning her attention to the mess in front of them, she rummages through another pile. The cool, leather-bound diary she stumbles across sidetracks the awakened beast thrashing around in her chest.

Soft under her fingers, she notes the passage of time fraying the edges. Flipping it open, the pages are yellow with age, the handwriting fluid. Written in a delicate hand, the fading ink is still legible.

"Conall," she nudges him with one elbow while holding the diary up for him to see.

"What is it?"

"A diary, or journal of some sort. I'm not entirely sure who it belongs to, but it's definitely old. Do you want to have a look?"

"No. I think it's best if you read it."

As the night inches closer, Keary struggles with her lack of energy. While her eyes burn and her head throbs, she realizes there's still too many unanswered questions. If they have any hope of finding Daigh and breaking the curse looming over the brothers, she needs to make use of every available moment.

Conall chuckles beside her when she covers her yawn with the back of one hand. "Why don't we call it a night? This stuff isn't going anywhere."

"I'm okay."

Pushing himself to his feet, Conall sweeps up the wooden horse with one hand and pulls her to her feet with the other. "It's okay to sleep, Keary," he adds.

Keary trembles as his deep voice dances across her skin, setting her entire body alight with a million pinpricks. Unable to move, trapped by the intensity of his gaze as he tucks her hair behind one ear, sending a shockwave through her. Time seems to stand still as his eyes trail down to her mouth. Operating on instinct, Keary's tongue darts out to wet her lips.

Instantly, his face is alive with want and desire, but just as quickly, the spark fizzles out. In the span of a heartbeat, chilly indifference smothers the craving that etches across his strong features. "I'm tired too." The gruff sound of his voice roughens his usual smooth baritone.

With a shaky nod, Keary clutches the journal to her chest and runs for the safety of her room. Glancing back once more, the sight of him standing still where she left him sends a tremble along her muscles. Letting out a deep breath, she ignores the scorching heat where his eyes land and hurries down the hall.

Bolting into her room, Keary shuts the door behind her, leaning against its cool surface. Her hands quiver as she opens the journal to stare at its yellowed pages. As much as her brain rants at her to dive into its secrets, Keary needs a moment to recover from Conall's close proximity. Once she's able to trust her legs, she stumbles forward to plop on her bed. While dragging a brush through the tangled mess of her hair, she reaches out to give Erin a gentle nudge. Less than a minute passes before Erin's soft buzz fills the space between her ears.

"You're up late."

Keary releases her breath knowing her sister won't feel the tremble in her hands as she piles her hair into a messy bun. *"Been busy working on your trunk. Why are you up so late?"*

"Finals are coming up soon. I'm determined to cram through as much information as I can."

"Just remember that rest is just as important."

"I'm going to bed soon, Kear. I love you."

"I love you more. Sleep sweet."

"You too."

Although brief, touching base with Erin allows Keary to breathe a bit easier. Crawling under the blankets, she tucks them around her legs, reclines against her pillows and begins reading under the meager candlelight.

While the handwriting is pretty and delicate, emotions color every word. Cherished by a doting father, annoyed by a younger sister, and stifled by her controlling mother. The beginning pages read much the same as the last. As she flips through, the early entries read so much the same, she stifles a yawn. Battling the fatigue, Keary re-reads the latest entry through red-rimmed eyes, before extinguishing the candle and succumbing to the slumber the darkness promises.

The loud bang that vibrates within the hall just outside her door jolts Keary awake. Heart racing, she sits up, ears straining against the dark, her hand on her chest. Behind her ribs, her heart thumps erratically as footsteps walk down the hallway, heavy and determined. Squinting through bleary eyes, she glances out the window to see the sky still dark. *What in the world is he doing now?*

Throwing her legs over the side of the bed, she inches toward the door, her bare feet padding softly on the cool hardwood floors. Balancing on the tips of her toes, Keary leans in just enough to put an ear to the door.

Another loud thump reverberates against her bedroom wall, Conall's soft, cursing quick to follow. His thick accent wraps around the syllables like a lover's caress, yet the words sound jumbled to her ears. Snagging her breath against her teeth, Keary opens the door and peeks into the hall.

Soft candlelight from the downstairs creates a mess of shadows on his imposing figure. Still, Conall without a shirt constricts her throat as he struggles with an oversized object.

"What are you doing?" she hisses softly.

Whirling around, he studies her in the doorway to her room, his eyes bright. "You should be in bed," he growls.

"Yeah?" Keary's lip twitches softly as she closes the distance enough to determine he's wrestling with her broken door. "I don't know why I didn't think of that. What are you doing?"

"I said I would fix your door for you," he mumbles softly, looking anywhere but at her.

An unwelcome surge of warmth explodes in her chest to send shockwaves coursing through her body. Thankfully, she relocates her voice after a serious mental slap.

"I appreciate that, but it's the middle of the night."

Bracing the door with his thigh, Conall rubs a hand across the back of his neck, drawing her gaze to the tightly corded muscles. "I couldn't sleep."

Stepping closer, she gives him more room to maneuver. The scent of sweat mixes with a hint of spice slamming into her senses, leaving her knees weak as if she's under some dark spell. Squaring her shoulders, Keary trains her attention to the task at hand.

"Let me help."

"No. I've got it," he grinds between his teeth. Muscles in his back strain and flex for several minutes before he drops the weight of the door back onto one thigh. "Your walls are too close together," he snarls, dragging an arm across his damp brow.

"You might as well let me help," she insists, grabbing the bottom of the door, and together they make their way down the stairs to the living room. "Where do you want it?"

"Here is fine. I can move it later."

Propping the door on the railing for the stairs with a grunt of effort, her breath comes rapidly. Keary locks a stare with him as her heart pounds in her chest like a timpani drum, while Conall remains emotionless, his breathing deep and steady. It's as if all the air is being sucked from the room to feed his oxygen-starved lungs, leaving her gasping like a wild animal.

Bracing his hands on his hips, a hint of amusement etches onto his rugged face. "You're out of breath."

Keary huffs. "I'm fine."

"You're not," he insists quietly before taking a step towards her.

Alarm bells sound off inside her head, causing her to side-step his advance. "I need coffee," she grumbles. When his soft chuckle reaches her ears, she refuses to acknowledge the blush creeping up her neck.

"Coffee would be grand," he purrs behind her.

As Keary fumbles around the kitchen, Conall leans against the counter, his legs crossed at the ankles. Heat flares in his golden eyes as he watches her every move with a bemused expression on his face. The heat of his stare only serves to ramp up her frustration as she taps a finger on the counter while the coffee pot brews.

"Do you need help?"

"Nope. I've got it," she declares in a cheery tone before filling two mugs in front of her.

"I make you nervous."

Pressing her lips tight, Keary sets the mug down in front of him with a little too much force. "I'm not nervous," she argues. "I'm just not a morning person."

"Ah," he muses.

Keary's eyes flick up to his face, taking in the hint of a smile tugging at the corners of his full lips. Despite the situation they find themselves in, a thrill of attraction still runs through her veins. It's as if a part of her can't resist him, even though she knows it's a dangerous game to play. "Just drink your coffee. I'm going to go change my clothes."

Conall nods, taking a sip of the coffee as she turns and makes her way upstairs. With every step can feel his eyes on her as she heads back up the stairs, and it only serves to make her more uncomfortable. Once her breathing slows and her heart no longer thumps in her chest, she wanders over to her closet and flicks through her clothes. Settling on a pair of black leggings and an oversized sweater, she dresses quickly. Running a brush through her hair, Keary gathers the length and secures it within a lopsided pile at the back of her head, then grabs the journal before returning to her cup of coffee.

When she re-enters the kitchen, Conall is on his feet, looking every inch the powerful warrior that held her captive just days earlier. His eyes light up when he sees her, his gaze raking over her from head to toe. Keary kicks herself for noticing even as her cheeks turn pink. Forcing air in and out of her lungs, she avoids his stare as she makes her way to an empty chair.

The two of them fall into an uncomfortable silence, Conall lost in his thoughts, Keary searching the journal for where she left off the night before.

She's nearly half-way through before the entries change. Soon, excitement replaces the dragging monotony of every day before. After a chance meeting with the miller's son, Ren, the author's emotions become palpable.

A smile flirts over her lips as Keary reads about their whirlwind romance. The young couple, so caught up in their feelings for one another, they overlook the consequences. Until the girl records an entry where she vents her fear laced excitement over missing her monthly flow. Suddenly, the prospect of dealing with their parents looms over their happiness like a brewing storm of impending emotions.

Between the occasional sip of her coffee, Keary learns that one of the maids takes it upon herself to notify the author's mother. Tears stain the pages as she writes of her mother's outrage, encouraging tears to prick at Keary's eyes as well. The hopelessness that the author experiences settles in her gut like a pallet of stone.

Keary forgot about her coffee she reads on, becoming increasingly invested in the story of this woman's life. She pages through it eagerly, her breath held until she finds a resolution for the forbidden love. Her eyes brim with tears as her fingers land on the last entry; unfinished.

Despite the girl's tears and declarations of love, her mother deems the boy unfit for a woman in her station. Forbidding the author of ever seeing him again. With the pregnancy looming over them, the situation forced her mother to work fast. As luck would have it, two of her father's business part-ners were due to arrive any day. Surely one of them would make an offer of marriage. It had to be done.

Sitting in her chair, Keary wonders what became of the young woman. Did she end up with Ren or another? Was she happy? Or did she live the rest of her life alone, nursing a broken heart? Her heart ached for the woman, for all the paths lost to her.

Retracing her steps, Keary's eyes skim over the passage written on the inside cover of the journal itself. A chill slips along her spine to twist her heart painfully as she reads it over and over until even breathing becomes difficult.

To my star, Geillis. The moon to Darby's sun. I hope this journal can help you break away from whatever chains plague you. May the love that binds us never be diminished by time or fate, Pa.

Keary's voice cracks as her mouth opens, no sound escaping from her swollen throat. Her eyes clench shut as she forces a breath past the lump trapped in her esophagus. Desperate for him to hear her, she pushes out one last call- his name echoing off of the walls with an anguished quaver. "Conall?"

CHAPTER 17

The sound of Keary's broken voice snaps him to attention. Studying the hunch in her shoulders and the quivering of her chin sends his heart into a furious rhythm. Rushing to her side, Conall pulls her into his arms. Hushing her softly, one hand rubs gentle circles across the small of her back. "What is it?" He demands, his voice carrying a hard edge he's unable to disguise. "What's wrong Keary?" After giving him a tiny shake of her head, Keary buries her cheek into the wall of his chest. Dipping his chin, he searches her gray complexion, left with nothing to do but wait as she battles with the emotions flooding her system.

"I'm sorry," she whimpers, swiping at her face with one hand.

"There's no reason for you to be sorry."

Instead of offering comfort, his words fall like a hailstorm, pelting her with fresh anguish. Light green eyes shimmer with unshed tears that want nothing more than to drip over her skin like shards of broken glass. The sight she makes punches through his chest like a warrior's spear. Arms tighten around her slight frame as each sob she holds back threatens to rip apart the very fabric of his soul.

"What's happened? I don't understand."

Heavy, bone aching gasps make her words nearly unintelligible. Nearly. "I kn… I know. W-why. Y-y-you we-were c-cur-cursed."

His blood runs cold as Conall pulls back to search her face. Growing still, he meets her statement head-on. "Why?"

Keary's words rush out, her breaths still coming in shallow bursts, but she meets his gaze without hesitation. "This journal reveals a passionate love story between a young woman and the miller's son. Once her mother learns of their relationship and the unplanned pregnancy, she forbids them from ever seeing each other again."

"O-kay?" Conall's forehead furrows as he tries to understand why Keary feels so strongly about this. In his time, marriage was a common way for women to increase their social standing. The tremble in her lower lip soothes his need to pace.

Turning in his arms, she shows him a small passage written inside the front cover. "The woman was Geillis."

The instant her words take hold, agony shoots through him like a lightning bolt. Beneath him, the ground seems to fall away, causing him to stumble backwards. Bile rises up into his throat as his mind races with the implication. "You're saying she," Conall pauses long enough to swallow around a thick throat. White heat coats his words as he spits them free. "She cursed us because her daughter was with child and needed a more suitable husband?"

Keary nods, her fingers gripping onto the journal tightly. "I believe so."

Conall's eyes burn as he takes in the weight of her words. Muscles tense and coil within him like a tightly wound spring. "Why us?"

"I don't think that was planned. I think you and Daigh were in the wrong place at the wrong time," Keary murmurs, her eyes darting warily across his face.

He gulps, his eyes wide. "Does it say how to undo the curse?"

"No. It cuts off before I believe you arrived."

"So, we're back to the beginning."

"At least we know why."

"Yeah, great," he snaps, fists clenching tightly at his side. "A lot of fucking help."

"You don't have to be an ass."

"Me? Your ancestor was a monster! She stole away years of my life and suddenly knowing why is supposed to give me some sort of comfort?" Shoving a hand through his hair, Conall stomps back and forth across the kitchen. "That gives me more than enough reason to be an ass."

"Sure, if she was here to bear the brunt of it, but she's not. I am," she growls. "And I'm trying to help you."

"I'm still not sure I should even accept your help."

"What's that supposed to mean?"

"Your bloodline is evil," he spits, cursing the wounded expression his words cause. Grinding his teeth, Conall charges onward. "For all I know, you're trying to lock me up again."

"That's not fair."

"Fair?" Conall sneers. "You want to talk about fair? This entire situation isn't fair to me or my little brother. You've been here, living your life while we've been stuck for centuries. Do you expect me to trust you without question?"

Her cheeks flush pink as heat crackles within her tired eyes. Bridging the gap between them, Keary lifts her chin. "I'm not the one who cursed you. I had nothing to do with any of this. And yet, I'm doing everything I can to not only find your brother, but help you find freedom."

"Yeah. So, you keep saying."

Conall watches in tense silence as Keary's expression shifts from one emotion to the next, culminating in a heart-wrenching pain. Her fingers twitch uncontrollably, each movement sharpening his anticipation of the impending onslaught. On a hiss of air, she snatches her hands away before whirling around and stalking off, leaving him alone to battle the ache in his chest.

"You don't want my help? That's fine." Shrugging into her sweater, she stops long enough to jam her feet into a pair of boots. "I'm certainly not going to bang my head on a wall for you."

"Where are you going?"

Shivering, her hand clenches on the doorknob as if they became one. Seconds pass before she answers without turning around. With a razor-sharp undertone slicing through her words like a hot knife through butter, it's clear she could disembowel him in an instant with her tongue. "Someplace I should've gone the moment you fell out of my damn birthday present!" The soft click of the door behind her adds a new level of emphasis to her emotions.

When his words cut through her defenses so easily, the upset of his stomach took him by surprise. The instant his insults escaped his lips, Conall wanted nothing more than to snatch them back. His only reason for pressing on; Daigh. He couldn't afford to make the same mistake twice. Once the pain took hold of Keary, the heat boiled quickly, flushing her face and neck red. Standing in front of her, Conall noticed the moment that her shock and hurt morphed into an unforgiving resolve that hardened her eyes. Left alone in her kitchen, his head spins. Emotional girls drowning themselves in their own tears is something easily maneuvered. Sidestepping the ones ready to kill him had been Daigh's job.

"If only I had your barbed wit here with me now, Daigh." His brother's absence leaves an invisible void that sucks all the air out of his lungs. With a tightening in his chest, he imagines the unimaginable, Daigh out there somewhere, enduring who knows what horrors, and a wave of anguish washes over him, searing every inch of his soul. "You'd better be alive, because if I find out otherwise, I swear I'll never forgive you."

Cursing aloud, he buries both hands in his hair. A part of him wants to run after Keary, apologize, and beg for her help. The other part wants to push her away. Choosing neither, Conall relies on the analytical part of his brain to erect walls until her anger and hurt are so far away, it's nothing but a distant echo ringing in his ears. Pulling out a chair, he sits at the kitchen table, releases the air in his lungs and reads Geillis's journal. Every page is like peeling another layer of his own skin. Her story is beautiful and painful. In her own way, she too fell victim to Brigid.

In each black ink scrawl of her pen, he endures the weight of her pain. Each page giving a voice to emotions he didn't think was possible for the girl to feel, let alone express. By the time he finishes, his stomach knots as he places the book on the table with a resounding thud. The weight of her reality rests heavily on his shoulders, like a physical burden dragging him down.

Once again, he replays the venom he unleashed on Keary and the nausea grows until he's certain it'll consume him. I shouldn't have lashed out at her. Blaming her for something she had no control over. Suddenly, the thought of losing his one ally leaves him cold. He needs to make things right, but the idea of confronting her again covers his skin with sweat.

As the sun sinks lower in the sky, it casts a golden hue over Briar's quaint village. Pedaling her bike over the cobble streets, the wheels click rhythmically against the stones, echoing the turmoil churning inside her. Each turn of the pedals distances her from Conall's heated words. The sting of their exchange shrouds over her shoulders but while the cool wind caresses her cheeks, it takes remnants of her temper with it, leaving behind a resolute determination.

Stopping outside the shipping office, she exhales audibly. Bit of gravel rock crunches under her shoes as she crosses the lot and steps inside. The tiny bell above the door announces her presence with a cheerful jingle, starkly at odds with the heaviness in her heart.

"Good evening, Miss Keary," the man behind the counter greets after plucking the toothpick from his mouth.

"Evening Aaron, how is your better half?"

At the mention of his wife, Aaron's polite smile transforms into one of warmth. "Jolene's doing much better these days. I can't thank you enough for what you did."

"Actually, there is something you can do." Stepping up to the counter, Keary schools her features. "I need to see the shipping records for a specific item."

"That's easy enough. We should have a record of all of your shipments."

"Well, uh…" pausing, she taps a finger on the countertop in time with her increasing heartrate. "This would be one of the items my sister, Erin shipped."

Pausing in front of a tall cabinet, Aaron's brow furrows. "You want someone else's records?"

"She's my sister. I don't think she'll mind," Keary rushes to add. "Is it possible to find every place the item was ever shipped to?"

"As in, ever?" When she simply nods in reply, Aaron presses a finger against the bridge of his nose. "This is an unusual request. It's not standard poli-"

"Please," she cuts in quickly. "It's extremely important."

Aaron takes a moment to consider Keary's request, his expression unreadable. Resisting the impulse to pace the narrow lobby, she plants her feet firmly on the ground and waits for his response. As he chews on the end of his toothpick, her skin beginning to crawl and itch. "When Jolene first fell ill, our elders assured us that she would be at the top of the list when the doctor returned. But weeks went by without any news. Watching her health decline was one of the hardest things I've ever had to do."

Keary nods, reeling from the change in topic. Forcing herself to listen attentively, she ignores the uncomfortable sensation creeping across her skin.

"As a natural-born, I never really noticed a difference between us and the gifted, other than the obvious abilities they possess," he says. "And I know some people have strong opinions on both sides. If you were one of them and refused to treat my Jolene, I'm not sure I'd still have her with me today. So, for you, I'll make an exception."

After flashing her a quick grin, he turns to a nearby cabinet and rummages through a drawer before dramatically producing a folder and placing it on the counter. Silence stretches as he proceeds to make a list of all the dates and locations tied to her trinket box. Once he's finished, he replaces the folder and slides the sheet towards Keary. "Now this is only the places it's been declared. We're the only legitimate shipping company in Solstier, but there are cheaper, albeit illegal options that I can't track for you."

"This is perfect." Before she's tempted to scan the list, Keary tucks the pages into her bag for later. "I really appreciate this."

"Don't worry about it. I'd like to say this makes us even, but I came out ahead on the deal."

Keary smiles and offers his hand a soft pat. "Give her my best."

"I will."

The ride to the library is a blur, the wind whipping through Keary's hair as she puzzles over the list Aaron had given her. Colorful hues of twilight paint the rooftops in vibrant shades of orange and purple, but Keary is too preoccupied to pay them much attention.

Their library stands near the center of the village, a beacon of knowledge constructed in wood and dark stone. Bursting through the double doors, Keary's eyes immediately scan the expansive space for a familiar flash of fiery-red hair amidst the rows upon rows of bookshelves. A faint scent of old books and dust fills the library as Keary makes her way through several aisles before she finds Evie slowly but deliberately shelving books.

Her movements graceful and fluid, as if she's performing a dance. A soft light illuminates the dim surroundings, casting shadows on the walls behind her. When she notices Keary's presence, her face lights up with a smile that brings life to the dim surroundings. "Keary! What brings you here?

"I'm looking for any books you may have on curses."

"Curses?" Evie repeats, raising an eyebrow.

"Yes, specifically curses." Keary chews on the inside of her cheek as her friend carefully places the last book in its designated spot.

"May I ask why?"

"I'm just doing a little research."

"Research on curses? That's not something I would expect from someone who doesn't believe in such things," Evie said with a hint of amusement in her voice.

"Well, I had a patient last month who claimed his wife's mother had placed a hex on him." As the lie slips out of her mouth, Keary scrambles to offer some sort of explanation. "I figured understanding how curses work would help me better assist my patients if a similar situation were to arise again."

Evie's golden eyes darken slightly, narrowing into thin slits as she creaks out a short nod. Her voice is low and hesitant when she speaks, a hint of uncertainty coloring her words. "I can't promise they will help," she begins, "but any books we have on curses are this way." As she leads the way through the labyrinthine corridors of the library, the musty scent of old paper and ink fills the air, adding to the sense of mystery and urgency surrounding Keary's quest for answers.

When Evie stops at a section marked Mythology, her fingers skim thick shelves, dancing from spine to spine before pulling out several volumes. "Start with these," she instructs, handing the short stack to Keary. "But be careful. I know you don't believe in this stuff, but some of the things on these pages are better left undisturbed."

"Thank you," she breathes, twisting to the side to give Evie a one-armed squeeze. Settling in at an isolated table near the back, the silence of the library wraps surrounds her with only the occasional hum as Evie continues putting a large stack of books back on the shelves.

As she flips through dusty pages, Keary's thoughts wander back to Conall, his trinket box and the secrets it holds. The weight of time presses down on her, reminding her that his days are numbered. Every moment they spend fighting, keeps them from finding what they need to free him and his brother. She didn't bother to tell herself, that she'd sleep easy should they fail. So, with the library clock ticking steadily over her shoulder, Keary leans into the books, her quest for answers hiding beneath dust-laden tomes and fairytales.

Hours pass, the sky outside the window growing dark as the sun drops below the horizon. What if she isn't coming back? "It's her house. She has to come back," Conall grumbles. What if something happened? Is she laying in a ditch hurt? The click of the front door opening allows him to take a deep, cleansing breath.

Without a word, Keary sets her shoes on the small rack and hangs her sweater on a hook near the door. When she enters the kitchen with a purpose, he studies her silently, his throat dry but his chest free of the anchor he'd been struggling against. Before he can think better of it, Conall blurts the first thing that comes to mind. "I'm sorry."

Stopping an arm's length away, she lifts dark and stormy eyes. "I went to the library and checked out every book they had on curses," she says tightly. "I also grabbed a few history books so you can catch up on the things you've missed."

"Keary?"

"I would've been back sooner, but I had an idea. Took some convincing, but I got the shipping records for your trinket box. I thought if we could figure out where it originated, we could track it backwards to Daigh's."

Conall nods. "Thank you, Keary. I shouldn't have said what I did. It was wrong to take my anger out on you."

When she meets his gaze, Conall flinches at the shadows still lingering in her eyes. "There's a good chance if they sold one that they might've sold both. But it's a long shot."

"Keary. Talk to me."

"I am."

"No, you're avoiding me," Conall argues, stepping in front of her before she can skirt away from him. "I'm sorry."

"It's fine."

He nods again, his eyes flickering to hers before dropping. "No, it's not."

"Let's get started."

When she darts around him for a kitchen chair, Conall grabs her wrist and tugs her back towards him. His steel grip is unyielding as he crushes her hand inside his own and tips her chin up. When their eyes lock, a current passes between them like lightning, leaving him breathless. Despite the simplicity of her features, his heart beats wildly as he gazes into her light green eyes, so pale they almost appear colorless. Ensnared by the gentleness that shapes her face, he watches the tiny lights flickering in her irises.

"I really am sorry," he insists."

Keary shifts her weight from one foot to the other, eyes darting away for a brief moment. Her cheeks flush red with embarrassment before she gives a curt nod against the hand that still grips her chin. "I forgive you," she murmurs, the simplicity of her words belying the complex web of emotions roiling inside her.

His reaction is far from simple; heat coils in his stomach like a caged animal before invading his limbs. His breath hitches as he stares at her, unable to tear his gaze away. He swallows hard, the lump in his throat threatening to choke him as he struggles to process the enormity of what she has just offered him.

"We have a lot to get through." Separating herself from him, Keary takes a seat on the far side of the table. "My friend says there are several groups of witches in Solstier. One of them might share blood with the one who cursed you. She's going to track down their location so we can reach out to them."

"You think they could help us break the curse?"

"Maybe. It's worth a shot, right?"

"Absolutely." With a shaky grin, Conall takes a chair directly across the table from her.

With a shared sense of determination, they spend the rest of the night poring over the books, and manifests searching for any hint or clue that could lead them to the witches, or Daigh's trinket box. As he reads, Keary pulls out a map of Solstier, laying it out on the table before she marks important locations. Although the air is thick with tension, they work in silence, each lost in their own thoughts.

Finally, after several hours, Keary leans back in her chair and lets out a deep sigh. "That's everything I can find," she says, running a hand through her hair. "Working backwards from where Erin found your trinket, I've found several areas where it might've been. There's a good chance Daigh's trinket box was in the same areas, if not at the same time."

"There's at least a dozen marks there."

"We'll have to narrow them down. I might know someone who can help with that. I'll try to set up a meeting for tomorrow or the day after."

"Thank you, Keary," he mumbles gently. "I don't know what I'd do without you."

Teeth clamp over her lower lip as her face heats. Ducking her head to hide it, she shrugs. "Hey, I'm the only one of us who knows how to use a library card around here."

Conall chuckles, the hard edges around his heart softening in her presence. "True."

As they sit in a more comfortable silence, the weight of the task ahead is still daunting but a bit more manageable now that they have a direction to go. Keary breaks the silence, her voice whisper light. "Conall, can I ask you something?"

"Of course."

"How did Brigid convince this woman to unleash such a curse on you and Daigh?"

"There was a woman in Sloan's village, Etain. Most treated her poorly because she had a child outside of marriage. The first time I saw her, I felt sorry for her." As the familiar ache builds inside his chest, Conall rubs at it subconsciously. "The life of a smuggler isn't glamorous or steady enough to support a family and she thought her chances fared better with one of Sloan's knights."

"What happened?"

"After professing his love to Etain, this so-called knight bed her then asked another girl to marry him instead. They tied the knot almost immediately."

"That's a little harsh," Keary seethes, her voice reaching a fever pitch.

Despite the years, the events are fresh in his mind. "Heart-broken, Etain threw herself off the Dornhull Cliffs."

"I'm so sorry!"

"Unaware of the direction her sister's heart lay, Aoife blamed me for her suicide. I don't think it was difficult for Brigid to sell her on retribution."

Conall jumps when she reaches across the table and covers his hand with her own. "That's terrible."

"It is what it is," he murmurs with a shrug, only slightly distracted by the way his body relaxes under her touch. "It's a bitter pill to swallow."

"On that note, I think that's enough work for tonight." With a meager smile, Keary stands before gathering the books and manifests into piles. "I'm going to go get some rest. You should too."

Conall nods. "You're right. We'll continue the search to-morrow."

As they both head towards the door to retire for the night, he reaches out and touches Keary's arm. Turning back to him, her head tilts gently with an unspoken question in her eyes.

"Thank you."

CHAPTER 18

As the weeks pass, the gentle spring rain subsides, making way for summer's heat. Kneeling beside the garden, Keary's forehead glistens with sweat that also trickles along her spine. The garden itself is a sight to behold, a riot of colors and scents that dance in the warm breeze. No matter how many times Erin's forced to start over, she does so with determination. Once school finishes, Keary imagines her sister taking over, pouring her love to every leaf and petal. She marvels at Erin's ability to bring even the tiniest seed to bloom, a talent she silently admires. But instead of feeling tranquil in the garden, Keary finds it to be a delightful distraction from her own thoughts.

Keary scripts every moment of her days between the never-ending cycle of chores, the occasional patient with heatstroke and pouring through the books Evie gave her. Anything that distracts her from the memory of Conall's lips pressed to hers, igniting a fire she can't quell. But no matter how busy she keeps herself, the man himself remains a constant presence, his mere existence a reminder of her forbidden desires plaguing her thoughts and dreams. As if Keary needs anymore reminders in her already torturous state of longing.

Of their own accord, her eyes wander to trace the hard lines and curves of his body as he works in the yard. Under the merciless sun, he shed his shirt, exposing golden-skin damp with sweat. As he works the hand sander over the door to the tower, every movement if a work of art. Muscles bunch and ripple with each stroke of his arm, her own fingers curling in response.

"Stop it," she scolds, forcing her attention back to the task at hand. The struggle for steady breaths is real as she fastens an iron-grip on the primal desires stirring within her. "You're acting like you've never seen a man before." But even as she says the words, her mind argues against them. Not like this one we haven't. Teeth clench tight as she imagines those hands moving over her bare skin, feeding the monster kept too long in the dark.

Conall is a masterpiece, his body chiseled to perfection by manual labor. Every muscle defined and honed, ready for any hurdle thrown his way. Her reaction is primal, the impulses fraying bundles of nerves. She won't deny her physical attraction to him, but it's his mind that captivates her.

With every passing day, she finds herself infatuated with the useless bits of knowledge that occupies his brain. The way he tackles every obstacle with efficiency and purpose, never wasting an ounce of energy. When he succeeds and offers a satisfied grin, the crooked tilt of his lips never fails to make her heart flutter.

It's not as if he's uninterested either. More than once, she's felt his hot gaze warm her skin. Experienced the full body shiver as she imagines his thoughts. Pressing her lips into a thin line, Keary clears away the fantasies sprinkling glitter all through her brain. "Men like Conall are a heartbreak waiting to happen," she reminds herself before declaring war on the weeds seeking refuge in Erin's garden.

"Darlin'?"

The velvet lilt in his voice skims across her bare arms like a caress. Expelling a slow, controlled breath, she cranes her neck to meet Conall's strange expression. "We've been over this a hundred times," she huffs. "Keary."

"Of course." One hand reaches up to plow through the wet curls clinging to his damp skin. "I'm just wondering what it is you're doing."

The sound of her name on his lips forces Keary to squirm. "I'm weeding," she grunts, gesturing to the pile of weeds beside her.

"I was afraid of that."

"What's that supposed to mean?"

"You're pulling out the plants with the weeds, Darlin'." A smile flirts over one corner of his mouth. "Keary."

Eyes drop to her hands then her shoulders deflate *Stuff like this happens when you get distracted by a nice pair of shoulders and brawny arms.* With a wrinkle in her nose, she sorts through the discard pile. "I didn't even notice," she answers awkwardly.

His chuckle draws her skin tight, her lungs failing when he crouches beside her in the dirt. "It's an honest mistake."

"Erin is determined to have a garden waiting for her when she finishes school," she grumbles.

The hand he places on her shoulder momentarily sidetracks her meltdown. "Let me help," he offers with an amiable smile.

Resting back on her heels, Keary nods mutely. Soon, hands the size of hams move deftly to separate plant from offending greenery. *Would they be the same in the bedroom? Demanding but gentle? Where in the hell did that come from? Focus!* Too late, she realizes Conall is in the middle of telling her how she can identify plant from weed. Setting her teeth, she narrows her focus until all she can see is the damn garden in front of her.

Following his instructions, the two work side by side, replanting the good and pulling the bad. They're halfway through the last row when Keary sits back to admire yet another hidden talent with a laugh. "So, you were a gardener and a smuggler?"

"Not willingly. Moira had quite the garden behind her house. Whenever my brother and I were more rowdy than usual, she sent us to work in the garden." Lips curve softly. "I'm fairly certain Daigh slaughtered her plants, so she'd assign him a new chore."

"I'll admit. I can see the appeal," she confesses before meeting his grin.

"You have dirt on your face," Conall declares before brushing it aside with the pad of his thumb.

The instant he makes contact with her skin, Keary's core tightens. A simple gesture awakening a million nerve endings at once. She's certain he must feel the heat radiating off of her as he leans in even closer. As much as her brain is screaming at her to move, her body seems to be on a different channel entirely. Her mind races with thoughts of what could happen if she just closed the distance between them by a few inches. *Will he kiss me again? Can I resist him if he does?* When Keary peeks up at him under the veil of her lashes, her breath snags at the heat glittering in his eyes.

Frozen, she resists the urge to squirm as his eyes drop to her mouth. Suddenly, all she can think about is the velvet texture of his lips. The taste of salt from his skin. Enthralled, she's unable to stop her tongue from peeking out to brush across her lower lip. That one action turns the light off in his eyes as a strangled groan escapes him. Thankfully, the sound of a wagon bouncing down the driveway breaks the hold Conall has on her. When she spots the familiar bold colors heading her way, Keary groans aloud.

With a grunt, she heaves herself up from the ground, brushing off the bits of loose dirt that cling to her knees. As Evie sets the break and gracefully jumps down from the buckboard, landing on the dusty ground with a soft thud, she flashes a smile. "Well, this is quite a surprise," she says, forcing a light tone despite the butterflies in her stomach. The sun beats down on them, casting long shadows across the dusty ground and making the air thick with heat. Sweat glistens on their skin as they stand in the driveway, surrounded by acres of tall grass and endless blue skies above.

"You know how I live to be unpredictable," Evie chirps.

Glancing at Conall, Keary notes his blank expression. "Evie this is Conall," she says with a quick wave of her hand. "Conall, meet Evie."

"Nice to meet you Conall," Evie announces, covering the distance between them in long strides. Lips twitch as she shields her eyes from the sun to better study his face. "Now I see why all the buzz."

Keary frowns. "What buzz?"

"Seriously? How long have you lived here?" Evie's nose scrunches as she shoves thick flame-red curls away from her face. "You thought you could hide such a specimen at home, and no one would talk?"

"We're not talking about this."

"Fair enough. But a heads up would be nice. I damn near took out Mr. Soloman's fence coming up the driveway."

"Evie," Keary hisses, ignoring the sensation of Conall's eyes on her face.

With a soft pat on her shoulder, Evie soothes ruffled feathers. "All I'm saying is that you should warn people. Put out a sign. Better yet, charge admission."

Her next warning comes out in a growl so soft, Keary wonders if it'll reach her friend's ears before the breeze carries it away.

Rubbing a hand over the front of her long, flowing skirt, Evie directs her attention elsewhere. "Nevermind. Did I catch you two at a bad time?"

As Keary forms the words that will send her friend far, far away, Conall answers for her. "I was helping Keary with the garden."

"Hot and a gentleman?" Evie whispers close to her ear.

Instantly, Keary's face heats and her heart hammers against her ribs. "Don't start," she mutters thickly.

Evie raises an eyebrow but thankfully doesn't press any further. Instead, she turns her attention to the garden. "It looks lovely. Erin will be thrilled."

"So, what brings you out here? I doubt you came to see if any plants survived me." A ripple of tension flutters over her friends face, her gaze skipping between her and Conall. The bitter taste on her tongue offers Keary a tiny glimpse of insight. "You can speak in front of Conall. What's wrong?"

"I need your help."

As soon as the words escape her lips, the distinct metallic taste of blood floods her senses. She can't understand how she didn't notice it sooner, but now that she has, the bitterness is overwhelming.

Slowly, she makes her way toward the stench until she reaches the back of the wagon. With careful hands, she lifts one corner of the heavy blanket to reveal a young man writhing in pain. Buckets of sweat drench his clothes. His face pale and drawn from blood loss and exhaustion.

"What happened?"

"Don't ask me that. I don't want to lie to you, but I need you to trust me." Joining her at the side of the wagon, Evie runs a soothing hand over the man's damp hair. "Can you buy him some time until I can get him south."

"Someone is looking for him?"

"Help us," Evie pleads, her eyes offering a glimpse of the scorching heat she keeps contained.

Keary grits her teeth, holding back a barrage of questions threatening to escape. Her throat tightens as she notes his battered face and bloody knuckles, it isn't until she notes the amount of blood seeping through his shirt that her heart sinks. When she gently lifts the material away, her eyes widen at the extent of his injury. The steady flow of blood tells her that his wound is deep, the intense heat radiating from it reveals he is a Phoenix, like Evie.

"He'll never make it if I don't stop the bleeding." Squaring her shoulders, Keary nods at Conall. "Carry him inside, lay him on the table." Easing the blanket the rest of the way off him, she passes it to her friend. "Lay this on the floor beneath him."

Conall doesn't hesitate, powerful arms scoop the young man up as if he's weightless. While Conall's face is a blank mask, Keary knows him well enough by now to recognize the concern lurking in his eyes.

As they approach her house, she snakes a hand out to stop Evie from running ahead. "Who is he to you?"

Shadows flicker within her eyes, her smooth brow puckering. "He's someone from my past. Don't worry he's no danger to you."

"Considering he'll be bleeding out on my table, and Conall will be there, I'm not concerned about what danger he poses."

"I need someone to get the door," Conall calls over his shoulder. At Keary's nod, Evie runs ahead.

By the time Conall lays the man on her table, Evie's anxiety is palpable. Brushing past her, Keary rushes to her pantry. After emerging with an armload of supplies, she washes her hands thoroughly in the kitchen sink, then soaks several clean cloths. Wringing out the excess, she begins cleaning the wound, her eyes never leaving the azure flame burning within. Despite the urgent nature of the situation, Keary can't tear her eyes away, marveling at the sheer beauty of a raging inferno hidden beneath his skin.

"What's your name?"

Blazing eyes shift silently between her and where Evie stands over her shoulder. Keary follows the inner battle he has with himself, observing every pinch in his face. Lips thin as his square jaw tightens. "Orion."

"I'm going to give you something for the pain," she says in her calm and professional tone. "Before I can sew up your wound, I need to make sure there's no internal bleeding or further injury. It's going to hurt."

Handsome features contort slightly, but he meets her gaze with eyes so intense, Keary could swear she's staring into the sun. The sound of his voice, deep and slurred, reveals his struggle to maintain composure. "Do whatever you must," he responds unsteadily.

Keary nods, her hands steady as she measures out a spoonful of the potent mixture, adding water to the powder, she shoves the glass toward Evie's frozen figure. "Help him drink this. All of it." While her hand shakes for a brief second, she watches Evie steel herself and jerk a nod in response.

As she props Orion up to better help him drink, pain etches in every line and crease, but he keeps eye contact with Keary, his features softening. Minutes after the glass is empty, tension gradually leaks from his body, his ragged breaths falling even.

"You need to make sure you keep him still," she advises, releasing her breath when Conall steps over to lend a hand should the young man become too much for Evie to restrain.

With steady hands, Keary removes the bloody bandages to assess the extent of his injury. A chill creeps along her skin as she inspects the deepness of the wound, the precise edges and telltale signs of an infection. The weight of Evie's eyes burn with every movement, adding a soft tremor in her own hands. "This is bad," she murmurs. "He needs a real doctor."

Evie shakes her head. "The elders control the doctors. Please, help him."

Keary's heart sinks, Evie's plea acting as an anchor. Taking a deep breath, her face scrunches as her inhale pulls in the foul bitterness seeping from his wound. "I will do what I can. I need to treat the infection and stitch him up." Lifting her eyes from the man to her friend, her voice carries a hint of warning. "It won't be pleasant for him."

Evie nods and prepares herself for his struggle. "That looks really deep."

"It is," Keary snaps. "Deep enough I have to check for internal damage." As she probes inside the wound, she closes her eyes and concentrates on what she's feeling with her fingers. Orion's hisses turn sharp, his body coiled tight and shaking against the invasion. "The intestines appear to be intact," she observes loudly, meeting Orion's cloudy eyes. "You should count yourself lucky."

"How did this even happen?" Conall asks from beside Keary.

"I don't know. I found him like this."

Glancing up from arranging the supplies on the table beside her patient, Keary's voice drops. "What do you mean? Found him where, Evie?"

Teeth worry over her lower lip. "On my doorstep. Last night."

"And you're just bringing him to me now? If you brought him last night, the infection may not have been this bad!"

"It wasn't safe last night, Kear!"

Curling her fingers into her palms, Keary finds enough restraint to reign in her temper. "Safe from who?"

Evie's features twist into a petulant expression. "I don't know."

"I don't believe you."

"I can tell you this," Conall says with a darkness in his eyes, his voice eerily even. "That injury is from a blade. Too long and deep to be a dagger, so my guess is someone swiped at him with a severely sharp sword. Judging from the direction, possibly a left-handed swordsman."

"How can you possibly know that?"

The only answer Conall offers Evie is to shrug one shoulder lazily.

"If that's true, then we need to hurry," Keary grinds through her teeth and gets to work.

First, she cleanses the wound with a mixture of herbs and warm water, her touch gentle yet purposeful. For every careful movement, her mind races with how to combat the infection before closing the wound. "If I don't treat this infection, nothing else I do will matter."

"I trust you, Keary. I know you can save him." Her voice is barely above a whisper, but it carries a weight of hope that makes her heart ache.

"I need to you to look on the counter for a jar of white salve."

Her friend nods and skirts around the table while Conall remains at her side. She'll admit his presence offers her a sense of calm amidst the chaos. When Evie returns, Keary begins applying the salve onto the infected area, a surge of heat tingling along her hands. Soon the foul stench fades under a sharp, clean scent and she relaxes her shoulders. More than a few times, the young man shifts slightly, his eyes bright but unfocused.

After shaking the ache from her arms, Keary sets to work. With precise movements, she stitches up his wound, starting with the internal layers first. Occasionally, his pain seeps through her barriers to become her own, stealing the air from her lungs. Erecting mental barriers to protect herself, she strives to keep her hands steady. Once the last stitch is completed, Keary heaves a huge sigh, twisting against the deep ache in the muscles at her lower back.

Stepping back to the sink, she scrubs up to her elbows with soap and hot water. While her house reeks of blood and illness, the man sleeps peacefully. "Conall, can you open all the windows?" With a quiet nod, he pauses beside her long enough to brush fingers across the dampness gathering at the nape of her neck before moving around the house like a vapor to allow as much clean air in as possible. As she dries her hands, Evie avoids her shrewd gaze by checking the man's fresh bandage.

"Should I expect the vanguard to come here looking for him?"

As if caught off guard, Evie's hands still before she rights herself. "I don't know."

"Well, at least you didn't lie to me." Snorting more to herself than anyone else, Keary passes her a small jar. "Keep his wound clean, once the inner layers begin to heal, you can make a compress out of this. Apply it once a day and it'll speed up the healing process."

"Got it."

Grabbing her free hand, Keary forces her friend to meet her stare. "It's important that you wait until the inner layers heal first. And when this is all over, you and I are going to have a serious conversation."

"I understand, Kear."

Once again, Conall carries the now unconscious Orion back out to the wagon. From inside, soft traces of a conversation drift in through the open windows. With a sigh, she heads out to join them. The moment she steps outside, Keary's hit with a gust of fresh air and she breathes it in greedily, noting the crispness of it. "Everything okay?" she asks, approaching Evie and Conall.

Evie nods. Conall shoves his hands in his pockets.

"I packed you some bandages and herbs in case you need them on the road."

"Thanks, Kear," Evie whispers accepting the satchel and stowing it under the buckboard of the wagon before climbing into the seat.

"Link me when you're safe," Keary adds. "I need to know you're safe Evie."

"I will. Thank you for this Keary."

As the wagon moves carefully back up the driveway, Keary heaves a sigh. "Want to tell me what that was about?"

Conall shrugs. "I don't like that she put you in the middle of this. We don't know what he did or was doing when he was injured. As your friend, she should've taken him to another healer." Tipping his head back, he exchanges the air in his lungs before meeting her eyes again. "She wasn't overly fond of my opinion."

"I see. Well, thank you for voicing it, regardless." Looping her arm through his, she drags him toward the house. "Come on, we have some cleaning up to do."

CHAPTER 19

Stepping into the house, Keary's eyes fall on the table where Orion lay moments before. Devoid of the chaos and tension while she worked to save a man's life, the room itself seems to release a deep sigh. Ignoring the ache in her bones, she works beside Conall to clear away what remains of their impromptu infirmary.

"We need to bury these," the strain in his voice increases the soft lilt in his words, almost making them unintelligible. When Keary answers with a nod, he takes the blood-stained linens out to do just that.

After rubbing a hand against her lower back, Keary gathers up what remains of her supplies, making a mental note to replace some of the key items she used. The stench of blood still lingers in the air so she burns a bowl full of cinnamon and cloves, opening another window for good measure.

Her brain blocks out the trembling in her body as she attacks the floor with a broom and mop, her muscles screaming with every stroke. Beads of sweat form on her brow as she vigorously scrubs away the last remnants of the gruesome scene. When she pauses to catch her breath, Keary surveys the now gleaming floors. The refreshing scent of soap and incense mingles with the tang of her sweat. "Better than blood," she muses aloud, a hint of satisfaction in her voice.

"Wow, you work fast," Conall interrupts from just inside the back door.

Keary's laughter escapes her lips before she can contain it, causing her to subtly shake her head and utter a single word: "Practice." After storing the broom and mop in a nearby cupboard, she proceeds to fill the coffee-pot on the stove with water and waits for her addiction to brew.

"This kind of thing is normal?"

"Sometimes. Not usually so life or death, though."

"And Evie?" Keary stretches the ache in her back while she searches for the right words. "Evie and I have been getting each other into trouble since we were children. She knew I would help."

"You trust her judgment?"

"I do. She has a good heart, even if some of her choices can be reckless." A flicker of emotion flashes across Conall's face too swift for Keary to decipher. His lips tighten and a muscle twitches in his jaw, giving her a glimpse of his dislike for her best friend. Rather than press the issue, he redirects his attention.

"Do you think someone will come looking for him?"

As Keary considers her answer, a weight blankets her shoulders. Something heavy and dark, suffocating her with an acrid stench. She can't help but wonder who this mysterious man is and what secrets he holds. She begins to regret ever getting involved with him, knowing that she may have put herself and her loved ones in danger. "I'm not sure," she finally replies, her voice tight. "But whoever he is, he's caught up in something dangerous. And now that I've helped him...I might be too." Her words hang in the air, heavy with uncertainty. She can see the concern in his eyes as he steps closer to her, a protective stance that both comforts and unsettles her.

"What have you gotten yourself into, Keary?"

Before she can answer, the sound of hooves pounding against the ground does it for her. Exchanging a look with Conall, she notes the frown wrinkling his brow, adding lines to his mouth before she runs outside.

Scrambling off the porch, her lungs fail at the sight of a dozen horses charging up her driveway. The ground shakes beneath their thunderous hooves, sending dust and debris into the air. When her eyes land on the vanguard crest emblazoned on the horses' gear, her heart drops into her stomach.

Without a word, Conall appears beside her, his strong arm snaking around her waist and pulling her tightly to his side. Warm breath tickles her ear as he whispers, "Breathe." Taking a deep inhale calms the nerves that are stretched thin. Slowing her heart rate, she schools her features and plasters a polite smile on her face.

With a graceful dismount, the leader adjusts the weight of his sword at his hip before making his way towards her. The polished silver armor on his broad shoulders gleams in the sunlight, dazzling her eyes and forcing Keary to resist squinting. Every step echoes off the ground, reverberating through her bones. The clank and rustle of metal-on-metal ramps up the tension seeking refuge in her spine.

"Keary McKenna," he bellows in a thick voice, that easily reaches her ears. "We need to have a conversation."

Swallowing the lump in her throat, Keary unlocks her knees and gestures towards the house. "I just brewed a pot of coffee. Would you like to come inside?"

After some thought, he shares a glance with the man beside him. His almost imperceptible nod has her releasing the stale air from her lungs. "Broc, you're with me. Caleb, you and the others remain here." The sword at his hip tips downward from the weight of his palm on the pommel. "Station two men at the back. Just in case."

"Yes, Commander." His cool gaze on Keary once more, he sweeps an arm in her direction. "Lead the way, Ms. McKenna."

Despite the icy dread settling in her stomach, she smiles. "Of course, Commander," she says, ensuring the tremor racking her bones doesn't carry over into her voice. Briefly, her eyes dart to meet his before focusing on the path ahead.

As Keary leads the way inside, her movements stiff and deliberate, Conall hangs back, his arms crossing his chest. His gaze remains on the two soldiers in her kitchen as she begins to put cups of coffee together. Though silent, every muscle in him coils, ready to pounce at a moment's notice. Spying on the commander's quiet assessment, Keary isn't the only one to notice Conall's readiness. *Pay attention to what you're doing!* The tremble in her hands increases the difficulty of pouring the coffee without spilling, but somehow, she manages. *Thank the Maker for that.*

"Ms. McKenna, I'm afraid this isn't a social visit. I'm here on behalf of the council." The stern voice of the Commander cuts through the air, authority, and purpose lacing his voice.

Keary's throat tightens as she gestures for the men to sit. They maintain their stiff posture but lower themselves into chairs surrounding the worn wooden kitchen table. The words to withdraw Broc's invitation linger on her lips but the press of her teeth keep them from springing forward. Carefully, she sets a cup in front of each man, her hands trembling before she takes the seat that puts Conall behind her.

The air is tense and thick with unspoken tension, making it difficult for her to breathe. Yet, she sits in silence, waiting for the inevitable conversation to begin. Nerves stretch. Like an overused rubber band, Keary senses the tight bands cracking just under the surface of her skin. Dropping her hands to her lap, she searches the face of the man across from her.

With his perfectly groomed black hair, the commander exudes a sense of discipline and control. His onyx eyes reveal nothing of his inner thoughts, while his strong nose and determined jaw give off an aura of unbreakable willpower. The faint scar on his upper lip only adds to the aura of danger that surrounds him. She has no doubt he's a force to be reckoned with, commanding respect and fear in equal measures.

Swallowing to wet her dry mouth, Keary attempts to remain calm. "Since you know my name, it's only fair that I know yours."

A tiny spark of light flares in dark soulless eyes. "Commander Damien Emberstone."

"Thank you," she answers with a tiny smile. "What's this all about Commander Emberstone?"

While Broc begins to blow on his drink, the Commander ignores his cup altogether. "I need to ask you about a man you treated."

"I treat many people. Could you be more specific?"

"This man is different."

"I've seen Keary treat several people just in the short time I've known her. How do you expect her to recall one man?"

Onyx eyes harden as the Commander stabs a glare in Conall's direction. "I don't believe I caught your name."

"Conall."

"Well, Conall, this man sustained grievous wounds and seriously needed medical attention. As the healer for the gifted, that brings us to you."

After draining half of his cup, Broc sits forward in his chair. "We understand your desire to help those in need, but this man is dangerous, Ms. McKenna." The man's face appears younger with his small, friendly smile.

Conall grips the back of her chair, pulling a squeak from the wood. "If he's so dangerous, why aren't you out looking for him instead of interrogating their healer?"

The commander turns his glare on the man beside him, causing Bryant to sit a little straighter in his chair and scan the contents of his cup. When he turns his attention back to them, Keary takes heed of his severe expression. "The hope was that this man died from the injuries he sustained. However, we've recovered no body."

Keary's hands fist within her lap until the ache spreads into her stiff fingers. "I-I'm sorry, Commander. I see many patients. It's difficult to remember them all."

He leans forward, his gaze unwavering. "This man would stand out. I'm fairly certain he's a phoenix."

A chill runs down her spine as she recalls the man in question. *Evie.* "You said this man is dangerous?"

Broc jerks a nod as the Commander answers for him, his voice devoid of any emotion. "Working with the resistance. Their only aim is to start another civil war. Any aid would brand you a traitor to the Council."

As he speaks, his words fall like anchors into her chest, weighing her down. The sharp citrus scent she picks up from him only solidifies that he believes what he's saying. The clean, tangy aroma fills her until her stomach twists wondering what Evie is tangled up in now. "I'm sorry. I wish I could help you. But I have many patients on both sides and I don't recall treating anyone with a serious injury."

"This would've been a stomach wound. That's not something you'd trust anyone to treat."

"Many small villages have healers, Commander. It's possible he went to one of them."

"I suppose. But given the amount of blood he left behind, I doubt he'd have lasted that long." The silence in the kitchen stretches until the tension becomes fragile. "You're burning incense?"

"Yes, Conall dressed some small game he caught yesterday and the smell wouldn't go away." The commander nods, his finger tapping lightly on the table surface while he attempts to put puzzle pieces together. Fighting back the squirm that settles in her body, she remains still.

"I see. Forgive me for being direct, but you seem uncomfortable. Like someone who's hiding something."

Fingers twist tight together in order to keep her face impassive. "More like that of an older sister. You're man here was dating my sister and cheated on her."

"I wasn't aware." Something sparks in the commander's dark gaze, the faint scar twitching as he presses his lips together. As he sits quietly, mulling over her answers, liquid gold swirls within the dark depths of his black irises. "Ms. McKenna, you understand if I find out you treated this criminal and lied to me about it, you'll stand accused of treason?"

"I do."

"Very well." Pushing away from the table with a rough shove, the chair's legs squawk across the floor, no doubt leaving deep gouges in the wood floor. Keary grinds her teeth together to contain the quick strike on her temper as he stands to his full height. His arms form a deep v as he folds his hands in front of himself. "We've been unable to locate Evie Sherwood. Any idea where she might be?"

Keary's mind buzzes like an active beehive as she frantically searches for a believable excuse. "She mentioned something about a seminar north of Harper." Her gut continues to churn as she wrings her hands beneath the table. "I'm not sure when to expect her home. May I ask why you're looking for her?"

"We have reason to believe she had a personal relationship with this fugitive. She may tell us where he'd run to."

"If I hear from her, I'll put her in touch with you right away."

"I appreciate that, Ms. McKenna." Uncurling his fingers, the Commander moves to exit the way he came when something Broc whispers at his ear stops him in his tracks. Even under layers of armor and padding, Keary catches a soft ripple of the muscles in his back. "One more thing," he drawls, spinning towards her once more. "Is Erin around?"

The question hangs in the air, a sharp and sudden interruption to the silence. Once the weight of it settles around her, white-hot heat replaces the dread curdling her stomach. Squaring her jaw, Keary lifts her chin. "What could you possibly want with my sister?" The words are like fire on her tongue. She'll fight for Erin without backing down any day of the week.

"There are rumors she has the gift of persuasion. If that's true, and you helped this man, her help to apprehend him could mean immunity for you."

"Rumors? From who?"

The Commander stands before her, his gleaming armor fighting to contain his muscular frame. His face is stoic and chiseled, giving nothing away as he speaks. "I'm not at liberty to divulge that information," his deep voice booms through the room, sending a shiver down her spine. The man exudes an air of danger clarifying that he's not one to be trifled with.

"I see. Well, I'm afraid you're out of luck," she says, her palms clammy and slick with sweat as she clenches her fists. "I don't expect Erin to be home for another month. Maybe two."

"That's too bad. I'm sure by then we'll already have the man in our custody."

"I hope you do, Commander. For all our sakes."

While Conall escorts the soldiers to the door, Keary remains rooted in her seat. Her racing thoughts charge the surrounding air until it hums in response. Each thought compounds with the next building to swirl like a tempest, her insides quivering from the intensity. Trying to suppress the shiver creeping down her spine, she focuses on the weight settling heavily in her stomach. *What have I just done?* Not only had she given aid to a criminal, but now she's lied about it. In the eyes of the council, she's now an accomplice to his crimes.

Closing her eyes, she taps a finger against the pad on her thumb and replays snippets of her conversation with the commander. Despite his dangerous reputation, Orion had been in desperate need of medical attention. As a healer, she carries no regret for tending to his wound. But the mention of Erin and her gift leaves her with the taste of bile on her tongue.

"Tell me you know what you're doing."The tightness in Conall's voice rouses her from her musings to stare at him with blurry eyes.

"Um." Swallowing, the finger she taps against her thumb increases the tempo. "I d-don't know."

With a harsh sigh, Conall turns her in her seat, crouching to catch her eye, and covers her hands with his. "Why did you lie?"

Struggling to pinpoint one thought, Keary stammers, "I don't know ... it just slipped out." Dragging in a lungful of air, she focuses on regaining control over her emotions. The fact that Conall remains silent helps steady her erratic breaths. Once she targets each emotion, bringing them under logical control lessens the pressure in her chest. "Just because they say he's a criminal doesn't make it true," she reasons.

"You don't know him or the things he's done."

"But I know Evie. She'd never bring someone dangerous to my doorstep. Besides, his injuries were too severe for him to make it all the way here under his own power. As soon as I said I'd treated him, they're going to ask who brought him."

Conall shoves a hand through his hair. "Maybe."

"No way am I serving my best friend to the vanguard, Conall."

"We need to make sure we covered your tracks. And that when Evie comes home, she sticks to the story you just gave them."

"I know," Keary nods, running a hand through her hair. "To be honest, I'm more concerned with these rumors about Erin."

Conall nods, his expression grave. "Maybe it's best if she lays low for a while."

"And Evie?"

"Evie can take care of herself. Right now, we worry about you and Erin. Everyone else comes second."

"I couldn't bear it if something happened to my sister because of me, Conall." Her voice breaks as he sweeps her into his arms, tucking her head under his chin. As one hand rubs small circles across her back, he cradles her head with the other. "Nothing is going to happen to your sister. I promise."

Sniffling back the tears threatening to fall, Keary pulls away from the heat and comfort Conall provides. "I need to link Erin, and Evie as well. It might be best if they both steer clear of Briar for the time being."

CHAPTER 20

As Keary drifts into sleep that night, her bedroom walls disappear, and she finds herself standing on the edge of a stormy sea with rocky cliffs looming above. The scent of saltwater lingers in the air as a cool breeze prompts her to wrap her t-shirt snugly around herself. Breathing deep, Keary savors the briny flavor of seaweed, mingling with the subtle aroma from a recent rainfall and distant smoke. Turning on her heels, her toes curl within the soft blades of grass.

Nestled between towering cliffs on one side and the rolling sea on the other, a village sits quietly, almost forgotten. Cozy and quaint, it promises refuge from the cold weather and tumultuous elements.

The thatched-roof cottages, built from sun-worn stone, stand sturdy against the harsh climate while colorful shutters adorn their small windows. The smell of freshly baked bread, roasting meat, and the earthy scents of manure and hay from nearby farms fills the air, transporting her to simpler times. Several houses release thin streams of smoke that leisurely meander into the air, adding a hazy and picturesque touch to the sky despite the blazing sun high in the sky.

The heady scent of herbs and spices lingers in the air, emanating from the open windows. As she ventures closer, she catches a faint whiff of hot metal coming from the blacksmith's shop down the road. The streets ahead are unpaved and rough underfoot, with occasional patches of mud and straw, leading to what can only be described as a castle. Made of weathered stones and rough timber, it looms over the village below as a symbol of power and safety.

All around her, villagers walk around in simple clothing, their faces worn and tired. Mindless of the adults' chores, a group of children run among freshly churned dirt rows playing games. Their laughter and shrieks add a sense of innocence to the scene before her.

As Keary wanders aimlessly, she finds herself drawn to two particular voices just up the road.

"Wait for me!"

"No." The elder of the two girls sends a scowl over her shoulder toward younger one. "Just go home, Darby."

"But Mama said I should help you."

Keary slips behind a house as the girls turn a corner towards her. She immediately takes notice of the older girl's honey-colored hair and striking blue eyes. With her skirts held tightly in her hands, she carefully avoids a huge mud puddle before heading up a small hill.

Meanwhile, the younger girl splashes right through the middle of the puddle without a care for her dress, determined to close the distance. Dirty water and bits of mud cling to the bottom of her dress but she never breaks stride. As Keary watches them, she can't help but see the resemblance between the younger girl and Erin. They both have wild curls the color of apple cider and share a similar heart-shaped face. When the older sister turns to confront her sibling once again, Keary's heart jumps into her throat as eyes like Erin's harden in familiarity.

"Mama said to help bring back the flour."

"You need to go home, Darby."

"But Mama said–"

"I know what she said." With hands on her hips, the young lady stands firm in the middle of the path, refusing to budge. "I can gather the flour myself, so go find something else to do."

As if torn between following her mother's orders and the temptation of fun, Darby's shoulders tense and shake. "But–"

"Don't worry, if she asks, I'll tell her you helped bring the flour home."

A bright smile crosses Darby's face, so similar to Erin's that it fills Keary's chest with warmth. "Thank you, Geillis!" She squeals before darting off in the opposite direction towards a group of children playing in the open field.

Torn with following Erin's lookalike, or Geillis, Keary settles on the latter. Picking a path across the road, she makes sure to keep the girl in view as she creeps along behind her. As they approach the tall stone tower sitting proud at the top of the hill, a young man rushes out to pull Geillis into his arms. Her soft squeal of surprise draws Keary's attention to the young man. Judging by her reaction, Keary assumes this is the young man Geillis wrote about in her diary. Evan.

Too far away for her to make out their quiet conversation, Keary hides behind a large boulder, straining to catch any snippets of their exchange. Despite the chill, she gives a silent thanks to the breeze that carries fragments of their words close enough for her to decipher.

"..you know I can't stay away for too long."

"... just had to see you."

"I think Mama... "

He brushes a strand of hair behind Geillis' ear, his touch tender and intimate. "Please … careful."

Keary's heart clenches at the sight of their intimacy. Here, in this moment, she sees a glimmer of the love and connection she's only ever read about. The way Evan holds Geillis, it becomes clear that their love is genuine and strong.

The tender embrace lingers for only a moment before they reluctantly pull apart and the young man disappears back into the tower. Seconds later, he re-emerges with two sacks. After a fleeting touch of hands, he dips his head gently and returns the way he came.

The flour forgotten, Geillis stands there, gazing after him with a mixture of longing and fear. Even from her position, Keary recognizes an inner battle raging within the girl, torn between love and duty. After another long second or two, Geillis tears her gaze away from the tower, gathers the flour and descends the hill, her steps hesitant and deliberate.

Unable to resist the pull, Keary shadows Geillis closely, taking care to remain hidden. After several minutes of traversing muddy roads and bustling villagers, the girl begins up the path towards the authentic-looking castle. Appearing from behind a tall, narrow structure, a tall and slender woman steps out of the shadows and latches onto Geillis' arm. Geillis gasps sharply, her blue eyes widening in either fear or surprise.

Before Keary can decipher her reaction, she wakes from her dream with a jolt.

Screwing the heel of her hands against her blurry vision, she struggles to calm her racing mind. Taking a deep breath, grounds her in reality. The remnants of the dream cling to her like cobwebs, refusing to let go. The taste of saltwater still lingers on her tongue, and the scent of freshly baked bread teases her senses. It takes a moment for Keary to fully recognize her surroundings. Glancing around her bedroom, she finds solace in the familiar sight of her own furniture and decorations. Until the furious pounding on her front door finally registers.

Keary's heart jumps in her chest as the knocking grows louder and more insistent. Throwing off her blankets, she revels in its warmth for a moment before running to answer the front door. The trickling moonlight casts eerie shadows across the walls as she navigates her way towards the source of the disturbance.

The sight of Conall standing at the open door with only a pair of jeans hugging his lean hips scatters Keary's foggy thoughts. Silver light highlights a chiseled chest and muscular arms. His caramel hair falls in unruly waves against a strong jawline, adding a level of rugged to the allure. Unprepared for his presence, she freezes just inside the living room, her mind swirling with a mixture of longing and anticipation. A stout reminder of the desire she's tucked away in an iron-clad compartment.

"What's this about," he demands, though the ripple in his shoulders tells her he's aware of her presence, Conall stands firm between her and their unexpected visitor with an effortless confidence that makes Keary's stomach flip.

"Please, I need to speak to Keary."

Crossing the room, she draws closer to Conall. Teeth set, she ignores the heat radiating off his body that draws her close with an unseen hand, to peek around the wall of his back at the tall, broad-shouldered man darkening her doorway. Dark hair falls wildly around bare shoulders, thick with sweat and dirt. Wearing nothing but a loose pair of shorts, his clenched hands uncurl the moment his eyes land on her, tucked against Conall's side.

"Keary."

"Samson?" Giving her head a quick shake, she attempts to kick-start her rational thinking. "What's wrong?"

"We need your help," he gasps, his voice ragged.

Opening her senses, Samson's fear and urgency suddenly overcomes her body. A searing white-hot pain scorches across her ribs, constricting her lungs and threatening to overwhelm her. Swiping a hand across her brow, she tries to shake off the cold sweat that coats her skin as she fights to stay standing. With trembling hands, she grips Conall's arm and pulls him away from the door, urging Samson to step inside. Every inch of her body screams with tension as she braces for what comes next.

"Many of my pack has fallen sick. Including our healer." Samson sucks in air, his wild eyes pinning Keary in place. "And my daughters."

Keary's heart sinks as she absorbs Samson's words. She knows how important family is to him, especially after losing his mate years ago. "What kind of sickness?" she asks, her voice steady despite the tightness in her chest.

"I'm not sure. Marcus, my son-in-law, was the first to show symptoms. Fever and muscle spasms that were unlike anything I'd ever seen before. At first, I thought it was his beast trying to shift, but now I don't know. In the past hour, more members of our pack have fallen ill."

"Take me to your pack. I'll do everything I can."

Relief washes over Samson's face as he nods eagerly. "Thank you, Keary."

Conall's arm wraps protectively around her waist, holding her close. When he tilts her chin up to look at him, she notices the tension in his jaw and the tight line of his mouth. "Are you certain about this? It could be dangerous."

"My pack won't harm her."

"In their right mind," Conall reminds Samson in a strained voice. "But it sounds like they're not in their right mind."

Placing a hand on top of his, Keary speaks softly. "I can't just stand by and do nothing. Plus, I won't be alone… you're coming with me." As she meets Samson's weary gaze, she can see some of the stiffness leave his posture. "Just let me change and gather my things."

By the time they arrive on Samson's pack lands, Keary's nerves reach a breaking point. She's never treated a Lycan before tonight. Because of their enhanced healing and long lifespans, they rely solely on their own healers. Having their healer affected by whatever's running rampant through the pack members is a serious stroke of bad luck. As the wagon jolts and bounces over the rough terrain, she tries to find a sense of inner calm, sandwiched in between Samson and Conall.

The scent of pine and damp earth fills the air, mingling with the anxious energy that hangs heavy around them. Keary clutches her bag tightly, containing the herbs and potions she hopes will aid in their battle against this unknown sickness. Based on the symptoms, she returned to the house long enough to grab the activated charcoal she kept in the pantry. Hopefully, the few minutes she spent retracing her steps won't prove fatal for his pack members.

As they approach the heart of the pack's settlement, Keary's heart races. The howls of wolves echo through the night, a haunting chorus that sends shivers down her spine. Flickering torches illuminate the faces of worried pack members as they gather around a long wooden building.

Just as Samson brings the wagon to a halt, the door swings open. Conall offers a hand for Keary to climb down when a young woman with wild curls rushes out to meet them. Her eyes widen at the sight of Keary, smoothing tired lines dotting a freckled forehead.

"Thank the moons," she breathes, latching onto Keary's arm with a surprisingly forceful grip for someone so small. "I haven't been training with our healer long enough to know where to start."

Keary offers a reassuring smile to the young woman. "Don't worry, we'll figure this out together," she says, her voice steady despite the surrounding chaos. "Where are the affected pack members?"

Stepping forward, Samson gestures towards the long cabin on her right. "Amelia here moved everyone, experiencing symptoms in our pack hospital. Including my daughters."

Darkness clouds a pair of remarkable green eyes before Amelia hangs her head. "I've tried everything I can think of. Nothing is working."

"I'm sure you've done everything your healer has taught you. There's no shame in that. Can you take me to them?"

Slipping her hand into Conall's, Keary follows Amelia towards the long cabin. Even with the cool night air filling her lungs, every inhale carries the scent of herbs, sickness and sweat. While dozens of pack members hang around outside of the hospital, inside several members huddle over their loved ones. Forced to squeeze between two giant bodies, she hands her bag to Conall and climbs up on the nearby desk.

"Excuse me." Keary stands quietly until she's certain she has everyone's attention. "I know you're worried. I understand your fear. But having this many people in here at once will only make it more difficult to treat and monitor your loved ones."

"I'm not leaving my pup."

Addressing the voice over her left shoulder, Keary turns slightly, her smile gentle. "I'm not asking you to. All I'm asking is that you limit your vigil to one family member at a time. Is that do-able?"

The older woman bobs her head gently before resuming her seat beside a cot, holding a man barely out of school.

As the extra family members file out the front door, Keary climbs down and begins assessing the sick individuals. It's clear that this illness has taken hold of them rapidly, their bodies wracked with fever and convulsions. She starts by examining Marcus, Samson's son-in-law, who was the first to fall ill.

His body trembles uncontrollably as she places a gentle hand on his forehead. As if her touch brings more pain than comfort, he reacts violently. Back arching, arms flexed, every breath leaving him on a grunt or a savage growl.

Beside her, Conall stands like a stalwart pillar amidst the chaos, his unwavering presence a comforting anchor for her. She steals a glance at him, but his bright amber eyes are now shrouded behind unfathomable shadows.

For a moment, their gazes lock and she notes the weight of the world reflected in his eyes. With a silent nod, he offers her strength and without hesitation, Keary draws it in like a lifeline. Taking a deep breath, she steels herself against the overwhelming task ahead. "I need someone to write the symptoms as I list them."

"I can do it," Amelia announces, turning up with a pen and paper in hand.

As she works, her mind races to locate all the puzzle pieces. Keary recites his elevated fever and severe seizures for Amelia to jot down. When she notices his labored breathing and the agitation of the beast just underneath his skin, a sinking feeling fills her stomach. She glances over her shoulder and sees

Samson standing between Marcus's cot and the two holding his daughter's. "I need to check his pupils," she informs him. "If I'm correct, his Lycan won't be too pleased."

"I've linked Reika's beta. He'll turn on the lights when I give the signal." Samson says as he positions himself at Marcus's shoulders. As soon as the lights flash, Marcus lunges forward, snarling and snapping at Keary's face with his sharp canines.

Emitting a growl of his own, Conall lunges forward and pulls her back, pressing her into his chest as his arms clamp around her waist. When the lights go off again, Marcus falls into another violent seizure that Keary fears will break more than a few bones.

Her heart pounds furiously against her ribcage while Keary tallies the symptoms together. On the cot, Marcus falls victim to the darkness of his inner beast. Thrashing and convulsing with terrifying snaps and snarls. Conall's protective embrace tightens, his solid presence grounding Keary amidst the havoc. With a sense of urgency, Keary calls out to Samson over Marcus's frenzied cries. "We need to sedate him!"

Amelia rushes forward with a well-used silver syringe. "This should calm him down, but be careful," she pleads in a whisper soft voice.

Taking the vial in her trembling hand, Keary steadies herself and approaches Marcus cautiously. Conall stands rigid, ready to jump in if needed. Time stretches against her as she waits for a lull in his violent thrashing before seizing the opportunity to plunge the needle into his arm. Once she depresses the leather plunger, she counts the seconds until the sedative takes effect. When Marcus's movements slow and eventually cease, Keary releases the breath clawing for freedom inside her.

"Do you know what this is?"

Samson's booming voice echoes around her, drowned out by the chaotic buzzing in her mind. The healer in her rejoices at finding the culprit, but a numbness spreads quickly through her body, rendering even the simplest movements impossible. She swallows hard, trying to dislodge the lump in her throat, and raises her face to meet Samson's pinched features. "It's strychnine poisoning," she chokes out, ice coursing through her veins as she realizes the gravity of the situation.

The room falls into a stunned silence as Keary's words hang in the air. Strychnine poisoning. The deadly toxin causes uncontrollable muscle contractions, convulsions, and ultimately, death. Panic surges through the pack members gathered around, their eyes wide.

Samson's voice breaks through the hushed atmosphere, his tone brittle. "But how? How did this happen?"

"It's very rare. It only grows in the warmer climates. My guess is someone either laced your food or tainted your water supply."

The protective mother steps forward, her eyes dancing between Keary and the cot where her son thrashes violently. "Who would do this?"

"I don't know," she admits, her voice barely above a whisper.

With a hand on her shoulder, Conall draws her attention to his lips, set in a grim line. "What do you need us to do?"

"Which ones have been sick for longer than two or three hours?"

"Marcus and Logan, one of my hunters."

"Okay, I have activated charcoal in my bag for everyone else. Mix it up and administer it as gently as you can. We need them to keep it down."

"What about Marcus and Logan?"

Fisting her hands at her sides, Keary forces herself to say the words. "All we can do for them is to keep them comfortable."

Samson's face blanches at Keary's words, his eyes wide with a mixture of horror and disbelief. "You're not serious."

"I'm afraid the poison is too far into their system. All we can do is keep them sedated and cool. We also need to monitor their breathing. We also need cool sheets or towels for the ones running a fever. The ones that can drink should. We need to keep them as hydrated as we can."

As she outlines her plan, Conall's grip on her tightens. His eyes reflect the flickering shadows of despair, but he nods in silent agreement. Keary knows Conall is grappling with his emotions, torn between wanting to protect her from the harsh reality and facing it head-on alongside her. She squeezes his hand reassuringly, silently letting him know they're in this together.

Time blurs as they scramble to execute Keary's plan. Amelia distributes the activated charcoal to those who can still ingest it, while others gather cool sheets and damp towels to ease the feverish bodies. The air in the room becomes heavy with urgency and determination, as if every pack member is willing their loved ones to overcome this dire situation.

CHAPTER 21

Just before sunrise, Marcus's body gives up the fight. In a chair by his side, Keary's heart is heavy as she watches him take his last breath. Taking a seat beside him, she places a trembling hand on his cooling forehead. The weight of loss hangs heavy in the air, suffocating the hearts of those who loved him even as his body finally stills, the ferocious energy that once consumed him gone.

Behind her, Conall wraps his arms around her shoulders, offering solace amidst the sorrow. Samson's expression twists darkly, his hand shaking as he gently runs it through his youngest daughter's damp hair. On a cot beside her, Reika slumbers deeply, thanks to the sedative. Tears prick at Keary's eyes as she considers the fact that Reika unknowingly sleeps through her mate's passing.

Still, amid their sorrow, glimmers of hope emerge. Logan, one of the hunters afflicted, shows signs of improvement. With every passing minute, his convulsions subside, and his breathing stabilizes. Others not as affected as Marcus, settle peacefully without the sedative, their bodies exhausted but healing.

While the original confusion subsides, the underlying threat of the poison lingers. When the first rays of dawn filter through the windows to bathe the room in a golden glow, Keary's feet are dragging. Sweat gathers on her brow as she tends to each patient, her hands steady despite the ache in her muscles. A heavy hand on her shoulder has her staring up into Conall's piercing, amber eyes.

"Everyone is resting. You need to do the same."

"Some of them have me concerned."

"Amelia can keep an eye out." Using a hand at the small of her back, Conall steers her toward an empty chair in a far corner. "You won't be much help if you collapse on your feet."

"If we don't know where the poison came from, all this could be useless."

"Samson left earlier to speak with the Beta. I'll go see if they learned anything."

With a somber nod, Keary all but drops into the chair. "Thank you for helping tonight."

"It's the least I could do." Though tiny lines of exhaustion plague his face, his smile is full and bone-melting. When he bends down to place a kiss on the top of her head, heat floods her cheeks. "Rest."

She couldn't say how long she sat there after Conall left, but Keary couldn't move if she wanted to. The knots in her back scream with every movement, her head still throbs from a night full of stress. She blinks to soothe the burning sensation in her eyes before leaning back in her chair and resting her head against the wall. But just as she closes her eyes, Amelia is shaking her frantically.

"Something's wrong."

Conall's stomach churns as he checks to make sure Keary hasn't left her chair. He'd been speechless most of the night as she worked tirelessly, her movements graceful and urgent moving from cot to cot. Despite the disheveled state of her clothes, the dampness of sweat on her skin and the wild tangles in her hair, Conall can't recall anything more breathtaking. Even with the dark circles underneath, her eyes radiate with an inner light, a testament of her unwavering dedication to saving lives.

Once he's content, she intends to rest, for now, he steps outside.

As he explores the community, Conall notes the strange stillness that has taken over since the commotion of the previous night. Despite the early hour, many members of the pack are already awake and busy with their daily tasks. Some men chop wood while others gather fresh produce from a well-tended garden. Even the children take part in their own small ways, moving about with care and purpose.

It's as if everyone holds their breath, waiting for something to happen. While he wouldn't call the occasional glance in his direction hostile, Conall couldn't call them friendly either.

He runs his rough, calloused hand through his hair in a quick motion, the tousled blonde locks falling back into place. Stretching his shoulders as he walks, releases the remaining tension and discomfort. As he looks up, he notices a tall figure with a thick, dark beard and briefly extends his hand. "Excuse me. Any idea where I can find Samson?"

His piercing gaze, a mesmerizing blend of golden hues and varying shades of brown, studies him shrewdly. After a moment, he jerks his thumb towards the towering building behind him. "You'll find what you're looking for up at the pack house," he grumbles in a deep, gravelly voice that echoes through the air like thunder. Even as he moves on, his tone holds a hint of warning, as if the pack house is not a place meant for outsiders like him.

"Thanks."

Ignoring the now curious glances, Conall strides down the worn path, his steps heavy with purpose. The events of last night leave a lingering unease in the air that fills him with a sense of urgency to wrap this up. I need to get Keary home.

Like a majestic stronghold from a fairy tale, the Lycan's packhouse looms over the lands against a backdrop of vibrant, green forests. Tall windows that eagerly welcome the sunlight adorn the three-story building constructed out of dark wood and sturdy stone. Flags bearing the intricate emblem of the pack dance joyfully in the wind, swaying innocently to their own rhythm. As the sun rises higher, the rays highlight exquisite carvings and engravings decorating the massive front door. The place boasts of a rich history and power.

When he steps inside, his eyes sweep over the open floor plan, taking in the warm glow of the fire crackling in the mammoth stone fireplace. The sweet scent of pine and cedar fills his nose, mingling with a hint of wood-smoke to add a coziness to the atmosphere. Without a soul in sight to guide him, he follows the sound of raised voices towards the heart of the building.

Worn wooden floors creak and groan underfoot as he bypasses the large kitchen complete with scents of spices and cooking. Dipping down the long, dimly lit hallway, he absently scans the family photographs and dented picture frames lining the walls. As he draws closer, the muffled voices grow louder, filling the space with an intense energy that prickles at his skin.

"... need to retaliate."

"Without ... it'd be a war."

Conall's hand glides over the cool, polished surface of a tall wolf statue before he pauses outside the only closed door. With a thud of his knuckles, he raps twice before the door immediately swings open to reveal a young man with mussed, dark hair and intense yellow-gold eyes. The subtle scent of lemon and musk emanates from the man's tall frame. Sunlight behind him stresses his sharp features as he stands with a cool confidence, a guardian protecting what lays beyond the door.

"Can I help you?"

"I'm looking for Samson."

"Let him in Bodie," Samson's gruff voice sounds from inside. While the man is quick to comply, Conall catches his pinched expression and the furrow between his brows.

Stepping into the room, he takes the few steps needed to bring him to the large wooden desk Samson sits behind. After sparing a glance at the papers scattering the top of the desk, he meets Samson's tired gaze. "What do we know?"

"Who are you?"

Quietly, Conall assesses the man on his left, making note of his tense posture and his folded arms. Unwilling to show the crack in his calm façade, Conall couldn't help but tighten his own stance slightly. His sharp gaze catalogues the man's unbalanced stance, noting the weakness of his right knee for later, should the need arise. "Conall O'Corr," he announces clearly. "I came with Keary." He extends his hand to the mountain of a man, his voice lightening in tone. "And you are?"

The man seems to study the hand he offers for longer than required before finally accepting the handshake. "Grant. I'm Reika's Beta." Pointing to the man just over Conall's shoulder, he continues. "That's Bodie, Reika's Gamma."

Samson's eyes widen slightly, his mouth opening and closing. "O'Corr? Have we met before last night?"

"I doubt it."

"Are you sure?" Leaning forward in his chair, Samson rests his arms against the top of the desk, oblivious to the groan the wood emits. "You look familiar."

"Pretty sure." His eyes dance over the men gathered for a half second before asking his question again. "Have you learned anything?"

"Why do you want to know?"

"Look, I'm not trying to step on anyone's toes here, Bodie. Keary is completely drained. If we have neutralized the danger, I'd like to take her home."

"I understand," Samson says, his voice heavy. "I've spoken with some of the other packs. It seems we're not the only ones dealing with this poison."

Bodie narrows his eyes at Conall before turning back to Samson. "We shouldn't be discussing this with an outsider. Let alone a natural."

"Keary trusts him. And in case you've forgotten, we're in her debt at the moment." Samson counters firmly before addressing him again. "One pack lost its Beta and another its Luna."

"We tracked down the source of the strychnine poisoning, here at least," Grant snarls, his meaty hands curling into impressive fists. "I told you those hunting parties weren't a good idea."

"Wait, hunting parties?"

The three men lock eyes, each one bristling with tension before Conall spots the same look Keary had when she mind-linked him. After a silent exchange, Samson offers a weary nod. "The elders require some of our older pack members to team up with natural born hunters," he spits through clenched teeth. "They're desperate to increase our catches before winter comes."

"Tainted meat makes that task damn near impossible." Lowering himself into the nearest chair, Bodie takes a deep breath, pinching the bridge of his nose between his thumb and middle finger.

"Someone tainted the meat?"

"That's the only common factor," Grant cuts in. "If it was the water, more people would be sick."

Conall takes a moment to digest this information, his mind racing with the implications. If you can link the strychnine poisoning to the hunting parties, it can't be a mere coincidence. "You think someone did this deliberately?"

Bodie leans forward, his voice low and steely. "We questioned everyone thoroughly. No one saw anything suspicious before they gave us our share of the meat."

"You think the natural-born hunters are capable of this?"

Samson's gaze flickers to Grant before he answers, "That's hard to say."

Grant scoffs. "They're capable."

"Do you have any proof that this poisoning occurred during the hunting parties?" Conall presses further.

Samson shakes his head lazily. "No concrete evidence yet."

"Well, you have a lot on your plate. I'm going to take Keary home. Let me know if you need any more help." Conall gives the three men a quick nod just as Samson rushes to his feet. The blood drains from his face, the hands he places atop the desk trembling.

"Something's wrong with Reika."

Conall's heart seizes. Keary. Without hesitation, he shoves himself towards the door. Grant and Bodie exchanging anxious glances before they both follow Conall. Heavy footsteps thunder through the dimly lit hallway as they sprint out of the pack house and back towards the hospital. While the pack members understandably worry about their soon-to-be

Alpha, Conall's concern rests on the healer he'd left unsupervised. A cold weight settles in his stomach as he runs.

As they reach the hospital, Samson bursts through the door first, his eyes widening at the sight that greets him. Stepping around his enormous frame, Conall takes in the sight of Reika lying on her cot, her slight frame wracked with convulsions. However, it's Keary beside her that makes his blood run cold.

"Reika took a turn for the worse," Amelia cries, her voice thick with unshed tears. "Keary is drawing the poison from her and into herself!"

"What?!"

Surging past Samson's frozen stance, Conall shoots forward. Mindless of the cost to herself, Keary has a hand across Reika's brow, siphoning the poison into her own body. Sweat drips freely from her forehead, her face tight as she continues to draw more and more from her patient. When he raises a hand to stop her, someone jerks him backward.

A low, guttural snarl escapes from his lips as he rounds on Grant, his body tense and ready for a fight. He takes a step forward, forcing the man back, raising his hands. "If you touch her, you'll end up poisoning yourself. You have to wait."

"It will kill her!" Conall's eyes narrow as he studies Grant, weighing the risk against the potential consequences. The room fills with a tense silence, broken only by the sound of Keary's labored breathing. Wild, his eyes dart between Keary and the others gathering around the small cot. "We can't just stand here," he pleads.

"There's nothing any of us can do."

As Conall weighs the options, the pressure between his ears builds. The tiny voice in his head concedes Grant is right. That realization, however, does nothing to stop the bile filling his mouth. Out of options, Conall settles on the drastic. Stepping around Grant, he speaks with a hard edge in his voice. "I'll share the load."

Grant's eyes widen, stepping forward to intervene before Samson lays a firm hand on his shoulder. After sparing Samson a quick nod, Conall focuses on Keary.

Despite her needing to gasp for air, she never removes her hands from the pack's Alpha. Her pale face, strained features and the sweat glistening on her forehead no match for her stubborn determination.

Taking a breath, Conall steels himself for what's coming. The moment his hand settles gently over Keary's smaller one, her eyes shoot open. Lips part before a surge of energy closes them again. The air is thick as it crackles with intensity as Conall and Keary drain the toxins from Reika, absorbing it with their own bodies.

A fiery inferno rages through his veins, searing every nerve and tissue. Conall grits his teeth as each wave of agony crashes over him like a tsunami, threatening to consume him whole. Locking his limbs, he remains resolute, grinding his teeth against the searing poison that ravages through every fiber of his being. The only sounds he can make out are Reika's weak moans and their own labored breaths, as they fight against a torrent of pain.

Time becomes a blur, seconds stretching into eternity as Conall's strength drains with each passing moment. He can feel himself slipping towards a deep, all-consuming darkness when someone jerks him away. Pushing away the arms that restrain him, Conall leaps forward to catch Keary when her knees buckle. Cradling her close to his chest, he supports her weight as he sinks to his knees on the cold, unforgiving floor.

Conall's heart races as he embraces Keary tightly, the weight of exhaustion circulating throughout his body. In his arms, Keary is damp with sweat. Her forehead glistening as she struggles to catch her breath. Wordless, he uses his thumb to stroke her pale cheek, silently promising to stand by her side and face whatever challenges come their way together.

Kneeling beside them, Amelia swipes at the tears rolling down her cheeks. "I never should've let her do this," she whispers, her voice unsteady.

His chuckle turns into a guttural cough that rattles within his chest. "No one lets Keary do anything," he gasps. He can sense the faint pulse of Keary's heartbeat through his fingertips, but it's weak and erratic, like a fading drumbeat signaling the end.

"Is she going to be alright?" Samson asks as he and Grant hover nearby, their expressions a mix of concern and awe. The weight of their gazes only adds to the pressure building within his head. He knows the risks he took by sharing the burden with Keary, but in that moment, it was the only choice he could make.

"I don't know," inhaling, he gives himself a moment to steady the tremor in his voice. "She needs rest."

"I'm sure we can spare a room for you both to recover in," Bodie offers, scrubbing a hand across the back of his neck. "Especially after what you did for our Alpha."

Brushing hair away from Keary's face, Conall gives his head a gentle shake. "I think she'd like to be in her own bed."

"You'll let us know if you need anything?" Samson holds his gaze, forcing Conall to nod. "You both have permission to link me anytime. I'll have Grant see you both home." When he holds his arms outward, Conall can only arch a brow in his direction. "I can carry her out to the wagon for you."

Arms tighten involuntarily around her sleeping form. "That's not necessary. Just a hand up will suffice." Accepting Grant's offer, Conall pins her tightly to his chest as he surges to his feet. After spending a moment adjusting her weight against him, he carries her out to an empty wagon. "Does anyone have a link with her sister?"

Silence hangs heavy in the air until Samson's powerful, commanding voice rings out, demanding an answer. The sound of it echoes around the room, booming like thunder, leaving no doubt of his authority. "Who among us is capable of linking Erin McKenna?" The weight of everyone's gaze falls upon the potential candidates, their eyes searching for any signs of hesitation or uncertainty.

Bodie's sheepish smile and the way he scratches at his head betray his nerves as he speaks up. "I can."

Samson's steps falter at Bodie's words. "Let her know what's happened and that she needs to come home."

"You want me to tell her everything?" Bodie's expression shifts from nervousness to concern.

"What's the problem?"

Bodie winces. "I'm just wondering how she'll react to know we did nothing to stop her sister from almost killing herself."

Conall gently hands off a drowsy Keary to Grant long enough to climb into the wagon before settling her in his lap once more. He takes a moment to run his fingers through her hair, soothingly. Then, he meets Bodie's gaze. "Tell her everything," he says firmly.

CHAPTER 22

Bright rays of afternoon sun spill through Keary's bedroom windows where she slumbers intermittently. In a chair beside her bed, Conall counts the tiny purple flowers stitched into her quilt. Anything to distract him from the furious pounding in his head.

They were only halfway home when Grant told him Bodie had reached Erin. All Bodie relayed was that she'd be on the next train home. Initially, Conall absently wondered what a train is before occupying himself with Keary's comfort during the trip. The tension didn't leave his shoulders until he'd tucked her into her own bed.

Even now, she tosses restlessly, all color absent from her face. Sweat continues to bead against her skin, evidence of the raging fever heating her body. When she jolts awake, Conall winces at the sight of her dull and unfocused eyes. Once bright with life, he fears the infection is sapping away her spirit. Every breath is a struggle as she croaks a gust of air past dry lips.

Snaking an arm under her shoulders, he nearly recoils away from the scorching heat radiating from her body. Gritting his teeth, Conall props her up with one arm while offering cool water with the other. After several careful sips, he lays her gently against the mound of pillows beneath her. Despite the fever and her sickly appearance, one could mistake her for simply being exhausted.

Propping his chin up with one hand, he considers what he might have done differently. Reluctantly, he replays the events in his mind, searching for missed opportunities or signs that could've prevented her from taking such a risk. The truth, he realizes quickly, is that she's fiercely independent and driven. It's part of her nature to push boundaries even if they come at a great personal cost.

Still, he swore to protect Keary, keep her safe. The end result of his effort is plain in the way she lays limply against her pillows, her body struggling to function as the poison rampages inside. Shackles of helplessness tighten around Conall, squeezing until drawing breath is a chore.

In his natural life, he's faced countless battles, triumphed over unimaginable odds, this is different. As he faces the chance he'll lose Keary, her vibrant spirit snuffed out, it fills him with a ravenous ache that threatens to consume him.

The loud bang of the front door hitting a wall snaps him from his thoughts a second before he springs up from his chair.

Conall's heart races as he bolts from the room and down the stairs, his eyes scanning the first floor for the source of the commotion. The sight of the young woman just inside the entryway nearly causes him to miss a step. He can't tear his eyes away from her, mesmerized by the stark contrast of her petite form against the raging storm of coiled muscles and sharp angles. Every movement she makes is like a bolt of lightning cutting through the air.

She gathered her soft red curls into a messy knot at the top of her head, giving him an unobstructed view of her face. The bright flush of her complexion almost conceals the delicate sprinkling of freckles across the tops of her cheeks and the bridge of her nose, adding to the illusion of strength and power radiating from her. But it's her steely gray eyes that hold his attention, burning with a familiar fire despite their bloodshot whites and swollen lids. What he sees in her face is not softness, it's a fierce determination that reminds him so much of Keary, for a moment, Conall can't breathe past the pressure in his chest.

Absently, Conall notes her lips are moving but the words seem to be lost in the space between them. Swallowing, he inclines his head gently. "Say that again?"

Though her fists may appear small and insignificant, they clench tightly at her sides, ready for whatever battle lies ahead. She is a warrior through and through, unyielding and unbreakable. Her bag hits the ground with a thud as she fixes her gaze on him, frozen in place on the stairs as she crosses the living room. Conall's first instinct is to wince. Not from the danger the tiny pixie-like girl poses to him, but from the fierce and frenzied expression twisting her delicate features. Her fury and fear radiate off of her in waves, making Conall's heart race. "You're Conall? Yes?"

"Correct. And you are?" Conall demands, his voice low and threatening as he steps in front of her, effectively blocking her path with his imposing frame.

A humorless smile tugs at the corners of her lips, but her delicate jawline pulses with tension. Her eyes darken with a predatory glint before flickering with a raw energy that seems to fuel every movement she makes. "I'm Erin," she spits out through clenched teeth, her brow raising defiantly as if daring him to stop her.

Without hesitation, Conall twists to the side and allows her to lead the way with a sharp motion of his hand. "Thought as much."

As they enter Keary's room, a heavy, pungent stench hangs in the air, a mixture of sweat and sickness that makes Conall's heart twist. In a bundle of sheets and blankets, Keary rests in an agitated mess. Her once vibrant body now pale and weak, ravaged by the poison. Each ragged breath she releases is barely audible in the quiet room, her lips cracked and bleeding from dehydration.

Conall leaves Erin at the door as he steps around the bed to dip a cloth into cool, clean water and carefully drips several drops of water into her dry mouth. His eyes snag on the strands of hair as dark as the night sky, cling to her damp forehead and scatter across the pillow beside her. Knots and tangles from her restless tossing and turning ruin the once smooth texture.

"How did this happen?"

Lifting his eyes, Conall sees Erin hovering just inside the door. At the sight of her sister's condition, her warrior stance deflates, leaving a small child in its' wake. Taking two small steps into the room, Erin lays a gentle hand against one of Keary's feet.

"Bodie didn't tell you?"

"All he said was that the pack had fallen sick and their Alpha nearly died. Since he was telling me to come home quickly, I assumed Keary had used her gift to save her." Tearing her eyes away from her sister, she levels a broken expression on Conall. "I never expected this."

"The pack's meat was tainted with strychnine. Keary and their junior healer worked through the night to save as many as they could. At some point their alpha took a turn for the worst. Your sister refused to give up."

"Why did you let her do this?" she demands, her voice barely under control. Her words sting with the venom of a snake as it's something he berates himself for over and over again.

Taking a deep breath, Conall gives her the only answer he'd found during his quiet musings. "I didn't *let* her do anything. You know your sister better than I. Do you think I could've stopped her?" For several minutes the room falls quiet aside from Keary's shallow breaths. Standing over the bed, Conall's body tenses until he's certain more than a few muscles are stretched to their limits.

"No," Erin breathes softly, her voice heavy. She reaches out and takes Keary's hand in her own, her grip tight as if trying to transfer strength and healing through touch alone. "She's always been stubborn like that."

Conall's shoulders relax slightly at her acknowledgment, but the weight still hangs heavily upon him. He watches as Erin tentatively reaches out and brushes a strand of damp hair away from Keary's face, the tenderness in her touch a stark contrast to the anger and determination that radiated from her moments before.

"I just... I can't bear losing her," she admits, her voice barely above a whisper.

Conall moves closer, standing beside Erin, their shoulders almost touching. He places a comforting hand on her back, offering silent support. "You won't."

"I knew she was strong-willed, but I never thought she would go this far,"

"Keary has an incredible spirit. It's what drew me to her in the first place."

Erin looks up at him, her gray eyes now tinged with sadness. "You love my sister, don't you?"

The question catches Conall off guard. He hesitates for a moment, his gaze shifting to Keary's fragile form lying on the bed before returning to Erin's searching eyes. The room feels heavy with anticipation as he searches for the right words.

Love is a word he's never been comfortable using, never truly believed in until Keary came into his life. But now, as he stands beside her fragile sister, witnessing the fierce determination etched on Erin's face and feeling the raw ache in his own heart, he realizes it's more complicated than he wanted to believe. "I don't know," he finally admits, his voice stretched thin.

Erin's expression softens, the fire in her eyes replaced with a glimmer of understanding. She squeezes Keary's hand gently before turning to face Conall fully. "Then we're in this together," she says, her words clear and resolute. "We'll fight for her."

Together, they spend hours at Keary's bedside, tending to her every need. They take turns soothing her fevered brow, feeding her small sips of water, and whispering words of love and encouragement into her ear. The poison continues to ravage Keary's body, testing their resolve with each passing hour. Days blur into nights as they refuse to call a retreat.

It isn't until the third day when Keary finally opens her eyes, the pale green depths clear of the fevered haze. Conall smiles, an unspoken surge of relief building between him and Erin. He steps forward and takes Keary's hand, lightly brushing her cheek with his thumb. "Welcome back."

"Am I..." Keary struggles to speak, her voice little more than a whisper.

Without missing a beat, Erin replies, "Alive? At least until you're well enough that I can kill you." Despite the small smile she offers her sister, Erin's voice is shaky.

Pressing a hand to her forehead, Conall's shoulders deflate to find her skin cool. "You're fever broke. Get some sleep. We'll be here."

When Keary slowly rouses from her slumber, she's unsure how much time had passed. The lingering pain in her bones suggests it'd been quite some time. Every inch of her skin throbs, as if it had been stretched and pulled beyond its limits. Turning her head gingerly, she squints to bring the figure next to her into focus. Conall.

Hunched in a contorted position, his chest rises and falls with each breath. The lines on his face tell a story of worry and exhaustion, etched deep into the chiseled features that once exuded strength and confidence. His hand gently holds hers, providing a sense of warmth and comfort despite the pain she feels. As she looks at him, she finds the effect the weight of their struggle has on his body. How many hours has he been sitting there, holding her hand? Whatever the answer, a sense of safety and comfort attempts to smother the deep-seated ache in her body.

Turning her head once more, her eyes fall on Erin curled up in a chair her body tucked over her knees with a tightness that speaks of immense strain. Several wild curls escape the bun she restrained them with to fall against the soft swell of her cheek. Even in sleep, Keary notices the tension in her sisters shoulders as if she were carrying the weight of the world on them. The faint light filtering through the window casts a warm glow on Erin's face, illuminating the worry etched in her forehead. Keary's heart wrenches as she catalogs the pain and concern staining her sister's face. When did she get home?

With a trembling hand, Keary reaches out and brushes hair away from Erin's face. The familiar touch of her sister's silky curls sends a wave of emotions through her, overwhelming and almost painful in its intensity. The two of them had always been close, but she's never experienced such a fierce protectiveness rolling off her sister, as if their bond had suddenly been forged into something unbreakable, crafted from blood and fire.

When Erin's eyes flicker open, Keary spots the unshed tears first. "I'm going to be okay," she croaks beyond the dryness in her throat.

The sisters pass the next few seconds in silence as Erin appears to fully digest Keary's words. Once she does her expression hardens and the softness disappears from her face. After a heavy exhale, Erin's gaze flits over the open window to the soft sounds of windchimes dancing in the wind. When she turns her attention back to Keary, there is a subtle change in her demeanor. Her jaw tightens slightly, complimenting a blaze of something in her typically soft gray eyes. "You need to eat something."

Keary's heart sinks as Erin abruptly rises from the comfortable armchair and quickly disappears down the hallway. The sound of her feet slapping against the hardwood floors echoes in her ears, a clear indicator of her anger. Each step reverberates through the house, a sharp contrast to the tense silence between them. Lying there, Keary can't shake off the feeling that Erin will have some harsh words for her soon enough.

"You're awake."

Keary tries to ignore her queasy stomach from Erin's strange behavior long enough to give Conall a small smile. "If that's what you want to call it," she mutters, attempting to sit up, Keary winces when her body protests the movement. Towering over her, Conall lifts her easily, sitting her up against the mound of pillows. The moment he retreats, she suppresses the cold shudder skipping over her spine at the absence of his touch. "How long was I out?"

"Five days." Conall's eyes dance from her to the open door. "How do you feel?"

"Like someone dropped a mountain on me," she sighs, her voice still nothing more than a hoarse whisper. "I suppose that's an improvement though."

"Very much so."

"When did Erin get here?"

Conall winces, recovers and scrubs a hand across the back of his neck. "The afternoon you collapsed."

Fiddling with a loose thread on the quilt, Keary's stomach drops. "Who told her?"

"Bodie."

"He shouldn't have done that. It's not safe for her to be here."

"You mean you'd rather I didn't know about your reckless behavior," Erin cuts in, her tone slicing against the rising tension in the air. Balancing a tray of food in her hands, she picks her way across the room carefully.

Skipping over Conall's weak smile, Keary finds a simmering heat waiting for her in her sister's eyes. "Conall, can you excuse us a moment?"

With a wordless nod, he shifts toward the door until Erin stops him with a look. "There'll be time for that later," she clips, laying the tray across Keary's lap. "You need to eat, and I need a shower."

"Erin –" Keary sighs when her sister simply vanishes from the room, shutting the door behind her with a furious thud.

"Just give her time."

Forcing a nod, Keary takes a few bites of the bread and soup. Despite the broth's rich flavor, every swallow is an effort, her stomach already launching a savage rebuttal. After several more spoonful's, she rips off a chunk of bread to munch on. "Has there been any news from the Lycans?"

"Grant and Samson were here yesterday. Everyone appears to be fine. No ill effects from the ordeal."

"And Reika?"

Conall's bright, piercing eyes momentarily darken with shadows, but he quickly blinks them away. "She's fully recovered."

"But?"

"But it was too much for her unborn pup," he adds gently. "Once you're recovered, she's requested your presence at the ceremony for the tiny soul and her mate."

With a grimace, the rough bread scrapes against Keary's tongue until she forces it down her throat. The weight of missed opportunities weighs heavy on her mind as she considers how things might've ended differently. "I was hoping for better news. Maybe if I'd acted sooner –"

"You did everything you could. And possibly something you shouldn't have even tried. No one blames you."

Keary sighs, the tension in the room beginning to choke her. "I'm sorry for what happened. But I thought I was strong enough to overcome it."

"I know. You did what you thought was best at the time. And you came out of it alive."

Keary swallowed hard, trying to match Conall's level gaze. "Do you think Erin will forgive me?"

"That's up to her," he mumbles running a hand through his hair, pulling at his scalp. She can't help but feel responsible for the strain she sees in his eyes. "She was terrified she'd lose you. I'm not so sure all of her emotions are anger, I'm certain there's relief in there. Just give her time."

The longer Keary sits there, the more she can sense the storm brewing in her sister. It's only a matter of time before the storm breaks, the dam bursts, releasing Erin's pent-up emotions. She tries telling herself to be patient. Allow her sister to say her piece, but the gravity of the situation isn't lost on her.

When Erin finally re-emerges in the doorway, her eyes are red and swollen from the tears she let fall. Standing rigid less than five feet away, Keary picks up on the faint traces of her anger, along with something bitter. Without a word, Conall gives her hand a quick squeeze and slips from the room.

"Erin, I," she begins only to have her sister quietly raise a hand.

"First. You listen."

"Okay."

"When mom and dad died, you and Gran were all I had left. Then Gran died." Wrapping her arms around her middle,

Erin begins pacing back and forth at the foot of the bed. "You're all I have left, Kear."

"I know."

"Maybe it's selfish, but I'm not willing to trade you for anyone. No matter how noble the cause." Other than a slight tremble in her voice, Erin continues calmly.

"I never meant–"

"If I had done what you did, you'd have put me in lockdown. You wouldn't trust me out of your sight until you were old and gray and lost your sight. It's like you have no regard for your own life."

Keary bristles. Although promising herself just a few moments prior that she'd allow Erin to say her piece, heat begins to build in her stomach. "I didn't ask for this gift."

"None of us did."

"But you expect me not to use mine?"

Her question snaps Erin to attention, her back ramrod straight and her shoulders pulled back in a display of rigid control. The twitching in her left eye betrays her façade of calm, giving Keary a glimpse at the raging turmoil within. "What I expect," she says through gritted teeth, her voice icy and dangerous, "is for you to be damn careful. You know, like you've been drilling into my head for years!"

"I am careful."

"You say that as you literally wake up on your deathbed!" Just like that, the façade shatters as Erin's emotions boil over, her words laced with an intensity that makes Keary's head throb. "How could you be so reckless? Do you even think about the danger you put yourself in? What were you possibly thinking?" Heat radiates off of Erin, her eyes blazing with a fire that could set the whole room ablaze.

Keary's hands shake as she grips the quilt tightly, her nails digging into the fabric. "I was thinking about helping some-one!"

"And that's worth dying for?"

"Helping someone? Yes," she snaps.

"But what about me? What about my life?"

"This isn't about you, Erin!" The pain in Keary's head throbs and she struggles to find a measure of calm.

"You act invincible, but you're not! You're just one careless mistake away from death!" Erin grabs a letter opener off the dresser and thrusts it towards Keary with a snarl. "If you won't listen to reason, then kill me now and spare us both the misery!"

The air crackles with tension as their eyes lock in a battle of wills. Keary's muscles seize and tremble as her gaze falls upon the sharp, glinting silver blade lying innocently on the tray beside her. "You can't be serious," she mumbles, but the intense look in Erin's eyes confirms that this is no joke. Cold dread climbs up her spine once she realizes that her sister is willing to sacrifice her own life just to not be left alone by a risk she may take in the future. A wave of nausea crashes over her at the mere thought of her sister's life hanging in the balance. "I could never," Keary pleads, her voice thin and broken. As she pushes aside the blankets and clambers out from under the tray, her legs threaten to buckle beneath her, but she clings to a nearby bedpost for support. "You are everything to me, Imp."

"Then stop making such reckless choices with your own life."

"You're asking me to let someone die...knowing I could save them."

Erin shrugs indifferently, but her eyes shine with unshed tears as they scan the floor before locking onto Keary with a chilling gun-metal steel glare. "That's exactly what I'm asking, and I don't give a damn," she spits out, her desperation morphing into a ruthless determination. "If you won't put your own life above others', then at least value mine. Because I can't survive without you."

"Yes, you can. You're stronger than I am."

"Maybe. But it'll change me, Keary. Forever. So, I want you to promise, swear to me you'll never do this to me again."

Her heart pounds in her chest as the weight of Erin's request bears down on her like a mountain. "You know what you're asking of me, "she hisses.

"I know as an empath, your word is your bond."

"You can't ask me to do this."

"I just did. If you can't give it then I have to protect myself," Erin responds coolly, her eyes hardening with resolve. "Even if it means cutting ties with you in order to learn how to live a life without you."

"You mean, you'd leave? Never come back?" Erin's curt nod has Keary increasing her grip on the bedpost until it feels like it might snap. Closing her eyes against the lightheaded sensation, she discreetly sniffs the air. "You're not trying to persuade me?"

Erin bounces one shoulder absently. "It doesn't work on you. Besides, this needs to be your choice to make."

"Fine," Keary finally concedes, "but with conditions."

"Okay?"

"Children, animals, friends and family are an exception," she insists.

Erin hesitates for a moment before nodding in agreement. All tension melts from her body as if she had just been holding her breath the entire time. "Now let's get you cleaned up," she says lightly, trying to diffuse the heavy atmosphere. "You smell like shit."

CHAPTER 23

Once the sun begins its descent towards the horizon, casting a shimmering reflection over the serene lake, the rumbling of a wagon alerts Keary to Samson's arrival. Tucking her sweater tighter against her body, she rounds the back corner of her house just as he brings it to a stop with a loud creek.

Leaping over the side, he pulls her in for a hug designed to squeeze the air from her lungs. His breath tousles her hair, his voice hardly perceptible to her inadequate human hearing. "Thank you for everything you've done."

For a moment, Keary wordlessly stands there, enveloped in his embrace. Closing her eyes, she pulls in the scent of fresh dirt and pine trees clinging to his clothes. A small smile tugs at the corner of her lips as she returns the gesture by slipping her arms affectionately around his waist, unintentionally pressing her cheek to the hard wall of his chest. While the ordeal with his pack had been harrowing at the time, and almost fatal for Keary, she established a deep connection with the former Alpha.

Pulling back a little, he looks her over with a hint of relief visible in his eyes. "It's good to see you upright, Scamp." The warmth she detects in his voice forces her heart to swell.

"How is everyone?" she asks, her voice wavering.

"Most are unaffected. Initially, some children took longer to bounce back, but now everyone is doing well."

"And Reika?"

Deep, weathered lines etch themselves across the man's forehead, a roadmap of worry and experience. A shadowy heaviness, evidence of the toll this ordeal has taken on him, dulls his bright eyes. "As well as can be expected. She has her good days and bad days. I'm certain that she'll overcome this. She's one of the strongest women I've ever known."

Keary lets out a gentle chuckle, her warm breath mingling with the cool breeze. "Only one of?"

"Until I saw what you'll sacrifice for not just my Alpha, but my pup, I would have said the strongest." He pauses, his words heavy with emotion. "I can no longer say that and truly mean it."

Ducking her head, Keary tries to hide the light blush spreading across her cheeks as Conall and Erin join them outside carrying an armload of medical supplies.

"Just set these in the back?"

Samson nods, releasing Keary from their embrace to greet Conall with a firm handshake and a nod before tipping a wink in Erin's direction. "Miss Erin, always a pleasure to see you again."

A rosy hue spreads rapidly across Erin's cheeks before she can hide it from Keary's shrewd gaze. A garbled murmur eludes her lips as she climbs into the back of the wagon, drawing a hearty chuckle from Samson.

Pausing with her calloused hand resting on the side of the wagon, Keary exchanges a glance with Conall. "Did I miss something?"

Conall's grin is swift as he extends a hand to help her up onto the wagon's seat. "While you were unconscious during your sister's outburst, she threatened to skin Samson and peddle his fur to a pleasure house if he ever let you do something like that again." Once she's settled next to Samson on the wooden bench seat, he hovers for less than a full heartbeat before stepping away.

Erin's eyes narrow at the retelling, but her lips curl into a soft smirk. "Might be more ass than he's ever gotten in his life," she grumbles before pulling the hood of her cloak up to hide her hair and most of her face.

"Erin," Keary hisses, turning sideways in her seat as Conall rocks the wagon sideways, climbing in the back with her sister. Instead of a look of shame, Erin meets her chastisement with a hard glint in her eye.

"She's fine, Keary." Samson chuckles before nudging the horses forward. "Besides, I can't say she's mistaken."

Keary nods after making a mental note to have a conversation with Erin later before settling in for the ride out to pack-lands.

While the wagon jolts violently over the uneven roads, Keary's unable to shake the tension from her fight with Erin lingering like a poisonous fog, suffocating her with its bitter words and sharp barbs. Her sister's rigid determination cuts deep, a constant reminder of all the pain and loss they've endured together.

As the landscape blurs into a hazy mess of green and gold, she can feel the weight of their shared past bearing down on her. When the sun sinks lower, she can't help but admire the transformed canvas of fiery pink and blood orange hues.

"Thank you for agreeing to this," Samson says, his deep voice pulling Keary from her wandering thoughts. The gentle breeze ruffles his hair, adding a touch of wildness to his otherwise composed appearance.

"I'm still not sure it's a good idea." Keary fidgets with a loose piece of yarn, her fingers tracing the intricate pattern of the delicate material. "I would think this type of ceremony is closed to outsiders."

"You're no longer an outsider," he reminds her with a warm smile. "You've become an integral part of our community, and Reika holds you in high regard."

Even though I couldn't save her mate or her pup, Keary's mind argues, the thought vibrating against the shell of her skull. Whatever argument she can offer has to be set aside, however, as they roll into the center of Samson's small village.

Once the wagon comes to a stop, Conall is there to assist her down from the wagon, hovering for an extra moment as Keary settles on still shaky legs. Around them, the crowd parts, allowing them access to a clearing. As they approach the gathering, Keary could see people had already started to gather around a large, circular structure.

Intricate designs of wolves and trees decorate the smooth, stone surface, while flowers and fresh herbs line a path against the tall grass. The golden glow of the setting sun behind them creates an ethereal touch to the atmosphere.

Flickering torches cast shadows on the reverent faces filling the open space. The sweet scent of incense mixes with the forest's earthy aroma to brush a soothing hand across Keary's nerves as Samson leads them deeper into the crowd. The closer they get to the center, the stronger the bitterness and loss Keary picks up from those attending. As she licks her lips to moisten them in the dry, cool air, the saltiness of her sweat clings to her tongue.

After they finally come to a stop, her eyes land on Reika less than three feet away. Though her eyes are red and puffy, it's hard to mistake the slow-burning fire blazing to life in their startling green depths. After offering Keary a tiny smile, she gestures for the men beside her to begin.

As one man steps forward, Keary directs her attention to the ground beneath her bare feet. The damp earth and the cool caress of grass against her skin. After a long moment, a gentle breeze fills the clearing, carrying with it the essence of the forest just beyond.

Every swallow scrapes her throat like a fresh cut as Bodie and Grant shovel dirt onto Marcus's grave. Unwillingly, her gaze falls to the tiny headstone beside his, the weight of it crushing her heart. Gasping for air from the reality of Reika's loss, Keary turns to escape into the crowd when Conall's hand clamps down on hers. Unforgiving and grounding, his touch is a lifeline to anchor her amidst the storm of her emotions.

Despite the deafening buzz in her head, Keary allows herself to cling to the shelter Conall provides. *Just this once,* her brain warns. While everything else around her blurs significantly, it isn't long before the dull throb in her head returns.

Ritual complete, a heavy silence falls over the clearing. One by one, the mournful wolf cries accompany the cacophony of suddenly howling winds to crescendo into a symphony of grief. Frozen, Keary's skin breaks out in goosebumps as the gravity of the moment takes hold. Even the surrounding woods seem to hush in reverence for the lost Lycan warrior, their branches bowing with respect for a fallen packmate.

Clearing his throat with a cough, Samson steps forward to address the crowd. "We've said our goodbye's. Now we celebrate his life, and the life my grandson could've had!"

Immediately, the crowd erupts in cheers. The sound of their voices echoes through the clearing to bring a flutter to her heart, reminding Keary that even in the darkest of times, light can still be found.

One by one, the group moves toward the back of the pack-house and the mouth-watering scent of food. Rounding the corner of the house, Keary's feet still, her toes curling into the lush grass as she drinks in the sight before her.

Nestled snugly amongst a few enormous trees, stand dozens of wooden tables heavy with food and drink. Vibrant flowers and candles in various shapes and sizes adorn every flat surface. The aroma of grilled meats, roasted vegetables and savory herbs tease her senses, eliciting a rumbling growl from her stomach. People gather quickly, the air buzzing with dozens of quiet conversations held at once.

Chairs and benches sport soft blankets and pillows inviting her to sink into the warmth and comfort. The once again gentle breeze carries a cool touch to brush against skin, while the damp earth underfoot grounds and connects Keary to nature. The candles flicker like fireflies, casting a warm and comforting glow over the gathering, as if the night itself offers its condolences through gentle illumination.

Stepping around the row of tables, she's steering Conall and Erin to a table near the back when Samson's hand on her shoulder quickly squashes that idea. "Tonight, you three will join Reika."

Conall's quick acceptance smothers Keary's hope for a polite refusal, though he appears oblivious to the glare she stabs in his direction. Gritting her teeth, she clamps her lips tight and forces her legs to move in the opposite direction toward the front, center table.

Spotting Bodie's warm presence on Reika's left, Erin excuses herself to take a seat between him and Reika's younger sister Sonja. Tipping his head in Grant's direction seated on Reika's right, Conall pulls out a chair for himself and Keary beside him. As she sinks carefully into her seat, Keary shoots Conall a scowl he's sure to notice. His lips twitch in response, clearly enjoying her discomfort as he leans back into his chair.

"Can I have your attention?" Yet again, as if gifted with telepathy, Samson sidetracks her murderous thoughts as he stands just in front of Reika's table. "Marcus was more than just a packmate. He was a son, a brother, husband and protector. Let us raise a toast in his honor!" Moving as one entity, the pack lifts their glasses, toasting to Marcus's memory. While they drink deeply, several eyes drift to Reika, who remains steadfast despite the pain etching across her face.

Soon, the clinking of dishes and the low murmur of conversations from nearby tables provides soothing background noise. While the two moons cast a melancholic glow on the pack below, they huddle together with heavy hearts. Yet, somehow, they carry on. Sharing memories and laughter about Marcus throughout the meal. Alive with a mix of emotions, time passes slowly, weaving a tapestry of grief, joy and hope.

Still, with each passing hour, Keary slowly opens up to the community of Lycans. With a pair of fresh eyes, she realizes they're not just fierce warriors fighting for their pack; they also know how to celebrate life and honor their connections with each other. Every shared story fits like a piece of a puzzle, coming together to create a vivid picture of Marcus and the impact he had on those around him. With each one, Keary laughs and cries with them in an unexpected sense of camaraderie with kind-hearted and resilient people.

So engrossed in the moment, Keary doesn't notice Grant's close proximity until his voice floods her ear. "If you're finished with your meal, Reika would like a private word with you and Conall."

Lifting a delicate brow, Keary peeks around Grant's imposing frame to note the warm smile Reika offers. Nodding her agreement, she pushes back from the table. Conall offers her a hand to help her up and she takes it without hesitation, her body zeroing in on the steadiness of his grip. When did I become the girl that requires help standing? Dropping his hand quickly, Keary takes a moment to chastise herself before following Grant and Reika towards the pack-house. As she passes Erin engrossed in a conversation with Sonja and Bodie, she stills. Judging by Erin's tinkling laughter, the conversation is an easy one, perhaps too easy?

"She'll be fine. Sonja and Bodie will keep an eye on her."

Keary flashes Reika a half-hearted smile, her head tipping to assess the Lycan nearly falling into her sister's lap.

Lean and muscular with broad shoulders and well-defined arms, Bodie watches her sister intently, his yellow-gold eyes sparkling with mischief. Dark hair falls in messy waves against a strong jawline complete with light stubble. He carries a quiet fearlessness privy to someone who's known great pain and came out the other side. Scars still visible but no longer deeply felt. His voice carries a hint of huskiness that only adds to his charm and when he laughs easily at something Erin says, Keary can't help her own hesitant smile.

"It's Bodie that concerns me," she admits gently, earning a nod of understanding from Reika.

"He's a good guy. Your sister would be lucky, but Bodie knows the importance of waiting for his mate." As if to emphasize her words, Reika lays hand on Keary's arm. "I give you my word, Erin will be just fine."

As they follow Reika into the packhouse, Keary studies every framed photograph and trinket. Anything to distract her from the heat of Conall's touch at the small of her back. To her, Reika's home resembles a cherished book. The pages are dog-eared and the spine sports a few cracks, but the story it tells is one of love. Every nook and cranny harbors a memory, every inch of space holds a story. This isn't simply a home, but a sanctuary where the very foundation echoes with the voices of those who have lived and loved within its walls.

When they dip into a long, narrow hall, Conall's touch on her back grows heavier, almost possessive. Grinding her teeth, Keary searches for the reaction she'd had when Jeremy attempted something similar. Digging deep sends a sharp ache through her stomach, taking away her breath. Instead of the bitter insult over him staking his claim, Keary finds a slow burning fire waiting for her. One that's certain to singe and welt if it's ever released.

Reika pauses in front of the only closed door, pulling Keary back from her thoughts as she opens it and gestures for them to enter. A stark contrast from the dark hallway they just left Keary struggles to adjust to the warm glow of several candles as Reika and Grant follow closely behind. As Reika shuts the door behind them, Keary can't help but look over her shoulder, her breaths turning into soft puffs of air. Each creak of the floor and rustle of clothing sends her heart racing, as if the room itself holds secrets waiting to be uncovered.

Large and spacious, the candles flicker brilliantly while moonlight floods the tall windows on her left. Various maps and intricate diagrams of pack territories cover two of the three remaining walls. The desk in the far corner, carved from dark wood carries designs so exquisite, an itch to trace each one crawls into her fingertips. Conall's touch lingers on her back, the warmth of his hand now fanning into a small flame. When she shuffles sideways, she can't miss the sly smirk on his lips as he catches her reaction.

Clenching her hands into tight fists, she quickly steps away, sinking into the thick cushions of the long couch and putting as much distance between them as possible. When he lowers himself onto the cushion beside her, Keary fights with the urge to change her seat. Her face a cool mask of indifference, she instead directs all of her attention to Reika. "You wanted to speak with us?"

"Yes," Reika begins, her voice strong and steady as she perches on the corner of the mammoth desk. "I wanted to thank you for coming tonight to celebrate Marcus. And for what you've done for my pack when I was unable."

"I'm sorry I couldn't do more."

Reika's fingers dig into her lap as she grips the delicate silver bracelet, spinning it frantically around her scarred wrist. As the silver spins, Keary's gaze is drawn to the fresh welts and patches of pink skin each pass creates. Finally, Reika meets her gaze with unshed tears sparkling in her eyes. "That was in the Maker's hands," she chokes out, voice trembling. "Not yours." Minutes pass with a mounting tension filling the room before she speaks again. "My father is the other reason I pulled you both aside."

As if the man trains countless hours to hone his telepathy, Samson chooses this precise moment to waltz into the room with a giant book in his hands. Without a word, he flips through the many pages, his focus razor-sharp until he lands on one he wants. His exhale is heavy in the quiet room as he lays the book down on the coffee table in front of them.

Conall's sharp intake of breath reverberates in the air, drawing Keary's attention to his tightly clenched fists. She considers his white-knuckled grip and the way his nostrils flare as he takes in a deep breath. Silent, his jaw tightens until a small tic emerges in one cheek. Searching for the cause to his sudden distress, Keary turns her gaze to the open book. Taking in the lifelike depiction of Conall and another man standing side by side, her stomach tightens into a bundle of muscle spasms and frenzied nerve endings.

Briefly, she studies the man beside him. A complete stranger stares back at her from the page. Bright, silver-blue eyes and chiseled features soften the jagged scar over his left eyebrow. Jet black hair cascades down his back in wild, untamed waves, coiling around his broad shoulders like a serpent ready to strike. A thick braid runs from just behind one ear to rest over the front of his shoulder, the sole hint of order amidst the chaos. While Conall's smile is warm and inviting, the other man's expression remains stoic with only a minuscule quirk of his lips hinting at any emotion beneath the surface.

The two of them stand in front of a tiny, weathered cottage with the setting sun behind them. The vibrant hues of the setting sun enveloped them in an intimate embrace, revealing the depth of emotion between the two figures and the bond they share. Silently, Keary studies the picture a moment longer before she comes to a startling realization. "Daigh?" she asks, her voice little more than a croak. Conall's jerking nod his only reply.

"I found this in the pack's archives," Samson begins. "Your name was familiar, but I couldn't recall where I'd heard it before."

"H-how? "How did you...?" Swallowing the tremble in his voice, Conall merely gives his head an unsteady toss.

"When you and your brother went missing, my grandfather commissioned this painting." Samson sits down heavily in an armchair across from them and continues in a gentle tone, as if he is afraid of triggering something in Conall. "He used to tell me stories about you both when I was just a pup."

"Your grandfather?" Despite the deadly grace in his tone, Conall's shoulders visibly tense with inner turmoil. Keary takes his hand in hers, subtly drawing away some of his anxiety.

"William Shorden. He believed the war was a tragic loss for both sides and wanted to make sure history wasn't one-sided. He hoped to keep the memory of you and Daigh alive in our pack's history." Samson's revelation eases the tension in Conall's body until he nearly collapses against Keary's slight frame. She tightens her grip on his hand, projecting quiet support. "Your father and my grandfather were friends long before the war. When your father died, my grandfather lost track of you both. Imagine his surprise when you reappeared years later to influence the opposite side in the war."

"I never knew," Conall offers quietly.

"The whereabouts of you and your brother were a mystery to everyone. He searched tirelessly for years, only coming across myths and rumors before finally meeting with Sloan McKenna." Samson reclines in his chair and scrubs a hand across his face. "The story he told certainly set my grandfather back on his heels. On the chance that Sloan spoke true, he began searching for the two trinket boxes."

"Is that why you have called us here tonight?" Keary raises an eyebrow, finding it difficult to contain her need to protect Conall.

"I called you both here tonight with a proposal, approved by my Alpha." Reika, sitting quietly nearby, nods her agreement.

Whether from the anxiety she's pulling from him, or the support she's pouring in, Conall straightens. His grip tightens on her hand. His voice gravelly as he speaks. "What's the proposal?"

"If you agree to help us against those who attack us from the shadows," Samson takes a deep breath, his eyes shifting between Conall and Keary before the rest of his plan falls from his lips like an anchor in a dry dock. "I will give you Daigh's box."

CHAPTER 24

The room's atmosphere is heavy, almost touchable, as if a sharp knife could slice it. No one speaks, as if afraid to disturb the tense silence that settles over him. Internally, Conall's mind races with a thousand thoughts, each one fighting for attention as he struggles to pinpoint one. "Y-you," he croaks, his voice breaking just beyond his throat. Swallowing hard, he tries again. "You h-have my brother's box?" His question hangs in the air, oppressive. Samson nods. "How?"

"When my grandfather learned of your fate, he spent his remaining years trying to track down the infamous trinket boxes." Samson pauses, his eyes a battle of light and shadows. "He could only find one."

Conall takes a shaky breath, his eyes locked on Samson as the weight of his words settles in his chest. He gazes around the room, searching for Reika's eyes, trying to determine whether they are genuine in their offer. The prospect of his brother being within his reach twists his stomach until every breath is a struggle.

Beside him, Keary holds her shoulders rigid. Wordlessly, she grips Conall's hand tighter, as if to offer strength and support. "Why do you need his help?" Keary asks tentatively. "You have your pack, your Alpha."

Samson sighs while Reika takes to pacing the small area behind him. "Life has changed since the war. The lines between gifted and natural are more clearly drawn than ever. It will help to have someone like Conall on our side to navigate those lines."

Reika utters her words in a gentle tone one would use to soothe a wounded animal. "I know you suffered a lot with this betrayal. But my soul cries out for justice for my mate and our unborn pup. I truly believe that with your help, we stand a better chance at achieving it."

"Something like this could take time," Conall spares a glance at his hand, joined with Keary's. The intensity of the emotions spilling out of him could drown a small village. "What happens to Daigh during that time?"

Samson nods, making a promise with his words. "Once you agree to assist us, I'll hand him back to you," he says firmly. "I have faith that my grandfather had good intentions. The inability to bring the two of you together haunted him until the end."

Conall's gaze flickers between the two, their faces full of raw emotion. It's a daunting proposition, one that requires him to give trust. Trusting the gifted goes against the very marrow in his bones.

What about Keary? She's different, he argues internally. Trusting her came slowly, over time spent with her, not out of some deal. Though if he's honest, Conall can see where Samson and Reika are coming from. Can he walk away with his brother's future hanging between them? Is a future possible with this curse?

"Did your grandfather ever uncover a way to break the curse Brigid McKenna purchased from Aoife?" In an instant, Samson's shoulders tense up, his hands curling into fists. The slow, yet definitive shake of his head has the ground falling away.

The weight on his shoulders bears down, crushing the flickering light Conall didn't even know he held close. Brigid's actions have haunted him for far too long, trapping the brothers in a cycle of eternal life and loneliness. It'd be easy to surrender to the shadows nipping at his heels. But when he catches a glimpse of Keary, her gaze radiating unwavering support, surrender isn't an option.

Straightening his spine, Conall meets Samson's eyes. "I'd like to help you," he states simply, his blood pumping quickly through his heart. "However, this curse consumes my available time here. I want your word if my time runs out, you'll leave Daigh with Keary."

"No!" Shaking her head furiously, Keary's eyes snap with an inner fire. "We'll break the curse." The flames of resolve flicker in her gaze, daring anyone to challenge her conviction.

Conall manages a tight nod, though he can see it offers her no comfort at all. Brushing his thumb against the back of her hand, he tears his eyes away and regards Samson quietly. "Do we have a deal?"

Samson's face softens. "You have my word," he says solemnly. "If your time runs out, Daigh will be safe with Keary. I promise."

With a wrinkle on her forehead, Keary re-reads the last three chapters of the latest book. The words on the page blur and twist before her eyes. Breathing through her nose combats the urge to rip the pages free from their binding, from shuddering too far into her hands. It's been two short days since they met with Samson and she's still no closer to finding a solution. With each passing day, she witnesses Conall's strength and determination dwindle, like a candle burning out.

As the clock ticks on, each tick ramps up her already overly-sensitive nerves. Time for Conall is running out. The curse that plagues him weighs heavily on her mind, fueling her determination to break it.

Lost in thought, she doesn't register Conall's presence until he lays a hand along her shoulder to coax her back to the present. Whiskey eyes twinkle, poorly disguising the exhaustion hidden from anyone else.

"You've been up here since Erin returned to school," he says softly while taking a seat beside her on the loveseat. "I know you're worried."

Closing the book with a sigh, Keary rests her hands on top of the printed pages to keep them from pulling him close. "I will fix this. I won't let you just fade away."

A fragile smile tugs at the corners of his lips. "If anyone is stubborn enough to do it, it's you."

"Have you thought anymore about Daigh?"

"I have." Tearing his eyes from her, Conall pins them on the dark night sky just beyond the thin windowpane. "Your papers say a McKenna woman needs to release him, but I won't do that, while there's no chance for him to have a future."

"That's fair." Tapping a finger against her thumb, Keary studies the closed book in her lap. "There's a way to lift this curse, I know it."

"Perhaps," he concedes while covering her restless hands with one of his own. "We've given Brigid and this curse all of our attention. Maybe it's time to take a break."

Pursing her lips, Keary's nose wrinkles. "Yeah, I'm don't know how to do that."

"Don't you ever just relax?"

"Of course I do."

Conall chuckles, a deep, melodic sound that warms the surrounding air. "I fear, for you, this is relaxing. Researching and finding solutions to everyone's problems."

"It's better if I keep my mind occupied."

The moment he leans closer, Keary's body stiffens. "Better than what?"

Her heart flutters in her chest as heat warms her cheeks. Despite the weight of his circumstances, the pull he awakens inside her sidetracks Keary's analytical thinking. Swallowing around a tight throat, she clenches her fingers together. "Better than the alternative."

"Ah," he whispers, hot breath caressing the shell of her ear. "What's the alternative?"

When she risks a glance at him, instead of the usual whiskey color, his eyes darken to resemble an aged cognac. The hand he sifts through her loose hair sends a shiver straight to her core. A slight quirk of his lips tells Keary he's aware of the effect he has on her body.

Still, her brain is relentless in its warning signals. Puling in a slow breath, she gives her head a shake. "I don't think this is a good idea."

"Probably not." With a soft nudge of his hand, Conall tips her face upward, his eyes scorching her soul. "But I'm done fighting it. The question is, are you?"

His question hangs in the air, heavy with anticipation and possibility. Keary's heart pounds as she grapples with conflicting emotions. Giving into these feelings will complicate the situation. Skew her clinical focus. Is that the only reason? Her mind challenges, forcing her to catch her sharp gasp behind teeth.

She'd be lying if she didn't admit to a bit of apprehension. The few times she'd tried to be intimate, it ended prematurely. The feelings invoked inside her both pitiful and trivial. What are the chances this adventure ends like previous ones?

As if sensing her inner struggle, Conall brushes his thumb against the back of her hand until her grip loosens. "What is it?"

"Huh?" Nipping the corner of her mouth, Keary shrugs. "Nothing."

"Keary," he says softly, "you have many qualities. Some are endearing, others are bothersome. However, being coy and cowardly is not among them. So please, talk to me."

"I've always thought emotions cloud judgment. Erin being the only exception." Bracing herself, Keary continues. "This situation is already tense. Crossing this line could make it worse."

"In what way?"

"What if our feelings cloud an already confusing situation? What happens if we follow our hearts and overlook something crucial?"

Conall's expression softens, his tawny hair dropping over one brow to tempt her fingers into sinking deep. "I'm not saying we should forget everything else going on. But what if we let our minds rule and we miss out on something truly magical?"

Laughter bubbles up from her lips, too quick for Keary to contain. The deep furrow between his brows only increases the intensity of each giggle. "I'm sorry," she gasps between breaths. "I'm not... I'm not laughing at you."

"Fair enough. Which part did you find funny?"

Coughing, Keary attempts to contain the laughter still building in her gut as she searches for the words to explain. "The few times I've been intimate, magical is not a word I'd use to describe that experience."

Conall stares at her, eyes wide, mouth open. "I beg your pardon? Are you telling me..." he trails off, his voice dropping into a hushed whisper. "You've never truly experienced... that before?"

Keary frowns, her lips twisting into a half-smile. "It's not that I haven't experienced it. It's just... less than satisfying, if I'm honest." She sighs, her fingertips sweeping over her own lips as she speaks. "I've always been more focused on understanding the world around me. And that's left me, well..." She shakes her head, her eyes dancing between his and her clenched hands. "Left me slightly disconnected."

His expression softens, and he reaches out to cup her face between his calloused hands. "This thing between us doesn't have to resemble anything else. It can be its own journey, its own story."

His fingers trace her jawline, sending shards of heat into her core. Swallowing against the sensation saps the strength from her voice. "I... I don't know." Conall's thumb brushes over her bottom lip, exploring its gentle curve. Unprepared for the wave of longing blooming in her stomach, Keary leans into his touch.

"I won't push you," he murmurs, his voice rough against her skin. "But I can't deny this any longer, Keary. I've fought it for far too long."

Every fiber of her being screams for surrender to the allure of his touch. His words hang in the air between them, their gravity pulling her closer. The intensity of his gaze mirrors the tempest of emotions swirling within her. Closing the distance, Keary softly presses her lips against his. His breath is a soft gasp, and while trembles rack his body, he remains motionless, true of his word.

As her lips linger, heat scorches her insides. Calloused hands cradle her face, as if she's the most fragile treasure in the world.

Slowly, she pulls back, avoiding his eyes full of feelings she can't name. "I'm tired of fighting it too," she admits.

Her confession has the air draining from his lungs in a whoosh of air. Eyes search hers as Keary swallows the lump growing in her throat. The tension between them hangs in the air like a palpable wall; a wall she's no longer interested in maintaining.

The heat from his hands seeps through her clothes as he drops them to her waist to pull her flush against him. When he lowers his head, Keary's expecting another soft brushing of lips. Instead, Conall devours her in a kiss meant to curl her toes. She'd be lying if she said it doesn't have its desired effect.

The passion is overwhelming, leaving her with nothing but the pounding of her heart and his lips against hers. Under her hands, Keary absently notes the heat from his body and the rhythm of his heartbeat pulsating inside his chest.

Earlier, she believed she comprehended their allure, but it extends beyond the physical realm. The connection they've built, the trust between them, is what it's all about. It's the way he knows her thoughts before she speaks them, the way he understands her in a way that no one else ever has. How their souls seem to dance together, intertwined in a beautiful symphony of emotion. In this moment, Keary realizes that what they share is something extraordinary.

As the kiss deepens, Keary's mind races with a whirlwind of emotions. Every touch, every brush of their lips, sends a surge of electricity through her body, awakening a longing she never knew existed. Conall's firm hands roam her body, leaving a trail of fire in their wake. The sensations are intoxicating, overwhelming. Yet amidst the passion and desire, there's an undercurrent of tenderness that makes Keary's heart flutter.

Breaking apart, gasping for breath, Conall cradles her face in his hands once more, his eyes searching hers with a hunger that sends shivers down her spine. The world around them seems to fade into the background, leaving only Conall and herself standing in a bubble of suspended time. She traces the lines of his face with her fingertips, committing every detail to memory. The roughness of his jaw, the creases around his eyes that deepen when he smiles.

With a newfound resolve, Keary leans in to capture Conall's lips once more. They meld together with a hunger and urgency that ignites a bonfire within her. Their bodies press together, fitting like two puzzle pieces that were always meant to find each other.

With each kiss, her mind fogs, consumed by the intoxicating sensation of Conall's lips pressing against hers. Her entire being tunes in to his slightest movements, every brush of his fingers along her spine sending sparks through her body. When he daringly slips a hand under her shirt, tracing the curve of her back, she can't control the primal urge to pull him closer. She releases a soft sigh as he positions her to straddle his lap.

Once she registers the evidence of his desire pressing against her core, his hands are everywhere. Nerve endings stutter as his hand trails over the soft skin of her back before pressing her tight against him. The other hand tangles in her hair for a full heartbeat before cupping the nape of her neck, holding her hostage for his assault.

Mindless, her own hands grope and explore, her fingers aching with the barrier of his shirt between her and his skin. Reading her frustration, Conall tears his mouth away long enough to pull his shirt over his head then fits his mouth to hers once more.

As Keary finally allows herself to explore his tawny skin, her hands twitch. Caressing over shoulders, dipping along the collarbone, then drifting along the length of his arms. The muscles beneath his skin ripple at her touch, and she can't help but let out a soft gasp as she discovers new contours and planes to trace. His soft guttural groans of approval barely satisfying the beast inside her.

As her fingers dance over his chest, they pause at the faint scars that mar his skin. Without hesitation, Keary leans in to press feather-light kisses along each mark. She knows they must hold stories of battles fought and wounds endured, but in this moment all that matters is Conall and the intense connection between them.

Conall's hands ravage her body with an insatiable hunger, tracing every inch of her skin with a fervent urgency. His touch ignites a blazing fire within her as he brushes his thumb over the hardened peak beneath her bra, sending sparks of electricity through her body. His lips leave a scorching trail from hers to taste her neck. The searing kisses he leaves along the length of her throat have her trembling in response.

Keary's moans escalate into desperate cries as pleasure consumes her, every inch of her body shuddering. Arching into his touch, her nails score gently along the ridge of his ribs, reveling in the shiver of his response.

With practiced ease, Conall removes her shirt, baring her heated skin to the traces of cool air. When he pulls back, Keary struggles with the urge to squirm as his heated gaze burns a path over exposed skin. Even with the shield her cotton bra offers, she recognizes the need to cover herself, her fingers curling with the temptation.

Before her insecurities win, Conall turns to lay her back against the plush cushions of the loveseat then places tiny, nipping kisses against her lips. Hands journey over the skin he just uncovered, leaving a trail of heat in his wake. Eyes close, the first few moans escaping from her lips as she arches and writhes under his touch.

As soon as his lips make contact with her hardened peak through the thin fabric of her bra, Keary's eyes snap open. A surge of fiery electricity courses through her body, causing her to arch into his touch with a wanton cry. Fingers dig into his shoulders, nails leaving angry marks. His low growl vibrates over her skin, sending shivers down her spine and an aching throb to her core.

The rash of goosebumps on her skin serve as a warning of Conall's slow retreat. Canting her head, she can barely make out his twisted expression in the thick haze clouding her mind. Suddenly, a relentless pounding breaks through the fog and Keary jolts upright, crossing her arms protectively over her exposed chest.

A quick glance at Conall renders her speechless as he shoves a trembling hand through his disheveled hair. His entire being tenses, skin quivering with the strain of repressing what she has awoken within him. As he takes a deep breath, every muscle in his body taunt, flexing and releasing in sync with each slow inhale. The raw power radiating off him, threatening to break free at any moment, forces Keary to press her thighs tightly together.

As the knocks downstairs escalate into loud, angry thumps, Keary frantically pulls on her shirt and gasps for air. "To be continued," she whispers, her voice barely recognizable as a husky growl. In an instant, flames ignite in Conall's eyes, his gaze daring her to go back on her word.

CHAPTER 25

While Keary scrambles toward the main floor, Conall allows himself a moment to reign in the emotions she unleashed. He doesn't need to close his eyes to recall the taste of her lips or the scrape of her nails on his skin. As vivid as reality, the memories send a shudder down his legs. "Soon," he vows quietly.

Curling his hands until his knuckles ache grounds him enough to sweep his reaction aside to drag his shirt on and follow after Keary. By the time he catches up, she has the front door open.

Soft light from the candles she lit inside illuminates enough of the night for him to make out Reika's elegant features. As the evening chill creeps around like an uninvited guest, she clutches her thin cloak tighter around her shoulders.

"Reika," he says, his voice carrying the same level of surprise that Keary's face reveals. "What brings you here at this hour?"

"May I come in?"

After trading a quick glance with Keary, Conall steps aside. "Of course."

Once she steps over the threshold, she removes the cloak covering her mahogany hair. Rolling it into a ball, she tucks it under one arm while smoothing her hair with the other hand. "I apologize for just showing up on your doorstep, but I fear this couldn't wait."

Keary gasps and automatically clenches his arm, seemingly oblivious to her actions. "Is it the pack? More poison?"

"No, nothing like that," Reika reassures them with a gentle smile, tucking a stray hair behind her ear. "I stumbled upon something... a rumor, really. But I felt it was important to share with both of you."

"Sit," Keary offers, gesturing toward the living room with a sweep of her hand. "You look like you've been wrestling with the shadows."

Reika sits down in front of the fireplace and stares at the dancing flames. After a moment, she speaks, her voice barely audible over the crackling fire. "There is a rumor among the elders that one of them is a direct descendant of Aoife. And although the gift did not pass down to him, his granddaughter may have inherited it. If this tale is true, she could be the one to help break your curse."

Silence fills the room. Wordlessly, Keary's hand once again finds his, a harbor for the storm brewing to life inside his chest. Aware of the battle he fights with his emotions, Keary breaks the quiet.

"Is there any certainty to these rumors?"

"No," Reika admits with a slight shake of her head. "But where there's smoke, there's a spark."

"You believe she'll help us?" Keary prods, her voice soft yet carrying the strength of steel.

"I believe it's worth asking."

"Then we go now." Conall's decision settles along his shoulders like the wind after a storm.

"Her grandfather is protective," Reika warns. "Gaining his cooperation could be difficult."

With a lift of her chin and the familiar spark reflecting in her eyes, Keary speaks calmly. "But not impossible."

"It may be easier if Erin comes along."

Reika's words add a furrow to Conall's brow. How does any of this relate to Erin?

Sensing his confusion, Keary's teeth worry over her lip. Her eyes dart, searching for a discreet way to offer an explanation.

"Erin possesses the rare and powerful gift of persuasion," she answers simply, but Conall doesn't miss the hint of admiration in her tone. But as she turns toward Reika, her tone hardens, her gaze sharpens. "Even if I'm willing to expose Erin's ability to the elders, which to be clear, I'm not. She's already left for school."

As the two women regard each other, the air simmers with tension. The unspoken dynamic between them crackles like a forest fire. Every word; calculated. Every movement; precise while they engage in this battle of wills. In the background, the ravenous fire in the fireplace increases their individual determination.

Conall's mind becomes a battlefield, torn between the right thing and the easy. While Erin could make this task easier for all involved, he'd expose her to the elders. What are the chances they wouldn't use her and her gift for their own benefit? Can he betray Keary's sister in order to secure his brother's future? The voice in his head argues that Daigh deserves nothing less. It's the bitter taste of bile rising in his throat that cements his decision. "We keep Erin out of this."

Reika opens her mouth to argue while Keary exhales all the stiffness from her muscles. His brain calls him every form of idiot that ever existed while he basks in the gratitude Keary offers. The gentle quirk of his lips places a knot in his stomach.

"If that's your decision," Reika cuts in, her voice telegraphing the argument she's holding back.

Conall nods. "It is."

"I've arranged a meeting with him, but you should prepare yourself. There's a chance he'll shut you down."

Conall nods again. Now, the movement is clear and intentional. "I have to try."

Individual footsteps whisper across the cobblestone pathway, shadows elongate in the light offered from the inside. Freshly, baked bread and wood-smoke seasons the air, reminding Conall of simpler times.

As the three of them approach the elder's modest home, his heart thrums against his ribcage. Suspicion as delicate as the lacework displayed in the windows builds in his gut. Before they can get closer, the door creaks open.

"Reika," the man greets, his voice the timbre of aged oak.

"Elder Grayson, thank you for seeing us on such short notice."

Beady eyes narrow under a pair of bushy brows while he scans each of them. "You didn't give me much choice." They spend a moment in silence until he moves from the door. "Come inside. I've no desire to heat the outdoors."

Conall moves aside for Reika to go in first, then quietly guides Keary by placing his hand on her back. Her breath catches in her throat as heat floods his palm before a blush crawls up her neck. Good, she craves my touch as much as I do hers. When the elder leads them toward a small, round, battered table, Conall secures a grip on himself and takes a seat beside Keary.

Though dimly lit, the light from a single candle and the roaring fire offer Conall the chance to survey the room. Small and simple, he notes the worn-out furniture and faded tapestries adorning the walls. The air itself carries a musty aroma, reminiscent of old books and forgotten memories.

Taking a seat at the far end of the table, elder Grayson eyes them with a mixture of curiosity and skepticism. Weathered hands trace several deep grooves on the table. "Suppose one of you tells me why this meeting is so important?" he asks, his voice heavy with authority.

After a cough to clear her throat, Reika begins. "There's been talk elder of your granddaughter."

Grayson's gaze never wavers, yet the wrinkles around his eyes tighten ever so slightly. "What about her?"

"They say Shannon is a descendant of Aoife," Reika finishes after a brief pause.

A hush falls between them, laden with the weight of ancestral secrets and unspoken fears. Conall sits in silence as memories flicker in the elder's eyes, like the dance of firelight upon the walls.

"Rumors," Grayson dismisses with a scoff.

Keary's hand tightens around Conall's, her fingers cool against his skin. "All rumors have to begin somewhere, elder."

Grayson's gaze softens for the briefest of moments, offering Conall a glimpse of the kindness deep under his grizzly layers. "Let's pretend there's a hint of truth to these rumors. Why are you here? What are you asking of me?"

Conall takes a deep breath, steeling himself for what he's about to reveal. "If Shannon truly is a descendant of Aoife, then she possesses a power that could break a curse Aoife created."

Grayson nods. "I know the curse you speak of. Our ancestors passed stories of her disregard for human life, of the darkness she opened herself up to." Gnarled fingers curl. "Are you aware a curse is a double-edged sword?"

"How do you mean?" Leaning forward in her chair, Keary places a small hand over his from across the table.

"My grandmother told tales of Aoife's undoing. How the ripples of her actions will carry for generations. After losing her mother and then her aunt, young Iseult was never the same. Over time, she found love with a young stable boy and the two were married a short time later. Her husband, Ren, died a month shy of his daughter's birth when a horse he was training became violent."

"I'm sorry," Keary murmurs heavily, her voice unsteady with emotion.

"He wasn't the last." Despite the empathy evident in Keary's expression, Grayson continues to speak, deaf to any consolation. "Since then, love was our curse. So much so that for the longest time, I refused to open myself up to my wife. Refused to feel anything beyond respect for her. Over time, I got sloppy." Dragging in a ragged breath, he pins his tired gaze on Keary's pained features. "I came to love her. This fall will be five years since she passed, and it still hits like yesterday."

Conall's heart aches as he witnesses the raw pain bloom on Grayson's face. The weight of loss and regret blankets the room, enveloping them all. Reaching across the table, his hand finds Keary's trembling fingers and intertwines with them.

"I'm sorry for your loss," Conall begins, his voice fragile against the air rife with grief. "Perhaps by breaking the curse Aoife started, Shannon will also lift the curse on your bloodline."

Grayson's gaze flickers back to Conall. Shadows battle glimmers of light in his eyes as he leans back in his chair. "I've lived long enough to know hope brings both comfort and burden."

Keary's eyes brim with tears as she squeezes Conall's hand tighter. The weight of Grayson's words settles over them, the heavy silence punctuated only by the crackling of the fire.

"Isn't it worth a try? If we're successful, she may never know the pain you feel now."

"Why is this so important to you?"

The three of them share a quiet glance. In the end, it's Conall that answers. Filling his lungs, he fights to keep his voice steady as he speaks. "The curse Aoife put on my brother in me not only stole our present, but our future as well."

Grayson regards him with a contemplative look, as though weighing his words with what he knows to be true. After a moment, one brow lifts. "That would make you over five-hundred years old."

Emotions churn in his gut, clawing their way up into his throat. Clasping Keary's fingers tightly within his own, Conall manages a stiff nod. "Yes, sir."

"You believe Shannon can save you."

More statement than question, Conall recognizes the flash of sympathy in the elder's eyes, clenching his jaw in response. "I do."

Grayson leans back in his chair, his gaze locked on Conall's face. The room seems to shrink, as the air grows thick with anticipation. After what feels like an eternity, the elder breaks the silence. "Wait here."

Pushing himself up from the table, Grayson limps from the room with heavy footfalls. Once a door shuts behind him, Keary releases her breath in a deep sigh. "Do you think he believes us?"

Reika shrugs one delicate shoulder. "We're about to find out."

When the door opens, instead of Grayson's awkward gait, the footsteps are light and whisper soft. Lifting his eyes from the hand he joins with Keary, Conall takes in the tiny woman.

Thick, luscious strands of chocolate hair cascade in varying shades, from rich mahogany to warm chestnut, creating a stunning frame around a heart-shaped face. Deep pools of dark hazel eyes peer out from beneath the silky curtain of hair, their natural allure enhanced by thick lashes and subtle hints of golden flecks. Soft, pink lips stand out on the smooth, unblemished canvas of a fair complexion. The overall effect is ethereal and breathtaking.

With a hint of nervousness in her voice, she introduces herself. "I'm Shannon." As she ventures deeper into the room, the tension notches further up Conall's spine. After a deep breath, she takes a seat at the table, her gaze skipping between the three of them. "My grandfather says you wish to speak with me about Aoife's curse."

Conall's heart thumps erratically as he locks eyes with Shannon. The last piece of the puzzle had finally fallen into place, and despite his better judgement, light blooms within him. When Shannon's velvety gaze meets his, it's as if time stands still. A delicate breeze rustles through the air, and a strange sensation tingles in his hand as he grips Keary's. Gazing into her eyes, his heart falters at the sight of Etáin's intricate pattern hidden within her irises.

Clearing her throat, Keary leans forward in her chair. "I'm Keary, this is Conall and Reika," she begins. "I met Conall a few months ago when he climbed out of a small trinket box my sister, Erin gave me for a birthday present. Does that sound familiar to you?"

For longer than Conall cares to contemplate, the only sound in the room is the crackle of the fire on the far wall. Across the table, Shannon's features shift from surprise to concern, and she looks to her grandfather for confirmation. When he gives her a quick nod, her attention returns to Conall. "I had heard stories, but after so long many of us just assumed that's all they were. There isn't much information about Aoife after she cast this curse, but everything before said she was a gentle soul."

"She was," he admits slowly, extending his jaw to relieve the ache.

Shannon's brow wrinkles and her nose scrunches. "What happened?"

Conall closes his eyes and draws in a deep breath. "Aoife had a younger sister who tragically ended her own life. After that, Aoife was never the same. She shut herself off from others, unable to cope with her grief, which made her an easy target for Brigid McKenna." His skin prickles with the remnants of past emotions, but he forces himself to concentrate on the hand he holds onto for balance. "I don't know exactly what Brigid told Aoife to get her help, but I'm certain it had something to do with Etáin."

"You're saying the curse my ancestor created, the one that's caused hell for my own family, was used on you?"

"I understand your skeptical," Keary chuckles quietly, giving her head a tiny shake. "I know how you feel," she says softly. "Given the chance, we would let you come to your own conclusion. But time is not on our side." A sense of urgency creeps into her gentle voice as she continues. "Conall's time is running out and his brother is still trapped. We need a solution, and fast." The gravity of their situation clings to him like a heavy fog, casting a shadow over this conversation.

Without a flicker of emotion on her face, Shannon sits and absorbs Keary's words with a quiet grace. The hands she places on the tables surface betray no tremor as she draws small circles across the top. "My mother spent her life seeking a way to untangle ourselves from this curse," she says in a hushed tone. "She believed there was an antidote for every dark spell." A wistful smile touches her lips though from his position, Conall recognized the hint of sadness. "Before my father passed, she had hope. Afterwards," Shannon's voice trails off as memories assault her, painting shadows beneath her eyes. "She became a mere echo of herself, a shell wandering through the rest of her days."

"Then you understand our urgency," Keary nudges verbally.

"I do," Shannon replies with a heavy sigh to follow. "But Aoife was not some simple practitioner. The curse that weaves into the fabric of your fate is sophisticated. It'll take some searching to find the thread that will unravel it all."

The usual warm tone of Keary's voice disappears under a brittle edge. "Time isn't something he has a lot of right now."

Shannon regards him with an empathetic look. "I understand," she says gently. "It won't be easy. I'll need to consult the old texts and perhaps even seek the assistance of my old mentor."

Conall releases a long held breath, a sense of relief slowly creeping over him. "We thank you for your willingness to help, Shannon." Shoving himself to his feet, he pulls Keary up beside him. "I think we've taken enough of your time for one evening. Should you find anything …"

"I know where the McKenna's live. If she comes across something, I'll bring her to you," Grayson adds with quiet authority.

"Fair enough." Dipping his head toward Keary's he offers what he hopes to be a carefree smile. "Ready?"

CHAPTER 26

On their way home, Keary's mind buzzes with everything they learned tonight. With Shannon's agreement to help, it seems as if they are one step closer to breaking the curse and saving Conall and his brother. When Rika first suggested the meeting, Shannon's help seemed almost too much to hope for. After meeting her, Keary's doubts eased. There's something about her, something sincere. Even without the sharp, citrus fragrance of her emotions, her eyes held a wisdom beyond her years, a knowingness that settled Keary's nerves. Each step forward lands like a victory, each breath a reminder of the ticking clock.

Conall walks alongside her, his gaze fixed on the path ahead. More than once tonight, the stench of his desperation threatened to suffocate her, but under all that, Keary found the familiar woodsy scent of his resolve. Reaching out, she takes his hand and gives it a gentle squeeze. Lifting his eyes from the road, Conall glances at their hands, and a small smile tugs at his lips.

"Thank you."

Tilting her head to one side, Keary watches him from the corner of her eye. "For what?"

"Everything? For believing my story. Helping me put the pieces together." Conall's grip tightens as he pulls her to a stop and turns toward her. "For going with me tonight."

"You don't need to thank me for any of that."

A mixture of emotions flashes across Conall's face, too fast for Keary to catch them all. Without a word, he pulls her into a tight embrace, tucking his face into the crook of her neck and inhaling deeply. The press of his hands on her back combines with the heat from his touch to leave Keary trembling before he releases her.

In silence, they continue walking, but this time, Conall doesn't let go of her hand. Distracting herself from the warm, calloused fingers against hers, Keary considers anything else. Despite the warm summer days, the night air carries a bite of crisp air. Tree's heavy with fruit for harvest sway, the breeze carrying the distant call of a nightingale to her ears.

As they approach home, the warm glow from the fire beckons them inside. With a smile, Keary pushes open the creaky, wooden door and steps inside. The flickering fire casts dancing shadows across the wall, engulfing her in its comforting embrace. Instantly, heat seeps into her bones, soothing the weariness from the walk home.

While she hangs up her sweater on the short row of hooks, Conall adds another log to the fireplace. Flames roar, high-lighting the lines of worry etching across his face.

Hanging back, Keary observes as Conall's troubled expres-sion softens in the warm glow of the fire. The flickering flames seem to ignite a glimmer of hope within him, casting away some of the burden that weighs on his shoulders. She moves closer and stands beside him, their shoulders almost touching while the crackling wood and the gentle hiss of the flames fills the silence between them.

"I can't help but wonder," he begins, his gaze fixed on the fire. "If we can trust Shannon."

Her brows furrow, mirroring his concern. She watches the flames dance for a moment, contemplating her response. "What's your hesitation?"

"The last time I was in front of a witch doing magic, I lost five-hundred years."

"I can certainly understand your doubt. But something about Shannon feels genuine."

Conall sighs, the lines on his forehead deepening. "I suppose you're right," he murmurs, finally tearing his gaze away from the fire to meet her eyes. "It's just so hard to trust the gifted after everything I've been through."

A flicker of searing heat travels up into her chest. "I'm gifted," she reminds him. The sharpness of her tone clears his features.

"I didn't mean it like that."

"How did you mean it?"

Conall's gaze falters, a mix of guilt and vulnerability flashing in his eyes. He takes a step closer, his voice wavering with emotion. "I meant, I've seen how power can corrupt, how it can twist someone's intentions and darken their heart. What happens if I put my trust in the wrong hands again? Lose everything because I believed in someone who turned out to be something else entirely?"

"But you trust me, don't you?"

A slow smile tugs at the corners of Conall's lips as he reaches out to gently cup Keary's cheek. "With everything that I am," he whispers, his voice full of enough passion to make her heart skip a beat.

Her breath hitches against her lungs as she leans into the heat of his touch. The moments suspend in time as they stand there, the warmth of the fire and Conall's touch enveloping them. Keary's mind is a blur. Thoughts of him and how much she's come to care for him pinball back and forth against her skull.

Her eyes meet his, shimmering with unshed tears. In that moment, she sees not only her own fears reflecting at her, but also the weight of his past. The countless betrayals, the shattered dreams, the years lost in an endless cycle of despair. And yet, despite it all, he stands before her, his hand warm against her cheek, willing to open his heart once more.

The second his head dips, Keary prepares herself. Once his lips brush against hers, a surge of white-heat courses through her veins. As he deepens the kiss, Keary searches for leverage, her hands settling at his shoulders as he palms the back of her neck.

His touch is gentle but insistent, and she melts into him, relishing in the fervency of his desire. By the time he pulls back, Keary is a bundle of raw nerves. Dragging in lungfuls of air as Conall heaves a sigh and rests his forehead against hers.

"To be continued, yes? That's what you said?"

She hesitates, wrestling with the urge to play coy. Now is my chance. She could act like she's no clue what he's hinting at and shut down any further advances. The words cling to the tip of her tongue, but when she opens her mouth, they evaporate into thin air.

Swallowing, she tries again while her heartbeat echoes in her ears. Keary attempts to steady herself as every breath leaves in quick gasps. Then she catches his signature scent of sage, mint, and cedar, and her entire body softens with a light hum.

"Yes," she murmurs. "That's what I said."

Conall stills, his shoulders tense. As her admission hangs in the air between them, she's unable to tear her eyes away from the heat in his stare. In this moment, bright amber eyes darken with a primal hunger. Nostrils flare and his jaw clenches so hard it looks like it could shatter teeth. His face holds a look of desire and longing, heavy enough to send delightful shivers along her spine.

Without another word, Conall closes the distance, his lips claiming hers in a kiss that curls her toes and the outside world falls away in an instant. For once, her mind is quiet. Drawing her closer, Conall's worship of her mouth speaks volumes of unspoken promises and pent-up emotions. It's a dance of passion and longing, a silent confession of feelings that have been brewing beneath the surface for far too long.

As they break apart, breathless and dizzy with emotion, she searches his face. The soft drag of his thumb along her bottom lip is a spark in the dry timber containing her beast. With a long, languid stretch, eyes open before it offers a slow purr of approval.

When he tips her face towards his, Keary's lips part. Instead of another searing kiss, his voice, hoarse and savage, dances across exposed nerves.

"There's no turning back this time, Keary." He gulps, causing his throat to tense up. "Tell me you understand."

Not giving her mind a moment to sober the mood, Keary nods. "I understand," she says, the sound of her throat creaking and scratching like sandpaper fills the room. She lets out a high-pitched squeal as Conall sweeps her up into his arms, causing her body to tingle from the fluttering butterflies in her stomach.

Each step towards her bedroom takes an eternity, every inch of her skin vibrating from the light kisses he peppers along the side of her neck. The warmth from his hands seeps through her clothes, sending shivers down her spine. Finally, he kicks the bedroom door closed behind them, and Keary can't help but let out a breathless, shuddering sob. Her heart races as she turns to face him, her eyes locking onto his in a heated gaze.

Conall's lips descend once more in a slow exploration that has her knees buckling. One powerful arm encircles her waist, taking her weight just as his tongue travels along the seam of her lips. Her fingers curl against the solid wall of his chest as her lungs struggle to take in oxygen under his delicious assault. When their tongues tangle, scorching and sleek, she can't help but release the moan building inside her chest.

One hand tangles in her hair, pulling her head back as the other tastes her lips with a hunger Keary's never experienced before. Every brush of his fingertips against her skin ignites a wildfire, sending sparks flying through her veins. His touch trails around to her stomach, eliciting an animalistic groan from deep within her.

Conall breaks the kiss, teeth baring in primal need as he tears off his shirt before dragging hers up her out-stretched arms. Her bra is quick to follow. A cool rush of air sends shivers down her spine as she commits the feel of his bare skin against hers to memory.

Fingers digging into his shoulders, she pulls him closer until their bodies press together in a desperate embrace. Tracing delicate kisses along his chest and up to his neck, she drags her teeth over the sensitive flesh. When his entire body quivers under her touch, it shreds what remains of her patience.

With a hunger that rivals her own, he guides her to the bed, sending the world spinning on its axis. Overwhelming sensations flood Keary's senses as he settles beside her.

"Look at me," he demands softly, drawing her attention to the way the moonlight intensifies the rugged angles and lines of his face. She can't help but admire his strong jawline and sharp features.

Conall's hand travels up her side and pausing just under one breast before he leans in to kiss her again. The embrace is slow and deliberate, each movement calculated to drive her wild. The amount of heat pooling in her stomach takes her breath away. Lips trail along her jaw, adding a tremble to her legs that has her head spinning. *What is he doing to me?*

Quickly, Keary scours through her memories to recall ever having a reaction so visceral. The hitch in her breath, the sweat gathering on her skin. When his velvet touch draws a line over her exposed throat, she notes her muscles twitching in response.

Her previous encounters had been enjoyable. Enough to make her heart race. But every one pales in comparison to the buzz she's battling now. The musky, fruity scent Conall gives off bypasses her head, lodging in her chest to amplify everything.

Breath trembles against her lips. Once her skin shrinks to be too small for her body, Keary squirms. The button popping on her jeans snaps her eyes open, her hips lifting of their own accord as he drags the material from her legs. For a moment, Keary considers covering herself, but the heat in his eyes squashes the instinct.

Sitting back on his heels, Conall inches one hand up the inside of her calf. For once, the niggling voice in her head pointing out the extra pounds she's battled her entire life is silent. Under the weight of his stare, her flaws don't seem as relevant as they have before.

"Beautiful," he breathes, his hand skimming over the inside of her knee. Toes curl, body arching under his touch as she latches onto the blankets beneath her.

His gaze roams over every inch of her exposed body, tracing every curve and contour with a predatory hunger. Keary's skin prickles as his eyes linger on her most intimate areas. The sight of his slow smile growing into a crooked grin replaces the pressure in her chest with a warm, tingling sensation. Soon, the tingle morphs into a live-wire when

Conall descends upon her center, pressing a firm kiss against the fabric.

Gasping, Keary clutches the bedding beneath her as Conall devours her through the thin barrier of her panties. Each intimate touch sends bolts of heat straight to her core.

Conscious thought loses to frenzied cries, her hips rocking against his mouth. Muscles tense, and her body throbs as her hips continue its search for something she can't name. Every graze of his lips sends shudders of need through her until her body heaves with each breath.

With one last kiss on her most intimate area, Conall pulls back with a groan. Hooking his fingers under the fabric, he guides her underwear down shaking legs. Material scraping against sensitive skin floods Keary with a rash of goosebumps. The restraint it requires to not shield that part of herself from him leaves her arms shaking.

Stealing shallow breaths, she lays under Conall, every nerve ending alive and humming. When she catches his piercing gaze in the dark, his eyes burn with a promise and a warning. Resting his head on her stomach, Keary shifts under the unfamiliar weight as he draws tiny circles over a hip bone.

"I'm going to do my best to show you the magic," he whispers. Between the warm breath on her skin and the low vibration of his voice, her heart squeezes. Movement against her skin tells Keary he's smiling as his hand ghosts over her hip and down between her thighs. The small voice inside her head voices its doubt while her body primes for what comes next.

Even with all the mental preparation, his fingers at her core send a shockwave through her chest. A low growl eludes him as he dips a finger into her folds. Thighs clench while her hips search for more. Gently at first, Conall explores with one finger, then escalates the pressure and speed until her moan slips free.

With the utmost precision, he continues to strum her body. Every stroke builds the waves assaulting her core. The intensity increases with each landing until her body bridges the gap between an ache and a flutter.

Hot breath washes over her stomach as he transitions seamlessly from one technique to another. As he explores, he seems to read her reactions and adapts.

"Oh-my-goodness," she pants. With her nails scraping against the quilt, her back arches, and her hips buck.

Conall's soft chuckle ramps up the pressure, balancing her on the edge of release. As he continues the sweet torture with his fingers, Keary's eyes flutter shut. "Conall." Her voice breaks as her head thrashes from side to side on her pillow. Everything lands at once, flooding her with savage intensity even as her body begs for more.

"That's it, love. Let go. I've got you."

The words against her skin are like a dream. His voice, his touch, and the fervency flooding her system make speaking impossible. Absently, she realizes she wants it to last forever and yet, she can barely keep her breath. Succumbing to these unfamiliar sensations, Keary abandons all inhibitions and sacrifices herself to Conall's skilled touches.

With one final push, he thrust two fingers inside her, sending shards of white heat through her body. Throwing her head back, her hips lift the second her orgasm rips free. Each cry and mewl fill the room even as her body continues to tremble under Conall's relentless touch. Her climax crashes over her like a tidal wave, swallowing her entire being and leaving her gasping for air.

"Amazing," he whispers, pressing a light kiss to her hip as she shivers and writhes beneath him.

Exhaling a long, shuddering breath, Keary opens her eyes to find Conall staring at her with a smile on his crooked lips. Eyes so dark, it steals the air from her lungs. His touch trails along her stomach, fingers brushing against her sensitive skin. "You're beautiful," he whispers again, his voice fragile.

As the afterglow settles in, Keary collapses against the bed. How have I never felt that before? While Conall places a light kiss over her belly button, she struggles to understand the completely spent yet invigorated sensation filling her chest.

The air is thick with sweat and the sweet scent of their lovemaking. Keary's body vibrates like a well-oiled machine, humming with energy and satisfaction. She can't seem to catch her breath as she lies against the bed, her eyes closed and her senses still buzzing from the pleasure Conall had just given her.

With slow movements, Conall moves to stand beside the bed, drawing her focus. Moonlight filters through the window to cast an almost celestial glow on his broad shoulders as he methodically unbuttons his jeans. When they drop to the floor, the whoosh the material makes is similar to the air leaving her lungs.

The bed dips under his weight as he settles beside her. With a gentle hand, Conall parts Keary's legs, positioning himself at the entrance of her body. His own body trembles, a testament to the emotions coursing through him. While his hands surf the sensitive skin at her sides, his lips trace the outline of her jaw. Skimming her hands across his back, she buries her fingers in his hair to drag his mouth back to hers.

As their lips connect, Conall's tongue dances with hers in a passionate exchange. Every breath falls ragged against her lips while his hand explores her curves. His touch, raw and unhurried, teases the bundle of nerves underneath her skin. When he rolls a hardened nipple between thumb and forefinger, she gasps.

Swallowing her whimpers with a shudder, Conall groans when she arches her back to press her breast deeper into his hand. Despite his reaction, he takes his time, teasing her with feather-light touches until Keary's a writhing mess.

A deft touch coaxes her body to respond in ways she never thought possible, leaving Keary speechless. His fingers continue to explore her body, charting a course of pleasure that leads her to the edge of ecstasy and back. With each touch, each kiss, each soft word whispered into her ear, she's drawn deeper into the web of their emotions, their connection. It's not long before feral growls tear up from her chest as her hands and nails urge him to continue with a desperation that borders on madness. After his sweet torture, every fiber of her being screams for more.

As her impatience and need grow stronger, Keary can't bear to look anywhere beyond his face. The moonlight highlights his chiseled features, revealing the serenity in his eyes, replaced by a hunger that mirrors her own. His breath is shallow and ragged, the rhythm of it matching the thudding of her heart against her ribs.

She reaches up to cup his face, fingers trembling as she traces the lines of his cheekbones and jaw, the subtle scratch of his whiskers against her skin. A low whimper escapes her lips as their eyes lock, the intensity of his gaze leaving her breathless. "Please," she whispers, her voice barely audible against the pounding in her chest.

With a low growl, Conall moves. The moment he enters her, she lets out a desperate whimper, her nails digging into the wall of his back. The sensation is unlike anything she has ever felt before, as a wave of pure ecstasy crashing over her.

Keary's body arches off the bed as Conall's hips move in a rhythm that is both intimate and fierce. Each stroke sends shivers of a ravenous demand coursing through her veins.

Hand's grip along her hips, holding her in place for the lips Conall travels down her neck. Keary shudders and groans when teeth nip at her collarbone. His tongue flicks against the sensitive skin, leaving behind a trail of fire that makes her writhe beneath him. Every inch of her skin is alive, tingling with the rampant hunger coursing through her.

Once Conall's thrusts become more urgent, Keary's body responds in kind, her hips bucking to meet his every move. The bed creaks in protest, the only sound in the room besides their ragged breathing and the slap of flesh against flesh. It's feral. Primal. Everything they've both been fighting.

Another growl eludes her lips as she reaches up to tangle her fingers in his hair, pulling him closer. The need to feel him against her, to be one with him, is painful. Wrapping her legs around his hips, their bodies rock together in a harmony of desire, each movement building a crescendo of pleasure that Keary never thought possible. "Conall," she whispers, her voice shaky with need.

The crest of the wave is approaching. Taking up space in her stomach, the pressure grows until it leaves room for nothing else. With one final growl, Conall pulls her even closer, his hips pistoning with a force that leaves her breathless. Her body trembles, electricity flowing along her veins, flooding her limbs as she nears the edge.

Once the ecstasy reaches its peak, Keary's body convulses. Her breath catches in her throat. Conall swallows every cry he rips from her as she rides the tremulous waves rocketing her frame. Heat spreads up from the tips of her toes, humming across her skin with a ferocious appetite.

Every movement is deliberate, each touch precise. Conall's heart thuds against her chest, the steady drumbeat pulsating in time with hers. His lips brush against her skin, leaving a trail of fire in their wake. When he stiffens under her hands, Keary wraps her arms around his neck to hold him closer as he reaches his release. Arms tighten around her as his face presses against her neck, his own body trembling as he growls into the crook of her neck.

Finally, as the waves crash, it leaves them both spent and breathless. Air shudders from her lungs as Keary collapses against the bed, her heart pounding in her chest. Conall drops beside her, one arm draped lazily around her waist, his leg hooked between hers. The feral groan he makes echoes in the silent room.

"Conall," she whispers, her voice thick. "I never imagined it could be like this."

With a soft smile, he brushes the hair back from her face, his eyes warm. "I told you we'd write our own story." Pressing a kiss to her temple, he leaves her long enough to come back with a damp washcloth. Heat stains her cheeks as Conall takes his achingly sweet time, wiping away the traces of their lovemaking from her body.

Once he's satisfied, he climbs in next to her and tucks her into the warmth of his side. The afterglow fades and Keary nestles closer, her breath hitching as his arm snakes around her. "That was," she trails off, searching for the right word.

Conall hums, his fingers tracing the curve of her back in lazy circles. "That was amazing," he murmurs. "Just as it should be."

Keary's heart swells even as she stifles a yawn with the back of one hand. Shifting closer, she rests her head in the crook of his shoulder. "I feel like I could sleep a hundred years."

"If that's the case, we should make sure we've done enough to last you that long."

She doesn't need to see his face to know his gaze carries renewed heat. The rasp of his voice combines with the musk of his desire to cause a stutter in her heart.

Instantly, her body reacts. Muscles clench and quiver, her breaths soft and shallow as she turns enough to brush a kiss against his chest. Salty sweat from his skin clings to her lips and Keary drags her tongue along their soft curve to collect more of his taste.

Conall's groan over her actions rumbles under her touch. When he drags her mouth to his, Keary succumbs to the still strange tingling climbing up from her core.

Even now, the brush of his fingers, the warmth of his breath, settles like a dream. A memory of something that never happened.

CHAPTER 27

As the sun climbs out of the horizon, it paints vibrant steaks of cherry pink, honey, and a subtle touch of apricot across the sky before emerging from the treetops. Cradling a steaming cup of tea in her hands, Keary lets the swing sway as Conall applies the last coat of lacquer to the trunk.

Birds overhead welcome the new day with a symphony of songs, each chirp as familiar to her as the evening crickets. Reclining against the swings back, Keary taps an absent finger against her cup. As her eyes close, she melts into the sounds and fragrances.

After spending all of yesterday in bed, Conall declared today to be productive. Typically, she plans each day meticulously to get the most done, but the temptation to stay in bed and lure him under the sheets is strong. Despite the twinge of discomfort in her lower half, her body stirs.

Lifting her lashes, her eyes devour the broad shoulders she clung to the night before. It takes no effort to recall the delicious shiver those calloused hands created running over her skin. The warm sensation of Conall's arms wrapped around her, skin on skin, the taste of his lips on her own; these memories send a thrill of longing coursing through her veins.

Oblivious to her scrutiny, Conall hums a tune under his breath, his focus on the task at hand. His hair, tangled and disheveled from their night of passion, falls around his face in loose waves. Keary's heart skips a beat at the sight of him, stunning despite the early morning light.

"You're staring."

The melodic rasp of his voice washes over her skin, producing a series of small shivers. Hiding her smile behind the rim of her cup, she gives the swing a gentle nudge. "I'm just impressed with what you've done with the trunk. It's like new."

Standing to his full height, Conall shoves a hand through his messy hair as a smile tugs at the corners of his mouth. "Thank you. But I doubt it's my woodworking skills putting that flare of heat in your eyes."

"You never know. I could have a thing for wood." Her smile turns to a smirk as a significant darkness floods his eyes. "Cedar," she moans breathlessly. "Pine. Oak." His body shudders as she groans over the last one.

"You're naughty."

"It's not my fault watching you is a turn on."

His gaze lingers on her face, his laugh a mild rumble in the morning air. "It's not watching me work that's turning you on," the low, husky growl of his voice causes her core to clench. Stepping closer, Conall brushes a lock of hair from her face, his fingers light on her skin. "It's knowing what we did last night. And the night before that."

His eyes never leave hers as he slides a hand behind her neck to hold her close. His hand is tender yet firm, a quick reminder of the nights they shared. Keary's breath stalls as her long, slender fingers tighten around her cup.

"We could always make work a bit more ... enjoyable," she suggests with a grin.

"And what would that look like?"

Embracing this unfamiliar boldness, Keary sends an image of the two of them across the mind link. Both naked and entwined, she straddles his lap. Her back arches as she throws her head back, the swing beneath them jerking and bouncing with their frenzied movements. A soft chuckle leaves her lips as Conall heaves a shuddering gasp.

"Another five-hundred years wouldn't satisfy this hunger I have for you." His soft murmur is barely audible over the birdsong, but her heart swells regardless.

Exchanging a look, Keary's body tightens as Conall's eyes continue to darken until only flecks of heat remain. Setting her cup on the knee-high table beside her, she reaches up and guides his mouth to hers.

Heat blooms in her chest as their kiss deepens. When he scoops her from the chair only to settle her across his lap, her body spasms with anticipation. Rough, calloused hands run up the outside of her thighs, placing a moan just inside her throat. The soft bite of his nails rips the moan free as he feeds snippets to the beast inside her. It's not long before the beast is wide awake, demanding for more. Heavy footfalls on the porch shatter the moment.

Scrambling off Conall's lap, Keary adjusts her clothes and smooths a hand over her tousled hair just as Commander Emberstone rounds the corner. With the sun rising behind him, too much of his face hides in the shadows for her to get a read on the reason for his unexpected visit. "Commander," she stutters, her fingers knotting in the hem of her shirt. "What brings you here so early?"

"Damien," he corrects without a hint of a smile. Dark eyes dance from her to where Conall stands resolute over her shoulder. "I hope I didn't catch you at a bad time."

Even as heat spreads across her face, Keary steadies herself and gives her head a quick toss. "Not at all. What can I help you with?"

"The council is requesting your presence."

"Wh-," as the question stumbles leaving her mouth, Keary draws a tremulous breath and tries again with more control. "Why?"

"I'm not at liberty to say," the commander replies, his tone almost apologetic.

"When?"

"Now, I'm afraid."

His response blurs her vision with tiny black dots, so Keary wraps her arms around her waist to stop them from trembling. There aren't many reasons the elders would summon her. In fact, only two scream out from inside her skull. Either their questions concern the criminal or Erin is involved. Both possibilities tighten her chest, but she can't help but hope for the former.

"Your friend is welcome to accompany you, of course," Damien adds, his lips twitching awkwardly in what she'd consider a smile.

After a moment, Keary rips her gaze from him and looks up at Conall beside her. "Will you come with me?"

"You don't even have to ask," he says, resting a firm hand on her back.

Needing time to compose herself, Keary nods towards the house. "Give me a moment to change."

"Make it quick. I'll wait for you out front," Damien says, already turning away from her.

As she makes her way through the corridors to her room, Keary's chest aches with a mix of emotions. Torn between putting Conall in danger by bringing him along and the state of her own sanity without his presence. Since he hasn't grown up in this society, the rules, and regulations aren't as vital to him as they are to her. Still, the thought of him not being next to her for whatever the elders wish to say covers her skin with a cold sweat. *When did I become so at ease around him?* Until now, she's always been self-reliant. Is it because she's finally letting herself feel emotions, or could it be that he's making her vulnerable? Whatever the case, she pushes these thoughts aside for later. She already has a lot on her plate and doesn't need to add Conall to the mix.

Using a brush, she untangles her wild locks, wincing as it catches on an especially stubborn knot. With swift hands, she gathers her hair into a messy bun at the back of her head. After another moment, she secures it with several clips, tucking away stray strands that refuse to cooperate. The scent of roses from her soap lingers in the air, calming her nerves for the task ahead.

Before she can talk herself out of it, Keary trades in her usual practical and comfortable attire and opts for a lightweight summer dress. The cap sleeves fall loose over her shoulders, the form-fitting bodice accentuates her figure, and the hem falls gracefully just below her knees. Delicate and airy, the dress hints at femininity without revealing too much. Grabbing a pair of light sandals, she hurries downstairs before she can give herself a final once over.

The moment Conall's eyes land on her, a rush of heat spreads through her body. Silent, his gaze lingers on her with a fiery intensity igniting a gentle shiver that travels from the top of her head to the tips of her toes. The weight of his eyes burns into her soul, causing a flutter in her heart and sending her senses into overdrive.

"You look beautiful," Conall growls, his eyes never leaving her. Taking her hand in his, intertwining their fingers, he leads her out to the front porch.

Sensing their arrival, the commander looks from one to the other, his expression never changing. "Shall we?" he asks, gesturing to the wagon waiting for them.

With a sharp exhale, Keary hoists herself onto the bench seat, her body wedged between Conall and the Damien. As she settles into her spot, she fights against the urge to tap her fingers together and instead folds them neatly in her lap. The horse-drawn carriage lurches forward, carrying them through the winding roads towards Briar. Countryside landscape whizzes by, dotted with vibrant wildflowers and rolling hills. A fresh scent of pine and rain fills the air, sharpening her senses. As the carriage jostles over bumps and dips in the road, a bitter sense of dread blooms in her chest at what awaits them.

The sun is high in the sky by the time they arrive. Chaos buzzes and hums with the sounds of merchants setting up their stalls and the clatter of horses' hooves on the cobblestone streets.

As they make their way through the bustling streets, Keary's unease grows. The commander guides the horses toward the council chambers, where the imposing stone building looms in the center of town, its entrance flanked by two stone lions. Once the crowd parts, Damien jumps from the carriage before it comes to a stop, holding the horses steady so Conall can help Keary to the ground. "This way."

Tugging on the hem of her dress as he leads them towards the imposing structure, sweat gathers on her brow. With his hand on her back, Conall follows closely as the crowd presses in around them.

Once they step inside, a heady mixture of old parchment, burning candles, and the faint hint of lavender welcomes them. The scent, both comforting and musty, resembles a forgotten, untouched library from centuries past. Massive stone pillars support the high ceilings that tower above them. Tapestries depicting scenes of bravery and valor adorn every inch of space, adding to the grandeur of the room. In the center stands a long wooden table, surrounded by high-backed chairs draped with rich velvet.

Every step Keary takes is a battle against the urge to turn and flee from this place. These chambers hold secrets and mysteries older than time itself. Shadows lurk in every corner, and whispers fill the air as if carrying the weight of centuries' worth of decisions - both wise and misguided. To her, this chamber is a temple of bones, filled with stories waiting to be told.

"Quickly," Damien urges as he leads them along narrow corridors. Despite her façade, Keary's heart thrums against her chest. When they stop outside a pair of double doors, it's impossible to hide the tremble in her legs.

Damien wears a thoughtful expression as his hand rests on the ornate silver handle. "Just be as honest as you can be." Keary's brow arches when his usual gruff tone comes off as soothing.

A moment passes with nothing but her own ragged breath. Then the doors swing open revealing the painted walls of the elder's inner sanctum. This is the heart of the council, where decisions are made, and secrets are kept.

An impressive row of bookshelves stretches across the far wall, each one filled to the brim with leather-bound tomes and colorful spines. Intricate paintings and tapestries celebrating Briar's rich history adorn the remaining two walls, their vibrant colors and detailed scenes capturing the attention of any onlooker. The coolness of polished stone greets her feet as she enters the room, her sandals providing little protection against the chill. In the center of the room sits an elegant oval table, its surface bearing subtle signs of years of important discussions and decisions made around it.

As Damien leads her further into the room, each elder becomes aware of her presence and takes a seat at the table. Their expressions are unwavering, their eyes fixed on her as she approaches. Elder Elias is the first to break the silence, his voice carrying a weight of authority. "Please, do take a seat Ms. McKenna." A sweeping gesture towards the one empty chair follows the soft command.

Keary takes a seat in the only vacant chair, purposefully making eye contact with the elders. Conall positions himself next to her without concern for permission, acting as a protective barrier with his unwavering presence. After receiving a nod from Elias, Damien delivers a deep bow before taking up a rigid stance by the double doors.

The silence in the room is deafening as she glances around the table, feeling the weight of each elder's gaze. When she catches Grayson's eyes, the slight flare of warmth she finds there settles her suddenly queasy stomach. If only for a moment. From her left, elder Thorne clears his throat, drawing her attention. The elder's piercing gaze lands on Conall, who stands stoically behind her right shoulder, causing her stomach churning once more.

"Who's your friend?" he asks while his lips curl up at one corner.

"This is Conall," she responds lightly.

"Correct me if I'm wrong, Commander. Didn't we send you to bring Ms. McKenna?"

"That is correct."

"Then why is he here?"

"I thought it would ease Ms. McKenna's nerves to have a friendly face," Damien explains.

Elder Thorne's jaw clenches as he glares at him. "You are not paid to think, Commander. You are paid to lead the vanguard."

Resting his palm over the tabletop, elder Grayson interrupts, his tone crisp and authoritative. "Given the sensitive nature of this discussion, I see no harm in allowing Ms. McKenna to have a companion by her side."

The two elders exchange sharp looks, a silent battle of wills between them before elder Thorne offers a begrudging nod. "Very well."

"The reason we've called you here is to set your mind at ease involving the criminal we've been searching for." Grayson pauses, his eyes sending a dark scowl towards Thorne before continuing. "Some of us believe you played a key role in saving his life. Now that he's in custody, he's been eager to clear your name."

"Custody?" Keary's voice croaks out, barely audible.

"He was apprehended by soldiers while attempting to sneak across the southern border."

"Has he told you anything else?" Keary asks, her grip on her fingers growing tighter.

"Just that he stumbled upon a healer east of here who tended to his wounds as best she could."

"You can understand why we had to investigate you?" elder Elias asks. The lines around his mouth make it feel more like a statement than a question. Her agreement simply a formality.

Managing a nod, she tries to steady her voice. "I understand. What will happen to him now?"

"We have come to a consensus regarding his punishment," Grayson answers tersely. "However, we are at an impasse when it comes to the woman we caught with him."

"A woman?" Keary's stomach crawls up into her throat and it takes all her concentration to keep from squirming within her seat.

"Your friend from the library," Damien offers, a flash of pain evident in his dark eyes.

A bone-chilling cold grips Keary's entire body as she struggles for breath. "Evie," she gasps, her lungs burning with every labored inhale. The weight of Conall's hand on her shoulder provides a fleeting sense of stability amidst the chaotic panic.

"That's correct," elder Thorne grumps. "She's currently being held in one of our cells until we can determine an appropriate punishment. But for now, your presence is required at the execution taking place shortly."

"Why do I need to be there?" Keary asks, mentally preparing for the answer.

Grayson's expression softens momentarily before hardening again. "Your presence will help put any doubts about your involvement to rest. Don't you agree, Thorne?"

Thorne grumbles under his breath before sitting taller in his chair. "I do."

"Let's finish this before the crowd becomes unruly," Elias commands as he stands up from his chair. One by one, each elder gets to their feet while Elias leads their small group back the way Keary had come from earlier.

Making their way back outside, Keary leans heavily against Conall's sturdy frame. His arm wraps protectively around her shoulder, drawing her close to his side. She hones-in on the steady rhythm of her heartbeat, focusing on its slow cadence until her body falls in sync.

The clink and rustle of armor draws her eye to Damien on her right. His profile is sharp and defined, his jaw clenched tightly and his full lips pressing into a thin line. Tension radiates off of him as he prepares for what's to come. As if sensing her gaze, he quickly turns to meet her eyes with a warning look.

"This is going to be unpleasant for you," he cautions, his voice a low whisper. "Breathe through your nose and whatever you do, do not react."

The air around her becomes suffocating, like a storm ready to break at any moment. She takes in deep breaths through her nose, trying to calm herself before the impending chaos.

As they approached the exit, the cacophony of the crowd grows louder. Shouts and jeers erupt from the group, their bitter sting palpable. With each step closer to the outside world, the stench of aggression overwhelms her.

Finally stepping out into the open air, she greedily gulps in deep breaths, her eyes watering from the suffocating odor emanating from those gathered to witness such a thing. Closing herself off from their violent presence, Keary steels her nerve as she directs her attention to the raised platform on her left.

The wood now aged and weathered, forms a formidable structure that towers above the crowd. The noose, sways in the breeze, dangling menacingly from its central cross-beam to send a chill down her spine and causing her lithe frame to shudder. The executioner, a tall figure shrouded in black, stands at the foot of the platform waiting patiently for the order.

Holding tightly onto Conall's hand, as they both look up at the noose hanging above them. She tries to inhale through her nose, but the pressure in her chest grows, until her face contorts in pain. "Breathe," she whispers to herself. However, the atmosphere ripe with hate and judgment makes it difficult for her to take the full breath that would calm her nerves.

Tears threaten to fall as she gazes at Orion standing in the center. Though he holds his head high, a shaky stance haunts his quiet assurance. His ragged clothes reveal the physical abuse he's endured in the vanguard's custody. Despite the constant barrage of food and insults from the bloodthirsty crowd, he stands firm, never flinching. The air is thick with the stench of rotten vegetables and the deafening noise of the spectators, creating a tense atmos-phere like a drawn bowstring.

From their position in the back, Keary struggles to see the criminal that the elders claim him to be. In this mo-ment, Orion appears more like a wounded animal, forced to endure the taunts and attacks from his predators. Yet even then, a soft smile plays on Keary's lips as she notices the glimmer of defiance in Orion's eyes.

As soon as Elias steps into the spotlight beside Orion, the audience falls into silence. "My fellow citizens of Briar," he declares, gesturing broadly to encompass the entire crowd. "Today, we bring you justice!" Keary has to resist the urge to cover her ears from the deafening cheers that erupt from the crowd. As it is, repulsive odor seeps into her clothing, tainting her skin.

"This man, Orion, has been apprehended by our vanguard for the heinous act of betraying the council and allying with the Crimson Claw. We don't yet know the full extent of their plot, but it's clear that their actions endanger all of us." Elias' voice pounds through the air, echoing the fear of the crowd. "For his crimes against the citadel and the council itself, we sentence this man to death."

The deafening roar of the crowd engulfs Keary, a violent symphony of unbridled anger and desperation. Her stomach churns and bile rises in her throat as if it wants to reject yesterday's meal. Despite her physical turmoil, her eyes remain locked on Orion, stoic and unresponsive as he awaits his sentence. When he meets her gaze amongst the sea of onlookers, she tries to transfer strength to him through their intense stare, holding her breath in a desperate plea for his survival.

Elias's judgement hangs in the air, ominous and heavy. The executioner, clad in a dark robe, moves swiftly towards the lever that will release the board supporting Orion. Keary flinches at the sound of gears turning and wood shifting as he pulls the lever. She gags with the realization that the sudden drop isn't long enough to quickly end Orion's life. Instead, his bound legs flail wildly, trying to find purchase on anything solid. His shackled hands leave him unable to defend himself against the sudden constriction around his neck, caused by the weight of his body pulling on the rope.

A strange hush falls over the previously raucous crowd as they witness the intense struggle. As Orion's movements become more frantic, the onlookers hold their breath in a mix of horror and fascination. Keary gulps. Every fiber of her being wants to reach out to Orion, to pull him from the noose. Yet, it is the piercing glare of elder Thorne that keeps her rooted in place, powerless to do anything but watch as the light fades from Orion's eyes.

As Elias gives another command, the executioner moves closer. Keary's vision blurs with tears, but she can't bring herself to look away as Orion's body is gently placed on the ground. His once vibrant eyes are now vacant, staring off into nothingness. Being a healer, she shudders at the loss of life as she fights the to contain the bile rising into her throat.

As if aware her resolve falters, Conall pulls her closer, his strong arm enveloping her shoulder. Gently turning her towards him, he holds her tight against his broad chest and lowers his head into the curve of her neck. Wrapping her arms around his waist, she clings to him as her body trembles uncontrollably. "Come on, I'm taking you home," he whispers against her skin, the promise almost causing Keary's legs to give out beneath her. Teeth set as the rasp of his voice and warmth of his breath on her skin create a soothing balm for the turmoil in her mind that she knows she doesn't deserve.

CHAPTER 28

The journey home was a somber one, with Keary remaining unusually quiet. It didn't take an empath to see the weight of Orion's death bearing down on her. As they made their way back, the heaviness in the air settles like a thick cloak of grief and guilt. Each step is listless, every breath labored as she carries the weight of loss and regret all the way home.

With a gentle guiding hand, Conall leads her into her cozy living room and helps her settle onto the soft couch.

Despite the warmth of the season, she still trembles from the emotional turmoil, so Conall removes the blanket from the back of the couch and drapes it across her shoulders. Her eyes sweep over the familiar floor, searching for some sense of grounding amidst her swirling emotions. Sensing her need for space, Conall takes a step back and gives her room to process

Tears well up in her eyes as she speaks, and her usually melodic voice is replaced with a soft, hoarse rasp. "I-I could've done something," she stammers out. "I should've been able to save him."

Kneeling down so they are at eye level, Conall tips her chin, forcing her to meet his gaze. "There was nothing you could've done without ending up next to him."

"Maybe I should've been."

"And where would that leave Erin?"

As soon as her sister's name crosses his lips, the shadows hiding in her eyes, dissipates. "You're right," she says, clasping his hand between hers. "That doesn't make me feel less guilty."

"You need rest." With gentle hands, he shifts her so she can lay down on the couch. Arranging pillows under her head, he covers her with the soft blanket. "I'll make you some tea," he offers, already moving toward the kitchen.

The vast difference in their society never fails to catch him off guard. In his time, public executions were a regular occurrence. When he first woke up here, the news that the gifted had not yet regained control of the council brought him a sense of relief.

The civil war had claimed many friends, if circumstances had been slightly different, he's certain his own name would be added to that list. But now, as he looks upon the society built upon the bones of those lost in the war, a sharp pain twists in his gut. The dull ache in his chest causes Conall to wonder if the civil war was truly for the betterment of all, or just another ploy for power. One he helped see to fruition. How could so many have gotten it wrong? How could he?

Before he can fully succumb to his own guilt and self-reflection, the high-pitched whistle of the tea-pot jolts him back into the present moment. With a practiced hand, he prepares a small cup and pours a generous amount of boiling water over a carefully selected blend of fragrant herbs. Steam rises in thick wisps as the herbs swirl together in a dance of colors and scents. As he waits for the tea to steep, the soothing aroma fills the room, calming his racing thoughts. He nearly groans aloud when there's a soft knock on the front door.

Stepping into the living room, Conall's eyes immediately fall on Keary who is already sitting up, tense and ready to answer the door. Crossing the room, he lays a hand on her shoulder.

"We don't have to answer it," he offers.

There's a brief pause as Keary weighs her options, her gaze flickering towards the front door. Just when he's certain she'll lay back down before a muffled voice filters through the door from the other side. "Keary, it's me, Shannon."

Conall's heart skips a beat at the sound of Shannon's voice, and without hesitation, he turns and moves towards the door. As he grips the doorknob, he notes a tingling sensation spreading from his hands into his arms. He no sooner cracks the door to let her in when Shannon sails past him, mindless of the tension.

Dressed casually in jeans and what Keary calls a tank top, she gathered her hair into a messy knot at the back of her head, revealing the tattoos that adorn her skin. Like twin serpents, the intricate tattoos coil around Shannon's shoulders and slither down her arms, each line and curl weaving its own tale of mystery. The delicate swirls and patterns hold secrets of their own, adding to the enigmatic allure that surrounds her. In this light, the ink seems alive, pulsing with unseen magic that draws all eyes to its captivating beauty.

"I've found it," she declares, drawing his attention to the thick tome she clutches to her chest. "I know how to break the curse."

Like a sudden blow to the chest, Conall's body sways and staggers. The unexpected surge of hope inside his chest makes it hard for him to catch his breath. His throat tightens with emotion, as he absently rubs a hand against the pressure building under his ribs. His mind is a jumble of thoughts, each one vying for attention as he fights to keep his legs from collapsing beneath him like two felled trees. "Say that again?"

With a gentle, almost cautious pause, Shannon turns to face Conall, her eyes locking onto his as she speaks. Every word that falls from her lips is precise and measured, like delicate brushstrokes on a masterpiece canvas. She seems keenly aware of the turmoil her revelation stirs within his body. As if treading on fragile ground, she utters the words that hold such weight: "I can break your curse." Just like that, the air around them charges with anticipation and possibility. The slightest hint of hesitation offering a slight tinge. It's a moment that holds the power to change everything for him.

Keary's soft touch on his arm startles Conall, bringing him back to the present moment. Her gentle voice breaks through his thoughts, "Why don't you sit, and I'll make two more cups of tea?" When he tips his head to stare down into her face, he's able to draw a full breath. The breath of hope glittering in her striking green eyes releases the pressure lodged under his ribs. Conall manages a nod as he stumbles to the overstuffed chair behind him, grateful for its support as he sinks into it like a weight has been lifted from his shoulders.

Taking a seat across from him, Shannon gives Keary a moment to prepare the tea. The gentle clinking of porcelain against porcelain fills the air as Keary carries a tray with three cups on it into the living room. Setting it down on the coffee table, she takes a seat next to Conall and gives Shannon a quiet nod. "Okay. There's been a lot of questions about how Aoife was able to cast such a powerful curse," Shannon begins, her voice calm but tinged with a hint of excitement.

"Everyone said Aoife was a powerful witch," Conall interjects, his brows wrinkling.

"That's true, Conall. But power eventually has its limit," Shannon explains, laying the book she brought across her lap. "Aoife not only pushed beyond the limit, but she cursed her own bloodline in the process."

A heavy stillness descends upon the group as they process this new information. Shannon runs her fingers delicately across the cover of the book she brought with her, lost in thought. Keary's eyes darken with conflicting emotions while Conall sits in a stunned silence. Keary is the first to snap out of it.

"But why would she do that?"

Shannon sighs and meets their gazes. "I don't think it was intentional. I believe we were punished for her tapping into such dark magic."

Conall turns to share a quiet look with Keary. "Punished by who?"

"Derunid," Shannon proclaims with a wide grin, as if she had just solved a previously unsolvable mystery. However, her face falls slightly as she takes in their puzzled expressions.

"You see, magic is not meant to be used for dark purposes. It is supposed to represent nature in all things. When Aoife cursed you, she stained her own soul in the process. To maintain balance, the Derunid had no choice but to curse Aoife's bloodline as well."

Conall takes a moment to process this revelation before speaking again. "So, your entity or something like that?"

"Something like that," Shannon confirms with a slight nod of her head.

Keary's delicate features twist as she nibbles on the corner of her lip, a habit that Conall finds endearing. "She angered the big bad when she meddled with this kind of magic, I get that. But how was she able to do it in the first place?"

"According to Iseult's granddaughter, Aoife used blood magic to create this curse. Specifically, McKenna blood. Brigid's intense hatred for you and your brother fueled the curse far beyond its intended power."

"That adds up."

The dry chuckle that escapes him earns him a silent glare from Keary. Shaking her head, a dark scowl casts over her face. "How do we break something like that?"

"It took some time, but I managed to craft an unbinding spell that should be strong enough to sever your connection with the cursed box. With Keary's help, of course."

"Not a chance," Conall spits, sitting up straight in his chair.

Ignoring his outburst, Keary leans forward on the edge of her seat. "What can I do?"

"Because Aoife used McKenna blood to cast the curse, we need your blood to break it."

Conall shoots to his feet, a hand reflexively rubbing the back of his neck. "Absolutely not. We have no idea what this could do to her."

"She wasn't the one cursed, Conall. It shouldn't affect her at all."

"What happens to Conall if this doesn't work?" Keary asks.

"I don't know for sure. I can't simply send him back to his own timeline. Ideally, breaking the connection to the trinket box will allow him to finish out his remaining years here."

"Ideally?" This time it's Keary who shifts uncomfortably in her chair.

Shannon softens her voice as shadows drop into her eyes. "Some things are never certain." Tucking her book under one arm, she rises from her seat. "Take today to prepare whatever you need to prepare. I'll be back tonight."

"Tonight? So soon?"

"It must be tonight, Conall. Tomorrow the moon's cycle will return and it'll be too late."

With a determined glint in her eyes, Shannon leaves Conall and Keary staring at each other in silence. The weight of their impending decision hangs heavy between them like a thick fog, suffocating the air with uncertainty. Keary's fingers fidget nervously in her lap as she searches for words that refuse to come.

Conall paces back and forth, the cogs of his mind turning furiously as he grapples with the magnitude of what lies ahead. Breaking the curse could mean freedom, but at what cost? His eyes flicker to Keary, her presence a comforting anchor in the storm raging within him.

"Keary," he begins, his voice low and steady. "You know, this...this is an enormous risk. I don't want to put you in harm's way."

"We can't risk not trying," Keary counters, walking over to him and wrapping her arms around his waist. Resting her head against the wall of his chest, Conall inhales the sweet fragrance of her soap. "I won't stand idly by while you remain trapped in that thing. Or worse, just fade like a distant memory."

Conall tears her hair free from the loose knot so he can run his hands through its silken length. Somewhere, the unseen clock ticks down with relentless intent. Yet, within the confines of this room, he refuses to bow to the tyranny of fear.

"Keary," he whispers, his voice soft but a resolute blade cutting through the suspense. Gazing into her eyes, those deep wells of courage bolster his nerve. "I won't let these last hours be stolen by dread. If this is my last day, I'm going to love you through all of it."

Understanding flickers across her face before her breath hitches. Stretching on the tips of her toes, their lips meet. Unlike the slow pleasure they've enjoyed previously, the fervor of souls intertwining for what may be the last time fuels this kiss. Just like that, the world outside fades away, leaving only the two of them. Conall's hands cradle Keary's face, his touch a mixture of tenderness and urgency.

The sear of her fingertips slipping under his shirt creates a burning sensation that spreads quickly, leaving him gasping for air. Cupping the back of her head, Conall deepens the kiss. Every soft sigh or moan he pulls from her stokes his own hunger. Gentle pressure from her fingernails scrape a trail across his back that has his hands trembling. His fingers fumble once or twice over the dozen buttons on the front of her dress, but a sharp hiss escapes her when the material falls open.

Taking a step back, Conall rakes a hungry look over smooth skin. After he takes in every inch of her, his eyes roaming over every detail, his throat goes dry. A hard, gnarled knot forms in his stomach, burning with the intensity coursing through his veins like a forest fire.

As he pauses to allow her to tug his shirt over his head, Conall's heartbeat echoes in his ears. With a gentle shove, he discards her dress from her shoulders, letting it fall to the floor in a forgotten heap. His hands glide over her skin, skimming down her arms, eliciting a soft moan from her lips.

Closing his eyes briefly renews his determination to take his time before he unclasps her bra, removing it from her body in slow increments and tossing it over one shoulder. Dropping to his knees, he peppers small kisses across her ribcage and along her stomach. Grinning as she squirms and dances under his touch, each breath more ragged than the last. She releases tiny mewls of pleasure when he guides her panties down her legs, waiting as she steps out on unsteady legs.

Slowly, Conall rises to his full height, the tip of his tongue leaving a wet trail up the center of her body. Keary shivers as his thumbs brush over hard nipples only to descend far enough to palm her ass and pluck her off the ground. His groan sticks in his throat the instant she presses the heat of her core against him. Even through the stiff denim of his jeans, Conall nearly loses the iron grip on his control.

Sinking into the couch behind them, he settles Keary in his lap. The air in the room seems to crackle and spark as their eyes meet, both unable to look away. Conall's gaze is intense and dark as he studies every inch of Keary's face, committing it to memory and etching her image into his soul.

With a tenderness that belies the raging inferno blazing just beneath the surface, Conall captures her lips once again. He nips at her bottom lip gently with his teeth before deepening the kiss, his palm splayed across the width of her back and his other hand teasing a sensitive nipple between thumb and forefinger. As her body responds with soft whimpers, Conall's hunger only intensifies.

Leaving her lips, Conall trails kisses down her neck, tasting the sweet saltiness of her skin as he goes. He grazes his teeth over her shoulder before trailing lower, causing Keary to gasp sharply. Her body arches off his lap as he takes one nipple in his mouth, sucking and flicking it with his tongue while his fingers work on the other. Keary's hands tangle in his hair as she revels in the sweet torture, her pleasure ringing in his ears like music.

The air is thick with the musky scent of arousal, mixing with the sweet fragrance of Keary's soap. The smell of sweat and heat has the beast inside him rattling its cage. Her hips rock and sway with increasing intensity, the sounds escaping from her throat more primal and urgent. Pushing her to the edge, Conall's lips roam between each of her nipples, his hands following closely behind, eagerly taking over where his mouth leaves off applying gentle yet firm pressure until she's gasping for air.

She lets out a deep whimper as her pleasure builds, her body straining against his touch. Then, in one explosive moment, Keary finds her climax. Hips buck and grind against him, her moans raw against his ears. The sensation sends shivers down his spine and causes his jeans to feel two sizes too small as she rubs herself against the bulge underneath.

As Keary's pulsing contractions begin to slow, Conall gently lifts her off his lap and lays her back onto the couch. Exhaling, he replaces the stale air in his lungs while brushing hair from her sweat-drenched face. The room still buzzes with the intensity of their lovemaking, but the tension in his chest eases. Not for long, though.

Careful to keep his movements precise, Conall stands, and the taste of anticipation lingers on his tongue. The sound of his zipper descending sends a jolt of electricity through the air. Keary's soft moan in response draws his stomach tight. As if in a trance, Conall sheds his jeans and lets them fall to the floor with a dull thud. His gaze never leaves Keary's as he stands before her, naked and unashamed. With each breath, his cock stands at attention, throbbing and hard in the cool air, eagerly awaiting their next encounter.

Standing before her, Conall steals the opportunity to stare at her speechless. Her skin is flushed and glowing from their passionate lovemaking. She meets his eyes with a mixture of desire and impatience glittering in her eyes to send a shiver down his spine. Taking a deep breath to steady himself, he crawls onto the couch and settles between her parted thighs.

The warmth of her body against his ignites a fire within him as he slides his hands up her legs, tracing the soft skin of her inner thighs. Her body responds to his touch, shifting slightly and causing her eyes to flutter closed in anticipation.

"Keep your eyes open," he commands in a voice that sounds foreign even to his own ears. Without hesitation, Keary complies and meets his intense gaze. Her bright green eyes captivate him, making his heart race and his breath catch.

Their eyes remain locked as he positions himself at her entrance. She swallows hard, her hips already lifting to meet him. The slick friction between them has Conall gripping her hips tightly to restrain her movements. "Stop moving, or this will be over too quickly," he warns, unable to tear his gaze away from her mesmerizing eyes.

Keary's lips curl into a sly, mischievous grin as she leans in closer, her breath hot and tantalizing against his stubbled jaw. "We have hours until nightfall," she whispers in a thick voice, her tongue flicking teasingly against his skin. "Let's make the most of them." With just one touch, she unravels him completely, overwhelming his senses with a fiery desire that consumes him.

In a swift, fluid motion, Conall thrusts himself inside Keary, the pleasure both agonizing and ecstatic. Her cry of surprise is music to his ears. His hands grip her firmly, and with a low growl, he begins to move, establishing a rhythm that sends shockwaves of bliss coursing through his body. Keary arches her back, her nails digging into his back as she meets his every thrust.

The next thrust of his hips causes her to gasp softly and her eyes to flutter shut. Nails dig into his shoulders, punctuating their passion with a sharp sting. "Look at me," he commands softly, his voice rough with desire. Her eyelashes open, revealing piercing eyes that flash with impatience. Hips rock in perfect synchronization with his, but then she adds a subtle twist that threatens to rip all restraint from his grasp. "Gods, Keary!"

Her eyes, dark and full of longing, bore into his as he continues to move within her, each stroke drawing forth a whisper of pleasure. Sweat drips down their bodies, mingling with the scent of their arousal and creating a heady aroma that fills the room. As their pace quickens, so does their breathing, their hearts pounding in sync with the rhythm of their bodies. Keary's moans grow more desperate, her nails digging deeper into his back. The pain mingling with the pleasure to send a shudder down Conall's spine.

When she next meets his gaze, there's a raw hunger that consumes him wholly, and he knows that she's as lost to him as he is to her. "Harder," she whispers, her voice hoarse with need.

Growling deep, Conall complies. Adjusting his position slightly, he increases the intensity of his thrusts. Within seconds, Keary cries out, her body arching off the couch as her fingernails leave bloody trails on his back. Her body tightens around him, forcing Conall to grit his teeth as she rides out her next orgasm with blind oblivion. His heart races as he thrusts deeper within her, the animalistic need consuming him. It's as if he's standing at the edge of a precipice, the fall to the unknown calling to him with a siren's song.

Keary's eyes bore into his with an intensity that ignites a fiery passion within him. Her expression is a mix of unbridled desire, longing, and something entirely primal, causing his heart to race and his body to ache with need. Suddenly, she screams out in ecstasy, her body writhing in a mixture of pleasure and pain under his touch. The couch groans and creaks beneath their frenzied movements, mirroring the urgency and intensity of their passionate embrace.

As he nears the edge, Conall lets out a guttural growl, his gaze locked onto Keary's while her legs wrap tightly around him. Her nails dig into his skin, drawing lines of crimson that blend with sweat and arousal in a sticky mess. The intoxicating mix of sensation only ignites his desire further.

With a surge of liquid fire, Conall releases himself into Keary, thrusting one last time as he buries himself deep within her. Collapsing on top of her, his heart hammers against his ribcage. The sound of their ragged breaths and the smell of sex and sweat riddles the room as they each bask in the afterglow. Keary runs her fingers through his hair, caressing his scalp as he raises his head to hold her attention. "I love you," he rasps before claiming her lips once again in a fierce kiss.

As they lay together, their breathing gradually returns to normal, and the room begins to settle. The aftermath of their passion lingers in the air, a testament to the intensity of their love. Conall's heart still races in his chest, the echoes of their most primal and intimate moments reverberating through his being.

Seemingly lost in thought, Keary breaks the silence. "Tonight, we'll make the most of our hours," she says softly, her voice heavy with a renewed sense of determination. "We'll explore every inch of each other's bodies, tasting and touching in ways that will leave us both breathless."

A sense of anticipation washes over Conall, bringing with it a wave of arousal. He can already feel the tension in his groin, the echoes of their earlier passion still resonating through him. "Whatever you desire."

CHAPTER 29

The water laps gently against the smooth, porcelain edges of the tub as Keary submerges herself deeper, reveling in the luxurious heat. long lashes flutter against the thick steam rising from the surface, creating a hazy barrier between her and the outside world. As she surrenders to the tranquility of the moment, the tension fades away, leaving her alone with her thoughts and the calming sensation of the hot water surrounding her body.

The faint imprint of Conall's touch still lingers on her skin, sending gentle ripples through the water with each beat of her heart. The rough and calloused texture of his hands sent delightful shivers coursing through her body with every brush. As the sun set, casting an orange glow over the sky, they had spent the day doing things she had only ever dared dream of before. The twinge of soreness in her muscles, a small price to pay.

As she scrubs the suds from her hair, a mix of emotions flood over her. Memories of their wild escapades bring a smile to her face, before the tight sensation in her chest overshadows them. Today had been a fleeting moment of happiness, a mere glimpse of what could be possible if not for the dark force that looms over them. Keary clings to the memories with all her might, but deep down, she knows they may not be enough to withstand the days she'll face without him if this spell fails. Teeth worry over her lip, her heart twisting between holding on tight and letting go altogether.

Keary lets out a long, wearisome exhale before mustering the strength to sit up. Water droplets glide down her arms as she reaches for the towel, each movement calculated and slow to delay leaving this sanctuary. The steam curls around her body like a protective cloak, seemingly hesitant to let go of its captive. She inhales deeply, taking in the refreshing scent of eucalyptus that adds to the tranquil ambiance of the bathroom.

Slowly, she steps out of the bath, the chill of the air against her now-sensitive skin making her shiver. Wrapping the towel around her body, she pads barefoot across the cool floor, past the sink to the short stack of clothes. Too soon, the steamy bathroom loses some of its warmth, and the cold reality of their impending fate seeps in. Opening her eyes once more, she readies herself for the task ahead. As much as she wants to hold on to the past, she knows it's impossible. Time waits for no one, and the clock is ticking down the hours they have left together.

The plush towel, still warm and damp from her bath, clings to her body as she pads barefoot across the cool, tiled floor. She passes the polished sink, its gleaming surface reflecting the soft glow of the bathroom lights to the short stack of clothes. Too soon, the steamy warmth of the room dissipates and a chill that mirrors the cold reality of their impending fate remains.

Closing her eyes, she takes a deep breath, trying to hold on to the comforting heat just a little longer.

As she dries off with the towel and hangs it on the hook near the door, time slips away. Prying her eyes open, she prepares herself for what's to come. Though she longs to cling onto the past, Keary knows it's impossible. Time stops for no one, and now they must face the ticking clock, counting down their remaining hours together.

When she pulls on a clean pair of panties, the image of Conall kneeling before her to drag them down her legs just hours prior floods her mind. A shiver runs through her body in response, causing her breath to come out in unsteady gasps. With a quick shake of her head to dislodge those thoughts, she finishes getting dressed, her tense shoulders relaxing as she moves onto running a comb through her long hair. Gathering up thick sections of her long locks, she weaves them with practiced ease into a tight braid that cascades down just past her hips. Puckering her lips in concentration, she attempts to tuck stray strands behind her ears before finally stepping out of the bathroom.

Before she can search for Conall, a sharp rap on the front door slices through the room, causing her heart to race in irregular bursts. "Keary?" Shannon's voice pierces through the wooden barrier, carrying a sense of urgency that mirrors the frantic beating of Keary's own heart.

"Coming," Keary calls back, her voice steady despite the tremor that quivers through her veins. Leaning against the door, Keary takes a deep breath, plasters a smile on her face, then opens it far enough for Shannon to squeeze through.

"I left my house as soon as the sun went down," Shannon explains while untying the dark scarf that had been hiding her appearance, revealing her serene features and intense gaze. "Are you both ready?"

"I think so. Let me get Conall."

"I'm here." With his jaw set and his lips drawn into a thin line, Conall steps into the living room from the kitchen. The light overhead highlights the shadows that dance in and out of his brilliant eyes, evidence of the stress he shares with her. He drags a hand through his already tousled hair, giving him a disheveled look that adds to the intensity of the moment. He looms over the room; his powerful presence emanating tension and resolve as he stands next to Keary. "How do we do this?"

"We'll go out back where there is a clear view of the sky." Tapping a hand over the hefty bag draping off one shoulder, Shannon grins. "I brought everything we should need. All I need is the trinket box. The rest is up to Keary."

With a gentle grip, Keary rests her hand on Conall's shoulder, offering him a warm smile. "You go ahead outside. I'll run up and grab it." To avoid any argument that may arise, she spins around and climbs the stairs.

The sound of the back door opening and closing is faint as she navigates the narrow hall with cumbersome steps. As she enters her bedroom, her focus lands on the rumpled sheets, still carrying Conall's distinct scent. A pang of agony twists in her chest with each inhale as she picks up the small box from the nightstand beside her bed. Despite its innocent appearance, she knows the turmoil it has caused him. Soon, he can rid himself of it, breaking free from the chains her ancestor created for him and his brother. Or he could be gone, her inner voice warns. That thought causes Keary to gasp and push it away into a dark corner of her mind before rushing back downstairs.

Slipping out onto the porch, Keary pauses to take in a deep breath before descending the wooden steps. The gentle sounds of a one-way conversation, carried by a distant breeze, guide her through a thick stand of trees and into a small clearing. As she emerges from the shadows, the vibrant greenery that surrounds her momentarily overwhelms her senses. The soft summer breeze plays with strands of hair that have escaped from her braid, while the leaves on the heavy branches sway and rustle in response. In the center of the clearing, Shannon has set up a large circle of candles around Conall, their flickering flames casting dancing shadows on the surrounding ground.

In the distance, insects chirp their melodies while a curious squirrel leaps from branch to branch, adding its own playful notes to the symphony of nature. Each step takes her deeper into the peaceful oasis, the plush grass brushing against her bare feet to release a fresh and earthy scent into the air. The combination bombards every sense at once. The flickering orange glow of the candles, the symphony of nature's sounds, the coolness of the grass beneath their feet, and the mingling scents of damp soil and sweet flowers all add to the delightful agony.

The clearing seems to hold its breath as the trio stand together, the air crackling with tension and the weight of their impending decision. Shannon turns her face upwards, her eyes closed in deep concentration as she focuses on the ritual at hand. Keary, unable to resist, sneaks furtive glances at Conall beside her, her small hand gripping the box tightly.

Legs spread, Conall stands with his hands behind his back in a stance of solemnity. His expression is grave and unreadable as his eye fall on the box in Keary's hands. Though he says nothing, a muscle twitches in his jaw, betraying the intensity of his emotions.

Moments tick by, time grinding to a halt. The candle-light dances across Conall's strong features, casting an eerie, otherworldly glow. Shifting on the balls of her feet, Keary tries to regulate her breathing, although the air is thick, almost oppressive. As Shannon recites the ritual, the words are ancient and far-reaching, echoing through the clearing and resonating with the surrounding energy. A gust of wind whips through the trees, as if the fate they decide upon is more than just a simple decision.

"Place the box on the ground at Conall's feet."

With a tentative bite of her lip, Keary follows Shannon's instructions with awkward, clumsy movements. She turns to face Conall to find him standing resolute, but the flicker in his eyes betrays the inner turmoil he must be feeling. As she takes a deep breath, Keary can taste the salty tang of fear building in his chest. With determined steps, she approaches him and sets the box at his feet, then closing her eyes, she taps into her power and sends gentle ripples of calm energy towards him. When the shadows infesting his eyes clear, his lips curl into a gentle smile before he reaches out to clasp onto her hand.

With a deep breath, Shannon recites more words foreign to Keary. In response, the candles flicker before growing brighter, casting eerie shadows on the ground. The air thickens, becoming heavier than before, as if the very it's bending under the weight of unseen forces. Her heart races as she clutches Conall's hand, her grip white-knuckled and unyielding.

In a split second, Shannon appears in front of her, hand outstretched and reaching for hers. Keary's eyes widen as she notices the glint of silver from a blade in Shannon's other hand, placing a knot under her ribs. Helpless, she watches as Shannon turns her own palm upward and drags the sharp edge of the blade across Keary's skin. The burning pain spreads quickly, shooting up her arm before settling like an ember in her chest. The metallic stench of blood fills the air as Shannon positions her hand just right, allowing several drops to fall onto the lid of the trinket box. Each drop leaving a dark stain on the once pristine surface.

Shannon's voice fades under the deafening roar of blood pulsing through Keary's veins. She blinks, while the small ember of pain in her chest explodes into an all-consuming inferno. Her vision blurs and contorts, like a funhouse mirror, as she struggles to stay upright on unsteady feet. Swaying from side to side, a tangible jolt of energy crackles through the air, causing her heart to stutter and her skin to prickle. As the darkness reaches out with gnarled claws, wrapping around her like a suffocating blanket, Keary can just make out the look of pure panic on Conall's face before everything goes black.

Slowly, Keary pries open one eye and then the next, only to be greeted by a searing pain that pounds within her skull. Gradually, as the haze clears, she exhales, registering the familiar bedroom ceiling above her. Tiny cracks and stains from years of wear and tear mar the soft moss paint she'd selected so many years before. When she struggles to sit up, Keary battles with the urge to be sick. Once she's certain she has a firm grip on her stomach, she gingerly swings her legs over the side of the bed and perches on the edge for another moment.

A delicate tremble courses through Keary's body, as she finds her balance and pushes herself to stand. She squeezes her eyes shut, her mind grasping for any memory of what happened before she passed out. But all that fills the void is a jumbled montage of fragmented images. Wrinkling her nose, she adjusts her jeans and t-shirt. The scent of stale sweat clings to her clothes, evidence that she slept in them for quite some time. Her hands shake as she hastily gathers her tangled hair and ties it haphazardly into a loose ponytail.

"Conall," she croaks, her voice barely a whisper.

No answer.

"Conall, where are you?" Keary calls out, her voice growing stronger as the blood rushes back to her head.

Silence.

Frantic, she rushes out into the hallway, her heart pounding in her ears. Hurrying down the stairs, she nearly topples sideways when she stops quick at the sight of him sitting quietly at the kitchen table.

Without sparing her so much as a glance, Conall tilts his head back and takes a slow, deliberate sip from the cup in front of him. The rich aroma of freshly ground coffee beans fills the air, enticing her senses. Collapsing into a chair with a thud, she studies Conall's cool demeanor with furrowed brows. While his strong features set in a mask of indifference, she can sense a simmering storm beneath the surface.

Keary's breath catches in her throat. "What's wrong? Did it work?"

Conall's response comes slow, while his smile never reaches his eyes. "So, Shannon says."

"Thank the Maker." Keary slumps back in her chair, a smile on her face as she whispers, "I thought you were gone."

Conall's smile turns brittle, lacking its usual warmth. "I figured I'd hang around until you woke up, at least."

His words dangle between them. "What do you mean 'hang around'?" Her voice trembles as she searches Conall's face for a trace of the warmth she's come to expect. All she finds is emptiness, like a fire that has burned out.

"Considering everything you've done for me, it's the least I could do to make sure you would wake up." His hand reaches out to gently touch her shoulder before he rises from the table, pushing back his chair with a loud scrape. The remnants of his coffee swirls down the sink, leaving behind a faint aroma of dark roast. Shaking off the disorientation she turns to find Conall packing his belongings into a shoulder bag.

"You're leaving?" Keary's voice trembles, barely audible amidst the deafening rush of betrayal in her ears.

"I'm a free man now. A large part in thanks to you." Her heart aches at the thought of Conall leaving, but she forces herself meet his gaze. His words a sharp knife, cutting through the remnants of their shared past and leaving her exposed.

"So that's it then. You don't need me anymore so it's time to move on?"

"More or less," he replies without hesitation.

Each word from Conall's lips is a shard of ice, burying deeper into her heart. The delivery is a punch to the gut. *I'm an idiot. How could I ever put my trust in him? Give him my heart? He was only ever looking out for himself.* A part of her wants to scream and lash out, but another part is consumed by the agonizing ache in her chest. *How could I have been so blind? So foolish to trust him and give him my heart?* While she berates herself for being naïve, the inner turmoil rages on, tearing at her until she fears she'll unravel completely.

Sitting frozen in her chair, a sensation twists and turns inside of her, like a sharp knife twirling within her gut. Nails pierce the soft pad of her palms as she battles with the urge to throw him out on his ass. Every nerve is on high alert as she opens her senses and tunes out the words spilling from his mouth and focuses on the other signs around her.

The tight pinch in his brow immediately draws her attention, followed by the white-knuckle grip he has on the bag in front of him. A sickly-sweet odor wafts off him, making her nose scrunch. She sits taller in her chair, unconsciously trying to distance herself from the repulsive smell. When she pushes against his mind, instead of the calm, cool demeanor he's presenting, she finds a tumultuous storm of fear swirling inside. It's suffocating and overpowering, causing her own heart rate to quicken with unease.

"What...what are you doing?" he manages finally, a lone tremor in his voice enough to set her mind at ease.

"I don't believe you."

Conall's expression tightens, his eyes flickering to meet hers for a brief moment before he averts his gaze. "Keary," he begins, his voice a low growl, "I've said my piece. It's time for me to go." He finishes loading up the bag and slings it over his shoulder, his movements purposeful and resolute.

"You're lying."

The room crackles and swells with an unseen force, filling the air with a palpable energy. For a moment, the pressure between her ears builds to a painful degree, threatening to split her skull. White-hot heat sears across Keary's skin, causing her to writhe in discomfort. Tiny whimpers leak from her lips as she twists and turns, searching for relief from the heat coursing through her body. Just when she thinks she can take no more, the pressure suddenly eases, leaving her gasping for breath.

With a start, Keary's eyes snap open once more, taking in her surroundings as the clearing comes into slow focus. To her left, Shannon and Conall hover over her concern etching onto their features. The air still crackles and pops with residual magic, like tiny bursts of electricity dancing through the atmosphere.

Shannon let out a sigh of relief, her voice barely above a whisper. "It was a test of trust," she explains, taking a step back so Conall can help Keary to her feet.

Her fingers tremble as she reaches out to grasp Conall's hand, the warmth of his skin a comforting contrast to the coldness that still lingers from her nightmare. As their hands intertwine, there's a strength and solidity of his grasp, grounding her in the present moment. Sensing her emotional turmoil, his strong arms wrap around her, enveloping her in warmth and making her forget the chill that still clings to her bones. Closing her eyes, Keary allows herself a brief respite, basking in the heat radiating from his body. But just as she begins to relax, a nagging thought creeps into her mind, causing her eyes to snap open.

"What about Daigh? Did I break his curse as well?" Her voice quivers as she watches Shannon, searching for an answer amidst the storm of emotions swirling inside her.

Conall's grip tightens around her, the intensity of the embrace momentarily stunning her.

"The test was solely for you and me. Having never met Daigh, I don't think you'd have passed a test where he's concerned anyway."

Frustration tinges her voice as she asks, "Then how long must we wait until I can break his curse?"

A shadow crosses Shannon's face as she speaks. "I'm afraid breaking Daigh's curse will require fresh McKenna blood. Using yours to break Conall's has left a lingering taint within you. I can't use it again."

Keary's heart sinks as she listens to Shannon's explanation. She glances at Conall, who meets her gaze with a mix of relief and grief. "I'm sorry."

"There's nothing for you to be sorry for. You freed me." Laying an arm over her shoulder, he guides Keary back towards the house. "We'll find a way to free him as well."

Keary rubs a finger against her temple, trying to soothe the persistent ache that has settles there. Freeing Daigh requires McKenna blood, and she knows just where to find some. But the thought of manipulating Erin, weighs heavy on her heart. She can only hope that her sister will understand and forgive her when all is said and done.

ABOUT THE AUTHOR

Sarah is a Michigan native, living in Northern Iowa. A mother of four, she still copes with the idea her youngest is in college. Married seventeen years, Sarah and her husband learned quickly that communication, laughter and resisting the impulse to maime makes their marriage work. He continues to be one of her most energetic cheerleaders. Writing had been a secret passion of hers since high school, after an English teacher knocked the dust off. While being the typical stay at home mom, she took classes and workshops to refine her skills. After a lot of anxiety, and a bout of self-doubt, she's excited to introduce the characters that live in her head to the world.

When she's not writing, she's a grandmother of four granddaughters and a soon to be grandson, as different as the
seasons. Between the rambunctious nature of children and the
neurotic nature of her three Great Danes, life is interesting. If
asked, she'll tell you she loves every minute of it. Even if some
of those minutes result in ice cream, buckets of coffee and a
little solitary confinement.